MW01256114

ʼhatever Happened to Lori Lovely?

Also by Sarah McCoy

Mustique Island

Marilla of Green Gables

The Mapmaker's Children

Grand Central

The Baker's Daughter

The Time It Snowed in Puerto Rico

Whatever Happened to Lori Lovely?

A Novel

Sarah McCoy

wm
WILLIAM MORROW
An Imprint of HarperCollins*Publishers*

HarperCollins books may be purchased for educational, business, or sales promotional use. For information, please email the Special Markets Department at SPsales@harpercollins.com.

hc.com

FIRST EDITION

Designed by Michele Cameron

Library of Congress Cataloging-in-Publication Data

Names: McCoy, Sarah, 1980- author.
Title: Whatever happened to Lori Lovely? / by Sarah McCoy.
Description: New York, NY : William Morrow, an imprint of HarperCollins Publishers, 2025.
Identifiers: LCCN 2024042056 (print) | LCCN 2024042057 (ebook) | ISBN 9780063338746 (hardcover) | ISBN 9780063338760 (ebook)
Subjects: LCGFT: Novels.
Classification: LCC PS3613.C38573 W47 2025 (print) | LCC PS3613.C38573 (ebook) | DDC 813/.6--dc23/eng/20240927
LC record available at https://lccn.loc.gov/2024042056
LC ebook record available at https://lccn.loc.gov/2024042057

ISBN 978-0-06-333874-6

25 26 27 28 29 LBC 5 4 3 2 1

For Mother Dolores Hart,
who blessed me with her friendship

With love's light wings did I o'erperch these walls,
For stony limits cannot hold love out,
And what love can do, that dares love attempt.

Romeo and Juliet (Act 2, Scene 2)

Whatever Happened to Lori Lovely?

Lu

Be Kind, Rewind

The Abbey, Connecticut
October 1990

So where do you want to begin?" she asks.

"Wherever you want?" I reply.

"No," she says, and it isn't gentle. "You're the one writing this, Lu."

My hand flinches and leaves a pencil dash across the page. "What do you mean? This is about you, Aunt Lori."

"Is it?"

She turns to face me. Originally Lucille Lorianne Hickey, formerly Lori Lovely, christened Sister Jude by the Queen of Praise Benedictine Abbey, and now Mother Lori by choice. My aunt is an icon like no other. The gold cross pendant around her neck swings. The veil of her wimple frames her pale face, concentrating all color into her eyes. Blazing blue, like the sky fresh after a storm. Crystalline. I can't look away and neither could audiences for a time.

I had a crush on her when I was young. Torn between wanting to be her and wanting to be so close that my body and bones melted into hers. It's hard for anyone who hasn't met Aunt Lori in person to understand. I wish more people could see the real her.

My eyes are blue, too. That's about where our physical similarities end.

I didn't inherit the golden hair, the cherubic bone structure, or starlike twinkle. I'm all angles and dark curls, presumably from my dad's Welsh side. But I get a kick out of seeing that blue streak of DNA reflected in film footage. I'm a little vain about our eyes, admittedly.

They named me Lucille-Marie because I was born eight days before Aunt Lori's birthday. I'll be honest, it was hard growing up when your first, middle, and last names already have a face and history. I was given the nickname Lulu to distinguish me, but by elementary school, *Lulu* became the popular playground satire: *Lulu is cuckoo; Lulu does voodoo; Lulu takes a poopoo; Screw you, Lulu . . .* Kids can be savage, and once a stigma is attached, it's hard to change public opinion.

In an effort to renew myself the summer before I started high school, I locked myself in the bathroom with a magazine photo of Pat Benatar and my mom's sewing scissors. I chopped my long brown hair into a pixie cut. Each time the blades came together, there was a liberating resistance and release. When I came to the dinner table, my parents were shocked, naturally. I told them I wanted to go by just *Lu* from then on. Dad passed Mom a look. She teared up and excused herself to the kitchen.

"What made you decide this?" Dad asked.

"I don't know," I said, running a hand up my bare neck. "It just felt right."

He nodded silently and forked his slice of meatloaf.

Mom returned with a bottle of ketchup. "I forgot this."

And on we went.

In all my high school photos, it's hard to tell if I'm a girl or a boy. Looking back, I wonder if that was my problem. I wasn't sure who I was or who I wanted to be. I can't say I've figured it out yet.

I'm in my fifth year at Mount Salem College and still don't know what I want to do with my life. I sampled a few majors (English Literature, Forensic Science, Journalism) before landing on History, which even now I am floundering in. Nothing's quite fit. My silent fear: the problem is me. *I* don't fit . . . anywhere. Never has it been so official as printed on a college transcript. A laundry list of unfulfilled requirements, unfulfilled hopes.

I changed my major this last time after taking Professor Proctor's course "Controversial Music History: 1900 to the Present," wherein he evangelized on the untold story behind the public life of American musician Billy Tipton, born Dorothy. It flipped history on its head.

Professor Proctor was an old soul with furry white eyebrows that accented his round spectacles and made his eyes look theatrically animated. He showed outward compassion in ways the others did not, like a grandpa with a butterscotch disc in his breast pocket. I never knew either of my grandpas. Grandpa Tibbott died before I was born and Grandpa Hickey when I was four. Professor Proctor is what I imagine of grandpas.

So, when he called me to a meeting before the department board, I knew I must be in serious trouble.

"Miss Tibbott, I don't want to see all your hard work come to naught."

It warmed me—the *naught*. It was so historical, so Professor Proctor.

"My colleagues have discussed your academic record. Unfortunately, no matter how much potential we see in you, the board is in unanimous agreement that we cannot graduate a student who has not completed the final opus of her academic journey."

He took off his glasses to wipe the moisture away. His face was flush. It pained him to say it and made me adjust uncomfortably in my chair. The Shaker-style spindles grated my back.

"I've spoken to the board on your behalf and they've agreed to give you one last chance to complete your thesis. You have enough credits to graduate, so your current courses will be audited and listed as Thesis Colloquium, for which I will serve as your advisor."

The head of the department, Dr. Gibbons, gave the kind of overly emphatic exhale that a livid parent gives a child or an ill-mannered dog.

"Professor Proctor has vouched for your scholastic capacity. As a colleague, we are honoring *his* recommendation," said Dr. Gibbons.

"Thesis or no, you will not be admitted to Mount Salem College for subsequent semesters."

I got the point. They wanted me to fish or cut bait. The problem was, like my major, I'd started and stopped writing various thesis topics but couldn't land on one interesting enough to sustain a dissertation. The longest essay I'd written was ten pages, double-spaced. And truth be told, I'd increased the margins before printing to hit the length requirement.

The skin behind my ears went hot. An agonizing itch crept dewy down my neck. But I refused to let them see me squirm.

"Are we settled, then?" Dr. Gibbons checked his watch.

It was nearing noon, and their kind held a strict lunchtime dictum.

I nodded. "Write my thesis. Graduate. Got it."

"Good. That will be all," said Dr. Gibbons.

I was dismissed. Professor Proctor accompanied me down the hall. The History Building's steam radiators gave off musty gurgles. He put a consoling hand on my shoulder.

"Let's discuss your thesis. I believe the issue you've experienced with your previous subjects is that they have no personal affiliation. They lack . . . passion. Don't think of history as a list of names, dates, and facts. It's not a static entity. Think of it as a living thing—a person you want to sit down beside to hear his or her story so as to better understand the happenings."

Once he reframed it as a person, the task changed. Immediately, she came to mind.

"My aunt Lori Lovely," I said. "I wrote that paper for you last semester about her."

It hadn't been a profound piece, a one-thousand-word essay. The whole of it was me spouting off about being the niece of a bygone movie star. But Professor Proctor had handed it back saying, "Well done, Miss Tibbott! Utterly riveting. I could read an entire book about Lori Lovely. I always wondered whatever happened to her."

I got the sense that he was asking for more information, but I hadn't any to share. She is my aunt and an enigma. I've always been drawn to her, but she has secrets. A known fundamental of religion is keeping and sanctifying secrets. So, I can't be sure if the mystery is in her occupation, her person, her relationship with me, or all three. For years, I wanted to ask certain questions. Questions I sensed might upset my mom and dad. Questions that under other circumstances might be uncomfortable for a niece and her aunt to discuss. But this—my thesis!—is a professional construct. At least on paper. I needed to write this. Everyone would agree. I have to graduate. And if I finally got answers to questions I've been afraid to ask, well, God works in mysterious ways. That's what Aunt Lori tells me, at least.

For Professor Proctor's sake, I pitched it differently: "I'm going to write about the 1960s musicals and the film industry . . ."

His brow had furrowed in a ponder.

"But really, it's about Aunt Lori. Her untold story. The stuff nobody knows. Why she became a cloistered nun, and all that."

"Splendid. I think that will go over well. Final manuscripts are due December twelfth and not a day later. Don't let me down, Miss Tibbott!"

He'd patted my shoulder and walked away. The click of his shiny loafers and smell of Old Spice decrescendoed.

My mind had raced. It was the beginning of October. The clock was ticking.

That's how I ended up driving over six hundred miles from North Carolina to Connecticut with every radio tower playing Janet Jackson's "Escapade" and Paula Abdul's "Straight Up" on maddening repeat. Somewhere in Virginia, I turned it off. Ten hours on I-95 was a good time to figure things out.

First off, I needed to get my story straight. If I rode in on a wobbly horse, Aunt Lori would see my Trojan aim immediately. I had to arrive brandishing a thesis statement with philosophical heft. I needed that for Professor Proctor, as well. Two birds, one stone.

Here's the catch: I don't particularly trust history. It lionizes model citizens, but it seems to me the only ones that are ever worth their salt are the men and women who break the rules. Meaning, a person can make all the right choices by civilization's standards and still end up all wrong. History is a tangled web of half-truths we tell ourselves. The trick is to figure out which half are truer than the other. *That* is my goal for Aunt Lori.

At a rest stop in New Jersey, I got a Wendy's Frosty and scribbled on the brown napkin:

My Aunt Lori was one of the most famous movie stars of the 1960s. She became a Benedictine nun. Whatever happened to Lori Lovely? Herein, I shall attempt to provide the details of her story for historical record and to finally unveil her journey from sex symbol to saint.

Sex symbol to saint. Alliteration. Yeah, that was good.

❀❀❀

"Aunt Lori, I'm here to write my senior thesis. On you and your work in musical films," I say as confidently as possible. Still, I can't quite bring myself to look her in the eye.

Aunt Lori has always had that quality. Like she knows what others don't. I've heard people like her called an old soul, a mystic, a prophet, a witch. Believe what you want, it doesn't change the truth: she's been through stuff. And that *stuff* is exactly what I've come to find out.

She turns to face me with eyes like steel and raises an eyebrow, purses her mouth—just like in *Roman Ragazzi* where she played a boy-crazy college kid on spring break in Rome. It's one of my favorites of her films. Despite being all nuniified, she's never lost that nymphette sparkle. It's still here, underneath the religious habit and parenthetical lines around her mouth.

"Fine," she says.

Fine? As in, *Fine, you're right, let me start at the beginning* or *Fine, I'm going to make you work for this given that you showed up unannounced at my abbey insisting that I spill my guts to save your thes-ass?*

I don't know what's going through her head. She has the same veneer in front of the camera. I've watched her movies so many times that the ribbons on the VHS tapes unspooled, and I had to get new ones.

"That's my aunt," I'd told the Best Buy video clerk.

He'd shrugged. "Great."

"Great," I say now and move my pencil down to the next clean line. "So, we'll start at the beginning."

"I'd never presume to know the discography of musical theater," she balks. "Marni Nixon sang every on-screen note that came out of my mouth."

Dubbed singers were common practice in the early cinema. Professor Proctor had noted that in his lecture. Nixon sang uncredited for Audrey Hepburn, Deborah Kerr, Natalie Wood, and more, including Aunt Lori. That's what performers did back then. They performed! Wherever the studio needed them and wherever there was a paycheck.

"Right. Well, the thesis isn't so much about the hard facts of musical theater as it is about *you* in it. A biographical account of how you rose to Hollywood stardom and then ultimately found a greater calling."

I add that last bit to sweeten the pot. She likes the altruistic nugget, the *greater calling* business. She's been a nun for half her life.

She laughs. It surprises me.

"Sure, Lu. Whatever you say."

Our eyes lock, and for a second I wonder if she's clairvoyant.

Sepia papers on the corner of her desk threaten to tumble over at any second. Around the room are dusty book towers. The soft pink glow of a switch lamp turns the stacks into a quiet landscape of shadow mountains. A single, large window looks out to the abbey's meadow where the sisters' prized Holstein cows graze gently on twilight grasses. A cocoon of an office, this is the space Aunt Lori keeps for meetings with the laity:

the pilgrims and gentiles, believers and skeptics, the lost and the looking-to-be-found. The world is restricted from the abbey's inner holy of holies with one caveat, those looking for sanctuary.

I am looking for sanctuary. It helps that I'm a blood relation of the Mother Abbess, too. That matters, even to strict religious orders like the Benedictines.

She clucks her tongue at the Siamese cat named Maid Marian asleep in a homemade basket filled with wooly yarn balls the colors of autumn leaves. Maid Marian lifts a dark face, stretches ivory arms, and yawns a set of fangs.

"Treat?" Aunt Lori produces a Lilliputian purse from her habit pocket, pinches inside, and pulls out what looks like weed.

In a flash, Maid Marian is in her lap.

"Catnip," she says. "It's practically taken over the herb garden. The mint family does that, you know. Once it gets its tendrils into the soil, you can't tell where it starts and stops."

She stows the purse back in her pocket. Maid Marian nestles into her skirt and watches me with probing sapphire eyes. Aunt Lori runs a hand from the cat's black chin to its white belly. Cats don't show their private parts as explicitly as other animals. Maid Marian was the son of Aunt Lori's first cat, Robin (of the Hood). She likes wordplay. They adopted out Robin's other kittens. Maid Marian was the runt of the litter, so Aunt Lori kept him close. His testicles remained unknown until he came down with a cat cough and the sisters called the local veterinarian. By then, he was three years old. Cats are relatively androgynous in behavior and looks anyhow. *A cat by any other name*, to misquote Shakespeare.

I didn't grow up with cats. We had dogs named after baked goods: Biscuit, Muffin, and Cookie. My parents got Biscuit when Grandpa Hickey died and we moved to North Carolina. We adopted each subsequent dog in five-year increments. Mom said it would ease the suffering. It didn't. The heartbreak when Biscuit left us was worse than Grandpa Hickey. I hadn't known him all my life like I had Biscuit.

Maid Marian purrs sweetly in Aunt Lori's lap. Long eyelashes bat at the gathering fog of sleep. His nose looks velvety. I dare to lean forward with a hand outstretched. Fast as lightning, the cat's eyes taper with a warning *meow*, and then he leaps back into the basket of yarns.

"You've heard the phrase 'Let sleeping dogs lie.' Same goes for cats," says Aunt Lori. "Maid Marian doesn't like to be disturbed."

"Clearly."

"So first, you tell me why," she says.

"Why?" I repeat to Aunt Lori, momentarily confused. Are we talking about the cat still?

"Why now do you want to know about the past?"

Good, back to the business: "Because, A, my major is in History, so in order to graduate, I need to tell a story. B, you're famous. And C, you are the only one I could ever really talk to."

My cheeks warm at that last one. It's the God's honest truth.

Aunt Lori listens without doling out penance. She's the only one in my family who gets me. Was it an ethereal characteristic of holy Mother Lori or something unique to Aunt Lori and me? Everybody likes to think they're special. That the kinship zing is the universe magnetizing atoms together.

I gesture to the wooden crucifix nailed high on the wall. "You're under oath. You can't lie."

She eyes the cross, leans back in her chair, and threads her fingers. "First off, fame doesn't amount to a hill of beans," she answers. "And secondly, who's to say I won't lie? Memory is made of human stuff."

Part 1

Lucille/Lori

Let's Start at the Very Beginning

1

Pufftown, North Carolina, to New York City
1964

Nobody remembers the very beginning of their own beginning. If they say they do, don't trust another word that comes out of their mouth. We're all basically making up stuff from what we've been told.

So, according to the story, I was born during a fluke snowstorm in April 1946 in Pufftown, North Carolina, which has since been incorporated into the greater Piedmont Triad. I was the family miracle—a nice way of saying an accident. It was the American baby boom. In the postwar years every bundle was a blessing.

My dad, Bert Hickey, was an accountant by profession and a vaudeville performer by pipe dream. A romantic with a glint in his eye and a shimmy in his step. My mom, Henrietta, was an all-American pragmatist, blond, blue-eyed, and an admirer of Rosie the Riveter. Their communication skills were twofold: barking like dogs or hiding like cats. Opposites really do attract.

They met on a church hayride under a moon like a washed peach. It didn't take long for one thing to lead to another. They got hitched and immediately had Marie. Mom's cousin was in the tobacco trade back when cigarettes were considered a health food and fields were flowing with nicotine. That's where the money was. Knowing they'd have a new mouth to feed, Mom put Dad's tap shoes in a trunk and bought him a pair of field boots so he could walk the red dirt farmland with the tobacco men. Each morning, Mom worked at the Mercantile, Dad went to the trade office with her cousin, and Marie went to the schoolhouse. They'd just saved up enough to buy acreage and a new, mechanized harvester that they planned to share with her cousins when—surprise!—Mom was pregnant again.

My parents had given up on having another child. It hadn't happened in nine years, so they figured Marie was their one-hit wonder. They'd just come through the Second World War. Sugar was still being rationed. A baby was the last thing they'd expected.

We plan, God laughs. A popular saying in the church.

I may be a Roman Catholic now, but I started as a Southern Baptist. It was the only religion in Pufftown. My parents were God-fearing people, so they joined the local congregation. When I was young, I thought heaven was one way: full of Baptized Born-again Believers: the BBBs of the B-I-B-L-E. I didn't know there were other faiths besides the Baptists until I went to New York. I met all kinds: Lutherans and Jews, Muslims and Buddhists, Taoists, and, of course, Catholics. God is far more diverse than we give him credit for.

With a new baby on the way, my parents decided it was best if they kept the jobs they had. Dad was relieved. He was a man who liked shiny shoes, the smell of brilliantine, and an audience. So instead of buying farmland, they used their savings to build a three-bedroom house with a wraparound porch. Quite something for its time. Mom had a knack for making a dime stretch a dollar. They painted it yellow and called it the Canary House.

Dad's fate was sealed. He didn't have to be a farmer, but he was going to be a businessman to keep a happy household of four. Lucky for us, the trade was much like putting on a show. Dad channeled his dream of stardom into charming buyers. He became the number-one tobacco man in Forsyth County.

I grew up in the Canary House with my mom, dad, and big sister, Marie, thinking the whole world was tied up in the sheaf of Pufftown.

Then one day, a young fellow named Bill Tibbott got off the train in what he thought was Smithfield for a photography assignment, only to discover he was a hundred and fifty miles off. He decided to stay and take photos anyhow, and bumped into Marie coming out of the Pufftown Public Library. The rest, as they say, is history. They married a couple months later in the fall of 1961, and off she went to New York City.

It's funny, there are moments of childhood when you feel the world shift. Everything around you changes and you change in the process. You want to go back to how it was, but at the same time you're excited to see how it's going to be. That's how I felt about Marie getting married.

On her wedding day, she was a vision, otherworldly in her white dress and lace veil. She got a chic haircut, the bob. Her honey-brown hair cupped her cheeks like two neat parentheses. It was the first time I'd seen her wear proper pumps, too. Our mom fashioned a camellia from the garden as a wrist corsage and a matching boutonniere for Bill.

Not a big to-do. Bill's kin were out West. Idaho or Nebraska, I can't recall. They were a decade older than our own parents and in poor health even then. So, Marie and Bill had the preacher ceremony in Pufftown. When the newlyweds kissed at the altar, I felt lightning flash through my core. It was the closest thing to God manifested that I had known up to that point. I went with my parents to see them off at the train station. The echo of the steam pistons was like a heartbeat. From where I stood, the iron rails led straight to the horizon where they jumped into the blue beyond. A place I saw in the mirror when I stared down the tracks of my own ambitions. I knew I'd follow her into the world.

And I did a few years later. My parents were reluctant to send me north on my own, but Dad couldn't leave the trade and Mom couldn't do the travel. She'd begun to experience chronic fatigue and aches in her joints, later diagnosed as fibromyalgia. But back then, nobody gave a name to it. Dr. Keaton, the local physician, had shrugged his shoulders and said it was probably "the change." Women's health was the no-man's-land of medicine. One day of gardening would land her in bed for three. I'd never seen her take so much as a catnap before then. The doctor told her to limit exertion while she made the transition. She did the best she could, but sitting was not a skill she'd practiced. She took up knitting, reading, painting, piano, anything she could to keep her mind occupied on the days she had to sit on the sofa for hours.

Marie came home to visit each summer since becoming Mrs. Tibbott. But the summer after I graduated from high school, she called to say she couldn't get away. Bill needed her help. They'd just opened a little photography shop on Fifth Avenue in New York City. The overhead costs for the space were such that neither could afford to take a full hour lunch, never mind a vacation. I found out later that they were trying to have a baby and it wasn't happening.

I was to attend the local Christian college's secretarial school like most of my fellow Pufftown schoolmates. The college was nicknamed Mount I Do because so many couples met and married there. Going to New York seemed my shining opportunity to step out before settling into domesticity.

The plan was for me to help Marie and Bill until school started in the fall. I packed a couple of day dresses, one Sunday dress, a pair of cigarette capris, and some cotton button-down shirts. We'd go to the laundromat on Fridays, so I'd wash and re-wear. Mom filled my suitcase corners with gifts for Marie: a knitted blue shawl for cool New York nights, a painted wooden ring box, nettle tea, and a new novel she fancied called *A Wrinkle in Time*. Nothing for Bill.

"He'll have both my daughters. That's more than enough," she said.

Dad took me to the Pufftown train station and bought me a first-class ticket, which included complimentary meals served on bone China, three kinds of soda to choose from (Coca-Cola, 7-Up, ginger ale), and a reading selection of every recent magazine from *Life* to *Time*. I was giddy. The getting there was as impressive as the destination.

"Don't tell anyone about the ticket." Dad made me promise. "Your mom wouldn't approve of the extra expense. Just enjoy yourself and be safe."

He smiled with a little showman's bow of his fedora. His hair had thinned on top so that when the breeze passed, it swept back the strands and exposed the white of his scalp. I was suddenly conscious of the fact that my parents were growing older. That they were old. It dawned on me that time was a bell curve. I was on one end, and they were on the other.

The sight of my handsome dad graying and my mom at home nursing her pains made me sad. I was grateful to be going. It hurt too much to be close to their declines. Dad saw my gaze linger on that bald spot and quickly put his hat back on.

When you're living minute by minute, you don't think about the effect of your cursory actions. The side glances. The sighs. The smiles and frowns. We think them minuscule in the greater arc of boarding a train and starting the journey to becoming someone in the world. Only in hindsight do I recall the embarrassed tremor in his fingertips. I wish I had kissed his cheek and told him he was the handsomest man in the world.

Instead, I nodded excitedly and tried not to clutch the ticket too hard. I felt everything like a raw nerve: the sharp peal of the overhead train whistle down to the pounding of my heart. I wanted to go before anything stopped me. Nothing did, and in my haste I barely said goodbye.

We assume the familiar will always be familiar. That our parents are part of us at that age. God is merciful in not allowing us to remember the pain of cutting the cord.

I waved from the train door. "I love you, Dad! I'll call you from Marie's!"

He waved back. "Get the pie in the club car, not the ice cream!"

Which I did. After the chilled tomato soup, buttered hot rolls, baked cod with tartar sauce, and vegetable du jour. Two cups of frothy Coca-Cola to wash it down. I wasn't even hungry when the dessert arrived, but I ate every caramelized crumb. How could I not? It was boysenberry pie. I'd never even heard of a boysenberry before! And that was merely the lunch menu.

I arrived at Manhattan's Penn Station before the dinner meal with a bellyache to beat all bellyaches. I was sure I might've died if served more.

Marie and Bill met me at the platform.

"Lucy! I'm so glad to see you!" Marie pulled me close. The pressure made my stomach gurgle, which she wrongly interpreted as hunger. "You must be famished. When we took the train, they hardly gave us a cracker."

They had been in Coach Class, and I couldn't explain my discomfort without breaking my promise to Dad.

"Not to worry." She led me forward by the crook of my elbow. "There's Jell-O salad ready at home, and I just have to warm up the chicken pot pie."

At the mention, a sourness—tartar sauce and boysenberry—came up my throat. Before I could gulp it back, I vomited on Marie's suede Funster pumps.

Like the impact of a bomb, the passengers scattered, the station snuffed into silence—minus the ringing in my ears. Marie spoke inaudible words. Bill took my suitcase. My shoes slipped on the tacky floor.

I would never be able to eat pie again—boysenberry or otherwise. Cooked fruits in general make me queasy.

I hardly noticed the city. I spent the first twenty-four hours in bed with a cold washcloth over my eyes. Or, more accurately, on Marie and Bill's sofa in their East Harlem one-bedroom. Marie tucked a sheet over the T-cushions with a daisy-chained Afghan, and I slept snug as a bug. I didn't have to move a muscle to watch *Candid Camera*. There was something about feeling homey in a place that puts one at ease, no matter how foreign a setting.

When the nausea settled, I ventured to the fire escape window, the coolest place in the apartment. Up high, a light breeze from the unseen Hudson River brought with it the briny tang of far-flung places. Down below, taxi cabs honked, engines purred, kids played Freeze Tag on the street, radios hollered out the Yankees game, and somewhere near but far a man sang out, "Piraguas! Ven aqui, piraguas!" Like a game of "Hidden Pictures" in a *Highlights* magazine, there was something curious to discover in every corner, and that was just our block. I was jealous that Marie and Bill got to live there permanently.

Tibbott Photography was on Fifth Avenue. Marie wanted to cut back her hours with my arrival but never found the right ones to snip. So, all of us took the subway to the studio each day—a ride that seemed as exciting as the train from North Carolina. Although, I was grateful for the lack of a dining car.

At the shop, I was tasked with styling customers while Bill adjusted the lighting and camera angles, and Marie ran the storefront register. I learned that our job was to capture the best side of each paying customer. My first client was a shy fifty-year-old named Mr. Dubrowski. He had a glass left eye and two gold teeth on that same side. Both were the result of a childhood accident with a mean mule who'd kicked him in the face.

A lifelong bachelor, he confessed that he'd been on four dates in his entire life, so he'd finally signed up with a matchmaking service. The service required applicants to submit a completed questionnaire and two photographs: one head to toe and one closeup. Mr. Dubrowski was blessed with good height. He had just enough brawn to appear athletic and just enough softness to show that he wasn't obsessed with it. His nails and mustache were trimmed clean, and his hairline was graying but solid. If it hadn't been for his false eye and the unnatural glint of his smile, he might've been one of the most attractive men in New York City. Immediately, I saw the solution. Turn his right side to the camera and leave his left in the shadow.

Everyone has a preferred angle. One that emphasizes his or her attractive features—a straight nose, bright eyes, high cheekbones, a long neck—and de-emphasizes the negatives—a pimple, a bulbous chin, a crooked tooth, a scar. We all have things we like about ourselves and things we don't. Clients wanted to show their good sides and hide their flaws.

It's very similar to how people come to church, when you think about it. They confide in the individual behind the scrim to help them do that. The problem is, they walk out, and their eyes are the same color as when they walked in. Their noses are as crooked, too.

The photography shop was my early education. Have you heard the saying "All things work together for a greater good"? I believe that's true.

2

Mom's birthday was at the end of June. Bill came up with the cracker-jack idea of sending her portraits of us girls since we wouldn't be home to celebrate.

Marie sat first. It was the end of a long, hot day after she'd swept the shop, balanced the books, ordered more chemical developer for Bill, and scribbled a grocery list of *chicken, lemons, ketchup, thyme* on the memo pad. She plunked down like a sack of potatoes in front of Bill's lights and camera.

"You've got to smile, Marie," said Bill.

"Why do I have to?" She fought a yawn. "Mom knows I love her, smiling or not."

He gazed through the lens a beat, then stood back and shook his head. "No, no, that won't do. You're far more attractive than this. Push your hair off your forehead, turn your shoulders, raise your chin, open your eyes wider, and for God's sake, smile."

Marie sat unblinking, tired hands clasped in her lap.

Feeling the marital temperature rise, I stepped in. "Here, let me."

I combed Marie's hair with my fingers so it draped elegantly around her ear, pulled her shoulders back to give her poise, gently lifted her chin to the right degree, patted the skin beneath her eyes with talc powder, and brought her a compact mirror to see the results. She smiled then.

"You're a magician," said Bill.

Marie squeezed my hand. No thanks necessary. We were sisters.

In a flurry of snaps, Bill completed Marie's portrait. Her window of amiability was narrow. I was next.

Hair frizzed from the humidity, I combed my bangs back with pomade and hid the rest under a brimmed hat tied with a green velvet ribbon. The shop kept costumes for clients who wished to gussy up. I twisted my torso and gazed over my shoulder. The position elongated the neck and emphasized the bone structure of the face. I smiled, but not so much that my teeth showed and eyes crinkled. Everything in moderation. Just enough to leave the observer wanting more.

"Holy mackerel!" said Bill. "Marie, come look at your sister."

Marie laughed. She was in better spirits out of the spotlight. "I see her."

"But through the lens." He pulled Marie behind his eyepiece, and her smile broadened to toothy gums.

The flashbulbs sliced the air with electricity. The camera's shutter clicked. The heat of the lights seemed warmer than the sun. I basked in it. This was why customers came. When they took home their portraits, it wasn't the image they treasured but the glory of the experience. Film was indelible proof of existence. Long after memory faded and we were all gone, the images of who we were—or more accurately, who we *wished* we were—would remain.

Sitting in front of the camera that night was the closest thing to immortality that I had ever known, and I wanted to live forever.

The portrait came out so well that after Bill sent a copy to Mom in North Carolina, he made a larger duplicate for the shop window in the hopes of attracting clients. I was keen on the idea, as any teenager would be, but Marie was opposed.

"You're too young," she argued. "You're here to help with the business, not to be a glamour girl."

"But glamour girls *are* our business," Bill countered for me.

Marie pinched the bridge of her nose. "Mom will kill us if she finds out."

Bill had no retort, so I stepped in.

"What she doesn't know, can't hurt. Right?" I'd heard the church ladies in Mom's Bible study say this and figured it had to have come from the Gospel somewhere.

They looked at me wide-eyed. Bill with a grin, Marie with a scowl. I smiled like I had in the photo.

Within an hour of putting the image on display, we'd booked two new clients, socialites from Manhattan's Upper East Side.

I'd inherited Dad's showmanship. Marie inherited Mom's industriousness. The chime of the cash register was clemency. The portrait stayed and brought in more customers who were thrilled to see the same girl from the photograph styling them for their own. Attractiveness was attractive. People wanted a piece of it for themselves and would pay handsomely. The problem was that the charm didn't discern between the good and the bad.

Take Doug Barns, for example. The next Thursday afternoon, on a break from manning the ticket window at the Loews Theater between Fifth and Sixth Avenues, Doug came into the shop looking for the girl in the display photograph.

When he saw me, he leaned an elbow on the counter. "Hiya, cutie, what's your name?"

"Who's asking?" I replied.

"Doug Barns. I'm an MGM talent scout looking for the next big star, and I think you're it." He winked and made his finger like a pistol. "Love to take you out on the town—tomorrow night if you're free."

I turned to Marie stocking the back shelf and stuck out my tongue. She smirked as if to say, *You brought this on yourself.*

Doug was three inches shorter than me and younger by the same number of years. So wet behind the ears, he nearly dribbled.

"An MGM talent scout, eh?" asked Marie. "Where's your card?"

His face flushed piglet pink. "I—I left it in my jacket back in the office. Too nice a day."

True, it was too hot for a jacket. But Doug had no chops for acting, or even lying.

"Well, when you come back with your card and we have proof that you are who you say you are, then I'm sure my sister will give you the benefit of a reply."

Marie winked at me and joined Bill behind the studio curtain.

I stared down Doug with arms crossed until his resolve broke.

"Okay, okay, so I'm not a talent scout but I do work for MGM by way of Loews Theater, and I do think someone should send your photograph to MGM." He leaned in closer. "I can sneak you into my theater for a free show if you go on a date with me."

I might've been from a small town, but even small-town girls know that a date should never contain *sneak* and *free* as incentives. I was worth far more than that.

"You're barking up the wrong tree, kid," I said and waved him off.

"Aww, come on, be a good girl. Nobody likes a sourpuss."

"Nothing personal. I simply don't feel the *je ne sais quoi*."

I'd seen a French film actress use the term and thought it chic. It rolled off my tongue like warm chocolate.

"Jenny-what?"

"It means the indescribable. The special feeling that makes a person do anything for love. The spark!"

"Well." Doug stood back and shoved his hands into his pockets. "If you ask me, that's the dumbest thing I ever heard."

"But I didn't ask. You walked in here asking me for a date based on half-truths."

"Fine," he said and marched to the door. Before walking out, he turned. "Would you go for pastrami sandwiches at the diner sometime?"

I shook my head.

"How about a Coca-Cola on the corner?"

"How many times do I have to say no?" I huffed.

"As many times as it takes for you to get tired and say yes!"

I was flattered. I'd never had anyone ask me out.

Marie and I had a good laugh about it. But then I went to the studio mirror ringed with light bulbs for clients to apply rouges, eyeliners, toupees, and costumes. The heat of the lamps and the heat of the day brought on a sweat. My head went woozy and my heart beat in double time, tickling like piano keys under my rib cage. My eyes shone glassy, and my lips flamed red. This was who Doug saw. The woman in the photo was me. It was a side of myself that I suspected might be there underneath little Lucy Hickey from Pufftown.

So, a week later when Doug came back with a newspaper page in his hand, I only feigned indifference.

"I'm not here to ask you on a date," he began, then paused and scratched his chin. "Unless you changed your mind in my absence, in which case—"

"Doug." I stopped him.

"Okay, okay." He slid the newspaper forward on the counter. "They're looking for girls at an open audition. Not MGM but Paramount Pictures."

FEMALE DANCER CASTING
NEEDED AS EXTRAS IN MUSICAL FILM. DANCERS MUST BE ATTRACTIVE, 18–28 YEARS OLD, GREAT PHYSIQUE, UNINHIBITED, NEW FACES & INGENUES WELCOME. SEND HEADSHOT AND CONTACT INFO TO CASTING DIRECTOR CAROLINE MARION AT 1501 BROADWAY, NY. UNION ELIGIBLE.

The heat I'd felt in the vanity chair returned, flushing my face. This was a real opportunity.

"Caroline Marion," I read aloud.

Doug smiled. "Can you dance?"

I hadn't formal training, but growing up with my dad had made me an expert in the Buffalo Shuffle and soft-shoe choreography. His vaudeville days might've been over, but he never stopped dancing. He'd turn up the radio while we were doing after-dinner dishes, and we'd twist and kick-ball-change until our knees ached. Marie and I were his faithful partners. I got the feeling that Mom wanted to join, but abstained. Instead, she'd task herself with drying the dinner plates, mending the napkins, or suddenly needing to count how many soup cans we had in the pantry, parlaying the message that his stage days were a bygone indulgence.

"I can move," I said.

Doug nodded. "Most of the actresses I know don't have a lick of training. They just fake it till they make it." He turned to the portrait in the window. "Send that and I guarantee you'll get a callback."

Marie and Bill escorted a couple from the portrait studio.

"Oh, hello again," Marie said to Doug. "You're back." She looked to me with raised eyebrow.

I gave her a look that said, *He's not bothering much.*

"Hello to you too, Mrs. Tibbott. I'm just dropping something with your sister." He spun on his heels. "But if Lucy wants to go out dancing, I'm the King of the Mashed Potato." He proceeded to gyrate out the door and down the sidewalk.

"He reminds me of a Central Park pigeon. Flapping for crumbs," said Marie. "Brought you something?"

I didn't show her the newspaper, afraid she might quash the ambition that was just beginning to sprout. Some dreams are like that. Seeds bursting through the shell within. Instinctually, one feels the need to protect them, even from those we love most dearly. Sometimes *especially* from those we love most dearly. They're the ones with access to our tenderest roots. If those are damaged, there's no hope for a bloom.

So that night when Marie went home to start dinner and Bill was cleaning the darkroom, I quietly slipped one of the 5x7 promotional portraits into an envelope with the shop number as my contact and addressed it to Caroline Marion at Paramount Pictures. It wasn't stealing, I told myself. The image was mine even if the paper and ink was borrowed. If I got a job, the pay would help the whole family. If I didn't, what they didn't know couldn't hurt.

Two days later, the shop phone rang, and thank God I was the one to answer.

"Tibbott's Photography, how may I help you?"

"Tibbott's? I'm sorry, I was trying to reach Lucille Hickey. I must have the wrong number."

"No, no, this is the right place. I'm Lucy—Lucille."

There was a pause, an inhale, the clattering of something in the background.

"All right—I'm Miss Marion's assistant at Paramount," she said, "calling regarding *The Kid*, our musical gangster film set in Brooklyn. We got your headshot. Miss Marion thinks you've got the look. Can you come in tomorrow at nine a.m. for the audition?"

My hands went clammy. I choked to answer. Marie looked across the room with concern.

"Yes."

Another pause. Background clattering.

"Great. It's 1501 Broadway. Bring your résumé. No music. They'll have it. Be ready to improv. Sign in and they'll put you in the queue."

"Will do, thank you."

Click. No goodbye.

I hung up, the spiral cord juddering from receiver to wall.

"What did they want?" asked Marie.

For one of the first times in my life, I undisputedly lied to my sister.

"To see if we did on-site photography."

"Manhattan only," Marie corrected. "You should've said that."

"I will next time." The untruth burned, and I looked away to keep her from seeing my discomfort, because I was about to try my acting chops some more. "The lady wanted to know if I could drop off samples tomorrow morning at nine."

"She can't come here? I'm happy to talk to her about package options."

I thumbed through a stack of photography postcards on display. "I get the impression she might be housebound. One of those old-moneyed New York types. It's just a few blocks away on Broadway."

"She lives on Broadway? Fancy! That's fine, but make sure her building has an elevator. Bill's got a funny back. He can't be schlepping equipment up apartment stairs. Also, my obstetrician thinks I'm too active. He wants me to stop lifting things." She sighed with unspoken frustration.

She'd had a doctor's appointment that morning. *You aren't pregnant today, but next month you could be*, Dr. Fielding had told her. The same as the month before and the month before that. Endless ambiguity with an unchanged prescription: rest, drink honey tea, eat chicken liver, feet up, no alcohol, don't lift things, don't move too far, don't get excited, don't stress, don't worry . . . as if abiding by those might be the magic formula to make a baby.

It sounded complicated, and I witnessed how those complications manifested in Marie's marriage. She couldn't hide her tears when her period came. Bill's crestfallen shoulder slump was unmistakable. He was disappointed for them as a collective unit. Marie's pain became his pain. *Two become one flesh* had been the headline of their wedding announcement in *The Triad Herald*. Mom had put it in a scrapbook.

Still, Marie cursed herself, her body, her fault. I never did understand. When Bill argued that he didn't need children, she projected her frustration at him: "Don't say such a thing!" As if guardian angels of the unborn were listening and might take him up on the offer.

The walls were thin in the apartment. It made me glad not to have to worry about husbands and children and the intersect of those within my private sanctum. I wanted to keep it just me, myself, and I for as long as possible. The responsibility of that felt overwhelming enough.

Even if their voices hadn't carried, I wouldn't have slept much. My anticipation of the morning audition held me in a state. Each passing minute pricked like a bee sting.

3

The buzz of nine o'clock was a welcome relief. I arrived at the Paramount Building on the minute. Inside, the gilded ceiling sparkled in the summer sunlight, gold on gold. The bronzed elevator doors chimed open and close with a heavy bell that sounded either too tired or too posh for the work. Faces emerged laughing and frowning, talking and yawning, old and young, beautiful and plain. All dressed to the nines in Technicolor fashions and echoing well-heeled down the marble halls. It was the drone of somebodies, and I was one of them.

I wore my black cigarette capris and a black boatneck shirt, like Audrey Hepburn in *Sabrina*. I borrowed eyeliner from Marie's makeup bag and drew up the corners of my eyes, a touch of pink cream on my lips and cheeks. I'd seen patrons overdo it with cosmetics and end up looking like corpses at a wake. Less is more, Mom had taught us. It was true. No amount of furbelows could mimic natural attractiveness, and you didn't have to be beautiful to be attractive. The camera recognized that truth.

"Hi, I'm Lucille Hickey," I said to the woman at the reception desk. "Here for Miss Marion."

She cradled a phone at her neck while scribbling on a pad.

I held up my résumé. "The female dancer audition—"

The woman covered the handset's mouthpiece. "Casting is on the fifth floor." She pointed with her pencil to the elevator and continued her phone conversation.

A girl who looked about my age entered with a canvas dance bag slung sideways across her slim waist. She wore a pink wraparound ballet tunic and leotard. When she made a beeline for the elevator, I followed. We got on together. The lift was crammed shoulder to shoulder, but she stood a head above. If her exceptional height hadn't made her noticeable, her bright hazel eyes, flawless skin, and perfectly bowed lips would've. In the middle of the packed car, she applied a wand of shiny gloss that smelled of strawberries. Everyone inhaled with pleasure.

At the fifth floor, she pushed forward. I did the same. Young, lithe dancers formed a waiting line along the wall. A middle-aged woman in a pleated chiffon blouse sat at a table with a clipboard taking résumés and headshots.

Seeing me at her elbow, the tall girl smiled, and it was impossible not to smile back.

"Auditioning?" she asked.

I nodded. "You?"

"Yup." She eyed the leather-banded watch on her wrist. "I got dance class at noon though. So I hope they speed it up this time."

"You've auditioned before?"

"I was an extra in *Hey, Let's Twist!*"

I was too nervous for pretense. "This is my first."

She did a ball change, shifting her weight back on her heel. "Aw, no worries. You've got the look they want. Film's a cinch. You go, dance, hang out with the cast, and get paid. Oh—and they even give you free food. Craft services. It's swell. So much easier than theater work."

She pulled a slightly creased résumé from her canvas bag.

"I'm Ginny, by the way." She pointed at the bolded top line. "Ginny Wilde's my stage name. It's good, right? *The Importance of Being Earnest* was my first gig. I changed it then. Real name is Jennifer Cockburn. Can you believe my bad luck?"

She laughed, and the sound was like a jar full of pennies.

"I'm Lucy Hickey."

"Cockburn and Hickey!" She hooted. "Ain't we a pair!"

I laughed, too, momentarily forgetting my nerves. Ginny had that effect.

While typing up the week's client list the night before, I'd borrowed a page for my résumé, listing my name, height, weight, and that I'd been dancing since I was three years old. True, albeit open to interpretation. I showed that to the woman at the check-in table, who had called the day before, Miss Marion's assistant, Doris Leach. Talk about bad names. Ginny said some of the girls had nicknamed her *D'Leech* after a film of similar title (*The Leech Woman*), due to her ability to *suck the blood out of you with* you're in *or* you're out. It proved how a name could become a reputation, regardless of its merit.

Doris skimmed my résumé, checked her notepad, and handed it back.

"Stretch in the hallway," she instructed. "I'll call you when it's your turn. Have your résumé ready. They'll do a brief interview to hear your locution, followed by four minutes of dance."

"Come over here." Ginny led me down the hall past the other girls. "I sorta got this superstition—a theory really. I'll only share with you because it's your first day and you seem a little . . . I don't know, *unfamiliar*. So"—she lowered her voice to a whisper—"I always warm up by a coffee machine. The casting people come out for a cup and see you. I read an article that said it's a psychological fact that if a person sees your face once, they'll easily forget. But if they see you twice—no matter how briefly—the brain tricks itself into feeling like they know you. A facial déjà vu. I've booked every job that I've stretched near a coffee machine."

The hallway was quieter away from the mass, and the smell of the coffee beans brought with it a Sunday morning kind of comfort.

Ginny pulled out ballet slippers, tossed her canvas bag onto the tiled floor, and slid down into a wide splits position. Stretching from one side to the other like the needle of a temperature gauge, she changed her shoes.

"So, you're a professional dancer," I said, lowering myself to the ground, flexing and pointing one foot and then the other.

"I take classes, if that's what you mean," explained Ginny. "Dance, singing, acting. You've got to be good at all three to get noticed. But my goal is to be a professional actor—not supporting cast, either. I want to be a lead. I don't have an agent yet, so I've been submitting to cold calls the past couple years. It's worked out pretty good for paying the bills, but I'm ready to take the next step. I'm tired of being in the chorus line, plus I'm getting old."

I assumed she was my age, too young to worry about getting old.

"How old are you?"

She turned a cheek to her shoulder. "How old do you want me to be?"

Confusion must've shown on my face because she straightened up.

"If anybody at the casting table asks your age, that's what you say. Technically, I'm nineteen, but I've been eighteen on my résumé for the last two years, and I'll leave it that way for another two, if I can manage."

"The casting ad said ages eighteen to twenty-eight."

"Riiight. Eighteen is the legal working age, but if you're over the age of twenty, chances of getting hired dwindle. There's a fresh boat of eighteen-year-olds docking on Broadway every day. Most everybody fudges their birth date, like their names. So long as the execs can claim the paperwork, they don't go playing detective on an actor's background, particularly not the extras. We're the singing-dancing-smiling furniture on set."

I pulled out my résumé.

Ginny leaned forward to read, bisecting herself like the midline of an arrow. "Aw, yes, case in point. Still wet behind the ears. Stay eighteen forever. That's what they really want."

Just then, the door to the audition room creaked open and a short man with a purple scarf around his neck sidled out. He eyed the coffee machine, then us, and then the coffee machine again.

"Mind if I—" He pointed to the machine and rattled the coins in his hand.

"No problem," said Ginny.

"Come on, let's scoot over so he can get his coffee, *Lu-cille*." She enunciated my name and then gave me a look to pay her the same favor.

I did, awkwardly. "Okay, *Gi-nny*."

She smiled.

The man thanked us tactfully, got his coffee, and returned to the room.

"Works like a charm," said Ginny.

They called her first, and she was out in under fifteen minutes.

"How'd it go?"

She shrugged. "About the same as all the rest. I'm as tall as the male dancers, and they're always looking for tall girls who can high kick. It shows better on film. That's my signature move." She eyed her wristwatch. "Oh, shoot, I gotta run or I'll never make it uptown in time. Here—" She took my hand and a pen from her bag. "This is my number. Call me. I could use a practice partner. Most of the other girls I've met on auditions will sooner slice your Achilles than help you out. You're different."

She scribbled numbers inside my palm. The roll of the ballpoint pen tickled, and I fought the urge to curl up my fist.

"Good luck in there." Then, in a graceful dash, she raced down the hall, still wearing her soft ballet slippers.

She would become my first best friend. There are few things in life that are handed to you like that. Gifts that fall into your lap like ripe fruit. Ginny was one. I stood there, palm open, not wanting to smudge my only way of seeing her again.

So wonderstruck, I almost didn't hear Doris call my name.

"Hickey—Lucille Hickey—if you are still here, please come to the audition room!"

"That's me, sorry, yes, I'm here!"

She held out her hand. "Résumé." After briefly examining it on her clipboard, she met my stare. "All right. Deep breath. Ready?"

"Ready."

She was far from bloodsucking. I got the sneaking suspicion that she cared. I could've fooled myself into believing it was me—some existential favor I carried—but the truth was more practical. Doris's job was to administer order for the protection of each auditioner, and she was dedicated to it. She put a gentle hand on my back and ushered me into the room.

It was a large dance space with wall-to-wall mirrors and a wooden ballet bar running through the middle. The room was stiflingly still, lacking the usual whirl of motion. Instead, a panel sat behind a foldout table across one wall like a row of starlings perched on a fence.

"Miss Lucille Hickey," Doris announced, her attention directed to a woman wearing a black satin blouse, tortoiseshell glasses, and bold red lipstick. Miss Caroline Marion, I presumed.

The man in the purple scarf sat to Caroline's right and passed her my 5x7 headshot, recognizable as smaller than all the other 8x10s.

Midway across the room, Doris stopped. "Stand here," she instructed and then proceeded forward to hand Caroline the résumé.

Mr. Purple Scarf sipped his coffee.

Caroline set the résumé aside with hardly a look. "Hello, Lucille. I'm Caroline Marion, casting director for this film. It's nice to meet you."

"Hi, hello, it's nice to meet you, too," I said.

Caroline's expression remained neutral, but her eyes narrowed. She flipped over my photograph and lifted a sharpened pencil.

"That accent is charming. Where are you from?"

I hadn't thought I had an accent. Nobody'd ever mentioned it.

"North Carolina."

Caroline wrote it down. "I was on set in Asheville years ago. Lovely place."

"*Thunder Road* with Mitchum?" Mr. Purple Scarf asked under his breath.

She nodded without taking her eyes off me.

"That's western North Carolina," I explained. "I grew up in Pufftown. Kind of the middle."

"But now you're here."

"Yes, ma'am. My sister lives in East Harlem with her husband. They got a photography shop on Fifth Avenue called Tibbott's Photography. I work there."

She lifted my headshot. "Did they take this?"

"Yes, ma'am."

"It's one of the best headshots we received. It really captures you."

"Thank you." My cheeks went hot.

"So, what's your dance background?"

My flush turned cold. "Nothing professional. I didn't go to ballet school . . ." I gulped. "My dad did vaudeville. I grew up dancing."

Mr. Purple Scarf raised his head with a smile.

Caroline tapped her pencil. "Those fellows knew how to work a crowd." She gestured to the end of the table where a younger woman sat by a record player.

"When you're ready, show us what you've got."

No time to panic or worry. It was all happening fast. The younger woman began the turntable and lifted the tone arm.

I took a second to shake out my numb hands and wiggle my toes in my shoes.

"Right," I said. "I'm ready."

She set the needle on the record with a trip, and what do you know, Dee Dee Sharp's "Mashed Potato Time" echoed across the empty room. I had my moves ready, my pirouettes and double shuffles lined up, but I guess Doug was right about the audition and more. Without missing a beat, I twisted my heels, shimmied my hips, waved my hands, and danced like I was in the kitchen with the radio turned up. When the song ended, my fingers tingled from how hard I'd clapped along.

"I almost got up to join you," said Mr. Purple Scarf.

"She's got rhythm." Caroline scribbled something on the corner of my headshot. "Thank you, Lucille. That's all we need. Doris will be in touch with our final decision."

Doris's guiding hand returned to usher me back the way I'd come. I dared to look over my shoulder one last time before exiting and saw Caroline nod with a smile.

"Nice job," Doris whispered in my ear. Then she turned to the hall of waiting dancers. "Sally Jones!"

A freckled brunette jumped up, waving her résumé, and off they went.

I looked down at my empty hands to find my palms were stamped with the sequence of digits. Ginny's number. I couldn't wait to tell her all about it.

I was back at the photography shop by lunch.

"So?" Marie asked while busily packing up a customer's order. "How'd it go?"

"Good."

"Did you tell her that we won't climb stairs?"

"There was an elevator."

She nodded.

That was all that was said about it. For four days, life went on like clockwork, and I almost believed I'd dreamed up Ginny, the man with the purple scarf, Caroline Marion . . . the whole audition.

Then, on a blustery Monday morning with the weather outside pouring buckets, Doris called.

"You're in, kid."

I nearly dropped the lens I was cleaning.

"I am?"

"Yes. Dancers start rehearsal next week. Write this down."

She gave me the street address of the rehearsal hall, the choreographer's name, and instructions on what to wear. I hung up feeling charged, like the tip of the Empire State Building just before the lightning strike. When Marie walked in, my excitement turned to an anxious sweat. I'd be out of the shop during rehearsal and filming. I'd have to tell her the truth.

She gestured to the pad on which I'd written the information. "You book something?"

I gulped. "Yeah."

She raised her eyebrows at my prolonged pause.

I let it spool out as fast as I could: "Doug told me about a Paramount Pictures audition. I used Bill's portrait as my headshot. I got the job! It's to be a dancer in an upcoming musical film. Rehearsals start next week. I'll get a paycheck. Don't be mad, please . . ."

Her face went from confusion to anger to blank, where it rested, unreadable. I held my breath. Neither one of us blinked.

"A dancer in a musical?" she finally asked.

"Yes."

A smile stitched the edge of her mouth. "Dad will be thrilled."

I exhaled with relief and rushed to her side, wrapping my arms around her. "Oh, Marie! Isn't it wonderful? I wanted to tell you, but I didn't know how, and I didn't have a proper résumé, so I really didn't think I had much of a chance. But they picked me—they picked me!"

She kissed my forehead before pulling back with a stern look. "Mom."

Our mom had no patience for showbiz. She would not take kindly to her youngest daughter joining the thespian ranks.

"She'll have my hide if she thinks I had anything to do with this," said Marie.

"Like the portrait, could we maybe not tell her? If the job doesn't go well, I won't do another. She'd never be the wiser. But I'll never have the opportunity again."

Marie's eyes tick-tocked like a cat's, strategizing.

We'd been raised in a house that held firmly to the church's motto: *To lie is to sin and to sin is to do the devil's work.* Neither of us wanted bedevilment. But life is more complicated than what's taught in Sunday school.

"It pays," I went on. "I'm helping here, but I'm not bringing in any money. The extra would come in handy."

Marie shook her head. "Our finances aren't your responsibility, Lucy. I never felt comfortable with you working for us without pay. I told Mom that. She insisted because of the whole baby thing."

At the mention, her shoulders shrank a little. I gave her a squeeze.

"I'll only take it if you want me to."

It was a half-truth. I knew she wanted me to take it or I wouldn't have said it. And I wanted to take it no matter what she said.

Now it was Marie who squeezed me. "Do the job and keep the money. You earned it."

I buried my face in her neck and kissed the softness of her skin. She smelled like lilac soap and flash powder.

Bill came in. Seeing us noodled, his reflex was concern.

"Everything okay?"

We pulled back, both smiling.

"Tell Bill your news," said Marie.

"I'm going to be a dancer in a Paramount Pictures film."

"She used your portrait to get the job," added Marie.

Bill's eyes went wide, and then he raced forward with a hoot, pulling us together so that our heads met like a clover.

"Now, here's the thing," said Marie. "Mom and Dad can't know."

We made a pact there in the middle of the shop with the summer shower rhythmically tapping the front window, a corps de ballet of raindrops.

4

What was the protocol for calling someone you met at an audition? What if Ginny didn't get the job? I spent a long hour the following day turning digits on the rotary phone. Each time it spun with a satisfying vibration; but by the last number, I'd chicken out. Finally, and almost by accident, I let it fly.

Ginny picked up after the first chime. "Hello?"

I cradled the phone away from Bill and Marie, who were with customers in the back studio. I hadn't made personal calls since arriving; I hadn't known anybody else in the city until now.

"Hi, uh, this is Lucy—from the audition." She probably went to auditions every day. "The Paramount Pictures audition. I don't know if you remember me but . . ."

"Of course I remember you! I've been waiting for you to call. What'd Doris say? I'm sure you're in the cast, because they'd be dumb ninnies if you weren't. They'll sell at least a hundred extra theater tickets with you on camera." A cat meowed in the background. "That's Tulip, Mrs. Finkelstein's tabby. She's my landlord. Mrs. Finkelstein, not the cat."

I loved how Ginny made me feel as if we'd known each other forever and anything was possible. Like magnets, familiarity is the power of two.

"I got the job," I said.

"I knew you would. I'm in, too. Hey, there's a diner across from the rehearsal hall called Miss Pam's. They serve the best breakfast around. Want to load up before work next week?"

My first diner breakfast with my first New York friend before my first job as a paid movie star . . . up and up and up! The sky was the limit.

I met her in the Theater District the following Monday. Marie offered to take the subway with me, but that had an elementary-school feeling that I would just as soon avoid.

"I'm having breakfast with another dancer. Her name's Ginny," I explained.

She was glad that I wasn't going alone or on an empty stomach and loaned me the cash to cover everything. I promised to pay her back from my first paycheck.

There was a rhythm to New York City—in the wheels of the cars, the blinking lights of the marquees, the thrum of ten thousand feet in step with one another, hearts racing and minds fixed on a destination. No time to stop and worry, just move with the flow. A giant dance of daily commuters, and I was one of them.

Coming through the bell-triggered door of Miss Pam's, I spied the spritely corkscrews of Ginny's hair, still damp from a morning shower. She sat at the counter with one leg stretched across the neighboring stool, absentmindedly rubbing her hamstring while talking to the waitress. The sunlight was the color of green tea and hazy with dust motes wandering on the undercurrents of yawning patrons and bowls of steaming porridge.

When she saw me, she smiled and waved me over. "I saved you a seat."

She lifted her leg up an inch before bringing it down. The tiniest movement, but one only a dancer would do. And then she heeled the stool away from the counter to give me access.

"I ordered for us. Trust me, it's the perfect meal to fuel up."

Grace and spunk. I wanted to be like her and be with her and know everything about her. We had breakfast together at the diner every day and ate the same plates: two poached eggs, one piece of toast with butter, and a cup of coffee. She was teaching me how to be a New Yorker, a performer, and a friend. She was teaching me how to be a woman of my own making.

We danced our tails off in that picture. The biggest number was a choreographed contra-dance that was your basic Do-Si-Do. They call it clogging in North Carolina; tapping, in the big city. Semantics. The interweaving paths were the same. So we twisted and kicked around lead actors Mitzi Simmons and Rick Mooney while they feigned true love. Ironic given that they couldn't stand each other. Yet there they stood, passionately lip-locked in the middle of our chorus line. The magic of movies.

As soon as we hit our finale pose and the director called *Cut!*, Mitzi pulled back and wiped her mouth with the back of her hand.

"A breath mint might be nice next time, Rick."

"Sure thing," he replied. "If you lay off the gin for breakfast."

Mitzi gave him a look that did the job of a slap before marching off set.

"Girl, girls," called the choreographer. "That was terrific! But the director has a great idea for chorus only. He needs five of you to sing a line of the song."

All the dancers rushed forward. Ginny pulled me by the arm.

"Come on! Freebies like this never come along!"

Singing was not my strong suit. In fact, Marie had gone so far as to say I sounded like a cat in a puddle when we sang Sunday hymns, bless my heart. Which was southern for, you are not good.

Feeling my hesitation, Ginny frowned. "What's wrong?"

"My singing . . ." I whispered.

"Lucy, you can dance but that's not enough. You've got to be able to sing and speak without sounding like you're from anywhere."

While we talked, the choreographer had rounded up five girls eagerly humming notes in warm-up preparation.

Ginny stayed by my side, choosing me over the opportunity. The briefest blink of a moment that spoke volumes. Already there was a bond of loyalty between us.

"Don't worry." She softly pushed a wayward bang back behind my ear. "You've got the It factor. The rest is learnable. If you're willing to go out on a limb with me."

I wasn't sure what she meant, but she had the same glint in her eye as when she wrote her number on my palm. I was willing to go wherever she led.

"Come to my apartment. I want to show you something."

The director had gotten what he needed that day. We were paid by the hour, so the extras were sent home early to save production a few thousand dollars. Marie wouldn't expect me back at the shop until later, and it was the first time Ginny had invited me to her place. No way I was declining. It felt like another step in our grown-up friendship.

We grabbed hot dogs with sauerkraut from a street cart on the way. Both were gone by the time we reached her ground-floor studio, accessible through a hidden door in the courtyard. It was a Gilded Age mansion left to disarray during the Great Depression and then modernized into three apartment units. Mr. and Mrs. Finkelstein owned the first floor and basement, which the Finkelsteins renovated into a studio that they rented off the books.

"Welcome to my abode," said Ginny, throwing her bag down on the single bed, made up tidy with a pink comforter.

Film posters of *Showboat, Singin' in the Rain,* and *Funny Face* had been tacked to the walls, alongside actress portraits of Ava Gardner, Elizabeth Taylor, and Rita Hayworth. A set of fairy lights hung from the ceiling. One barred window looked out to the courtyard where the rainbow tips of the garden dahlias could just barely be seen. Under the window was a three-legged table, a chair, and a collection of paired dance shoes in a row.

"You might be the first guest I've had during the day." She gave a cheeky wink. "Have a seat wherever."

There were two choices: the bed or the chair. I chose the chair.

Ginny went to a stack of books arranged as a kind of filing system in the far corner. Folded papers, newspaper clippings, handwritten letters, and the like stuck out from between the pages. She picked up the top book, *The Lion, the Witch, and the Wardrobe*, and pulled out a folded glossy pamphlet from its pages. Wordlessly, she handed it to me.

The front read *Italia Conti Academy for Performing Arts, London, UK.*

"London?"

Ginny nodded. "They can teach us every*thing* we need to know and introduce us to every*one* we need to know. We're young and we've got great experience. All we gotta do is get in."

"Is that all?" I'd just as soon consider going to magic school on the moon as going to a performing arts school in London. It seemed so far out of my reality.

"How would we pay for it? Where would we live? And . . ." I shook my head. "Who's to say we'd even get in?"

Ginny took me by the hand and pulled me up out of the chair over to the bed so we could sit side by side. The polyester comforter was silky beneath my bare legs. Ginny unfolded the pamphlet across our laps. The delicate skin on the inside of her wrist leaned against the delicate skin of mine, and I could feel her heartbeat clean through to my toes.

"See." She pointed to the photographs and the information. "We submit our applications, which is no different than submitting our résumés and headshots for an audition. I've been saving up, and if you did the same, we could find a place to live together and work until we make it. I know a couple students. They say if you've got SAG credits, you're a shoo-in."

"SAG credits?"

"Screen Actors Guild. It's the Hollywood actors union."

"But *The Kid* is the only film I've done."

She smiled. "All it takes is one union gig and your actor passport is stamped. Even uppity theater folks in London look favorably on SAG members."

I knew little of England. Scenes of *Peter Pan* came to mind: cartoon characters flying past the illuminated face of Big Ben; *first star to the right* toward some unseen adventure. Simultaneously, scenes from *Oliver Twist,* homeless and hungry wandering dark alleys. Unlike Oliver, however, I had a friend by my side. I couldn't deny the flickering hope taking wing within.

Ginny saw the twinkle in my eyes. She wrapped her arms around my shoulders in an excited squeeze. “Imagine us strolling the streets with the royals!”

We fell back onto her bed gazing up at the ceiling, glittering like the Milky Way.

“This is just the beginning.” She lifted the pamphlet above our two faces. “This school will teach us how to be stars.”

So close, I could smell the piney rosin she’d rubbed on her dance shoes and the bold lily of her shampoo. I wondered what I smelled like and hoped it wasn’t pickled cabbage and perspiring doubt.

Lu

Holy Brews

The Abbey, Connecticut
October 1990

"I need a cup of tea," says Aunt Lori.

She rises and walks out of the office, with me still writing as fast as I can. My spiral notebook is a jumble of scribbles, and I feel the karma coming back on me for telling my secretarial course instructor that shorthand was a dying art. I wish I had paid more respect. The joint of my third finger has seized up. There's a red callus forming on the skin. I should've brought my tape recorder. It's in the back seat of my car. I make a mental note to grab it. I didn't get nearly enough of what she said on the page, and half of what I did get is indecipherable.

First off, Ginny Wilde! Being famous, naturally Aunt Lori would know other famous people. But nobody told me that she and Ginny Wilde came onto the scene together. Ginny was an international superstar! So great in name that the media often called her by initials alone, *GW*. Singer, dancer, award-winning actress—she'd done it all! I wanted to hear more.

"Wait a minute," I say, but Aunt Lori's already gone.

I follow, not exactly knowing the way. A breeze dashes through the atrium, bringing with it the copper bite of fall; the earthy smell of rosemary and brittle leaves; the happy tune of chickadees and titmice foraging. I catch a glimpse of the kitchen at the end of the hall and the garden beyond. The nuns keep the doors open on temperate autumn days like this so the air can flow from room to room, in and out. A breathing priory. Soon enough, winter will be here. Frost and ice will cap the abbey in a snow globe through May.

I know Aunt Lori must be close when I see Maid Marian. He follows her every move.

It's the hours between the Sext and Vespers. Sister Candace, a novitiate not much older than me, passes so quietly that I hear the fabric of her scapular brushing against her tunic. She smiles with her eyes and nods to convey that she's in silent meditation, communicating with the holy unseen. I nod back so as not to interrupt.

Then, a shriek from the kitchen. I startle and drop my notebook. The loud *thwack* echoes down, down, down the chambered hall. Sister Candace turns to me.

"Sorry," I whisper.

Even when I'm obedient, I break rules just by being me.

Aunt Lori leans across the kitchen doorway with a rainbow-colored parrot on her left shoulder. She eyes me, looks to Sister Candace, and then lifts a delicate sprig of flowering basil to the bird's beak. It nibbles. Purple petals flitter to the floor. Maid Marian pounces and the basil is licked up.

"You got a bird?"

"A macaw," says Aunt Lori. "Given to us by a shelter. A family bought it on holiday in Costa Rica. The children loved it when it had the wingspan of a Christmas tree angel and chirped like a mouse. All grown up and making a racket, not so much. God works in mysterious ways. He was meant to be with us. Isn't that right, Clarence?"

The bird takes the basil sprig in its beak and flies to a macramé perch by the open door.

"Why doesn't he fly away?"

"Why would he? We feed him, give him a clean home, spoil him with affection. Besides, he and Maid Marian are completely besotted with each other. How do you explain to a bird and a cat that they are fundamentally not supposed to love each other?" She shrugs. "We put rules on tablets and God breaks them."

I smile as Maid Marian climbs to a perch beside Clarence, curls into a doughnut, and falls asleep.

On the stovetop, a kettle simmers.

"Would you like a cup?"

Aunt Lori holds open the top of a brown teapot in the shape of a cottage. The strangest teapot I've ever seen.

"What kind is it?"

"My own blend. Holy basil, ginger, lemon peel, rosebuds, cardamom, and yerba maté. Helps with the time of the month. I've been crampy all day." Aunt Lori rubs her midsection. "Always worse at the beginning, right? Sister Candace is feeling particularly bloated. It happens, you know, when women live in close proximity. Menstrual synchrony. They've done studies."

She uses the back of a spoon to muddle a piece of ginger and a slice of lemon peel before dropping them through the roof of the cottage teapot.

An abbey full of nuns with PMS. I had to laugh.

It brought to mind when I visited Aunt Lori for the abbey's budding summer stock. I was thirteen—before the Pat Benatar hairdo. It was the first time I'd been on my own, without one of my parents as chaperone. It surprised me that my mom had been so agreeable to the trip. In every other aspect of my life she acted as a life preserver, so tightly buckled around me I could barely breathe. But when it came to Aunt Lori, she seemed to throw caution to the wind. Mom drove me up to Connecticut and dropped me off without a backward glance.

Under Aunt Lori's direction, the abbey was putting on a collection of theatrical performances for the community. They'd held open auditions, and a handful of amateur thespians, young and old, had been chosen. One of the program scenes was from *Anastasia*. Aunt Lori had suggested me for the role of young Anna. I was ecstatic. I dove headlong into the part. Borrowing one of the abbey's bikes, I rode over to the town's public library and read everything I could on Czar Nicholas II and the Russian Revolution. The firsthand accounts of the family's demise were profoundly tragic. Even after I'd left the texts, I carried the bitterness of their history like I'd eaten too many sour cherries.

When I stood up on the grassy hill outside the enclosure to read my lines with my fellow players, I felt something I'd never felt before. A sharp, hot ache folded low in my belly. Even my ears were sweating. Flecks of light floated in and out of my vision. My throat closed up. I couldn't get a word out.

Aunt Lori graciously suggested we wait to do my scene until after lunch. It was summer in Connecticut and while the sky was overcast, we stewed in the clinging humidity. Everyone needed a cool drink.

In the bathroom, I found a soft pink blossom in my underwear. I'd started my period. Some might call that a historic moment in a woman's life. Most of the girls in my middle school already had theirs, and my mom had shown me the dainty pink pads hidden underneath her bathroom sink. But I wasn't at home to swaddle myself in Kotex. I was in the middle of the woods, at a nunnery, with scenes of Anastasia's bloody end on my mind. I broke down in tears, mostly because I worried this one event might steal my opportunity to participate in Aunt Lori's program. I wanted so desperately to make her proud.

I'd stuffed my underwear with toilet paper and went to find her, waddling a bit.

"Honey, are you okay?" she'd asked.

"I . . ."

Silly as it sounds, I wasn't sure that nuns got periods. I figured those of religious sanctification relinquished all worldliness and lived in supernatural functionality, free from biological concerns. If the blind could see and the dead could live again, who was I to say what miracle of miracles took place behind consecrated walls?

I, however, was as mortal as they came.

"I started my period."

Aunt Lori's face had turned from concern to understanding.

"Aw," she'd said. "Your monthly. God be praised, welcome to womanhood! Follow me." She'd put an arm around my waist and led me to the little closet where the sisters kept their supplies. There were shelves of maxi pads in every size, some with belts and some with adhesive strips, pads with wings and absorbent cores. Even a small selection of tampons, which not even my mom had dared to stock.

"Do you have a preference?" she asked.

There was one brand under the sink at home. I had no idea there were so many options. I'd always been too embarrassed to walk the feminine hygiene aisle at the grocery store for fear someone from school might see me. So, in my first act as a newly christened woman, I chose the Stayfrees.

Aunt Lori waited for me beside the bathroom. When I came out again, she smiled proudly.

"Are we ready?"

"Ready."

She kissed my forehead, and we'd gone out together to meet the troupe. While I quickly realized that I hadn't inherited an ounce of acting ability from Aunt Lori, I came away from that visit closer to her than ever. We'd shared a life moment, and I intrinsically wanted more. She was living proof that the holy and unholy were on the same daily journey. Their socks were just as hard to reach in the morning. Their toes just as cold. And yes, PMS is dreadful for every woman.

The kettle whistles, boiling to a climax. Aunt Lori pours the water into the teapot. Steam rises from the chimney spout like a cartoon.

"I've never seen a teapot like that."

She pats the top.

"It's one of my favorites. Kensington Pottery. Handmade. I bought it in London. It predates the famous Brown Betty. The sisters swear it's got healing powers. Holy brews."

In the light of the steamy kitchen, her eyes are phthalocyanine, an alchemic blue that seems to glow. I see the young girl in the portrait my dad took those many years ago. The chemical film process in those days translated her eye color into something the world had never seen before and never could replicate in another era. Today's cameras are too slick. The apertures, too quick. Like a pair of scissors cutting a taut string, modern moments are snatched and thrown into development alkaline at the one-hour Fotomat. There's no suppleness to the image. No slight margin of grace for the mind to dream. The art is gone. That's what my parents say, at least. It's one of the many reasons they moved back to North Carolina.

I grew up hearing tales of New York City and young Aunt Lori's visit. If it wasn't for Aunt Lori's portrait, they'd have closed Tibbott Photography then. They'd used up all their savings and were too ashamed to ask my grandparents for a handout. The strain on their finances impacted their marriage, too. Dad jokes that he counted his lucky stars every day he woke to find my mom hadn't packed and gone. The tight look on his face as he cracked the joke belies how much he believes that. He always ends the telling with *No need for lucky stars, we got something better—you.*

They never openly discuss that Mom struggled to get pregnant, but I figure as much. They'd been married almost ten years by the time I came along. As a child, they were always hovering watchfully, like I might vanish in a blink. It makes sense. People who've wanted something for a long time act that way. Like they secretly worry that the universe might decide to snatch the blessing back.

It's strange to see my parents through Aunt Lori's eyes. My mom and dad before they were Mom and Dad; before they moved back to the Canary House to take care of Grandma Hickey after Grandpa died of lung cancer. Once upon a time, they were Marie and Bill running their own business and living the high life in New York City. Totally different people. Just like Aunt Lori seems a totally different person in her movies and celebrity photographs. Stranger still is that I feel like I'm getting to know those past people better than I know the present ones.

"So, you went to London when you were eighteen," I say, checking the dates in my notebook and flipping the page to a fresh one. "Can you tell me more about that?"

"*Mm-hmm* . . ." She opens the teapot lid, sniffs, and pours. Tea the color of harvest straw rolls out of the chimney spout into two clay mugs with no handles.

The abbey has a Monastic Arts Shop that sells artisanal goods: yarns, candles, soaps, teas, jams, and cheese; stationeries, leathers, wood, and metalworks; paintings, sculptures, pottery, ceramics, and more. The sisters are quite crafty. The kiln is fired year-round. I can tell these mugs were practice pieces. Their top openings are disproportionally too small for the bases, giving them the appearance of handheld beehives. There's a distinct thumbprint on the lip of the one Aunt Lori hands me. The shine on the firing is lovely, however, and to my surprise, the mug fits perfectly between my palms, warming without burning. The small opening allows just enough room to sip without spilling. I've never seen cups like these at Ikea. I'm wondering, why not?

"London in the sixties was, well, *London* in the *sixties*." She laughs.

"Right. But for the purposes of my thesis, let's assume I don't know what London in the sixties was like because I wasn't there. Tell me."

Before she can, the telephone back on her office desk rings. A beige rotary phone. It clatters so fiercely that it always nearly walks itself over the edge.

Aunt Lori clucks her tongue, awakening both Maid Marian and Clarence. The bird gives an echoing cluck with Maid Marian chiming *ack-ack-ack*. Then, on wing and paw, both follow her to collect the call before the phone crashes to the floor.

I follow, too.

"Hello," Aunt Lori answers without formality.

Hers is one of three phones at the abbey. The abbess and prioress each have a private number. The third is the Portress Office, a public line for congregants answered by rotating sisters during phone hours. So, whoever is calling Aunt Lori's office is familiar.

The soft jingle of her voice confirms. "Well, hey there."

She looks to me with a smile that turns to a pucker.

"Yes, Marie, she's here. Do you want to . . ."

I flap my arms *No!*, and the movement causes Clarence to squawk and fly to a perch atop the bookshelf.

"Sorry. Clarence is rattled." She narrows her gaze at me, razor sharp. "You're right, I should've called to say Lu arrived safely. She's here to write her thesis. *Hmm* . . . Well, she must've been in a rush to beat traffic. You know how it is around the city. I'm sure she meant to phone. I'll have her do so once she's settled."

I sigh with relief as she changes the subject to more benign topics: the garden and the programs for the abbey's upcoming advent season. I listen and pick at the paper threads caught in the notebook's metal spiral. Remnants of former pages I don't remember ripping out.

At the end, Aunt Lori laughs at something my mom says and is so tickled that she wipes tears from the corners of her eyes. I'm not privy, and despite waving off the phone I hate that I'm outside of their private conversation.

"I promise," she says to my mom. "Love you too."

The words echo in my own mind. *Love you too, Mom.*

I wish I could be more open with her, but I can't. My whole life she's been my rescuer. A hypervigilant guard sheltering me from the world and then bearing the guilt when I was inevitably wounded by it. But a person needs to be free to make choices that others might call mistakes. Not everybody wants a knight in shining armor.

I didn't when I gave my virginity to a boy named Kenny from school. I was curious after multiple viewings of *Fast Times at Ridgemont High*. I wanted to see what the fuss was about. So, Kenny stole a condom from his dad's sock drawer and picked me up on a Friday night. He was a year older and had just gotten his driver's license. Two young people sprawled together in the back seat of an Oldsmobile trying to figure things out. I didn't even take off my coat. The sex was as benign and satisfying as scratching an itch in my ear.

I had no regrets until Kenny subsequently began to treat me like a social outcast. He walked past me in the halls without a glance and had his younger brother tell me not to call their house. It was humiliating. Infuriating! And revoltingly cliché.

The only person I told was Aunt Lori. I knew I could confide in her in a way I couldn't with my mom. Mom never spoke of anything related to sex beyond *It's how babies are made*. Which I knew wasn't the whole truth.

"That boy is an ass," Aunt Lori had replied.

I'd gasped aloud. From the mouth of an abbess!

"An ass is the original Greek translation for *donkey* in the Bible," she'd continued. "I'd say it's apropos here. You're a young woman discovering the world. It's not a sin to be curious."

I'd waited for her to say more but she didn't. There was understanding between us. Woman to woman. Aunt to niece. Mother Abbess to child of God.

Now, Aunt Lori sets the handle of the phone back in the cradle with a heavy click and turns to me.

"Your mom called your dorm, and they said you were gone but didn't have any more information. It scared her."

She raises one flaxen eyebrow high, waiting for me to speak.

"I was going to call . . . when I got a minute."

Maid Marian jumps into her lap. She strokes the cat's tail. Four unblinking blue eyes. I'm outnumbered. The abbey bell chimes for Vespers and another round of Gregorian chants. Thank. God.

Part 2

Lucille/Lori

A Rose by Any Other Name

5

London
1964–1965

I thought nowhere on earth could compare to New York City's comings and goings. Then I went to London. It was a feast of happenings.

All the athletes had returned home from the Winter Olympics, and Beatlemania had crossed the pond to the United States, leaving the UK in a kind of post-carousal tranquility. The Queen was expecting her fourth child. Flower peddlers sold buckets of red roses along the Thames for Valentine's Day. The whimsical script of Charbonnel et Walker chocolate boxes were in nearly every hand. Sweet expectations permeated the city with Ginny and I dancing through the center. Or so it felt.

We'd spent all the previous summer working things out in New York, bulking up our résumés, and submitting the application materials. When the time came for me to go home to North Carolina, I told Marie our plan.

She looked me flat in the eyes: "That's not happening." And then she went back to plucking finished photographs off the dry line, as if I hadn't spoken.

I may have had doubts, but her flippant dismissal fastened my resolve.

"I'm going to London, Marie."

Once I said it decidedly, I believed it.

She hadn't argued back, simply put a hand to her hip and stared at me a long minute. Then she returned to the line. "You're making that call to Mom and Dad."

I knew if the setting had been different—if I had been face-to-face with my parents explaining that I was not returning to Pufftown or going back to secretarial school and planned to work as a dancer in New York City while I awaited admission to a drama school in London . . . my pie in the sky-ness would've smashed right in my face.

But I had taken the first step, and that was just enough to make me brave enough for the next. I called home and told them everything before either one could get a word in edgewise: about Bill's portrait that we'd sent for Mom's birthday, which I'd used to audition; about my first film role in *The Kid*; about the subsequent castings and extra money; about Ginny; and finally . . .

"There's a school called the Italia Conti Academy for Performing Arts."

"An Italian school?" Mom asked.

"No, that's just the name."

"Oh, thank God, I worried you might—"

"It's in London. I applied. I've saved up money."

Silence.

"Mom? Dad?"

"We're here," said Dad.

There were two landlines in the Canary House. One in the kitchen and one in the den. As kids, Marie and I were so proud to show our friends how well-to-do we were. Most only had one telephone. As we got older and multiple lines became the norm, the novelty wore off. Now, having only two on the main floor seemed sadly deficient.

I knew they were looking across the rug runner at each other.

"I feel a migraine coming on," said Mom.

"Why don't you go lie down and I'll talk to her," said Dad.

"I think that's best. Speak with your father, Lucille." She only referred to him as "your father" when she was upset.

There was a rustle of static and a click as Mom hung up the kitchen receiver.

"Is she okay?" I asked.

Dad paused, waiting for her to be out of earshot and climb the stairs.

"She worries . . . and misses you girls. It scares her to think that you and Marie are grown up and gone for good. Even if that's the nature of children."

It stung. I expected combat. I had my defensive rebuttals ready, finger on the trigger. The vulnerable response made me stumble.

"I—I'm sorry, Dad."

It felt like the right thing to say, but also a lie.

"Don't be sorry for following your calling. There are too many other things in life that you'll regret. Trust me."

I wondered what *his* regrets were. It pained me to know that he had them. I let it be. There was enough on the line.

"The academy is really good. My friend Ginny knows students. They have a flat that's part of the campus dormitory system with a room for us. We plan to work to save up until we get in."

"What happens if you don't get in?"

I had the same question at first. But after a summer of successful casting calls, I felt myself a veteran.

"We will. We have SAG credits."

"You have SAG membership?" Even he knew the Screen Actors Guild.

I wanted to make him proud.

"Yeah, I got lucky. My first film was union."

"My little Lucy. I knew my girls had talent. Marie too, but you . . . you have the twinkle in your eye. Always have."

"The Hickey Buffalo Shuffle helped."

He laughed.

"Think Mom will come round?"

"Let me work on her. Meantime, how about we make a deal. You get in, and we'll help fund your education. The same as if you attended college down here. The money you earn, you use for living expenses. If you're going to do it, do it right."

It was more than I'd dreamed he would offer.

"Oh, Dad, thank you!"

When I hung up, Marie and Bill popped open three Coca-Colas. We clinked bottles that fizzed over with crackling expectation and sucked the sugar foam. The sweetness clung to our lips for the rest of the night.

Still, it was agony waiting to hear if I'd been accepted—for Ginny, too. We submitted together in the hopes of being admitted in the same semester.

When the letters finally arrived, Ginny came to the shop in the middle of the day.

"I got mine," she said, breathless. "I'm in."

We both shrieked.

I turned to ask Marie if I could leave to check the apartment mailbox.

She read my thoughts. "Go!"

Together, Ginny and I ran the city blocks with the first autumn wind blowing chills down our coatless backs. The smell of pushcart pretzels and roasted peanuts swirled while we darted between men and women on lunch break.

While waiting impatiently to cross a busy intersection, Ginny looped her arm through mine.

"Don't worry. If I got in, you definitely did. You've got everything it takes." She kissed my cheek and my stomach cartwheeled.

No matter what the letter said, Ginny believed in me, and I believed in her. That kind of bond felt unbreakable. So, when I opened my acceptance letter in the foyer of Marie's building, we read it as evidence of a greater hand of fate. We were destined for this. All we needed to do was follow the path.

❋ ❋ ❋

We entered the Academy as dance students. Ginny's friends, Fern and Kitty, lived in a two-bedroom flat that was part of the Academy's housing. Dividing the rental fees between four seemed a great bargain. Fern and Kitty took the larger room with two twin beds. They offered us the other, which came with a full bed for Ginny and me to share, a bureau, and a bay window overlooking the cobblestone street. We had a kitchenette and a small living space pre-furnished with a slightly lumpy futon. Kitty bought a purple mandala tapestry from a gypsy kiosk on Brick Lane and hung it on the wall. Its psychedelic circles edged in silver and gold threading made the place feel like magic camp. The tinsel bits flickered alive by the slow dance of the aquatic lava lamp. It was perfect.

Back home, my family was relieved to hear that I'd moved into a domestic setting with three other female students. Our dorm was governed by a stern housemistress named Mrs. Coates. She made it known that her life's purpose was to ensure that trouble stayed away from the girls under her charge and the girls stayed away from trouble. During the week, she lived with the other housemistresses in the un-originally named Housemistress House. On the weekends, she was presumably with her husband, Mr. Coates, a groundskeeper. I never actually saw Mr. Coates. He could've been a figment of our imagination or a cover for Mrs. Coates.

"Poor woman," Marie had said over the phone. "No children. I bet she dotes on you girls like her own."

Knowing what I knew about Marie's struggle to conceive, I understood that she was projecting her own feelings onto Mrs. Coates. Because the real Mrs. Coates carried a clipboard and gave out demerits if our beds were unmade or our laundry or dishes were unwashed. If we ate fish and chips more than twice a week, she warned us of pudgy ankles. She told us to hydrate or our dance instructors would complain of sluggishness. She gave out candied prunes not to be kind, but to keep us regular.

There was a chickenpox outbreak that winter and Kitty caught the bug. Mrs. Coates called a doctor but never so much as dabbed an itch with calamine lotion. Lucky for Kitty, her case was mild, and all her scars were concealable. When it came to light that Ginny had been living on her own since the age of sixteen, Mrs. Coates barely batted an eye. Replying instead, "I see." She didn't inquire about our families, our feelings, or our dreams. She was balance check, not a mother.

Oddly, we all agreed that Mrs. Coates was preferable to having our real mothers in London. We depended on her boundaries to remind us of ours. In retrospect, it allowed me to appreciate my mom's tenderness more than I had.

The first month was a blur of Tube rides, paperwork, class schedules, and introductions. The jet lag and the fog didn't help my transition. Everything moved like overcooked giblets in gravy. Thank God for classes, and Ginny, and coffee. Together, they saved me from surrendering to the depressive state of London in winter.

Mrs. Coates had warned us during orientation that the first four weeks were the barometer for who would make it and who wouldn't.

"I've seen students with more God-given talent in their pinky toe than all of West End put together, but they hadn't the mettle to be a Londoner." She'd nodded sharply to signify that that was the end of that—the story and the students.

The fact that I was feeling more galvanized than ever in February meant that, by Mrs. Coates's assessment, I had the mettle to make it in London and showbiz. For Ginny, it had always been a given. The Italia Conti Academy was like finding a long-lost tribe. Our artist camaraderie became the drumbeat of London, and we marched beside our fellow students with confidence.

Ginny cut her hair to a curly crop like Rita Moreno while I did the opposite. I grew mine nearly to my waist, pinning it up in a pompadour for classes and letting it spill out however it pleased at night.

Fern introduced us to her friends, the troubadours, as she called them. A group of young men enrolled at the Academy who frequented the Troubadour, a coffeehouse and nightclub off the Earl's Court stop.

At our first meeting, I showed up in a pencil skirt, cardigan, and coat. Fern and Ginny opted for hot pants with stockings. It was February in London and, despite their names, neither hot pants nor stockings kept a body warm. I considered my outfit a prophylactic to stave off pneumonia.

"Hello, ladies," welcomed Benjamin Faith, a third-year actor, and the school's leading man. Ben was rakishly handsome with chestnut hair that he combed to the left side and brown eyes that kissed like the sun. He commanded the stage with the uncanny ability to make you feel not just seen but desired.

He casually flicked the butt of his cigarette into a frosted puddle, and I felt the heat of the cherry inside my belly despite knowing what we all knew. Ben Faith was terminally unavailable. While it was not publicly declared, the troubadours were men who kept company with themselves. They welcomed female friends but no closer than arm's length.

Free Love might've been the trademark of the decade, but history is a rippled reflection. Good families were illustrated in Norman Rockwell advertisements. Husbands with wives and children: familiar archetypes with a bit of gee-golly humor thrown in. Anything that colored outside the lines was not encouraged, and there were people ready to break all the crayons to ensure the picture remained pristine.

The troubadours threw glitter over everything. Highly combustible stuff. But they were careful to stay away from social sparks, which could readily turn into pyres.

"Ben!" Fern crowed, taking his outstretched hand and spinning in her go-go boots.

"Goddess incarnate, as always," said Ben. His Geordie accent made the words even more theatrical.

Fern blushed.

"And who do we have here?"

"My new flatmates. Lucy and Ginny. Trifectas."

Trifectas were students studying the three fundamentals of stardom: acting, dancing, and singing. But technically, we belonged to the Dance Department.

"Hi!"

"Hi!" I answered with the same effusiveness.

Ben's gaze moved from my face to Ginny's, and then he grinned. "Welcome to London. Maybe you two can teach me some new moves tonight. From America?"

We nodded together. Feeling our own awkwardness, I decided to break the duet.

"I'm from North Carolina."

"I'm originally from Oklahoma—like the musical," gushed Ginny. "But I'm more of a New Yorker now. That's where Lucy and I met. We worked together. Film mostly. The studios pay well, y'know, Paramount Pictures, MGM . . ." She name-dropped.

Ben raised his eyebrows high and cocked his head in a quasi-bow. "Seasoned pros. Very nice. The Academy is lucky to have you."

Five or six guys who had been finishing their cigarettes approached from behind, throwing arms around Ben as a means of entering our circle.

"What lovely dovelys have we here, mate?" said one with an arm looped around Ben's neck.

"Fern brought her flatmates. Ginny and Lucy. New ICA dancers."

"Brilliant! Dancers are the best. Singers rattle on too much. They love to hear their own voices. And actors, gawww. Glorified multiple personality disorders," he said.

The guys behind him hooted in agreement.

"So, which are you?" Ginny asked, her voice edged with annoyance.

None of us liked being shoehorned into a category. I was a dancer, yes, but I was there to become more.

He grinned like the Cheshire cat. "An actor, of course." He patted Ben's chest, and then sashayed between Ginny and me with arms spread wide so that his wool cloak covered us three.

"Name's Flynn Winston. Born Winston Flynn, but that sounds like an old fusspot, so I swapped it round for flair."

"Flynn's been Flynn since primary," said another troubadour. "Only his mother calls him Winston."

"And only when I've been particularly naughty." Flynn cut his eyes.

"That there is Jack. Second year. Talks too much—singer." He smirked. "Jack's jealous because he's just Jack and where's the fun in that."

Jack picked up on the rhyme and sang a ditty: "I'm Jack, just Jack. Where's the fun in that, you ask? Well, join the claque and please have tact whilst applauding my dramatic soundtrack."

Flynn uncloaked us with a showman's swirl and shimmied it to Jack's cadence. "In another time, Jack would've been a marvelous balladeer."

The others quickly introduced themselves. All were older ICA students with dashing names and handsome faces to back them up.

On our way to the club's entrance, Flynn pulled Ben aside, cleared his throat, and gestured to my attire. "Matron chic isn't really the troubadour vogue."

"She's with us," said Ben. "It'll be fine."

I wasn't sure what they meant.

Flynn frowned and came closer.

"Miss—remind me what your last name is?"

"Hickey," I said.

Flynn gasped histrionically. "Tragic! And with that accent. You can't even switch it around without it being satire—Hick E. Lucy, the Yank." He tsked and closed his eyes as if it profoundly wounded him.

Ginny took up arms beside me. "We're working on that."

"For crying out loud," I said.

It was my name, given to me by my parents, and utterly out of my control. I would never point out to Flynn that despite his good looks and charm, he had rather large ears. He couldn't see his ears without a mirror and having grown up with them, he probably didn't notice their unflattering nature. My name felt similar.

"I'm sorry my name isn't fashionable. If they won't let me in the club because of my name, then—"

"Oh no, lovely dovely," said Flynn. "It isn't your name. It's that outfit. You look like you're headed to the library, not a rave."

I was not at all regretful that I'd worn my sweater. Ginny's nose was bright red and the hairs on her arms were standing at full attention. Maybe I should've borrowed Kitty's red suede boots, since she stayed in. But again, why point out what I couldn't change?

"I'm going home."

"No! Don't leave," begged Ginny, hugging herself into my side for solidarity and warmth.

"My name, my outfit, I get the impression I don't pass muster with the troubadours."

Ben gave Flynn a disapproving look. "Cut her some slack. She's new."

"I didn't mean to hurt the poor dove's feelings." Flynn tossed his right cloak sleeve over his shoulder. "Dear, dear Miss Lucy Hickey . . ." He cleared his throat. "Everything is transformable." He lifted his hands, palms up. "May I?"

I wanted to go into the club. I wanted to be part of the troubadours' clique. I wanted Flynn Winston and Ben Faith and all the rest to like me. I wanted to be transformed. So, I agreed.

In a quick motion, Flynn came behind and shimmied my skirt waist up to my brassiere, making it a miniskirt.

"Scarf!" he called out like a stage director, and one of the troubadours tossed him the paisley-printed satin off his own neck. Flynn tied it round my waist to cinch the skirt material securely. Then, he unbuttoned my sweater down to my cleavage.

"Now you're ready to groove!"

The troubadours applauded at the costume change, with Ginny and Fern among them.

"You look hot!" said Ginny.

Heat went to my cheeks despite the chill sweeping under my backside. I dared not scratch my knee or everyone would see I'd worn *Tuesday*-printed underwear on a Saturday night.

"Let's get in and get warm," Fern chattered.

We fell in line with the guys. The doorman knew the troubadours and ushered us past the queue.

The front room was the coffee shop, dimly lit by old lamps and smelling of roasted coffee beans and heady tobacco, notes of herbal sweetness, too. The brass bellies of hookahs glimmered half-hidden on tables alongside copies of *Private Eye* magazine. The tapsters moved up and down the long bar like player piano keys. The air grew warmer and thicker with perfume and bodies the deeper we went into the basement of the club. The music grew louder with guitar riffs and bongo drums. A singer leaned into a standing microphone. The audience clapped in collective thunder.

It shook something loose in me and made me want to shake loose.

"Over here!" called a troubadour.

Ben and Flynn were already at a table with pints. Ginny, Fern, and I pressed in to join.

"Just a halfies," said Fern. "Mrs. Crawford told me I'm putting on a bit of bloat." She touched her cheek. "Too many nights out, she says."

Mrs. Crawford was the Academy's lead acting teacher, an expert on the Stanislavski Method. The Method, as it was known, instructed actors to imagine themselves facing the same circumstances and emotional motivations as their fictional counterparts. In essence, we were encouraged to become the characters for the duration of our performance. Marlon Brando was a disciple of the Method and was hero-worshipped for it. Rumor had it that Mrs. Crawford had been trained by Maria Ouspenskaya, a student of the namesake Konstantin Stanislavski. What you knew was important, but *who* you knew was even more. The direct lineage to the Method's godhead imbued Mrs. Crawford with hallowed authority. What she said was gospel, and not a soul dared contradict.

"Madame Crawford knows best," Flynn said to Fern. "Here, I'll help you." He emptied half her pint into his. "If you want a trick for bloat, I take a mix of water and charcoal before bed. Ben takes it too, even though he hates it."

Ben drank. The caramel ale wet his lips. "Tastes like licking an ashtray. The bedtime dram, I mean."

Flynn rolled his eyes. "Perhaps, but Crawford has never said either of us looks bloated and here we are nearly every night," he chided.

A drink was passed to me, and I sheepishly stared at it. I'd never imbibed before. Southern Baptists abstained. There was a great church debate in Pufftown about the definition of "the fruit of the vine" when Greek Orthodox monks in the Appalachian Mountains came through selling Christmas wine. For much of the area, the dogma of the Prohibition Era remained. Alcohol was moonshine and moonshine was outlawed. In the end, my parents chose to raise Marie and me in accordance with the local proclivities. For Holy Communion, the church bought grape juice from the grocery store's frozen concentrates section. A pitcher of water plus a can of concentrate, and voilà, water into pretend wine.

The problem with growing up under such well-intended shelter is that in the greater world, I struggled to make choices on my own. I was unsure if accepting the drink was breaking a family opinion, a national law, or a biblical edict. The margins were blurred.

"It's just ale," said Ginny. "Don't listen to Fern. Everything in moderation." Feeling my hesitation, she added, "But you don't have to if you don't want to."

It was hot and I was thirsty. If someone had told me it was lemonade, I'd have swigged it down without a thought.

"We'll share," Ginny told the guys and took a neat sip.

She was not the type to do anything for reasons of peer pressure. Nor was she the type to coax a friend to jump off a cliff because others were jumping—to borrow a parental platitude. But wasn't that exactly what I was doing in reverse?

I was abstaining out of fear based on what others had told me *not* to do. Rules enforced by my community, my parents, my sister, my friends . . . I couldn't go my whole life afraid of something I'd never tried. While a healthy amount of fear could save a person from harm, there had to be balance. *Moderation*, as Ginny had said. Reality was densely populated with varying people, cultures, and scenarios that all had their own methods for how to be a good person. I would never be able to act like someone else onstage if I was too afraid to find out who I was off it. As explained in Method practices, the only way to discover character was to tap into our own experiences.

So, I drank.

The beer tasted of sour bread dough, bitterly pungent. Not vile enough to spit back into the glass but not enjoyable enough to swallow with a smile. I choked it down. The troubadours laughed.

"An acquired dependence, for sure." Ben winked. "First go?"

I nodded.

"It's not our choice either, but they don't serve champagne here."

I'd have opted for pickle brine over another swig of that. Before I could say as much, an electric chatter filled the room.

"Who is it?"

"No, it can't be!"

"Is it really?"

"I don't believe it!"

Flynn leaned left and right trying to see through the crowd.

"Is it Bob Dylan?" Jack asked, his voice squeaking with excitement. "They say he comes a lot but just my luck, I've missed him every damn time!"

"Dylan's five inches shorter than me." Flynn put his hand at chin level to exemplify the height difference. "This guy's tall."

I caught a glimpse of jet-black hair. Shiny with pomade, it reflected the light as much as the leather jacket he wore. His name, whispered at first, grew bigger and bolder as seeing made for believing.

"Lucas Wesley . . . Lucas Wesley . . . Lucas Wesley!"

Lucas Wesley was the hottest star in Hollywood. The ultimate triple threat. He had four chart-topping rock and roll albums with another on the way. His songs were played on every radio and in every music hall from Honolulu to London, earning him the nickname Sing King, which many of the teen magazines had modified to Dream King, Supreme King, and a dozen other rhyming variations. He even invented his own dance, which every boy and girl was keen to emulate in living rooms and high school gyms across the globe. Now he was breaking into acting. The American tabloids had been full of speculation before we left, but I never expected him to show up in the same city at the same club on the same night. *That* was not the stuff of real life. Not mine, at least.

People use the phrase *I had to pinch myself.* I'd always thought it puffery meant to imply that reality was so good, it might be a dream. I'd never experienced a situation so extraordinary that I should inflict pain on myself . . . until that night.

I pinched myself. Lucas Wesley was, indeed, at the Troubadour Club.

Flynn gulped his pint and dabbed his forehead with the edge of his cloak.

Ben stood up straighter to catch a better look. "Great hair."

Jack and the troubadours clucked around us with bits of gossip collected from the room.

"He's here with his agent!" said one.

"I should start carrying my résumé on an index card!" said another.

"There's a director with him, too."

"Who? Is it Hitchcock? De Laurentiis? Carol Reed?"

"I think it's . . . Nico Cellini?"

"Is it?" Fern nearly jumped out of her seat. "Cellini just directed Elizabeth Taylor in her Shakespearean film debut!"

Ginny's mouth hung open. Elizabeth Taylor was one of the posters on her apartment wall, adorned in Renaissance costume with oversized eyes staring out seductively.

A younger troubadour rushed to the table. "Mates, I've got the scoop."

We all leaned in.

"I know Nico Cellini's assistant—we've bumped into each other a time or two—he says Nico and Lucas arrived this morning from Los Angeles to start work on a new film!"

"A new film!" gasped Flynn. "That must be what Mrs. Crawford was hinting at when she told us to mind our p's and q's this weekend, so we were on point Monday."

I only had an introductory course with Mrs. Crawford. It was a mixed bag of dancers, musicians, singers, and actors. She'd made no mention to us. The troubadours, however, were seasoned thespians in her upper levels.

"Auditions," Flynn whispered like a spell.

The temperature of the room rose to a fever. My sweater felt like a wool corset. Sweat itched under my bra's fastenings and along the raised skirt waistline.

"Did he say what they're looking to cast?" asked Fern.

The young troubadour shook his head. "No specifics. But apparently, it's being shot in *Italy*!" His eyes went wide.

Flynn threw both winged arms up. "We *must* get in this film! An Italian *vacanza*! Can you imagine? The food, the fashion, the flirting!"

For the briefest moment, Flynn looked to Ben and Ben to him, and then they both laughed and raised their glasses.

Meanwhile, across the room, the club's security had escorted Lucas, Nico, and half a dozen others over to a private table roped off from the bar crowd.

Seeing Lucas enter, the singer leaned into the mic: "Can I get a whiskey—gin—whatever you got back there?"

A waitress promptly brought him a neat cup.

"So, it seems we've a celebrity in the house. I will refrain from playing your songs and avoid self-destructive comparisons," he quipped.

Lucas magnanimously waved a hand high. I still hadn't really seen his face.

The musicians began an up-tempo beat led by the drummer. Table by table rose to the dance floor.

Ginny grabbed my hand. "Come on, Lucy, this is our chance!"

"Chance?"

She nodded. "Remember what I told you about coffee machines back at the Paramount audition?"

I did, but didn't see—

She pointed to the waitress approaching the VIP table with a tray under her arm.

"Just in from L.A. They're going to need caffeine. I don't believe in coincidence. I believe in right place, right time. That's destiny!"

She shimmied her shoulders and ponied on her feet. I followed suit. Hand in hand, we made our way through the gyrating crowd to where the velvet rope was the only thing between us and the stars.

There . . . we danced. The lights dimmed further. The music stirred our blood. We swung our hips in wide arcs, lifted our arms to the roof, kicked our legs so that our hems rode up even higher, and laughed until sweat washed away every speck of rouge.

Suddenly, the buzz and whirl of the club came to a hush.

"Well now, all right then," said the singer excitedly. "Folks, it looks like we got one last number. By request. It's a true honor and a pleasure to share the stage . . ." And then he faded into the black, and up to the mic stepped Lucas Wesley.

The club erupted in applause and screams. A single spotlight magnified the wonder. His skin radiated. His eyes were incandescent. He was cosmic. The room swooned, and me with it. The crowd fell forward to the base of the stage so that our bodies were pressed like grapes underfoot. The softness of Ginny's chest pressed dewy against my back, her thighs against mine; mine against Flynn; Flynn against Ben; and on and on to the front of the stage, where Lucas reached down to a fan. I couldn't see if it was a girl or a boy, just a longing, outstretched hand. When Lucas took it, the power surged back. My knees went weak. Chills ran the length of my body. I gasped audibly and felt the breath escape Ginny, too. The sound of one exhale multiplied to a roar.

"Is this really happening?" Ginny whispered at my neck.

The tickle of her words ran the length of my body, and I thought I might faint from it all.

Lucas raised a finger to his perfectly bowed lips, quieting the crowd. With that same finger he gestured to the guitar player. I expected an eruption of mania. To everyone's surprise, the guitar player strummed a slow chord.

"Ohh Lordddd, my God . . . when I, in awesome wonder, consider all the worlds Thy hands have made. I see the stars, I hear the rolling thunder. Thy power throughout the universe displayed . . ."

His baritone voice reverberated like the strings of a harp. Warm, rich, and wholly satisfying. My bones trembled in unrestrained places. Tears stung my eyes. He sang every verse of "How Great Thou Art." Not a person moved or made a sound.

In the void of its end, he bashfully ran a hand through his hair. "That's a poem that Carl Boberg wrote. I appreciate you listening to me sing it. Well . . . g'night then."

The spotlight cut out. The pub lamplights came on. A bartender hollered, "Pack it up, kids!"

I turned to Ginny behind me. She thumbed the wetness on my cheek and then wiped her own. We'd both been moved to tears.

It was my first time in a club, my first taste of beer, my first encounter with an honest-to-God celebrity, and the first time I felt total abandonment. It was rapture.

The troubadours dispersed with the crowd receding out into the foggy night. The VIP table was empty when we passed. They'd slipped out the back exit. Ginny was right. Not one pint or wine carafe was on the table, only empty espresso cups.

6

By Monday morning, word had spread across the Academy that Nico Cellini was casting for his first Lucas Wesley musical.

Ginny and I had dance class in the morning. Between port de bras and cambrés at the barre, the students whispered:

"It's a musical so they'll have choreography."

"Ballet or tap?"

"Not sure, but I bet we'll need to sing, too."

"Are any leads being auditioned?"

"Must be, they talked to Mrs. Crawford."

"Dancers!" shouted Mr. Stannus, our ballet instructor. "No talking, or you'll do pliés until your knees break. Your turnout is reprehensible—focus!"

We obeyed and silently pliéd to his *five-six-seven-eight*.

After our exercises, Ginny and I changed into wool coats, trousers, and boots. The February clag had turned to sleet that sheathed the trees and buildings in glassy dormancy. From the sidewalks to the brindled lawns, every step crackled underfoot. We clung together to keep from slipping and falling, to keep each other moving forward toward the convergence point of every ICA student that afternoon: the auditorium. A notice had been pinned to the main student bulletin that those with interest in film work should come to the information meeting during lunch hour.

The auditorium purred with the confluence of expectation and anxiety. Flynn and Ben sat in the second row holding court and seats for the rest of the troubadours. Ben smiled when he saw us enter and elbowed Flynn, who waved us over.

"It's our lovely dovelys," said Flynn. "Need seats?" He pointed to two beside him roped off with a similarly patterned scarf as the one he'd lent me at the club. I realized they each had one, a secret society token.

"Sure," said Ginny.

Flynn pulled away the paisley satin and we sat. So close, we were eye level with the chipped black of the painted proscenium.

On the hour of noon, the room hushed to attention. The clip of Mrs. Crawford's heels through the wings was steady as a metronome.

"Hello, students, welcome! I'm happy to see so many of you this afternoon." She projected her voice with perfect enunciation. From the front row to the back, every word was pristine as a bell. I could barely say my name without someone tilting a head in confusion. My accent was the first thing I aimed to change.

"I won't beat around the bush," Mrs. Crawford continued. "We're lucky to have an award-winning and much-admired film director with us. Please welcome Signor Nico Cellini." She lifted an arm to stage right in formal rhetorical pose.

On cue, Nico entered.

The audience stood in ovation.

At the club, I'd assumed the older, bearded gentleman in the VIP entourage was Nico. One ascribes paternal-like qualities to the title *Director*, an administrative type with stern gaze, commanding presence, and wizened age. But there stood a dashing middle-aged man with chiseled face, blond hair, and swagger in his smile. Dressed impeccably in a white collared shirt and tailored brown suit adorned with a blue pocket square. The chain at his neck glinted gold sparkles into the audience. He could've been a star himself.

He waved a hand and then plunged it into his pants pocket, making Flynn clutch his chest and fall back into his seat.

"*Ciao*," said Nico.

I felt myself mouthing the word back. Silently, trying on his Italian accent. Sweet as a scoop of gelato.

"Please sit."

We sat in dog-like adoration.

"*Ciao, e benvenuto*, Signor Cellini," said Mrs. Crawford. Her Italian was as refined as her English. "I will let you tell the students why you have come."

"Aw, *sì, grazie.*" He winked back, and I swear I saw old Mrs. Crawford blush.

"I come to ICA because you are the crème de la crème. That is exactly what I need for my film. It is a Shakespeare adaptation but not another same-same. A drama, a tragedy, a production to go down in the history books. The greatest love story of all time . . . *Romeo & Juliet*, *The Musical* starring Lucas Wesley as Romeo!"

The audience rose to its feet again. Singers squealed high notes, dancers waved jazz hands, actors gave each other high fives. It was official: a musical meant elaborate sets, embellished costumes, shooting on location, and Lucas Wesley!

"But here is my problem," Nico continued.

We quieted and sat.

"I have not found my Houses of Montague and Capulet . . . or my Juliet."

As sure as I live and breathe, Nico looked at me, second row on the right, and straight on. My skin prickled with a thousand tiny sparks.

"Looks like one lovely dovely caught the hawk's eye," whispered Flynn.

Nico's gaze remained while Mrs. Crawford explained that actors should come with short monologues from the original play. Singers should have their scales warmed up. Dancers should be ready to spin and leap to the piano's accompaniment.

"Signor Cellini needs to provide the studio with final casting and begin rehearsals as soon as possible. So please take the next couple of days to shine up your résumés and prepare. I'll post the audition schedule on the board. I'm confident that each of you will represent ICA to your fullest potential. Good luck, students."

Ginny pulled my elbow. The meeting was over. Mrs. Crawford escorted Nico off stage left. The students filed out in excited clusters. Regular classes had been canceled. It was like a holiday only with presents far superior to new socks and mittens.

"Do you think Lucas Wesley will be at the auditions?" asked Ginny.

Unwilling to venture into the cold yet, we gathered in the radiator-heated hallway outside the auditorium. Ben, Flynn, and Jack leaned against the splodgy plaster wall warmed by the steam pipes behind.

"Of course he will," said Flynn. "There's got to be magnetism between the lead characters. Juliet and Romeo, for certain. But even Tybalt and Mercutio have a love-hate chemistry. That's the director's job. Finding that magic."

"Who are you thinking?" asked Ben.

"Oh, definitely Mercutio. I would die happy to be Lucas Wesley's right-hand man." He threw back his head in mock martyrdom and quoted, "'If love be rough with you, be rough with love; prick love for pricking and you beat love down.'"

The troubadours laughed.

"Are you girls both angling for the lead?" Flynn asked.

"I could never be Juliet," said Ginny. "I'm way too tall. I stand four inches over most of the boys even when I slouch. But maybe I could be the Nurse," she mulled aloud.

"Does the Nurse need to high kick?" asked Jack.

Ginny raised an eyebrow. "I'll show you my high kick."

"Granted, my eyes are a bit bleary from gazing into the stage lights, but I could've sworn Cellini was looking at us," said Flynn.

Us, yes, *us*! The inclusive pronoun made me feel less self-conscious.

"Did he recognize us from the club?" asked Ben.

"Maybe," said Flynn. "Wouldn't that be our lucky stars?"

Ginny pressed her hip against mine, and it caught Flynn's attention.

"You're being awful quiet," he said to me. "What part are you thinking?"

I shrugged. "I'd take anything, really. I mean, beggars can't be choosers, right?"

Flynn stared at me, a long, dramatic beat. "So, your aim is to play a beggar?"

Jack guffawed.

"Come, come, we can do better." Flynn put a matriarchal arm around my shoulder and turned me slightly away from the others. "Remember what I said about transformation?"

I nodded.

"Well, this is your moment. You only get one chance to impress Nico Cellini. An opportunity like this is one in a million." He pulled his paisley scarf around my neck, satin skimming my skin, and then looped it back around his own. "Become who you were meant to be. And that, I promise, is not a beggar."

A more cynical person might've doubted the sincerity—or at the very least, the motivation of an ambitious young actor with a lust for fame. As much as the troubadours acted mature, they were boys navigating a harsh world in which they felt like outsiders. They recognized a similar spirit in me.

"First things first," said Flynn. "You cannot audition as Lucille Hickey."

If he had been the only person to say this, I might have waved it off. But Ginny said the same. The problem was, I couldn't think of a better name.

"Lucille Ball has your first name practically patented. Unless you want to do screwball comedies the rest of your life. And *Hickey* is unpalatable on a marquee. What about a middle name?"

"Lorianne."

"It's not bad but it needs to be punchier with a sexy spelling. Audiences eat that up. What about just Lori, lovely dovely?" He stopped and his eyes lit up. "Hey, that's nice. Lori Lovely."

"Lori Lovely," I said aloud, letting the dictation roll off my tongue without an ounce of Pufftown drawl.

It fit.

That night, while Ginny wrapped and pinned my hair for bed, I typed up a new résumé on the typewriter Mrs. Coates lent us.

Lori Lovely I put at the top and smiled at the look of it professionally inked.

"It's a really good name," Ginny agreed. "Should I still call you Lucy or do you want me to call you Lori?"

Her real name might've been Jennifer Cockburn but that wasn't the Ginny Wilde I knew. I wanted to be Lori Lovely in Ginny's eyes most of all.

"Call me Lori."

"Lori Lovely," she said in an exhale. "It suits you." And then she kissed my cheek. "Your hair's done. It'll be smooth as silk all week now."

She jumped in the bed we shared with a white table napkin, which she proceeded to tie over her curly bob.

"What do you think? Do I look the part? One of the other housemistresses who boards with Mrs. Coates used to be a wet nurse and said that sometimes their caps doubled as baby burp cloths. I am finding it very hard to Method this motivation because nothing could convince me to walk around with baby vomit on my head."

I turned off the lamp and climbed into bed beside her, being careful to lay my head on the pillow so as not to disturb the hair pins she'd placed. She leaned in, her sweet minty toothpaste breath against my neck in the dark.

"No wonder the Capulet nurse didn't have a lover. I mean, my God, the poor woman was leaking out her front and crowned with puke."

And then we rolled with laughter under the covers.

Before finally falling asleep, Ginny slipped her arm over my waist and whispered, "I think you have what it takes to be Juliet, Lori Lovely."

I squeezed her arm. I wanted to believe her.

7

Two days later was the first female audition and every trifecta student stood outside the Italia Conti Academy auditorium. I wasn't alone in having a newly minted résumé. Names, birth dates, hometowns, height, weight, and talents had been fudged to fit the bill. Actors had to be eighteen to get hired but under twenty to play Shakespeare's thirteen-year-old Juliet. That left a significantly diminished auditioning pool. So, liberties were taken and ICA turned a blind eye. Officially, ICA was merely providing the auditioning venue. It was a United Kingdom school. Paramount Pictures was a United States studio. Nico Cellini had an Italian film crew. Things were bound to fall through national cracks. It was 1965.

For many students, this was their first professional film experience, which differed vastly from theater auditions. Paramount Pictures' casting division was a well-oiled machine. Their brisk efficiency shook the courage of many confident students.

Per usual, the casting director's assistant sat outside the auditorium collecting headshots and résumés. He sized up each girl with a glance and placed the headshot in one of three piles, calling out, "Next!" without giving any indication of what the piles meant.

When Ginny and I got to the front of the line, he looked Ginny up, up, up, and said, "How tall are you?"

"Under six feet, but I've got dance heels on now, so I look taller."

That was half-true. She did have heels on and did look taller. But she was only under six feet if she hunched her back and bowed her head. I'd seen her do it in the mirror at home, testing the best way to slump so that her tunic hid the awkward pose. No one could be taller than the leading man, especially not the leading lady.

The assistant put Ginny's résumé in the thickest stack to the far left. Ensemble, presumably.

"I was in the film *Hey, Let's Twist!*" Ginny pointed to her résumé. "And Paramount's production of *The Kid* back in Brooklyn."

The assistant stopped. "My grandparents live in Brooklyn."

Ginny smiled. "I miss Highway Bagels."

"On the corner of Ocean Ave?"

She nodded.

"Yeah, me too. Best schmears in town." He grinned and moved her résumé to the middle pile.

She winked at him, and I wasn't entirely sure who was playing who.

"Next!" he called, and I stepped forward.

He looked up quickly, and then did a double.

"How old are you?"

"How old do you want me to be?"

He frowned. It hadn't worked the way Ginny'd said it would.

"I'm a first-year student."

He skimmed my résumé. "You sing, dance, and act. Already got your SAG card, too?"

"Yup, SAG in the bag."

I bit my lip. I sounded ridiculous. The gatekeepers were the ones who made me most nervous. Flippant decisions change the trajectory of an entire life. Like moving Ginny from one pile to another based on Brooklyn bagels.

He eyed my headshot, up at me, back at my headshot, and then he put it in the shortest pile to his right.

"Next!"

Ginny grabbed my hand. "Did you see? He put yours in the lead-roles auditions. I barely made it into the minor characters. Hopefully, I'll get a line or two. But you! I *told* you—you have the Hollywood It factor!"

She pressed her cheek to mine, and I wished we could go through life just like that—cheek to cheek, hand in hand, anchored by her steadfast belief in me. She didn't know how badly my knees were shaking.

The day before, Ginny and I had popped into the antiquarian bookshop to buy used copies of *Romeo and Juliet* to prepare. At Pufftown High, our English class had read the play. Classmates squirmed in their seats at references to maidenheads, kisses, and yearnings. The cheeks of those who had experiential knowledge flushed just as pink as those who didn't. Truth be told, beyond the pair of lovers, I'd had a hard time following what was happening—too much vestal livery and for-thou-art talk. We didn't act it out—heavens no! Our English teacher had enough trouble with the text. So, while I knew of it, I hardly knew it. Ginny and I picked what we thought was the easiest monologue to memorize: the balcony scene. Youthful desire was easy to decipher . . . and fun, too.

We each took turns playing Juliet sitting atop our bed and Romeo on the floor. Serious study was not an easy task with Ginny as my partner. She'd discovered Crunchie bars since moving to England.

"Chocolate is entirely different here. I can't stop eating these," she'd confessed mid-scene and mid-munch. "I bet Romeo had a devilish mustache." She'd smeared the Crunchie bar over her top lip so that every time I, as Juliet, leaned over the bed balcony, the smell of toffee made me hungry.

So much mooning, swearing, evoking of the gods and silver tips. We wondered what Shakespeare was smoking and giggled ourselves to spittle more often than completing the scene.

Still, even the most cloying lines resonated. I understood Juliet's longing to surrender to love even if it meant her life, and I was sure I could tap into whatever that feeling was.

In the audition hallway, however, panic displaced confidence. My mind went blank.

"If I call your name, please proceed to the greenroom. The rest of you—in the auditorium!" called out the assistant.

"Sophia Beauvoir, Lily Day, Miranda Saint, Jane O'Clara, and Lori Lovely."

"Lorrrriiiiiiii!" Ginny trilled.

I whispered through clenched jaw, "I don't remember the scene."

She took my face between her hands. "Yes, you do. Lori Lovely knows it by heart. Say it."

"Say what?"

"If you say something aloud, you tell the universe that you believe it. Believing is power. So say it: I am Lori Lovely . . ."

"I am Lori Lovely," I repeated.

"I am Juliet."

"I am Juliet."

"Now, every time you start doubting yourself, say that. It's like wedding vows with whatever it is you believe."

Ginny kissed me goodbye and good luck and then tied on her nurse's handkerchief and followed the majority into the auditorium.

The five named girls remained, and our collective breaths seemed to take up every inch of the hallway. We varied greatly in appearance—shades of blond to brunette, and even a touch of red in Jane O'Clara, which could've come by bottle, but she'd never tell. Despite our outward distinctions, there was something eerily similar. We were all wistfully young. The milk of our mothers still evidenced in our dewy skin, white teeth, and wide eyes. Our bodies were in that season when flesh blossoms to womanhood while marrow remains tender. Our desire to be seen mature enough to handle the title role made us all raise our chins, push our shoulders back, fake confidence, and act the part.

For those outside the theatrical fold, the greenroom is not green at all. It was the place where actors warmed up their voices, practiced their lines, and prepared to take the stage. Floor-to-ceiling mirrors encircled the room, plastic chairs had been aligned across the back wall. A table in the corner held an assortment of digestive biscuits, candied ginger, and instant Nescafé beside an electric kettle. It made me smile and think of Ginny. Coffee.

"Ladies," said the assistant, "you'll be auditioning one at a time. The rest of you will wait in the hallway. I'll bring you in that door." He pointed to the one we'd just come through. "And you'll leave through *that* door." He pointed to the one leading to the auditorium. "Signor Cellini is waiting for one more person to arrive before we begin."

We were all wired tight. Ready to do this. Fight or flight. My pulse beat in my earlobes.

"Follow me."

He lined us up against the tiled wall outside the greenroom. The radiator gurgled and spat. I tried to conjure the lines of the balcony scene, the lightness of Ginny's fingertips on my hair, the comfort of home.

I am Lori Lovely, I am Juliet, I mouthed to myself and then let the thought roll over and over in my mind: *I am Lori Lovely . . . I am . . .*

"Okay, they're ready," announced the assistant. "Miranda Saint, you're up first."

The coloring drained from Miranda's face, although it was hard to tell at first. She was platinum blonde, nearly translucent. The kind of fairy maiden that English knights died for in plays and poems.

I was relieved I wasn't first. Nobody wants to be the first or the last. The audience's expectations are too high at the beginning and patience is too low at the end. A nice cushy middle was the optimum, preferably after someone who fumbled a little. That was the truth no one spoke at the risk of superstitious ruin.

The radiator clicked on. Clicked off. Clicked on again. Had it been ten minutes or half an hour? None of us wore a watch. It wasn't Juliet's style.

The assistant returned and called for Lily and then Sophia and then Jane. The last one in the hallway, I was entirely convinced I was the last option. This is what I told myself walking in.

When I saw the panel, my stomach dropped. Lucas Wesley sat beside Nico Cellini.

"Oh!" I gasped.

In a cable-knit sweater, jeans, and white sneakers, he was somehow even more attractive beside the tailored Italians. The quintessential all-American boy. I half expected him to toss me a baseball and sing "God Bless America."

Lucas turned to Nico with a look of equal surprise.

The casting director cleared her throat and held up my résumé. "Miss Lori Lovely?"

"Yes, that's me."

There was a murmur among them.

"Tell me this," said Nico. "Have you auditioned for me before?"

I shook my head. "No, sir—*signor*."

He grinned at my attempted honorific.

"Very interesting. I feel I have seen you somewhere."

My résumé was passed across the line of panelists.

"I've done film work as an extra in New York City," I explained. "This is my first semester at the Academy."

A couple of the heads nodded, as if that must account for the déjà vu.

Lucas gently unfurled the lip of his paper coffee cup, deferentially glancing up from time to time.

"How do you like London?" asked Nico.

I expected him to inquire about my work in New York City, my education, my family background, my age, or one of the other items on my résumé. I wasn't expecting a conversation. It caught me off guard.

"I . . . I like it very much." I channeled the sound of Mrs. Crawford, clipping my consonance and using short sentences. "It's quite grand. Compared to where I grew up."

"It's real cold though," said Lucas. "Compared to North Carolina, right?"

The question evoked scenes of my childhood: sunny winter days when the neighborhood kids dared to throw off their parkas and race around the duck pond, careful to avoid the icy patches of the shade. That would never happen here. The London chill would snatch the breath out of you.

"Yes. I miss the sunshine."

Lucas smiled and it warmed me through. "Yeah, me too."

"Let's imagine ourselves in Italy, then, shall we? The city of Verona to be exact," said the casting director. "What monologue have you chosen?"

"Act Two, Scene Two."

"Aw, the balcony scene," she replied with a smirk and turned to Nico. "Three out of five. You owe me a drink after this."

The panel flipped pages of their bound plays.

"Let's cut to the *wherefore art thou* part," she continued, "and we'll feed you Romeo's lines."

"Okay." My voice shook slightly.

Nico heard it. "This is one of my favorite scenes. I'm glad you chose it." He nodded. "Please, Signorina Lovely, when you are ready."

I closed my eyes a beat to collect my courage and thought of Ginny playing Romeo with chocolate smeared across her lip.

"'O Romeo, Romeo! Wherefore art thou Romeo? Deny thy father and refuse thy name. Or, if thou wilt not, be but sworn my love, and I'll no longer be a Capulet.'"

"'Shall I hear more, or shall I speak at this?'" read the assistant.

And on we went until I hit the line *overheard'st, ere I was ware.* When practiced with Ginny, it had proved a tongue twister for us both. She'd accidentally spit toffee on my nose attempting to get it out correctly.

"'I should have been more strange, I must confess, but that thou overheard'st, ere I was ware . . .'"

I smirked at the memory, and suddenly couldn't remember what came after. I looked down at my feet to find Shakespeare's words again. Unable to meet the panel's stare, I stammered my way through the next line.

"'My true—true love's passion . . . therefore, pardon me, and do not impute this yielding to light love, which the dark night hath so discovered.'"

I'd broken character and shown myself to be no actress, no Lori Lovely, and no Juliet. I was a country bumpkin from Pufftown, Nowhere, trying to play a noblewoman.

Then came the smooth voice of Lucas Wesley.

"'Lady, by yonder blessed moon I swear, that tips with silver all these fruit-tree tops—'"

I inhaled sharply and lifted my gaze to his. Neither of us spoke. He grinned. I grinned. And it all came rushing back.

"'O, swear not by the moon, the inconstant moon, that monthly changes in her circled orb, lest that thy love prove likewise variable . . .'"

We finished the scene together, and the force of it knocked the wind out of me. I waited a long minute to be excused or for the casting director to make some remark, but no one spoke. Nico broke the stalemate. He gave a single clap that he held to his chest like a caught butterfly.

"Brava, *bellissima*." He nodded at Lucas. "Well done."

"That was all Miss Lovely," Lucas deflected.

I shook my head and was about to say that if it hadn't been for him, I would've bumbled the whole thing.

Lucas continued, "It came to me in the middle of your scene. Were you at the Troubadour a couple nights ago?"

Ginny was not going to believe any of this. Or maybe she was the only one who would.

"Yes, it's a popular place for ICA students."

"I knew we'd seen you before," said Lucas.

The dawning caused Nico to raise both eyebrows. "You were dancing."

"My friend, Ginny Wilde. She's auditioning for the Nurse's role."

Nico chuckled. "Your friend is far too elegant to be the Nurse. That part needs . . . *grossalona*, how you say?"

He looked to the casting director.

"Crass," she interpreted. "Someone more common."

"*Sì, corretta*," said Nico.

"Ginny's definitely not common," I conceded. "But she's an incredible actress."

"Thank you for this rousing audition," said the casting director. "Signor Cellini will now consider all of today's Juliets alongside the ones of the past few weeks. We will be in touch if needed."

Past few weeks? If needed? It made me question the sincerity of Nico and Lucas. Maybe the chemistry I felt was not me but their celebrity charm.

The assistant stood and ushered me toward the auditorium door.

"Signorina Lovely." Nico stopped me. "One more question, if you please."

I turned.

"You can sing, *sì*?"

I bit my lower lip. The truth could lose me the opportunity of a lifetime, but a lie could lose me a lifetime of credibility. I had to choose.

"I'm no Judy Garland, but I can get by if the song's got a catchy beat."

Nico laughed. "No matter. We dub. This is not Shakespeare's *Romeo and Juliet*. It is Cellini's! We make magic!" He turned to his assistant. "Call Marni Nixon." Then he patted Lucas on the shoulder before nodding to me. "*Grazie, Lori-etta*."

It would become his private nickname. A mythical hybrid. I was Lucille, Lucy, Lori, Juliet, and Lorietta all rolled into one. The person and the persona. So little separation, it was hard to know the difference.

Lu

Garden Dig

The Abbey, Connecticut
October 1990

The sisters sing seven times a day and once in the middle of the night. Every day, every night. It's the Rule of Saint Benedict called the canonical hours.

"Sacred music imparts serenity and arouses the response of modern people in common purpose," Aunt Lori explains when I ask how they got anything done with the incessant bell cueing Do-Re-Mi. "Gregorian chants outdate Rodgers and Hammerstein, but *The Sound of Music* is a wonderful picture."

Today, before the first note was sung, Aunt Lori left a handwritten one tacked to my door at the Women's Guest House:

Meet me in the garden after mass.

The garden? I'm supposed to be interviewing her again, but I'm not about to argue. Last night, after Vespers and supper, she was all business in her office. Meaning, we sidestepped the uncomfortable conversation about not telling my mom that I was coming here. Aunt Lori wasn't the fire-and-brimstone kind. That wasn't her way. Instead, she'd meet me in the garden.

I stop at my car parked in the gravel lot beside the Women's Guest

House. My tape recorder is underneath a half-eaten bag of Cheetos. The back seat is powdered in neon-orange dust. I pop in a blank cassette, but when I test it, the gears don't move. The batteries are dead. I'm sure the sisters have some, but it means I'm back to my notebook for the time being. I carry it dutifully to the garden.

It's one of those slate-gray days with clouds like laundered linens strung across the sun. The warmth is there without the threat of burn. Still, all the nuns wear brimmed hats over their wimples.

It's hard to tell Aunt Lori from the others. *Ora et Labora* (Pray and Work) is the motto of the order. The sisters are dedicated. They've etched the Latin on wood, metal, pottery, printed it on paper . . . even branded it into leather. All of which are sold in the Monastic Art Shop to locals and visitors. I have to hand it to them, they're an industrious bunch.

Working the land is a collective duty and passion for many of the sisters, an opportunity to nurture seed to fruit and celebrate life's seasons. It's autumn now, fade and flourish. The sisters remove the dead summer blooms, edelweiss skeletons, hydrangea tufts, and droopy zinnias, while simultaneously harvesting the bright squashes, cabbage heads, and leafy tops of radishes, parsnips, and carrots below. When they finish, the vegetable boxes will be raked flat and sprinkled with blood meal in preparation for winter and spring planting to follow.

One of the sisters stands to stretch her back, and drops her trowel. Another turns to pick it up. Face revealed, it's Aunt Lori. Wearing pink polka-dotted gardening gloves, she spritzes the downy sage leaves with a bottle of something.

There's a bold smell like peanut butter gone sour. My eyes are watering by the time I reach her. I can barely keep from gagging.

"For God's sake, that smells awful!"

"I welcome the invocation of the Lord. Good morning to you too, Lu."

She's in cherubic spirits. I'll take it—even if she smells like hell.

"That"—she squirts a fine mist into the air—"is the divine scent of Indian lilac. More commonly called Neem. A natural pesticide and fungicide. Highly effective. Sister Uma brought over a tree from India years ago. It took root over there." She points to the opposite side of the garden where a stone hedge demarcates the orchard of craggily bare branches removed of their fruits.

I wouldn't be able to tell a Neem from a coffee bean.

"We use it on everything," she continues. "Plants, animals, and mostly, ourselves. Skin conditions and digestive problems to arthritis. The Ayurveda have been using Neem for centuries, but our Western medicine hasn't caught on."

"I had a wart the size of Texas," says the nun who dropped her trowel.

She takes off her hat, and I recognize Sister Evangelista.

"Smack dab in the middle of my forehead." She brings her face so close that I can see where the sweat has dried to salt flakes. "See it? You sure don't. 'Cause it's gone!"

I take a step back. "It's a miracle."

"Yes, Christ be praised!" she says. "Neem be praised!"

Wart removal didn't seem to be on the same level as Christ, but who was I to argue with a nun.

"Got any warts, acne, or funny moles?"

I did not, and even if I did . . . "I'm not sure the price is worth the cure."

Sister Evangelista claps her hat back on like a cowboy mounting up. "When you're looking for a cure, there's no price you won't pay."

She kneels back down to pull a row of radishes out of the ground.

I lean into Aunt Lori and whisper, "Is she always so intense?"

She backs my way so the brim of her hat tents us in privacy.

"Sister Evangelista feels everything with great passion. It's one of her strengths and one of her challenges." Aunt Lori hands me her basket laden with vegetables and herbs.

I loop the handle over my arm and lay my notebook atop a row of carrots.

"I hoped we could continue talking today. You know, for my thesis," I gently remind. I don't want to upset her charitable mood.

She *spritz-spritzes* a plume of Neem on a nearby tomato plant.

"First, tell me why you didn't want to speak to your mom."

Right to the point. I'm ready.

"She would have wanted to come with me. If Mom were here, it'd turn into a family visit. I need to work—to ask serious questions, research and write when I'm alone in my room."

She scratches her chin with a polka-dotted finger and leaves the prettiest dirt fingerprint I have ever seen.

It was a good answer and true, mostly.

"Okay," she concedes. "But promise that you'll call her. She was really worried something bad happened to you."

I nod with my best solicitous face. "You know Mom. She worries that something bad is going to happen in the middle of something good happening."

Aunt Lori grins at that, but a shadow cloud passes over the ocean of her eyes.

"If your mom is guilty of anything, it's loving you too much. That can make people act in ways even *they* don't understand." She kisses my cheek, then gestures for me to follow her. "You can do your work while helping us do ours. Abbey rules, you know."

Everyone who stays at the abbey, including guests, is required to participate in the sisters' work. The goats need milking. The chicken eggs need collecting. The cheese and the whey need separating. The ripe fruits need to be picked before the birds carry them off. The vegetables need to be plucked, washed, and chopped. They work together so that they can be nurtured together, body, mind, and spirit. That's the abbey way.

If I'm going to unearth Aunt Lori's story, I'm going to have to step in beside her, dig and get dirty. So, I do, even though it feels like penance. I put down my notebook and sink my hands into the soft ground, rooting through the muck until I feel a round beet. I pull hard. A piece of the tail breaks off and the juice stains my fingers red.

"There are sets of gloves in the garden shed," Aunt Lori offers when she sees my black-ringed nails.

No point. My hands are already a mess. When we finish reaping our assigned box from the garden and Sister Evangelista is raking the soil, Aunt Lori leads me to the outdoor pump to wash up.

A bar of Ivory soap, mushy from lying in its own puddle, sits beside the tin basin. It squishes between my blackened knuckles. Aunt Lori primes the pump, and a minute later water *glugs* up from the well, ten degrees too cold for comfort. I lather fast to keep my fingers from going stiff. The beet juice stays in all the creases of my hands, making the lines of the M in my palms even more stark.

As a kid, I thought it stood for *Marie*—a flesh imprint of my mom. Then at sixteen, on a Southern Baptist youth trip to the Carolina Classic Fair, a group of us decided to be rebels and have our fortunes told. We popped into Madame Gabriella's tent adorned with sparkling celestial icons and ruby curtains. Besides being dangerously beautiful, speaking with an exotic French accent, *and* wearing the brightest shade of crimson lipstick I had ever seen, Madame Gabriella had a talent for reading palms—the work of the devil, according to our baptized-in-the-spirit youth pastor.

The youth pastor had shown us a VHS tape of a teen film called *Amityville,* where two friends played with a Ouija board. A lesson to us not to engage with demonic forces.

We opted for the palm readings at ten dollars a palm and asked that Madame Gabriella keep her velvet gloves on. She obliged.

She told Tom Larkin that he had "water hands" and was hiding his sensitive side from the world. The other boys made teasing remarks, and he'd gotten so pissed off that he left the tent. She told Ruth Beasley that her love line was splintered and she would have multiple great loves in her life. It was meant as a compliment, but Ruth turned flaming red and cried: "No, I won't. I'm not a slut!"

Two girls decided then not to do this wicked thing. Instead, they pooled their money to buy Ruth cinnamon churros and tickets on the wave swinger to help them forget about her promiscuous future.

I'd lingered in the back, watching, until the tent was empty. When I slid my bill onto the table and turned over my palm, Madame Gabriella didn't smile, but the dimple in her right cheek revealed itself.

"Your heart line is deep, but it begins between your index and middle finger. That means you are indecisive . . . caught between contentment and seeking."

At the time, I was neither. I had sat in her chair primarily to see if she could tell that I wasn't a virgin—because if she could, I worried others could, too. But she didn't speak of sex or conjure ghosts. She simply pointed out what was in my hand.

"Maybe that will change as you grow." She took off her glove and pressed her thumbnail into my palm so that it pained slightly and left a crescent moon between my heart line and my headline. "See that?"

I nodded.

She rubbed it away. "And now it's gone. Remember, you are transforming minute by minute. Keep your palms open to heaven and you will receive what you seek. *One cannot love without suffering* . . ."

She'd reached to her neck and pulled a gold chain. On the end of it hung a medallion with a woman holding a flaming anatomical heart. Circling the figure was the name *Sainte Marguerite-Marie Alacoque*.

"These are the words of my patron saint."

The Christian icon shocked me. Palm readers didn't have patron saints. Not according to our church pastors.

A couple mooning over each other while wiping funnel cake sugar off their chins came into the tent. Madame Gabriella squeezed my hand kindly without another word. My turn was up.

I didn't go on any more rides that day. I sat on a bench near the entrance, examining the lines in my hands, hearing Madame Gabriella's words echo. Something inside me changed and there was no going back.

The next day at school, I spent my lunch hour in the library reading about Sainte Marguerite-Marie Alacoque. A French nun from Burgundy who claimed that Jesus Christ appeared to her in a vision, Marguerite-Marie was one of the church's most venerated mystics. I nearly dropped the book when I saw the word. Clear as day, hot as hellfire: a *mystic*.

But how could a person who'd given her mind, body, and soul to the Catholic faith engage in mystical activities? I grew up under the doctrine that all things magical were wicked. Hell, I couldn't even watch *The Smurfs* cartoons on Saturday mornings because it was rumored to contain enchanted devilry. Parents beware: imaginary blue creatures who live in forest mushrooms are trying to bewitch your children's souls. Even more confusing were Sunday mornings when our pastor sermonized on the supernatural nature of the Holy Spirit. Where was the line between fact and fiction, good and evil?

When I'd asked my mom about Aunt Lori's conversion to Catholicism, she said that people created religious denominations, but God had none such. Aunt Lori chose to worship God in the way of Catholics, and we worshipped God in the way of Baptists. As simple as choosing to eat off a plate or out of a bowl, with a spoon or with a fork. The choice was ours. The food didn't change depending on the utensils we used and neither did God. I had countered that her theory held water so long as one believed in the supernatural, which I couldn't say for certain I did. The lines were all blurred.

Now, I flex my palm, washed clean but still tinged red in the creases from the beet root. My nail beds shade lavender from the cold. Aunt Lori brings me a kitchen hand towel. The cotton is warm. She must've set it by the stove a minute.

"Thanks, Aunt Lori."

"'Serve God fervently and constantly,'" she quotes with two fingers raised, "'without any other help than simple faith . . . your service the more pleasing to Him.'"

The daily chores have purpose beyond sacramental obligation. We eat these vegetables, braised in homemade chicken stock. Chunks of cheese are added to the bowl before the broth so that they soften to treasured bites. The abbey's handmade cheese smells like funky socks but tastes of heaven. It's one of their specialties. My stomach growls, but dinner is still a few hours away. The vegetables in our baskets are raw and bitter. They need the fire to mellow, the longer the better.

"Well, I'll *confess*," I say. "I'm not doing this to be pleasing. I want the stew."

Aunt Lori smiles. "And who do you think provided the ingredients and know-how to create that stew?"

Christ. Here we go again. Round and round. Everything always came back to this.

"Aunt Lori, you know I'm not convinced of God so much anymore. I mean . . ." It feels awkward to say aloud, the words stumble out of my mouth. "No disrespect. It's just . . . I'm grown up, and the whole idea of some bearded director dude pointing a commanding finger from a cloud, 'Stage left! Stage right! That's a wrap!' Well, it isn't something I choose to believe in."

"I never worked for a director like that, spiritual or human," she replies.

I take back my notebook and pen. "So, what were your directors like?"

She pauses a moment. The wheels of her mind rewind. "My first real relationship with a director was with Nico Cellini."

Hook, line, and sinker, I got her back where I want her.

Part 3

Lori

Set the World on Fire

8

London to Rome
1965

The week after my audition, Mrs. Crawford called me to her office.

"You are Signor Cellini's Juliet. Well done, Lori," she said without batting an eye, as if handing out life-changing news was a daily occurrence. "Lucas Wesley was particularly keen after meeting you."

That was flattering but also anxiety inducing. I wanted him to like me, of course. But what exactly did *keen* mean? I didn't dare admit that I'd never had a boyfriend or even kissed a boy, never mind everything I knew the stage required of Romeo and Juliet.

She clasped her hands together and cleared her throat. "One of the conditions of the role is that you keep it a secret for now. Paramount can't have the cast being leaked."

My enthusiasm sank with creeping doubt. If no one knew I was Juliet, was it real? They could cast another girl without anyone being the wiser. Mrs. Crawford interpreted my pause as fear.

"Given your student standing, I think it would be appropriate to tell your family. Your curriculum will have to be altered. The Academy will not penalize you for success in the skills you are here to master. So don't worry."

I nodded.

She unclenched her hands and patted my arm in congratulations. "I do hope you know how immense an opportunity this is. ICA is extremely proud that one of our students has earned the lead."

"Thank you, Mrs. Crawford."

There was an awkward pause. The radiator hissed.

"Well then." Mrs. Crawford consulted her wristwatch. "You best be off."

I flew through the streets of Bloomsbury without buttoning my coat. The too-long red scarf my mom had sent unfurled behind me, *thwack*-ing passersby.

"Sorry! Pardon! Sorry!" I said between skips.

I needed to get to our flat before Ginny left for class. It would be like a scene from a dramatic movie: running toward each other, breaths pluming winter white, when finally, we'd meet; I'd tell her the news in a whispered shout; and we'd dance for joy in each other's arms. I could nearly hear the orchestral score filled with horns and growing snare drums.

But I got all the way home with no Ginny in sight. "Ginny! Are you here?"

The flat was empty. The clock on the wall ticked a quarter past the hour.

The secret was like a balloon inside me, swelling larger with every minute. I had to tell someone! So I did what Mrs. Crawford suggested. I picked up the phone and dialed long-distance. An expensive call, the operator warned. I told her to break in at eight minutes. That's as long as I could afford.

"Hello?" came Marie's voice.

"Marie, it's me."

"Lucy? Is everything okay?"

"Yes, but I can't talk long." The seconds were adding up. "I got it. Marie, I got the part!"

"What part?"

"I wrote you . . ."

She hadn't received my letter yet.

Every Sunday, I wrote Marie and my parents. It had become my version of church. I'd stopped going to church since moving to London. None of my roommates attended, and finding a church on my own seemed a formidable task. So I'd swapped cleansing of sin for hair washings and prayers for letter writing.

In my last, I'd described the auditions to Marie, everything from Nico Cellini's dashing Italian accent to Lucas Wesley's blue eyes. None of that had reached Marie, however. So while I'd already told her everything, she knew nothing.

I gave the condensed version. "Director Nico Cellini did auditions for his new Paramount Pictures film, *Romeo & Juliet, The Musical*. I'm Juliet!"

The static was deafening. Had the operator cut us off? Then came a sniffle, the size of a mouse's.

"Marie, are you there?"

"Yes." She was crying. "And so is Bill. We've got the phone between us. We're so proud of you!"

I'd forgotten the time difference. It was six a.m. in New York and the shop didn't open until nine. I'd woken them and imagined their disheveled faces huddled together over the living room phone, sleep and tears in their eyes.

"Nico Cellini!" said Bill. "His last film . . ."

"*La bohème*," said Marie. "We loved that."

"We loved that!" echoed Bill. "And I don't even speak French or Italian!"

"*Romeo & Juliet* is in English," Marie told him.

"Of course it is—Shakespeare! I'm no dunderhead."

"Dunderhead?" teased Marie. "Somebody's been studying the *New York Times* crossword puzzle."

Their marital banter made me laugh and made me miss them even more.

"Have you told Mom and Dad?" asked Marie.

"Not yet."

"You're living Dad's dream. It'll mean everything to him," she reminded as only a sibling could.

"Miss Lovely," came the operator. "You are at eight minutes."

"Lovely?" asked Marie.

I had explained that in the letter, too.

"My professional name is Lori Lovely."

"Your middle name. Shortened. I like it."

"Do we still call you Lucy?" asked Bill.

"You'll always be Lucy to me," said Marie.

"You're now at nine minutes," said the operator.

"Oh, make it ten. We'll pay the charges," announced Bill.

"We love you," said Marie.

Ours was a family that said *I love you* only in goodbyes. I can't tell you why. Maybe it was because it was thought too precious to say glibly. Maybe it was my parents' way of ameliorating the pain of partings. They sweetened them with love. Looking back, I wish we'd said it more. For no reason. For every reason. Then I might've understood earlier in life that confessing love wasn't an end but a beginning.

"I love you too," I said.

"Call home, okay?"

I did, making a collect call this time, but no one at the Canary House picked up.

"Do you want to wait an hour and ring through again?" asked the operator.

My flatmates would be home for lunch then. I couldn't talk openly with them listening. While Fern and Kitty had become friends, I didn't trust either to keep a secret this big, particularly from the troubadours. If word got to the boys, there was no stopping it.

In the end, I told my parents a week later, and they never knew the difference. Marie was right. Dad was thrilled. Mom was apprehensive. They both asked a lot of questions. Dad about the film location and the costumes and the other actors. Mom about the contract and the pay and who would look after me on set. Neither asked how I was feeling. For the best. I had few answers to give and spent most of the call saying, "I don't know," which seemed to dampen the joy.

Conversely, that night when I told Ginny tucked in bed with the lights off, she threw her face into her pillow to muffle the squeals.

"It's mind-blowing! Utterly mind-blowing!" she gushed and pulled me in so we were cheek to cheek staring up at the ceiling. She'd hung a poster of the 1936 *Romeo and Juliet* film starring Norma Shearer and Leslie Howard as our inspiration.

"Look." She pointed. "That's you."

"And you," I said, not wanting her to feel excluded. "You may not be the Nurse, but that's only because you're too beautiful to be convincing."

Her chest rose and fell against my side.

"I don't think I got a speaking part," she confided. "I'll be in the dance ensemble if I'm lucky."

I wouldn't insult her with lies. We were too close for that.

"The lead dancer in the Ball Scene. I'm going to suggest it to Signor Cellini."

She pulled away abruptly. "Don't you dare! I won't have you asking favors on my behalf. I'll earn it on my own—or I won't. That's the only way. Promise me you won't say anything."

Her eyes were wide and wet in the dark.

"I promise, Ginny."

She exhaled and blinked away the tears.

"Don't ever ask for favors, even from the good people. They'll always expect you to return them."

Her body tensed beside me. It was the first time I felt Ginny withholding. The squeeze of her hand told me to listen but not ask.

"I heard they're already constructing sets in Italy," she said after a pause. "I've never been to Italy, have you?"

I shook my head. "I'd never been anywhere but North Carolina and New York until I met you."

And then we stayed up far too late talking about Lucas Wesley and Nico Cellini and *fair Verona, where we lay our scene . . .*

Outside of my family, Ginny was the only one I told. She kept that secret and many more.

9

The same day the Queen gave birth to bonny Prince Edward, the full cast list was posted on the ICA bulletin board. Royal gun salutes rang out from Green Park and the Tower of London. We thought they were firecrackers lit by celebrating students. *Romeo & Juliet, The Musical* was official. The wishes we sent up to the cosmos had come to pass. I was Juliet and Ginny was a dancer.

"We get to go to Italy together!" She did a celebration high kick, nearly clobbering a passing student.

Neither Fern nor Kitty had made the cut. Kitty took it personally and only spoke to us in single-syllable words: "Hi. Yes. Fine. No. Thanks." But Fern didn't seem too upset. Her boyfriend from Edinburgh was visiting and helped to ease her disappointment. Five of the senior troubadours had been selected in the roles of Montague maskers, torchbearers, and minstrels, including Flynn and Ben. Ben had procured a speaking role in Romeo's coterie. Flynn declared his feelings of injustice at not also having been given dialogue, but unlike Kitty, he didn't let it diminish his genuine joy for his friends.

"How could they *not* give Ben lines? Look at him. He's practically born of Zeus! It's a triumph for the troubadours. But the most deserving of celebration is that of our Lady Lovely, the world's next great Juliet!"

I'd been sitting on the secret for two weeks and was relieved to have it out in the open. Before any of us could rest on newfound laurels, Mrs. Crawford came down the hall projecting her voice at full capacity.

"Students! You've received the news, but this is still the Italia Conti Academy. Off to classes. Signor Cellini's filming schedule doesn't start until next week and only those listed are exempt from academics during it."

The students dispersed. Arm in arm, Ginny and I started toward the dance room.

"Miss Hickey—" Mrs. Crawford stopped us. "Or rather, Miss Lovely." She was well acquainted with students' name changes. "You have a certain Italian director waiting for you backstage. Miss Wilde, go on to Dance. Mr. Stannus knows that Miss Lovely will be late."

"Yes, ma'am," said Ginny.

She squeezed my arm before letting go.

Mrs. Crawford gestured with her head toward the theater auditorium.

"Off with you now." She grinned.

I rushed down the stairs to the backstage corridor.

"Signor Cellini?"

Standing in a pool of lantern light, he looked like a giant bear in a long fur coat. A cigarette hung from his lips, burning cherry red at the tip.

"Lorietta, please, call me Nico. Cellini is so formal . . ." He inhaled and exhaled a plume of sweet tobacco.

The smell reminded me of home and the sultry months when the stringers brought the tobacco leaves from the fields and hung the bundles in the barn. Dad would do inventory from sunup to sundown and come home powdered in tobacco dust. The herbaceousness stuck to him despite not lighting a stick.

Smoking was prohibited in theaters. History was riddled with horrific tales of fires. But Nico seemed to transcend law.

He beckoned me over. "I want to introduce you to someone."

We were not alone. Behind him and his enormous coat was a man who looked like he could take a punch and had. He was equal parts burly and jolly in an affable way.

"Darling, this is Lyle Dawson. I would like you and Lucas to work with him."

Lyle took off his cap. "Very nice to meet you, Miss Lovely," he said in the purest received pronunciation I have heard to this day.

"Lyle is an expert on the linguistics of Shakespeare, particularly iambic pentameter. You and Lucas share a similar American cadence that he is going to help us iron out."

By that he meant, we were going to unlearn our Southern drawls.

"When do we get started?"

Nico stared at me a beat, then smiled. "Lyle will be your dialect coach and will coordinate with the voice teachers. And don't worry, I won't make you sing. Marni Nixon is dubbing a *Pygmalion* adaptation with Audrey Hepburn and then she's coming to us."

Audrey Hepburn! I'd seen *Roman Holiday* with my parents and was smitten with everything about her. I hadn't known Hepburn didn't sing her own songs. I wanted to believe what I saw and heard on the screen. Participating in the dream was part of the pleasure. I was inexperienced in so many ways, most especially in moviemaking.

"A ghost singer. It's common practice." Nico waved his cigarette and continued. "But it needs to be plausible. You must only act the singing. We will do the rest. *Capito, mi Lorietta*?"

Before I could answer, he was walking away. "Tomorrow morning. A car will be at your flat at nine o'clock. It will take you to the studio on Dean Street."

Then he was gone, out of the dark theater into the white light of the winter day. Like magic.

"He's a genius, you know," said Lyle. "A direct descendant of Leonardo da Vinci."

I'd never met a genius nor a descendant of a genius. Nico Cellini was my first.

The next day, I was taken to the Dean Street studio, an intimate space meant for the lead actors to train and rehearse. From the moment I walked through the door, Lucas and I were never more than a few feet apart.

"Hey," he said.

"Hey," I replied.

His cheeks were freshly shaven but still wrinkled with pillow creases. His eyes were two blue crystals. In the dance mirror that stretched across the fourth wall, I noticed mine had a certain twinkle, too. The chill of the morning, I told myself, like waking up to the first snow with the world transformed. Old familiars are unrecognizable. The sky is taller. The buzz of the breeze in the trees has gone reverently still. Everything consolidates to a pinnacle, and you are standing at the apex.

That's how it felt to be in the room with Lucas Wesley.

I was less self-conscious when I looked at our reflections in the mirror. The mirror showed me what Nico and the crew saw. The camera, too. A matching pair: Lucas Wesley and Lori Lovely. Even our names sounded like they belonged together. It gave me confidence.

"Did you get breakfast?" Lucas gestured to the corner refreshment table of coffee, bananas, toast points, and Supercrema. "You gotta try the jarred stuff. It's hazelnut chocolate. The Italians . . ." He patted his firm stomach. "What's the saying—*la dolce vida*?"

"*Vita* with a *t*," corrected Lyle. "It means *the sweet life*. If you're going to quote like a Veronese speaking English, we must at least attempt to get things right. It's all so confusing as it is."

"However you say it, that stuff's good. Makes a guy want to sing." He smirked rakishly, took my hand like Romeo, and sang, "Supercrema, you're my dream-a, so sexy sweet, I just wanna scream ahhhh for the love of dolce vitaaaa . . ."

How could I not laugh? It broke the ice as only Lucas could. Then he insisted that everyone in the room try the spread on toast. Nico and his assistant arrived while we were licking chocolate off our fingers.

"You like?" Nico asked, seeing the empty jar. "We will order more." He turned to his assistant and the assistant made a note. "I like to see everyone enjoying."

That was Nico, the consummate host. Whether it was one or one hundred, people were his passion. He put the same energy, craftsmanship, and care into arranging a dinner party for a friend as he did with each scene he captured on film. He knew no other way. Life was story and creating story was life for Nico.

"Bring on the *dolce vita*!" Lucas welcomed. "*Buongiorno, signor* directoro."

Nico winced at the translation but benevolently let it pass.

"*Ciao*, Signor Cellini," I said.

I may have been from a little town, but even I knew how to say *Ciao*. When I was younger, Marie took me with her to Pufftown Pizzeria. The pizza boys were all in their twenties and notoriously flirty, catcalling *Ciao, ciao, are you Sophia Loren?* at Marie and her friends. I was skinny as a spaghetti noodle but thought it all so exciting.

"Aww." Nico shook a finger at me, smiling. "What did I tell you, *mia* Lorietta? Call me Nico."

I remembered, but sometimes what people say in private and what they want in public are different things.

"*Sì,* Nico."

"*Bellissima*." He kissed my cheeks and did the same to Lucas. "*Bellissimo*."

Lyle came forward with his hand extended. "Mr. Cellini, good morning."

Nico took it enthusiastically. "Lyle, my friend, are we ready to begin?"

"Indeed." He handed everyone bound scripts.

My fingers were sticky sweet. The pages stuck to them. On the top was printed *Romeo & Juliet, The Musical* in italics, and beneath it in bold block lettering was my name: LORI LOVELY as JULIET.

A handful of wooden folding chairs were set in front of the mirror. Nico, Lyle, and the assistant sat while Lucas and I stood in the middle of the room.

"Do not be nervous," said Nico. "This is practice. Lyle is the best in the business. He will make sure you are prepared. And I would not have chosen you for the roles if I did not believe you already have them inside you."

His faith in us—in *me* when I had no distinctions and no training of merit . . . Well, it goes without saying that without Nico Cellini, I wouldn't have been Lori Lovely. Some might think that self-deprecating, but too much stock is put in self-made proclamations. No one is self-made. We all have been graced with opportunities by others, and those gifts deserve recognition.

Nico was one of the gift-givers in my life.

"You are like seeds," he continued, pinching two fingers together for illustration. "My job is to water so you can bloom." He turned his hand theatrically and blossomed his fingers wide. "*Vedi, amori?*"

Lucas and I nodded.

"*Buono*!"

"I suppose that makes me your lingual horticulturist," said Lyle.

"Horta-what?" asked Lucas.

"Whatever Lyle says, we listen, and then"—Nico shrugged—"do what comes naturally."

Lyle turned, to explain or defend we'll never know.

"Okay!" Nico continued briskly. "Let us begin with Act Three, Scene Five. The morning after lovemaking."

I broke out in a sweat, even my toes went squishy in my socks. I'd expected to start at the beginning of the play. The morning after their first sexual encounter was practically the ending, never mind the culmination of their mounting passions. Lucas and I had yet to have a full conversation!

"I only prepared for the balcony scene," I said truthfully.

Nico nodded. "You did that very well at audition, but we will be shooting the *post coitale* as soon as we get to Italy."

I was torn between terror at the scene and elation at the promise of Italy. Beside me, Lucas shifted his weight. There was a tremor in his left pinkie finger. It was his first acting role. He was as nervous as I was. We were a couple of small-town kids, but we could be much more if we were brave together.

So, we began with *It was the nightingale* and *It was the lark* and the sweetness of hazelnut chocolate on our lips.

10

We spent all of March with Lyle doing dictation tutorials and scene rehearsals seven days a week, seven hours a day. After our lessons, we went to the costume designer, who took my measurements and draped velvet, satin, and silk brocades across my bare skin and then poked, pinched, and tacked with pins.

"You lose a pound or two from here, *sì*?" The designer cinched my waist with both hands. It was a rhetorical question.

Ginny told me to wear a girdle to bed and it would do the trick without having to miss a meal. But what I gained in hourglass figure, I lost in sleep. The girdle was torture and left bruises along my rib cage. Being Juliet was harder than anticipated.

When I saw the troubadours strolling home from the pubs laughing and smoking their cigarettes, I couldn't help being envious. I was a teenager with teenage yearnings: a bird longing to fly wild while also enjoying the safety of the golden cage. But you couldn't have both. In those moments, I'd remind myself that we'd all be together in Italy soon.

Each night after Dean Street practice, I went home to Ginny, my constant companion. She insisted that I tell her about my day while she pinned my hair for bed. Then we'd sleep the kind of deep, dreamless sleep that makes the sleepers believe in spells.

She left me notes on the bedside before going to morning dance class. Each day was a variation on the same message:

You are Juliet. You are Lori Lovely. Be you and let destiny do the rest. Lots of love, G

On our last day of London rehearsal before we were to fly to Italy, Lucas asked if I wanted to have dinner in his room. He couldn't stay at a normal hotel. Walking in and out would've resulted in mobs of fans. Luckily, Nico had friends who owned a townhouse a couple of blocks from the studio and lent him their upper-level suite. In addition to providing anonymity, the owner's wife cooked for Lucas and, according to him, had perfected a fried chicken recipe that rivaled Colonel Sanders back home.

"Nobody here appreciates fried chicken as much as we do," he said. "It's a Southern thing."

We'd become close through rehearsals. Nico wisely plunged us into the most vulnerable part of the story first, and it helped burn off the nerves. Celebrity had a way of extoling youth while simultaneously dismantling the very innocence that made it precious. I saw what the spotlight only flashed upon. Lucas was twenty-one to my eighteen and in many ways still a boy. Androgynous in his beauty and tenderness, he'd blink long eyelashes during our scenes with the bashfulness of a doe. Moments later, he'd say a line with such intensity that it made me want to cry. He was unlike any man or woman I'd ever known. It's a lonely thing to be unique. I recognized that in him once I got to know Lucas Wesley the person rather than Lucas Wesley the Sing King.

He was away from his family in a foreign city doing something he loved while fearing he might fail. Just like me.

So, when he asked me to come to his room for fried chicken, I trusted that it was that—fried chicken.

"Tastes like it came straight out of a take-out bucket."

It was the ultimate compliment for two homesick Americans.

We ate cross-legged on the shag rug in his room.

"I'm so full, I'll have to roll into bed," I said on goodbye.

"Roll in, but please don't roll out. That'd be a tragedy!" He took my hand and kissed my knuckles. "Goodnight, fair Juliet."

I curtsied as we'd practiced in the studio. "Your diction is on point, Montague."

"See you next at the airport?"

"I'll be the *Lady by yonder blessed moon*."

"*I swear!*" he mocked in a Southern twang.

We played this game together—throwing out lines to one another to test our memorization and coming up with ways of disobeying Lyle's linguistic culturing.

"You sound like a proper church lady!" I laughed.

I was still smiling with thoughts of Lucas when I came through the door of our flat and was met by the somber expressions of Mrs. Coates, Fern, and Kitty. My stomach dropped, weighted with chicken and dread.

"What's going on?" I asked.

"Oh! I'm fine, it's my own dumb fault," came Ginny's voice from the futon. She was lying down with her leg raised on a pillow, plastered from knee to toe.

"Ginny! What happened?" I rushed to her side.

"I'm a ninny is what. It doesn't hurt nearly as bad now as it did at first. After classes, the troubadours were walking over to the pub for a bite. You know how I love the curry, so I was in a rush to catch up. I didn't tie my laces properly and . . . well, I tripped and fell. Right into the street and in front of everyone. The doctor says my ankle's broke."

She drew in a deep breath and the tears started.

Mrs. Coates clenched and unclenched her hands. "It's a very lucky thing that you weren't run over by a car. Splayed out on the road like that."

"They stopped traffic—the people around. It felt as if my leg had splintered in half. I must've passed out because I remember falling but I don't remember how I got inside the tailor's shop. They laid me up on the fabric-cutting table."

"Oh, Ginny . . ."

I hated hearing that she'd been hurt and alone. If I hadn't been with Lucas, I'd have been with her. We would've been arm in arm and there's no way I would've let her fall.

Mrs. Coates eyed the clock on the wall. "It's late, girls." Fern and Kitty hung back with worried expressions. "You two have class in the morning. And you"—she turned to me—"must rest before your trip. I'll take care of Ginny. That's my job. Your jobs are to carry on."

"Yes, Mrs. Coates," said Kitty.

"Does this mean she's off the film?" Fern whispered while Mrs. Coates clucked around Ginny, making sure she was comfortable to sleep on the couch.

"She can't even stand," Kitty whispered back. "How is she supposed to dance?"

It knocked the breath out of me. I didn't want to go to Italy without Ginny. We'd dreamed about it, spoken the words aloud, manifested it to the universe. We were meant to go together.

"Did the doctor say how bad it's broken?" I asked Mrs. Coates.

"Broke is broke." She gave me a hard stare. "There's no such thing as a little broken."

"What I mean is"—I was flustered—"did they say how long it'll take her to heal?"

"Six to eight weeks."

I leaned into the hall shadow and pinched the bridge of my nose to make the tears go away. It was selfish to cry because my best friend couldn't come with me to Italy. Ginny was hurt and Mrs. Coates was right. It could've been a whole lot worse. So I put on a brave face and went back into the living room.

"I guess this means that we need to buy you pretty toenail polish."

Ginny smiled, more for my benefit than her own.

"I've botched it up for us. You'll have to go to Italy without me."

I knelt beside the couch and leaned my head against her side. "I won't be gone long. You know better than anyone, filming doesn't last forever."

She ran her fingers through my hair. The gentle pull made me miss her already.

"By the time I get back, you'll be healed up and summer will be here. We can go to the Troubadour with the troubadours and dance the night away."

"Yes," she said. The judder of tears threatened. "Say it again, please. I need to believe."

So I did, and I kept saying it until the pill that Mrs. Coates gave her for the pain took effect and she slept.

11

Rome

Italy was my dream of a fairy-tale kingdom. Sentinel cypress trees and parasol pines guarded the hilltops and lined the roadways connecting medieval towns, churches, and farms. Purple wisteria threaded the houses and hung in bunches. Pink Judas flowers peppered the roadways alongside pink and white azaleas. We saw it all from above first.

Our plane landed at the Aeroporto Internazionale Leonardo da Vinci. Nico instructed his driver to take Lucas and me directly to his villa, where we would stay for the duration. There were four of us: Lucas, Lyle, a newcomer named Miss Meriwether, who'd been assigned as the production assistant by the distributing studio, Paramount Pictures, and me. I liked Miss Meriwether. She was cheeky in a respectable way, and freely shared sticks of cinnamon gum from her pocket.

The four of us arrived at Nico's villa to a madhouse of languages, dramatic hand gestures, shouting, and fountains of espresso fueling the chaos. His estate was magnificent. Crafted of ancient limestone that sparkled gold under the sun and was laced with honey-smelling vines, it made romantic fantasies seem entirely plausible.

Principal photography had already begun in a village south of Rome. The ensemble cast had been taken there by bus and lodged in a smattering of *pensiones*, family-run hotels. The London troubadours were in the process of learning fighting moves from Italian swordsmen. For the more intimate scenes, sets had been constructed at the villa by the Cinecittà Studios set design crew.

At the center of the action was Nico. From the moment we set foot in his world, his arms were wide open.

"Welcome! You must rest and adjust to the time. Tomorrow, the great work begins!"

He wasn't exaggerating. Early the next morning, I woke to the knock of Miss Meriwether with my costume for the day's shoot: a cream nightgown two sizes too large with a lace-down neckline and nude underwear.

"It's a closed set," Miss Meriwether assured.

Nico had warned us. We were shooting Romeo and Juliet's postcoital scene first.

Breakfast was buffet style on the villa's veranda, a bounty of fruit and pastries. The bubble of morning chatter and frothy cappuccinos floated up to my bedroom terrace, but I had no appetite to join them.

It is the lark that sings so out of tune, I thought, *straining harsh discords and unpleasing sharps.*

Shakespeare was right. One person's morning was another's night.

Everyone else was excited for the first day of shooting, but I wanted to crawl into bed and hide. Staring at the gauzy nightshirt, it dawned on me that my first sexual experience would be in front of everyone on set. The next twelve hours would be captured on film for the world to revisit forever.

Miss Meriwether held out a crimson robe.

"A gift from Nico. We want you comfortable."

I took the robe, soft as mink. The initials *LL* had been embroidered in gold over the left breast.

"Hair and makeup are waiting," said Miss Meriwether.

"I still need to wash and change."

"Of course." She left with a quiet click of the door.

The warm morning shower helped settle my nerves. I practiced my lines while the steam warmed my throat and took away the raspy edge. Afterward, I dressed in the scant costume and cinched the robe tight. The HMU (Hair

& Make-Up) team applied their powders and sprays. Then I was escorted to Juliet's boudoir, constructed in what was once the villa's stables. It still smelled faintly of hay and leather bridles. The airiness of the venue allowed natural light to stream through in lemon tones, augmented by large halogen bulbs strung from the stable's wooden rafters. Below them, shiny boards and reflective scrims had been positioned around the lovers' boudoir.

The set was a tale of two worlds. One side, an enormous beechwood bed cascaded with muslin sheets and pillows, gossamer curtains, a religious triptych on the wall beside a standalone door leading to nowhere but a sumptuous Italian vista. On the other, a stained barn floor cluttered with modern equipment and men chewing gum while checking their wristwatches.

Nico sat casually in the director's chair wearing a linen caftan that billowed with the breeze. "I don't like the color of that one—too orange." He pointed to an overhead light. "It'll make them look like spawning salmon."

A crewman raced off to adjust it while another whispered in his ear and nodded toward me.

Nico turned with a grin. "Our Juliet!" He hopped off his seat, inspecting me with approval. "The hair is perfect. The makeup, too."

I felt as if I'd come through a London drizzle from the amount of rosewater they'd spritzed. My cheeks were slick, and my head was haloed in frizz. Apparently, this was what one looked like after sex. I was relying on others for accuracy.

"Do you like the dressing gown?" asked Nico.

"Yes, it's wonderful. Thank you."

"I always feel more comfortable in a dressing gown, don't you?"

I smiled in response. I'd never owned one. In the mornings, my family got up from bed and put on what they would wear for the workday. In the evenings, they took those off and put on bedclothes. We had nothing for lounging—no time for it.

Across the room was Lucas in a matching red robe initialed with *LW.* He gave a tentative smile and raised the orange juice he held.

"G'morning, Lovely."

"Morning. Sleep well?" My attempt at small talk.

"Not a wink." Lucas gulped. "You?"

I had, remarkably, but one doesn't tell the truth in such instances. *Salt in the wound*, as they say.

"I'm sorry," I replied.

"It's my first time doing . . . this. My first film, y'know, and I've never kissed anyone on camera." His voice was pinched, edging on shrill. A strange sound coming from him.

"My first time, too," I said.

We exhaled together.

"That's a nice robe you got."

"Dressing gown," I corrected with a smirk.

"Pardon me, m'lady, 'tis my first occasion with a . . . *dressing gown.*"

We laughed with ease a moment.

"*Va bene*, let's get rolling," said Nico.

Technically, it was a closed set. Only the essential film crew and Nico's inner circle were at the villa. It made sense for him to shoot the most provocative scene first before the ensemble actors were incorporated. Also, before the media got wind of our being in the area. In his way, Nico was protecting us. Critics would later argue that *Romeo & Juliet, The Musical* is a barbed statement regarding youth obsession and its ultimate self-destructive consequences. Who's to say? Celebration and exploitation sound so much alike.

What I remember from that first day of filming was that Miss Meriwether held my robe while I slipped into the bed and took off the nightgown. It was placed bedside for my stage cue. The sheets smelled of the wisteria draped along the laundry pergola and were sunbaked slightly stiff. I was naked minus the nude underwear. Nico instructed the stylist to cover my breasts with my long tresses. I fought the urge to itch. A gentle gust blew under the sheet. I twisted the cotton in my fists to keep it steady. Goose bumps rose while sweat snaked down my sides. I felt every sensation to an agonizing degree.

Lucas unrobed. I meant to look away, but it was the first time I'd seen a man's unclothed body. I was curious. He was sculpted of muscle, olive-skinned but pink in the hidden places, as artful as any painting hanging in the Uffizi.

He turned, with eyes downcast, and slipped into the bed. A flesh-colored modesty pouch had been systematically placed between his legs. A thin pillow hidden beneath the sheets acted as a barrier. The dip of the mattress didn't bring on the panic I'd anticipated. I was glad he was beside me. We were exposed and vulnerable together.

The film crew scurried into position with Nico waving his hand to begin. The giant eye of the camera loomed.

"Your lips are trembling," Lucas whispered. "Are you cold?"

I was frigid and on fire: the alchemy of terror.

Instinctively, he laid a shielding arm across my waist. It warmed me more than skin deep.

"Thank you," I whispered back, and then saw his lips were trembling, too. I leaned toward him and put an arm across his body so that we criss-crossed in embrace. The same way I slept with Ginny on cold nights in our flat, like best friends, like family, like lovers.

"You are my first and only Romeo," I told him.

He smiled. "You are my first and only Juliet."

"Get that camera rolling!" commanded Nico. "*Bellisimo*! Stay like that!"

And we did, staring into each other's eyes, blue to blue, blocking out the clatter of the crew. It was just me and Lucas. In that moment, I hoped to God I could make it look real and also . . . what if it was? The lines of fact and fiction were indistinct for two young people vulnerable and yearning for approval. I wanted Lucas to love me. I wanted to love him. We wanted Nico to love us. Our bodies against each other were hard to pretend away. We counted our breaths until the breeze settled and gooseflesh gave way to courage.

"Act Three, Scene Five, Take One," said the marksman.

"*Azione*," said Nico.

The clapperboard clacked. The film spokes hummed.

It was easier once we started. The play did its magic.

Juliet: *Believe me, love, it was the nightingale.*

Romeo: *It was the lark, the herald of the morn. No nightingale: look, love, what envious streaks . . .*

The cadence of Shakespeare's iambic pentameter carrying us through the portal of time and belief into another world where I was Juliet and he was Romeo.

Our first kiss was in that scene, which appears many kisses later in the actual film. The tender thrill I recognize on-screen is something that could never be described. I was kissing Lucas Wesley! And it came with a song.

With Lucas's lips inches from mine, he sang, "'I would kill and die, just to hold you by my side, let the sun and moon collide, all for my lovely . . .'"

The song had been written for the film. When my cue came to mouth the words of the chorus, I couldn't help myself. I sang along. Lucas's genuine smile told me that I wasn't nearly as awful as I thought. But I was no Marni Nixon. Nico would still dub my vocals.

Immediately following, when he called *Cut!* the crew erupted in applause. I'll never forget that moment. The bursting joy of it. Even Miss Meriwether wiped a tear from her eye. That first take was the one Nico used in the final film.

"*Stampa! Bellisimo, bellisima*! Before we go again—makeup!" called Nico.

Makeup? Lucas sweetly touched a finger to my ear. "Your ears have turned red."

The makeup artist powdered my ears, and Lucas and I kissed again. Kissing Lucas was fun. I never grew tired of it. A couple of times, he even slipped his tongue between my lips. While I laughed and swatted him afterward, I was secretly elated. The hardest kisses were the close-ups with the camera tight on our faces. Then, it was impossible to forget the hovering eye between us. Every wisp of hair was arranged, every second was counted. The lens, the audience, saw it all.

I learned quickly that getting a scene done in one take was the brass ring and much harder than it seemed. We were continually interrupted so that a camera position could be changed. I got tangled in my own hair. A fly unceremoniously landed on Lucas's nose. There were a myriad of things that made the sexiest love scene of all time entirely *un*sexy. At one point, the lighting assistant was in bed with us, holding the sheet down to keep it from fluttering in the breeze. The longer we lay there, the more comfortable we became, until I didn't feel the need to cinch the sheets across my breasts. In the end, I forgot my shyness, the lights and the cameras, and even my own nightgown.

When my rising line came, I stood, thinking only of Juliet's fears for her Romeo. "'It is, it is! Hie hence, be gone, away! It is the lark that sings so out of tune!'"

"*Taglio*," said Nico in a fatherly voice. "Lori, darling, the censors will burn us at the stake if we have you stand naturally like that . . ." He pointed to the gown. "So, let's try it with you slipping that over your head between lines while we do a cutaway."

Which we did, and I earned my second brass ring of the day.

"One-take Lovely, that's what you are!"

I took more pride in that nickname than in being his "Lorietta."

When we finished the day's shooting, Miss Meriwether helped me back into my robe. Lucas pulled his on. We hugged and held each other as ourselves.

"You were wonderful," said Lucas.

"So were you."

"The rest is going to be a cakewalk." He patted the robe knot at his stomach. "Speaking of cake, I'm starving."

I was, too.

"Think they'd mind if we raided the villa fridge? I got a hankering for food that doesn't look pretty on a plate. Biscuits, bacon, scrambled eggs with ketchup . . ."

His stomach audibly grumbled. It was so Lucas. More than anyone else, he was home when home felt far away.

So, instead of going to our rooms, we circled the back path that led to the kitchen where Lucas scavenged the refrigerator for ingredients and used the cook's fry pan to sizzle up pancetta and scrambled eggs dolloped with marinara sauce. It was the Italian version of American diner food. We each grabbed a fork and ate straight out of the skillet.

"Who taught you to cook?" I asked. "You're good at it."

Lucas shrugged. "Who taught you to kiss? You're good at it."

I must've blushed because he went on. "I never had a teacher. I just picked up one of my momma's pans one day when I was hungry. Sometimes the best teaching is doing."

I smiled and wiped marinara off his chin with my thumb. I could still feel the pliant give of his lips on mine. All at once, he kissed me—or I kissed him. I can't recall. But this time, it wasn't Romeo and Juliet. It was the real Lucas and the real me. He opened my robe, and I opened his. We pulled ourselves together like overlapping petals of a rose.

His skin felt softer than it had under the glaring set lights and rough muslin sheets. I closed my eyes, and by my own direction I touched the softness of him. His hairless chest, the gully that ran from the divot of his throat to the divot of his belly, and even the part that had been hidden before. His body. Sylph-like and strong. Bladed by coming-of-age. So were we both. A golden metamorphosis.

I might have lost my virginity against the warm sandstone walls of that kitchen if it hadn't been for the cook surprising us with his return.

"Cos'è questo?"

Seeing the eggshells, marinara sauce, fry pan, and two people canoodling in his sacred space, he threw his market bags down with dramatic flair.

"*Mia cucina! Dio aiutami!*" He raised pinched fingers to the crucifix hung over the doorway while we quickly cinched robes and fled, laughing and tripping over our velvet hems.

Was I in love with Lucas? In the same way that a bud is in love with the sun and moves toward it. Was he in love with me? That's not for me to say. Therein lies the beauty and the heartache of the past. We wish we knew more then. We wish we knew more now.

What I do know is that we were two people cast as *the* lovers of the millennium, and the romance of that was potent.

12

The cook told Nico, we're pretty sure.

The number of films that went off the rails because the leads had an on-set romance that ended badly was practically a Hollywood cliché. So while Nico advocated free love, he was first and foremost, a businessman. I suspect he carefully strategized a way to prolongate the unfulfilled desires between his young stars.

Lucas was sent to the village for sword fighting rehearsals with the Montagues. I remained ensconced at the villa with the Capulets. A house divided.

We found whatever moments we could to sneak a kiss, a touch, a whisper. There was never enough time to do much else before Miss Meriwether, a costumer, or a grip came to fetch us. Privacy is nonexistent when you are in the spotlight. I couldn't even scratch my nose without the makeup artist swooping in.

I was thankful when we finally began the ensemble scenes. I'd barely seen any of Italy outside of the villa. Cinecittà Studios had refurnished the nearby village streets into our *fair Verona, where we lay our scene.* The actual townspeople had been good enough to move their potted plants, TV antennas, and Vespas out of view for a courtesy fee and complimentary craft services after the actors were finished for the day. A table of free porchetta and limoncello quickly won over even the surliest of residents. If you look closely at the film, silhouetted heads of looky-loos can be spotted in many a window and doorway.

Of course, the first familiar face to greet me was Flynn. He had risen up the ranks from Montague male extra to *that guy* in Romeo's pack. His ad lib lines were not written by the Bard but made Nico grin. For Flynn, that was more validating than being knighted by the monarchy.

"Well, 'ello there, Lovely." He bowed.

"Flynn!"

"How goes fair Capulet?"

I raised my arms as far as they could go in my costume, which was no higher than my waist.

"They got me corseted in this dress on penalty of death by needle and pins if I tear it."

The costume designer arrived each day with his rolling rack, shoe boxes, veils, sewing kit, and one instruction: *Hold still*. I did as I was told. His needle came so close to my skin, I felt the heat of his thumb pressing it through the fabric. After we were tailored, Lucas and I would meet on the set for Nico to inspect us side by side. He wanted us to complement each other, right down to the points of our shoes.

Today's dress was for a scene in Friar Laurence's church. I wore an emerald gown with gold tatting on the sleeves that cascaded to the floor. I had to hold it up like a princess when I ran in and out to say my lines. With a high neckline and swaths of the softest material on earth, I felt beautiful and powerful by its fullness. It was my magic cape and my favorite.

The costume designer initially provided a matching emerald medallion, but Nico had dismissed it as gaudy. He'd gone to his bedroom and returned with a gold cross from his own jewelry box. That pendant is in every scene of the film.

"You know my motto: Fashion favors the bold," said Flynn. "Hoped you'd come down to the proletarians and have a cuppa vino. We've been having a ball with Lucas."

Lucas had been encouraged to meet up with the Montague extras to form on-camera *ragazzi* camaraderie. My single Capulet companion was Patricia Wood, a Scottish actress, cast as the Nurse. It was her film debut, too, so Nico put her in the room next door to mine. She had a booming laugh and a bawdy quip to nearly everything. I understood what Nico had meant by *grossalona*. Nearly two decades older than me and playing my nursemaid, ours was a kind of big stepsister, little stepsister relationship. We were casually friendly but not close enough to share a glass, if you know what I mean.

Nico was attempting to foster alliances. I might've only been a first-year at ICA, but I'd studied enough of the Method to see that he was orchestrating his actors' real lives so they might infuse the make-believe. He wanted me to be the saintly virgin ingénue, Juliet. He wanted Lucas to be the tenderhearted rogue, Romeo. The studio was paying for us to be those roles, and every minute in Italy was on their lira. It was a professional job, not a personal vacation. Reputation was everything in those days. If we sullied ours, it negatively affected ticket sales. If the film failed to achieve monetary success for the studio, none of us would work again. So, in a way, they owned us.

Still, I was a young, modern woman in Italy and couldn't help being jealous of Lucas's nights out. During our lunch breaks, I'd make him recount every minute so I could live vicariously. The Italian *ragazzi* had introduced him to grappa, which he greatly enjoyed: "It's like honey—on fire!"

I was keen on trying it and dancing. Good heavens, I missed dancing! It felt a cruel state of affairs to have the Sing King by my side but not be able to let loose with him. Nico had us doing nothing but the Moresca in preparation for the Capulets' ball.

After much wheedling, I convinced Lucas to help me sneak out one evening when he was on his way to meet the Montague men. I wore blue jeans and a couple of pieces pulled from the costume bin: a nude halter top meant to be a chest binder and a gold-beaded bolero. I thought it looked positively groovy. We'd gotten about a mile away on a Vespa when we came upon a slow-moving procession carrying a *macchina a spalla*, a religious parade float. Apparently, it was the feast day of Saint Catherine of Siena, patron saint of Italy and a virgin mystic. Neither one of us being Catholic, we didn't know. The local women were more than happy to enlighten. They gathered around with hands outstretched to pray overlapping words we didn't understand but got the sense were of the utmost solemnity. A loaf of peace bread was shared. Then one of the younger women recognized Lucas and began giddily shrieking, "*È* Lucas Wesley!" The hysteria caught on, and soon everyone under the age of sixty was singing Lucas's hit rendition of "O Sole Mio."

Suddenly, a lightning storm erupted. Italian paparazzi encircled the caravan, taking photos from every angle. We were caught red-handed. What we thought was a delay on our route became an impasse. The statue of Saint Catherine had been set down in the middle of the road. We had no choice but to jump back on the Vespa and return to the villa. By the time we arrived, Nico and the rest of the household were waiting on the terrace. He had a deal with the Italian paparazzi. Any photos of his young actors came to him first before they were leaked out to the rest of the world.

"Now, darling, this is not good." Nico was on his third cigarette. The stubs of the others littered the ashtray. "You can't be seen cavorting—in denim! You are my Juliet."

"But I'm also Lori. I miss dancing. I miss being me. I wear blue jeans!"

He stared a beat, then laughed. "That's the passion!" He chortled approvingly.

I was young, headstrong, and coming into my own. *Be who God meant you to be, and you will set the world on fire.* Saint Catherine of Siena said that. It was no coincidence that we were intercepted by her procession.

❁ ❁ ❁

Reuniting with the troubadours felt like a triumph of freedom.

"So, where've you been, lovely dovely?" Flynn pressed.

"In the villa tower," I joked. "We did all the closed-set scenes there."

"The director's villa. Bet it's posh."

Then came Ben from the craft services table, finishing a pizzelle cookie.

"Oh, darling, another? You keep gobbling those and you'll spread like a waffle."

Ben patted his belly with a shrug. "I can't help myself. The food is delicious. Hello, Lori." He kissed my cheek, and it carried the nostalgic scent of ice cream cones on summer days.

"He speaks the truth." Flynn sighed. "They've put us up in the local hotel with a morose landlady. But what she lacks in humor she makes up for with homemade gnocchi." He gave a dramatic moan. "Just last night I proposed marriage after eating a bowl. Clearly, I am bewitched!"

I laughed. I really had missed him and everyone back in London. Ginny most especially.

"Have you heard from home?"

"No, but you know how things are here. The mail still travels by donkey in Italian villages. Not to be relied upon. A letter could just as easily fall by the roadside as be delivered to the recipient. Little has changed since Romeo and Juliet. So don't tell your lover that you aren't dead but took a sleeping potion. We know how that turned out."

Correspondences were slow and phone calls expensive. I'd only written Ginny a couple of letters. Messages thrown into the proverbial ocean. By the time they arrived, whatever I had written would be weeks past. Nico's villa hadn't a return address, either. It was more of a *go south past the village until you see a ridge of cypress trees, make a right at the stone wall and that's Nico's house.* Nico did most of his business via the phone or at the studio office in Rome. His assistant handled everything else.

Hearing Flynn echo my own excuses relieved me of the niggling guilt. I should've written more. I should've tried to call Ginny at least once. It would've meant the world to her. She was back at school nursing a broken ankle, alone with the daily reminder that the opportunity of a lifetime has passed her by. It hurt me to think about it. Ginny would tell me to focus on the film—to feel and act as Juliet. That's what I told myself.

Flynn's gaze shifted over my shoulder, and he readjusted the faux dagger sheath at his waist. "Romeo, Romeo, *there*fore art thou Romeo!"

I turned to Lucas sipping a bottle of Chinotto.

"I think that's *her* line," he said.

Flynn shrugged. "A guy can dream." He put a hand under his chin daintily. "Wouldn't we all love that close-up?"

"Unless you wake up with a pimple!" I pointed to the bump on my cheek.

Flynn leaned in to inspect and then shook his head. "Hardly. The makeup artist has completely camouflaged it. You look radiant. Tell her, boys."

"Beautiful!" said Ben, who was joined by the Montague players.

"*Bella! Bella!*" they shouted.

"'Juliet is the sun! Arise, fair sun . . .'" said Lucas.

"'And kill the envious moon.'" I finished the line.

I remember the glint in his eyes. A flame that grew increasingly. We'd worked so closely, made love with words, and pressed our flesh to flesh. But throughout it all, we'd been stricken with self-doubt and insecurity, an impenetrable filter that kept us from embracing the magnitude of what we were becoming. Underneath the bravado, we were a couple of small-town kids with small-town sensibilities. We wanted to get carried away because we knew we shouldn't—couldn't—wouldn't. We respected each other too much to take things too far. That mutual respect was the axis on which everything revolved, the romance and the fame. Only Lucas knows the burning force of that on two teenagers. He lived it with me, the blessing and the burden.

Lu

Bees, Book, and Candle

The Abbey, Connecticut
October 1990

It's candle-making day. I'm meeting Aunt Lori in the chandlery as soon as she's finished singing. The abbey sells hand-dipped taper candles in pairs to visiting parishioners wishing to take home a little extra blessing for themselves, family, and friends.

At breakfast this morning over bowls of maple oatmeal, the inventory manager, Sister Mary Clare, explained that what makes their candles special is that the beeswax is produced in their cultivated hives. These consecrated bees collect pollen from the abbey's flower gardens. The flower garden seedlings are planted and watered by the sisters' hands, which are devoted to prayer and sanctified by God. So, according to Sister Mary Clare, a person breathes in the bees, the flowers, the land, the people, and the holiness of God with each lit taper.

It seems a rather high bar for a candle that burns to nothing. A light switch seems more practical. Which I use now to turn on the lamp in Aunt Lori's office.

On the roof, the growing pitter-patter against the timbers, a prelude to rain. The morning darkness should've given me a clue. Usually, there's a tipoff for storms: a televised forecaster, a radio disc jockey, a man carrying an umbrella on the street, a farmhouse weathervane spinning wildly. But at the abbey, the sisters let nature do nature. Prophesies are saved for more important things.

The choir continues, echoing through the abbey's stone portals in monophonic waves. It's enchanting in the same way as Christmas carols. No matter the season, one chord of "Silent Night" and I'm wishing myself into a romanticized Thomas Kinkade painting. The sung prayers have a similar effect.

I do as I promised and call my parents. I imagined them: Mom on the kitchen wall phone curling her fingers through the handset's spiral cord; Dad in the living room on the touch-tone landline. Talking to each other as much as talking to me.

"You're at the abbey with Aunt Lori?"

"Does your school know?"

"Yes, and yes. I'm writing my thesis."

"Your English Literature thesis?"

"I'm a History major now, Dad."

"She changed to History last semester, Bill."

"That's right. Must've mixed them up—Literature and History. All those Ken Follett books you read, Marie."

"Those are historical fiction, Bill."

"They're all set a long time ago."

"Right, but history is real and literature is not."

"Don't they sort of overlap?"

"Mom. Dad." They could go on like this for hours. "It's long distance. I gotta get off." Thank God. "I called so you wouldn't worry. I'll head back when I'm done interviewing."

They're mollified by the plan but make me promise to tell them when I'm on the road again.

"A lot of miles between the abbey and Mount Salem College. We just want to make sure you arrive at the destination safely."

Fair enough. We say goodbye.

I pull out my notes from yesterday and the tape recorder, armed and ready with a new set of batteries.

"Testing, testing, one, two, three," I say into the microphone, rewind, and press play.

Testing, testing, one, two, three, it plays back, only tinnier and distant, a mechanical echo. Not the real me but the old me. The minute-ago me.

The recorder keeps auto-memory of the facts as they are told and relieves me of the onus so I can concentrate on filling in the holes. Because, good Lord! There are a lot of holes in Aunt Lori's story. Not to mention all the super-cool stuff she skipped right over.

Like partying in London clubs—and the booze! I can't blame her for not liking beer. It tastes like stewed gym socks. I write in my notebook:

Recreational drugs?

It was the sixties. Pot, LSD, hallucinogens, hippies, flower power, herbals, and all that.

Did you get stoned with your friends?

It doesn't seem like an appropriate question to ask a nun. I need to keep it professional. I wouldn't put that information in my thesis anyhow. That's off the record. I'm just curious. But when people say *curious,* they're usually after gossip. Legit history shouldn't be gossip, even if the gossip was more fun to read. Moving on.

Ginny Wilde

I write her name down, first and last. There's gravitas in it. She's such a prominent figure in Aunt Lori's life, but this is the first time I've heard Aunt Lori talk about her.

Where is she now?

More questions. The troubadours. *Was that code for gay?* I think this, but don't write it down.

When I was seven, Adeline, the sweetest girl in the second grade and my best friend, kissed me underneath the playground slide during recess. Composition class was immediately following, and I wrote my heart between the lines in my best cursive, the scroll of fairy tales. It was the first time anyone had kissed me on the mouth. Besides my parents, I'd only seen the skunk named Flower get kissed in Disney's *Bambi*. The cartoon offered the most emotional context. So, I wrote of the color red filling my eyes and hot in my mouth; lips tasting of lunchbox licorice wheels; and feeling as if the world had spun head over tail. I didn't hesitate to script her name with all the furbelows.

Adeline, *my best friend*, my love, Adeline.

Writing it felt like reliving the kiss. Writing it made the memory realer. I turned to catch eyes with her three seats behind me in our desk row. She giggled, and I giggled. Just like we had under the slope of the slide. Not for a moment did I feel anything but joy. It was a kiss, innocent and full of devotion. And I was confident that writing of the experience would allow our teacher, Mrs. Mayer, to share in the extraordinary feeling.

I believe it's true for most that at our beginning, we experience love as an abstract whole. No divisions or subtractions. It's boundless and exists purely unto itself. We love with unmitigated equality: our family, our friends, our stuffed animals, our songs, our books, our dreams. Then there comes a moment when we start to discriminate, where we realize there are different types of love, and different ways to love different people and things. We call it growing up. But is it really?

This was that first dividing moment in my childhood.

Mrs. Mayer asked me to come outside the classroom. Alone in the hallway, she held up my composition book. Her neck flushed spotty.

"What is this?"

"It's . . . my composition."

"Yes, but what I mean is, what is this you wrote about *Adeline*." She whispered the name under her breath in the same way she'd whispered to the nurse that Abe Knight had peed his pants.

"She kissed me," I said.

Mrs. Mayer opened my book to the page on which I had written my love and ripped it from the seams. "Unacceptable. That's what gays do. That's how people are getting AIDS and dying." Catching herself, she swallowed hard. "You shouldn't . . ." She looked past me to the classroom. "I'll have to speak to Adeline about this."

Plunged into an ice bath of fear and shame, I couldn't stop the tears. I didn't want people to die. I didn't want Adeline in trouble. I didn't want Mrs. Mayer mad at me.

She gently wiped my face clean with her thumbs. "It's okay, Lulu. Just don't do it again."

She folded the paper in half, then fourths, and dropped it in the wastebasket on our way back into homeroom.

I learned that writing words could get me in trouble. Just because they were true didn't mean they could protect me. In fact, the truer they were, the more dangerous. I didn't mention any of it to my parents. Later, I found out that Mrs. Mayer had a similar talk with Adeline, who told her parents everything. They pulled her out of our public elementary during Easter break and enrolled her at a Catholic school two towns over. I begged my parents to let me go there, too.

"Just because a friend jumps off a bridge, doesn't mean you do it," my mom had countered. "Besides, we're Baptists."

"But Adeline isn't just a friend—she's my *best* friend," I cried. "And Aunt Lori is a Catholic so it's in our family."

I never kissed Adeline again and would often cry during recess. It was because of me she was gone.

The memory makes my pen judder on the page. Whatever Flynn and Aunt Lori's troubadour friends were doing in private was between them and, dare I say, God.

I shift to the next line.

Lucas Wesley

Here's the enigma. There was love between them, no doubt. So why the disconnect between the story and real life? Aunt Lori is now Mother Abbess, devoted to piety in the wake of *Romeo & Juliet, The Musical.*

What happened between them?

Thus far, the memories of Lucas are good ones. So . . . let's not beat around the bush.

Did they hook up or have a falling-out?

I have to be careful. Aunt Lori's started to talk, but if I push too fast, she'll jam up. I want her to trust me. This isn't a sensational tell-all. I'm recording her unparalleled rise to stardom as only she experienced it. Well, she and Lucas . . . but the dead tell no tales.

There's a void of echo in the abbey office. The choir has completed the chants. I collect my recorder and head to the candle workshop.

The sisters are already there, silently tying ropy wicks to short tree branches whittled into dowels. Beeswax warms in pots. The room smells of honeyed musk and fragrant herbs hung to dry. The prettiest ones are pressed flat between parchment to use as decorations. Lavender, chamomile, mint, pansies, marigolds, nasturtiums, wisteria, and zinnias. The collective smell is heady with summer and endless sunshine.

Aunt Lori is in the far corner on a stool dropping chunks of yellow wax into a pot. It will be nearly impossible to continue our interview in this austerity. Fortunately, there aren't just wicks being dipped. A couple of sisters in the adjacent room are doing carpentry. They turn on their woodturning devices. The loud whirl of the roughing gouge and click of chisels gives us some auditory cloaking.

I pull up a stool beside Aunt Lori. "Hey."

She kisses my cheek hello but doesn't break her silence. She drops another piece of wax into the thick, bubbling brew and stirs.

"That looks good enough to eat."

"Sister Evangelista makes lip balm with it," she says under her breath. "We use it on the cows, too."

"Lip balm for cows?"

"On their udders. They get dry skin just like we do."

I catch a shadow of a smirk. This is the Aunt Lori I wish more people knew.

I point to my handheld recorder.

She sets the spoon aside on a dish caked with layers of hardened wax dribbles, stands, and nods for me to follow her. In the drying room, tapered candles hang like rainbow icicles from rope lines strung wall to wall.

"Wisteria is my favorite. The smell reminds me of Italy."

She reaches up to a row of six-inch tapers studded with purple blossoms and runs her fingers across. They swing merrily.

"We only have one vine that's thrived here. It's along the stone wall of the lambs' pen. I want to think there's some spiritual connection, but it's the east wall and gets the most sunshine. God's creation doing what He made it to do. Visitors love to take photos, especially at Easter."

I quickly turn on my tape recorder.

LU:

Date: October 7, 1990. Location, the abbey in Connecticut. Aunt—Mother Lori with the candles in the chandlery workshop.

It sounds like we're playing the board game *Clue*.

LORI:

Help me cut these wicks. We sell in pairs, you know.

LU:

Sure, but I've got the tape running, so you're on the record.

LORI:

Record schmecord. If you believe in God, then you're always on the record.

LU:

Right, okay, but I mean for the record-record, not the philosophical one.

LORI:

Oh, that's right, you're not convinced of God anymore. Remind me why that is?

LU:

That isn't part of my thesis, Aunt Lori.

LORI:

It isn't? Seems to me that a thesis by its definition is a theorized premise based on personal research to be proved. So, you're writing about why my life has led me to the here and now. Is that correct?

LU:

Yes, but I don't see—

LORI:

God is the reason. So, whether or not the person who is acting as my storytelling proxy believes in the supernatural is absolutely pertinent.

LU:

(Audible sigh.)

I understand, but I really need us to focus on where we left off—in Italy, you just finished shooting *Romeo & Juliet, The Musical*. We can discuss why I don't believe we're going to eternally live in the clouds playing harps or burn in hell later.

LORI:

(Long pause.)

That's a reasonable compromise. I appreciate that you're on a deadline.

LU:

Excellent. I have questions about Lucas and becoming globally famous at such an early age.

LORI:

Being famous isn't an end point. If it were, my life would've ended by the time I turned nineteen. Besides, we were living in a protective bubble while shooting in Italy. The actors and crew were like family. It didn't feel real at the time—the fame. It was something we dreamed about in the same way that children dream of Santa Claus bringing them gifts.

LU:

Or God bringing them miracles?

LORI:

(Pause. A slicing sound—scissors through taut twine.)
Didn't we just agree to leave your disbelief alone and focus on the story as it is being told?

LU:

We did. I apologize. I didn't mean to—

LORI:

I know, honey. I know.

LU:

I'm trying to wrap my mind around what it was like being Juliet to the world. The hugeness of that for two teenagers. Men and women of every age swooning over you and Lucas. Love personified to a whole generation.

LORI:

Love personified? That's a bit overdramatic, don't you think? And I say that as an ex-actress.

LU:

Here, I'll read you some of your old reviews. *New York Times*: "The lovers, Lucas Wesley and Lori Lovely, are as young and full of life as they ought to be . . . a joy!" *The Guardian*: "Heartbreakingly beautiful actors on show, and all shot in a kind of honeycomb-sunglow light . . . ground-breakingly casting young actors close to the characters' supposed age." *The Herald*: "This Romeo & Juliet is no ordinary love story."

LORI:

Where did you get those from?

LU:
I'm majoring in History. I do my research. The reviews were on the film posters. MSC library has a sweet microfiche center. I used the quotes when I wrote the original essay.

LORI:
Original essay? You've written other things about me.

LU:
(Clears throat.)
It was a shorter assignment. More about being your relation. Anyhow! Back to filming and Lucas Wesley!

LORI:
I already told you, I lost my imaginary virginity on camera... in front of a film crew... of mostly men. My parents watched it in a theater with a hundred people, multiplied times a thousand theaters across the globe. And then there was the marketing. The international posters were stills from the film. Mostly of me lying naked atop Lucas in that closed-set boudoir. We didn't know those would be used until they were plastered from Milan to Tokyo. So much was out of our control, and yet we thought we had it all under control. I went from being little Lucy to Lorietta to someone even I was intimidated by—Lori Lovely, the marquee. When the film premiered, everything changed, and it would never be the same again.

Part 4

Lori

The Marquee

13

New York to Los Angeles
1966

When *Romeo & Juliet, The Musical* released, I was shot into the superstar stratosphere. The critics proclaimed that Nico's masterful musicality had transformed the Renaissance story into a modern classic. Marni Nixon made me sound like an angel heralding the second coming of the Bard. People hummed Lucas's love song everywhere. The radio stations and record stores had a field day. The public wanted to believe in this singing Romeo and Juliet more than they wanted to believe in God.

Overnight, Lucas and I became the most bankable actors in Hollywood. From newspapers and magazines to billboard posters and marquees, I couldn't go anywhere without seeing our pining faces. Audiences throughout Europe were in love with Romeo and Juliet.

So, Lucas and I thought it our chance, too. The problem was, real love isn't a game of Catch Me If You Can. Stolen kisses, secret embraces, and murmurs of desire couldn't sustain the required weight of relational intimacy.

On our first official date to a trattoria, a group of paparazzi asked us to kiss for the cameras, which we did. But it wasn't the same spark. With the world watching, my head had supplanted my heart. I was acting another role—Lori Lovely the actress, as seen on the big screen. I found myself unintentionally performing for the public each time Lucas and I stepped out together.

For example, I have a crooked smile. I compensate by tilting my jaw slightly to the right to offset, which makes my neck appear longer on camera. Lucas said he couldn't tell until I pointed it out. He argued that the lopsidedness was a part of what made me *me*. I couldn't explain to him that nobody wanted the *me*-me. Her name was Lucy Hickey. People wanted Lori Lovely, even him to an extent.

When I kissed Lucas, there always seemed to be an audience. I'd reflexively tilt my jaw and count *one-Mississippi*, *two-Mississippi*, *three-Mississippi*—the three seconds that Nico needed for the cameras to capture the moment. Then I'd pull back and exhale with adoring bliss. It wasn't that I was pretending. Lucas and I had simply perfected the art of the filmed make-out. The footage is irrefutable. I didn't know how to kiss him any other way. To this day, when magazines compile the sexiest kisses of all cinematic history, *Romeo & Juliet, The Musical* is always in the top ten.

The attraction between us was real. Lucas was beautiful from head to toe, and I was familiar with every inch. Moreover, he was one of the most compassionate human beings I had ever known. It seemed like it should work, but the timing was off. The burden of being the public's Romeo and Juliet put a strain on our private relationship—in which I was a virgin and he was not. This distinction would weigh heavily on both of us for different reasons.

Lucas felt compelled to give me the perfect first time; however, the responsibility of that often stole his ardor. In turn, his lack of brio incited my insecurities and fueled my conjuring of all kinds of unfounded suspicions. I was jealous every time another woman so much as looked his way. Because in the back of my mind, I suspected he'd find it easier to sleep with her than with me.

We had the first of many arguments when a stampede of women circled him at a nightclub in Rome, knocking me to the ground so hard that I broke a heel and ripped a hole in my stockings. Instead of coming to my aid, he gregariously signed autographs and kissed cheeks. One of the security guards helped me hobble out of the way before I was trampled by another herd of them. I was angry at the women, at Lucas, and at myself for feeling inadequate. I was nineteen, fueled by hormones, and sexually frustrated. But you can't see the forest for the trees when you're a sapling.

Later, Lucas said he hadn't seen me fall and assumed I was on the other side of the crowd greeting fans. He was genuinely sorry but still . . . It was hard for either of us to get in the mood after something like that. Over and over, a trivial argument would spin itself into a bigger issue than it needed to be. Before we made each other miserable and ruined our friendship, we decided to put a pause on our romantic endeavors. We couldn't handle the pressure of being lovers on-screen and off.

We had to keep our un-coupling a secret, though. Paramount Pictures publicized that the leads of the film were in a real-life courtship. The fans were mad for it and the studio was squeezing every drop out of the promotional optics. So we played our parts for the press junket, making googly eyes at each other and kissing for the crowds. The truth was, Lucas had moved on to a twentysomething model named Opal Margaret, who you can spy in the background of the later promotional stop photos.

I didn't mind that he was dating Opal. She was so different from me. Beautiful in a mischievous way. She ringed her eyes in the blackest of eye liner and smoked packs of slim cigarettes. The smell reminded me of the tobacco depot, sweetly sour and a little smoky. Most of the time, Opal could be found silently puffing on her cigarettes in the corner of the room while sketching Lucas. She had talent. Her drawings showed her sincere affection for him. She saw Lucas the way I did: boyish, kind, and optimistic, but a little lost, too.

I didn't begrudge Lucas for moving on. It had to have been equally frustrating dating a virgin celebrity. He deserved to . . . let off some steam, shall we say. I'd be lying if I said I didn't envy Opal for being the kind of girl with whom a man like Lucas could *let off some steam*. It didn't seem fair. But then, I'm sure Opal envied me for her own reasons. The grass is always greener on the other side, isn't that the saying?

We formed a little traveling troupe, crisscrossing Europe to give interviews, promote the film, and spontaneously (per the proprietor's agreement) pop into nightclubs. This, I learned, was the way marketers galvanized the locals, creating grassroots buzz.

The months added up fast, with too much happening too quickly. I'd gone to Italy intent on writing Ginny every day. But how could I between shooting and not having a reliable postal system? The only calls I'd made were to my parents and Marie, because Marie threatened to report me to Interpol as a missing person if I didn't . . . and she would.

So, my intended letters went from once a day to once a month to none at all. I kept telling myself that I'd wait until I could write Ginny of my return to London. Most of the film crew, the actors, the troubadours, even Miss Meriwether, went home after principal photography was completed. But Nico invited Lucas and me to stay to do the automated dialogue replacement—commonly called looping—in Nico's home sound studio. When we completed that, it seemed pointless to go back to London only to return for the film's Rome release and world tour.

These were all my rationales. But the truth was, I'd forgotten about Ginny. It shames me to this day to admit, but I had. I was wrapped up in *Romeo & Juliet*, Lucas and kisses, Rome and Nico. Every time I thought about Ginny, it made me homesick for somewhere I couldn't put a finger on. I didn't miss North Carolina, America, or even London. It wasn't an address on a map that I missed, it was a moment in time and the people in it. I was homesick for how things used to be but weren't anymore—the zeitgeist of my adolescence. It was the natural transition from one stage of life to another. But when you're in the middle of a rainstorm, you're too busy covering your head to see the cloud break.

I didn't find a solitary hour to myself until after the film's Berlin opening. Lucas and Opal had gone to a nightclub. My first taste of caviar and vodka had not agreed with me, so I'd returned to the hotel early. The quiet of the empty room brought on thoughts of Ginny.

I dialed our London flat, asking the hotel operator to charge the call to my room.

"'Ello?"

"Hello? It's Lori—Lori Lovely."

"Well, hi there, Lovely! Bloody hell—Kitty, it's Lori!" said Fern.

"Lori?" A sleepy voice. I forgot it was a school night. "Ask her when she's coming back."

"Kitty wants to know when—"

"Yes, I heard her." I laughed. "We're going over to the States next. New York City and L.A. The whole tour's been bananas. I'm sorry for calling so late!"

"I'm glad you did. Everyone will be crazy jealous when we tell them tomorrow. We're chuffed for you! We're all talking about how an ICAer is the star of our generation!"

I didn't deserve that kind of title. I went to sleep many nights anxiously wondering if I'd wake up back in my Canary House bed, like Dorothy in *The Wizard of Oz*.

I swallowed hard. The smack of salty fish eggs stuck in the back of my throat. "How is everyone?"

"Oh, fine. The boys returned from Italy like knights from the Crusades. Flynn threw a Welcome Home party at the Troubadour, of course. Nina Simone was there! It was a spectacle!"

"If Flynn's involved, it always will be. He made quite an impression on Nico Cellini."

I pulled the phone into the large, empty hotel bed.

"Is Ginny there? I was kinda hoping—I mean, I don't want to wake her if she's sleeping . . ."

The line went silent for a long beat.

"Uh, I don't know if she is or not," said Fern. "When you didn't call, I figured you'd heard the news."

My fist tightened on the phone handle.

"News?" I squawked.

"Ginny left. After her foot healed, she went back to dance but said it wasn't the same. She was always on the couch in front of the tube. We came back after class one day, and her room was empty. Mrs. Coates said she'd given her resignation and was going home to recuperate."

I squeezed my eyes tight, fighting off tears.

"Did she leave a forwarding address?"

"Yes, a Mr. and Mrs. Finkelstein in New York," said Fern.

"Anything else?"

A note for me was my hope.

"The only other thing she left was a poster on the ceiling."

Norma Shearer and Leslie Howard. I buried my cheek in the hotel pillow to keep my sob from traveling across the line. My heart was broken, and I'd done it to myself by breaking promises. I'd abandoned Ginny.

"Lori? Are you still there? Did the line drop?"

"I'm here," I croaked.

"Ginny was proud of you. She cut out all your articles from the papers."

I wasn't deserving. Ginny was the kind of friend you got once in a lifetime, and I'd been careless with her.

I told Fern I couldn't stay on. The charges were to my room and my room was being subsidized by the studio. I didn't want to be a spendthrift actress, I explained. But in ways that had nothing to do with coins, I'd already squandered the most valuable thing I had.

The next morning, no matter how long the makeup artist held the frozen spoons to my eyes, the swelling would not go down. In the end, they put a pair of extra-large sunglasses on me, which the German media headlined as *Lovely ist Juliet und modisch Italienisch.* (Lovely is Juliet and fashionably Italian.) Heartsickness was the vogue.

"You all right?" Lucas asked on our way to the airport.

I didn't answer. Instead, I leaned against his chest, and he put his arm around me.

"Just tired." It was half-true.

He sighed deeply, and I heard the rush of breath through his body. I wanted to curl up inside him.

"Me too." He reached down into his bag and pulled out a prescription bottle. "Here. My doctor gave me these. Quaaludes." He knocked one into his palm. "Take it when you get on the plane. It's the only way I get any rest."

Lucas was the only one doing everything I was doing and more. He wanted me to be my best. I trusted him. So when he asked the stewardess for a Coca-Cola to take the medication with, I asked for a second.

"To us." He clinked the lip of his soda bottle to mine and popped the pill.

I did the same.

"'That I shall say good night till it be morrow,'" he said.

It was the last thing I remember on that ten-hour flight. The rest was delicious and deep as death. It was addictive: the ability to turn off suffering with a swallow and awake reborn. Lucas and I shared that, too. I simply came to the realization sooner: we can leave one pain in the void, but life will always hand us another. The pills and alcohol didn't bring supernatural freedom. They made us believe the lie that the power was outside of ourselves. And if anyone truly saw our shame, traumas, and poisoned parts, they'd turn their backs. So we swallowed to get the job done, and we swallowed again because it was easy, and we kept swallowing because somewhere along the line, it became the thing we craved. It felt like love.

Much has been speculated about Lucas's drug and alcohol use. I want to say for the record, he had a problem, but it's wrong of history to highlight a fatal flaw and dismiss him. He was too good for that.

14

Lucas and I were on cloud nine when we flew into JFK airport. Lady Liberty welcomed us home with a wave.

The premiere party was at the Plaza Hotel across from the Paris Theater. Paramount Pictures rented an entire floor of rooms exclusively for the *Romeo & Juliet, The Musical* cast. I can't begin to imagine how much it all cost. Nico demanded that no expense be spared.

My room was lavish and next door to Lucas's with a door connecting the suites. The first thing we did was fling it open and compare.

"I see you have a French Château theme," Lucas said, swaggering around my room.

"French Renaissance is the official term," I corrected.

"Oh, *oui-oui*."

"I believe you have the same?"

"Give or take a gilded chair." He threw himself onto my chaise lounge. "I don't have one of these."

I ran my fingers over the petite pink roses that the hotel staff had left beside a plate of cursive chocolate: *Welcome, Ms. Lori Lovely!* A bottle of champagne waited on ice. Nobody cared that I was under twenty-one. In Italy the legal drinking age was eighteen. But to be honest, we were bouncing from country to country so often, it was impossible to keep track of such things.

"It's ironic," I said. "Two Americans in a French-inspired New York City hotel room who are famous for pretending to be Italian lovers as written by a Brit."

"Just goes to prove, we're all trying to be something else." Lucas got up and poured two coupes of champagne. "The stylists will be here in an hour. This will perk us up." He handed me one.

"Right." I rubbed my temples and took the drink.

We'd been spirited to the Plaza Hotel with a scant amount of time to change before the premiere's red carpet. *People began lining up at dawn*, the concierge had explained. They had to shut down the street and redirect traffic.

My stomach knotted. I was secretly terrified that despite all the European press praise, American critics would see right through me and pan my performance as clumsy, awkward, childish, not a professionally trained dancer or singer, and certainly not a real actress. In other countries, I couldn't understand the language. The shouts from the press pens could've been *You are wonderful!* or *You are terrible!*, so I had the blissful ignorance of being lost in translation. But now, I heard every word like a series of fire alarms.

Prior to our Tuesday premiere, the *New York Sunday News* did a phone interview for a feature that ran. In it, they asked if Lucas and I thought children should obey their parents. I said yes, but that it was more complicated than that. Children didn't stay children. They became adults who should think for themselves. Lucas agreed. The quote appeared in the paper as "The co-stars share a mod-minded opinion that children should think for themselves. 'It's complicated,' said Lovely, the chubby-faced, blue-eyed starlet."

The description completely nullified what I had said. As if I were the Gerber baby! I was horrified.

Lucas tried to make light of it. "They'll say all kinds of things to get readers' attention. Trust me."

"They didn't mention your chubby baby face, and you've got the same color eyes as me . . ."

"Don't read a word of it."

But I had read it, and looking out the windows of our hotel room to the waiting throngs at the Paris Theater, my terror doubled in strength. I took a cold sip of champagne. It helped. We had a long night ahead. But tomorrow was a day off.

"Get through the next twelve hours and you're free," I whispered. I needed the roses and the chocolate and the silk tapestries to hear me, even if no one else could.

I promised Marie that I'd taxi over to East Harlem in the morning. No need for her and Bill to trek downtown. I couldn't put a toe outside without the paparazzi on the hunt. I intended to keep Lori Lovely right where the world expected her to be—in a glamorous hotel room having champagne with her co-stars.

I didn't tell anyone about Marie and Bill either, to protect their privacy. That's the story I told myself, when really, I was embarrassed. I'd put so much energy into making a name and proving that I was no longer Lucy Hickey from Pufftown, North Carolina, that now I had to literally sneak back to my old world.

A knock at the door made me jump. Lucas opened it, and the room filled with a cacophony of chatter, the HMU style squad. They combed my hair, rouged my cheeks, and chose what I would wear from a lineup of designer fashions sent over on loan. In the end, a crimson velvet gown was decided. They did the same for Lucas, a matching velvet suit with gold-embellished shoes.

Nico came to give his approval, just as he had for our costumes.

"*Magnifico*, but . . . something is missing."

He locked eyes with me and tapped his chest so that his fingers splayed across his heart. Then he slid his hand under the lapel of his jacket and pulled the pendant from his inner pocket. The cross that I'd worn in the film.

"Please, Lorietta, I want you to have this."

"Nico, it's too generous," I declined.

"It's my gift for you," he insisted.

Before I could say no again, he looped the chain over my head and the weight fell against my breast like a talisman. I traced my thumb up and down the length of its bridge. So familiar.

"Miss Lovely?" Lucas extended his velvet elbow, and I released the cross to take it.

"My lovers!" Nico kissed our cheeks and then bowed for us to lead the way.

From the hotel to the hallway, down the elevator and through the lobby, our theatrical procession seemed to grow in number until we poured out into the New York City night sparking gold and silver by the cameras and marquee lights:

TONIGHT 7:30—SWINGING YOUTH PREMIERE
CELLINI'S ROMEO & JULIET, THE MUSICAL

The street was blocked off by policemen. Security guards the size of football linesmen chained arms to hold the crowd.

"Lori!"

"Lucas!"

"Lovely!"

"Wesley!"

"Romeo!"

"Juliet!"

I turned at each call, not knowing which I was supposed to heed. Lucas on my left. Nico on my right. The three of us pushed through the gauntlet. Reaching the theater was no relief. What had been intended as the red carpet had been usurped by teenagers in T-shirts and sneakers colliding with New York socialites in gowns and tuxedos. It was a pinwheel of frenetic energy, as dizzying and disturbing as a house of mirrors.

"Lori and Lucas, kiss for us!"

"Lucas, I love you!

"Lori, I love you!"

"Please sing 'Lovely You'!"

"Lucas, take me, I'll be your Juliet!"

"Lori, you've got great tits!"

The shouts became increasingly assaulting, frenzied in their urges. Then, out of the corner of my eye, a flash of familiar curly hair standing a foot above the rest. Ginny—was that Ginny?

I pulled away from Lucas and Nico in her direction, but they stitched me back in place.

"Ginny!" I called out.

The figure vanished into the shadows of the streets we used to dance across. The glaring spotlight grew wider and stronger, inescapable. My hands shook, my knees, too. It was a trick of my imagination, I told myself. It wasn't her. I didn't want it to be her—so near with so much unsaid.

"I'm going to faint," I whispered.

"We have you," said Nico.

Lucas's smile never wavered, but his hands were clammy; his eyes were gray as storm clouds.

The doors for the theater opened. I needed to get inside, find a quiet place, get a grip.

That's when I heard my name. My *real* name.

"Lucy! Luuuuccccccyyyy!"

There, behind a guard with arms outstretched, stood my parents with Marie and Bill. Dad waved. Mom wore a tweed coat and heels. Her bob had been hairsprayed high and wide in a bouffant. Bill smiled, but even at a distance, I could see Marie's brows furrowed with concern.

The sight of them in the flesh after so long clubbed me like a baseball bat. My vision blurred. Movement slowed. Sound muffled.

"Surprise!" Dad shouted and then said to the guard, "That's my baby girl!"

I tore away from Lucas and Nico straight into their arms. The guard moved aside but stayed vigilant.

"What are you doing here?"

"They insisted on surprising you," said Marie.

"Lucy—I mean, *Lori*!" Dad pulled me to him and whispered, "I like the stage name. We're so proud."

Mom leaned in too so that we were three in one.

The warmth of that embrace was everything I needed but didn't welcome. They could not witness their teenage daughter kiss a boy, lose her virginity, expose herself, and commit suicide in front of a massive audience. Not with me sitting beside them, at least. Make-believe or not, *I* wasn't ready to handle the real-life emotional upshot. I had responsibilities as Lori Lovely, and I couldn't break character.

"I—I can't," I said.

Lucas and Nico waved for me to come. The din of the crowd reached an ear-splitting decimal. The ticketed audience was about to be loosed. I couldn't be everything to everyone. A choice had to be made.

"I must go," I said to my parents.

I couldn't look them in the eyes. I knew the disappointment would shatter me. I kept my chin down, eyes on the gold cross on my chest.

Dad's arm went protectively to Mom's shoulders. She clutched her purse, knuckles white.

The only one whose eyes I could bear were my sister's.

"Please," I said.

She nodded and lay a wordless hand on mine.

Bill cleared his throat. "We told them this wasn't wise. So many people. They're calling it the movie of the century!"

"Tomorrow," I said, a promise and a resolve. "Tomorrow, I'll come."

Then the guard escorted me back to the theater doors where the cast posed for photographs.

"Do you know them?" asked Lucas.

"Everyone look at the cameras!" said Nico.

"Yes," I said quickly, and then chin angled to the right, neck extended, teeth unclenched, lips parted, breath bated, I smiled.

"Can we get a kiss from Romeo and Juliet?" requested a photographer.

"Sure!" someone answered for us.

Lucas took me in his arms and pressed his lips to mine. *One-Mississippi, two-Mississippi, three-Mississippi.*

I don't remember the conversations or steps that followed. I vaguely recall watching the film. I'd sat through so many showings already. An endless loop of out-of-order memories: the beginning scenes shot last; the ending scenes shot first. All credit to Nico. His technicolor enhancements and orchestral accompaniment wove it together like a magic needle and thread.

The premiere's afterparty was in the Plaza Hotel ballroom. I was there thirty minutes and left through the back staff exit. My head hurt. My feet, too. Everything in between was wrung out. I wanted to change out of this costume, get in bed, and fall into that dark worry-less chasm again. The connecting door between my room and Lucas's was unlocked. I had seen where he kept the quaaludes. So I rummaged in his bag until the clatter of the bottle made itself apparent.

The champagne from earlier was flat and lifeless but still golden in the cup. *Romeo, I come, this do I drink to thee.* I put the pill on my tongue and drank.

It's hard to say when the make-believes you tell yourself become your thoughts. The thoughts, your actions. The actions, your new memories, and on and on. The transformation is indistinct for actors. For everyday people, too.

15

Knocking woke me. I dreamt it was a clapboard, but it was the maid asking if I needed morning service. The clock read 11:11 a.m.

Biblical scholars of far higher rank than I maintain that the sequence of numerals 1-1-1-1 is used by the angels to indicate coming change. People are always looking for signs. Deep down, we want to believe in divine wonders. But in that moment, all it prompted was panic. The quaalude made me sleep too long. I'd promised Marie I'd be there for breakfast. In less than twenty-four hours, I'd be on a plane to Los Angeles.

The empty champagne bottle was sideways and beside it were three more. The door separating rooms was ajar, and through it I saw the pink of Lucas's skin. He lay face down on his bed. His smooth bare back rose and fell. A swath of blond hair draped across the pillow beside him. Opal's face was masked in the tangles. I thought I might be sick. Love came so effortlessly to Lucas. I wanted to love like that and be loved like that. One of them breathed with a pitchy nose whistle. I shut the door between rooms with a too-loud *clunk*. I had to get out of there.

I washed my face, brushed my teeth, and changed into jeans and sneakers. Lucas's cable-knit sweater was flung haphazardly on my chaise lounge. A gift from his mother. He'd mentioned that she endlessly worried he'd catch a cold. We rarely spoke of our family members. Funny how two people could be intimate and still not know so much.

I put on the sweater. The skim of the soft yarn over my bare breasts gave way to goose bumps. The smell of his skin and sweat enveloping me with tender familiarity.

A *thump* followed by an *Ow!* came from his bedroom. They were awake. Quickly, I grabbed a hat and dashed out the door.

In the lobby, the bellboys and patrons shuffled by with hardly a look. My pulse raced and my stride matched the cadence until I burst out into the open air.

It was a crisp, clear day. The kind that makes New Yorkers slow their hurry and look up between the buildings with the unconscious thought *Yes, blue skies are real.* I joined the city throngs but hailed a cab when I could.

"Corner of First and East 115th, please."

Lunchtime traffic was worse than usual—isn't that what they always say? I didn't arrive at Marie and Bill's until half past noon.

Bill answered the door. "Hi, Lucy."

The apartment smelled of waffles and maple syrup, patty sausages, and orange juice concentrate from the can. It smelled like my childhood and ordinary weekends in pajamas. I inhaled it as deep as I could, wishing it could fill me up like helium and help me rise.

In the hallway, I slipped off my sneakers and hung my hat, letting my hair fall long and messy down my back.

"They're waiting for you." Bill gestured to the living room.

Mom and Dad sat together on the couch where I'd slept those summer nights. So much had happened in two years. They leaned toward each other, their backs like two Cs bridging a gap. When I entered, they looked up. Mom's tear-streaked face was unrecognizable. A family trait from her side: ugly criers. We swell. It's for this reason that I accepted the menthol tear stick during Juliet's death scene. She needed to cry and die pretty. Not something I do naturally.

I'd witnessed my mom cry less than a handful of times. Stoicism was her best defense. Only a broken heart would bring her to this. I had brought her to this.

Marie stood by the fire escape window smoking a cigarette—in front of my parents! I hadn't known she'd started. I didn't like the look of the stick in her hand. She stubbed it out on the sill and faced me with a glare.

"You said you would be here for breakfast." Her voice was even but I heard the fury.

"It's been crazy, Marie. I woke up late and the traffic . . ."

"She made breakfast for you."

Mom exhaled. Her bottom lip quivered.

"It's gone now," Marie continued.

"I'm glad you ate—"

"I didn't," she cut me off. "Couldn't swallow a bite. Bill took the leftovers next door to the Russos. They've got five kids." Her voice broke.

A well of silence filled the room. Bill cleared his throat. "I'll make a fresh pot of coffee."

No one had asked. He went to the kitchen, leaving us to our own, mother-father-daughters.

Marie looked to my parents, then blinked hard at me. Sister Morse code. I got the message.

"Mom. Dad." I sat down on the couch. "I'm sorry."

It's what I should've said from the start.

"I was overwhelmed last night. I wish I could go back and do it differently. You are my parents. I should've found you seats—mine and Lucas's even!"

"We didn't expect you to do that, Lucy," said Dad. "We weren't there for the show. We were there for you."

His words splintered me like a twig.

"I—I should've tried . . ."

Mom lifted her chin, dew-skinned even at sixty. Her long eyelashes glistened. I'd inherited those, too.

"My sweet Lucille." She took my hand in hers, smoothing my knuckles with her thumb.

She'd done this since I was a child. The old habit made her real as only she could be. Bone of my bone, flesh of my flesh.

"You never have to ask. We'll always be here for you."

My eyes stung.

"I've missed you so much." The words brought a lump to my throat.

Marie sat on my other side. Four across on a sofa meant for two, our heads knocked uncomfortably into each other. We dared smiles, dared forgiveness, dared to choose love despite the hurt. Success or failure, my family would be there without my asking. Where once that seemed an anchor holding me back, I now recognized that it secured me against the tides. The same and yet different. The change was in me.

Bill brought us a box of Kleenex. "What'd I miss?" he said to lighten the mood. "Coffee's ready."

Marie rose to kiss him. "Thank you."

Neither of their marriages exhibited the passion of Romeo and Juliet, but there was an undeniable magnetism. They were safe to love each other and be loved, unconditionally. Bonded and yet free.

"Never you mind about last night," said Dad. "I remember the fans that would come to the back door of the theater after one of my vaudeville shows. It was a pandemonium!" He stood with a bounce of energy. "I'm glad to see you have excellent security. People can be overly familiar, and we can't have any Joe Blow grabbing my girl! Given the success of the film, you might consider hiring your own bodyguard. I believe Sophia Loren has one. Perhaps you two met in Italy—"

"Dad," Marie interrupted. "Let's give her and Mom a minute."

I was grateful.

Mom, my inherent plumb line. I leaned in. She smelled of garden herbs and kitchen bakes, of sweet sage and lemon thyme. Her hands were peppered with the freckles of sunny days in North Carolina and soft as the pages of old paperback books.

While Dad's enthusiasm was palpable, it was Mom's approval I sought most.

"Are you happy, Mom?"

"Happy? Of course. I have my two daughters with me again."

"I mean, are you happy with . . . what I've done?"

Are you proud of me? That's what I couldn't say directly. It felt too forthright, too self-important.

She ran her eyes across my face, tucked my hair behind one ear, and then looked at me in earnest.

"Are you happy with what you've done, Lucille? That's what matters."

I knew I ought to be exceedingly happy—and I was! But I was also kind of sad. The success felt like a belltower. From afar, the ringing sounded like triumph. Up close, it made you deaf.

"I think I am."

She kissed my forehead. "Your dad keeps reminding me that you are all grown up, but it's hard for a parent to let her children go their own way. First Marie, and now you. It's a strange thing to be the most consequential person in someone's life but with the duty of making yourself inconsequential. Because if the job is done well, your children won't need you anymore—they'll *want* you. And there's a great difference between requirement and choice. That's a parent's love. You'll understand one day when you have your own." She dabbed at her eyes.

We held each other until my stomach grumbled. The last thing I ate was a cheese Danish served in flight before landing.

"I'm really, really sorry I missed your waffles and sausages."

Mom laughed—a hiccup of a thing—but it was real.

"Give me a minute. I'll whip something up." She rose with renewed vigor.

In less time than it took the toaster oven to heat, she'd tied on an apron, fried fresh sausages, mixed lard with flour to make quick biscuits and gravy because "It's lunchtime!," and filled the Formica kitchen table again.

Dad, Bill, Marie, and I sat while Mom poured coffee into cups, washed up, and declined a seat when Bill offered. We knew it pained her joints no matter how cheery she appeared. Still, she refused to slow down.

"Newton's first law of motion. A body in motion stays in motion. If I rest too long, who knows if I'll get back up! Besides, I need to make Marie collards and beans. She needs more iron."

She filled a pot with water to soak the beans and stood over the sink tearing the stems from the greens.

"Mom brought her own shellies," Marie explained.

"Of course I did. Any old bean won't do. Who knows how it was grown or where it's been. Break a tooth on a pebble that way."

Marie shook her head with a smile.

The banter, the food, the sound of the white beans dropping into the pot, it was everything I didn't know I needed but desperately did. We filled our day that way, toe to toe and heart to heart. The light through the windows went butter to blue, and then we ate bowls of collards and shellies while watching *The Beverly Hillbillies*.

Dad got a kick out of Buddy Ebsen. "The slapstick is genius!"

Mom pulled yarn between her thumb and forefinger working the stitches of her knitting and chuckling whenever Irene Ryan as Granny came into a scene.

I could almost believe we were back at the Canary House on a regular Wednesday night.

"You're going to L.A. next?" Marie asked.

"Yes."

She turned back to Donna Douglas.

"Maybe you'll meet Elly May," said Mom. "Wasn't she in a musical recently?"

"*Li'l Abner*," said Dad. "It wasn't very good. She's better on television."

Mom nodded absentmindedly.

It was not meant as a slight. *The Beverly Hillbillies* was one of their favorite shows and they adored the cast. But just like that, I realized who I—Lori Lovely—was to millions of people. Entertainment.

16

New York to Los Angeles
1967

Our arrival in Los Angeles was a marked change from New York. It wasn't merely the palm trees, sunshine, and glittering Pacific Ocean. Los Angeles is a city that doesn't try to trick you with make-believe. It confesses right up front, I *am* make-believe. L.A. promises, if you work hard in pursuit of your dream, you too can attain make-believe. Magic is real, even if it isn't. The believing is what makes it so. Everyone accepts that with utmost sincerity. One could argue that's the basis of religious faith, too, so perhaps it shouldn't have surprised me that I took a liking to the town.

The pavement rose to meet our wheels in a yellow shimmer.

"It's like driving through pink lemonade," I told Lucas with delight.

"It's the air pollution," he said and promptly put on a pair of sunglasses.

It took an hour and a half with traffic to get from the airport to Nico's on the Santa Monica beachfront, but it was worth the crawl. Our town car stopped in front of a row of boxy condos trimming the oceanfront. Painted flamingo pink, lime green, and white, Nico's house reminded me of an Italian flag made of sherbet.

The dusk sun dipped below sea level and sent a dagger of light into our eyes.

"'More light and light,'" I quoted to Lucas, playing our old memorization game.

He'd been in a mood the entire trip, and I had a feeling it had something to do with Opal not coming with us to California. Their romantic flame had burned to its wick's end. I didn't ask the details. I wouldn't be able to feign sadness. I was glad it was just us.

He raised an eyebrow. "'More dark and dark our woes'?"

"That's Romeo's line. Juliet's is 'More light and light *it grows.*' I win."

It garnered a smile. "Tricky," he said.

A taxi pulled up behind us and out popped a young man in a crisp linen shirt, tortoiseshell sunglasses, and banana-yellow slacks that outshone the sun.

"Sorry, sorry! Nico had to go over to the studio and doesn't know when he'll get loose from the execs. I'm his L.A. assistant, Phillip—call me Pip."

He confidently stuck out his hand to shake each of ours. Pip had a face that could host a game show and the air of a Hollywood mogul despite being a mere assistant. This was the bravado of the town. People had unflappable optimism in themselves.

Our driver brought our luggage to the door.

"Thanks, man," said Pip, pulling a wad of cash from his pants pocket and fanning twenty-dollar bills into the driver's palm. The most generous tip I had ever seen.

He gestured for us to follow him to the fenced-in backyard.

"I'm sorry to bring you in this way. Nico had hoped to do it himself—through the front door! He wasn't expecting meetings today. He sends his apologies but wanted to make sure you were welcomed and settled."

At the back gate, he stopped and turned the numbers on the combination lock to 1-1-1-1.

I gasped. The number of angels again.

The assistant looked up at me. "Oh, I know, it's horrible, isn't it? I told Nico he should change it to his birthday or something, but he insists that nobody expects the simplest answer."

The lock clicked open and the door with it.

Nico's backyard was a zen garden of dove-gray limestones adorned with fleshy succulents in the shapes of hearts, teardrops, pinwheels, roses, spears, and elephant ears. Their soothing greens and blues were accented by small pink and yellow blossoms between needled spines.

"I honestly don't know why he owns the house," Pip continued. "He's rarely in L.A. When he isn't shooting on location, he prefers Italy. He could stay at the Miramar just as easily, but no . . ."

He knelt on one knee and without hesitation grabbed a prickly pear cactus by the head.

"It's plastic." Pip tossed the cactus to Lucas. "They're all fake. Nobody's here long enough to care for a garden. But nobody wants an ugly aesthetic. It's Nico Cellini's place, after all."

Then from the hollowed-out socket in the ground, he extracted a silver house key.

"For emergencies or when Nico needs someone to let in his celebrity guests!" He winked.

The key unlocked the sliding glass door that opened to the floor-to-ceiling windowed den perpendicular to the glass front door where our luggage sat under the portico. Glass on glass on glass. The California sun through the prism-fractured rainbows across the white shag carpet. Overhead a mirrored chandelier reflected their colors.

"Wow," said Lucas. "This place is far-out."

Pip sighed. "The real estate agent insisted the property is still in Santa Monica even though I swear it's the Palisades. Being so far from downtown, we don't get a lot of foot traffic or peeping paparazzi. That's the benefit. As you probably know, Nico likes to keep his private circle *privato*."

We brought in our luggage from the front porch, and Pip led us up the floating staircase to the second-floor bedrooms. We'd been traveling all day, all week, all month. Walking, flying, driving, or sitting, who could tell? All were measured by the same number of breaths.

"Lori, you'll be in the Seashell Suite." Pip pointed to a room decorated with whimsical conchs and cockles. "Lucas will be in the Sea Foam Suite." Across the hall, his was decorated with frothy green wallpaper.

Our arrival had unsettled the dust particles. My yawn sent them into an eddy of golden shimmer. It was evening in New York, already tomorrow in London and Rome.

Pip checked his watch. "I ordered Patsy D'Amore's. Best Italian takeout in town. I'll have the delivery kid leave it in the kitchen. Feel free to eat what you want and leave the rest in the fridge. The saltimbocca with Madeira sauce is Nico's favorite."

The doorbell buzzed.

Pip smiled. "Right on cue." He started down, but Lucas stopped him.

"Hey, man, I promised to call my manager, Tim. He's got me on a tight leash, y'know. I'm jumping on the plane as soon as we're done here. Gotta get back to Memphis and finish recording."

"Of course." He pointed to a corner desk in Lucas's room where a mint-green, push-button phone nearly blended into the wallpaper.

"Lori, if you need to call your agent or manager, there's a phone in your room, too. You'll just have to wait until Lucas is off the line."

"I don't have an agent or manager," I told him.

He frowned. "Well, you better get one. This town will eat you alive if you don't have someone on your team. Even I have an agent."

The doorbell gave a double *buzz-buzz.*

"Coming!" he called down the stairs and was gone in a yellow streak.

"Do I need an agent or a manager—what's the difference?" I asked Lucas.

"I don't know. I've been with mine all my life. He's my uncle. He takes care of all the business stuff. Got anyone like that?"

I shook my head. Marie and Bill were busy with the photography shop and still trying to start a family. My parents were expecting me to have dinner with the Clampetts, for crying out loud. As for uncles, I didn't have any. The closest thing I had were Carolina cousins, but they were all in tobacco, not moviemaking.

The smell of oregano, basil, and rosemary wafted up from below. The delivery boy's Italian lilt was sweet and familiar.

"Ciao, buon appetito."

Lucas went to phone his uncle Tim. I unpacked my suitcase and changed into cotton pajamas.

Our event was at two o'clock the following afternoon. A sunny, red-carpet premiere. After the show, Nico was hosting a party for his investors, cast, and crew at a local vineyard in Topanga.

So, tonight was the first night in what seemed like an eternity that I got to sleep in a bed that didn't smell like hotel bleach, and I didn't have to worry about maid service knocking at sunrise. It's funny how often we dream of being waited on hand and foot—ultimate luxury! But those who've experienced it know that excess is a lost and lonely island. Less really is more.

In that moment, a quiet room of seashell spirits with an ocean view was my sanctuary. I fell asleep effortlessly. Sunrise, sunset.

Lu

Library of Grace

The Abbey, Connecticut
1990

I catch Aunt Lori just before sunrise Lauds. It's too early for any normal person to be awake, but it was the only time I knew for sure she'd have to be out of her room.

While Aunt Lori gave up all her worldly goods, she was permitted one trunk of the past to accompany her into the sacred sphere of the vestal kingdom, a bridal trousseau of sorts. The sisters at Queen of Praise Benedictine Abbey decided back before anyone could remember that it made good sense to retain documents of their former existence: diaries, journals, cards, letters, medical records, and other significant paperwork. I agree with whoever thought this up, though no doubt it was for practical reasons rather than sentimental ones. It lessens the burden of keeping files for the older generations. The details are delegated to the individual. Quite democratic. I'm not sure if other abbeys make leniencies for keepsakes, too, or if this is just what they do here in Connecticut.

"I don't mean to pry, but you know how technical History folks are. I gotta have footnotes and primary source credentials and all that," I say as a means of asking to see the contents of her trunk.

There are so many confusing and contradictory parts of Aunt Lori's timeline. I don't think she's lying, but I have the sneaking suspicion there's a lot of stuff missing. Studying history is often prying with a badge of authority. I'm just doing my job.

"Sure," Aunt Lori says. "It's full of old bits and bobs—newspaper clippings, photos, medical records, sentimentals . . . If it helps your research, feel free to have a look."

It's been so long since she's opened it that the latch sticks. Flecks of corrugated metal chip off when we finally get it loose. An earthy must rises like the fallen leaves outside, not unpleasant. Stacks of journals are held together with rubber bands. Decades are demarcated with colored ribbons. Correspondences are tied with twine. The glossy edges of headshots shuffle with the matted tear of sepia newspapers.

"It's my Library of Grace," she says.

A nun's filing cabinet.

"We choose the things we keep." She lifts a photograph of my mom and her as girls sitting on the front porch of the Canary House. They look nothing alike. I see myself in Aunt Lori more than in my mom.

"History is a recollection of what we decide. The rest gets mulched. Kind of like what a lot of people do with religion. Cherry-pick." She runs her hand over folded lace, yellow as mustard, and I recognize the embroidery.

A memory, quick as a tadpole in the shallows.

I'm at a wedding. Aunt Lori is decked out in white lace and holds a posy of lavender. My smocked dress matches its palest hue. I'm in love with every gossamer thread of her. She practically levitates down the aisle. When she passes me, our gazes lock like I'm the only one in the room. Tears bud and make the blue of her eyes sparkle. The sight makes mine do the same. Her mouth moves to speak. "My child," I hear. It's one of the nuns, the Mother Abbess. Her face is wrinkled soft as the folds of my cotton skirt. I want to ask something but then the sisters sing, and I forget what it was. All around me, there's a questioning feeling.

"I remember that," I say.

"A bridal veil. It was your mother's. I borrowed it for my Clothing ceremony, the day I took my vows."

Aunt Lori tilts her head with a penetrating look.

I meet her gaze straight on. "I was there."

"You were," she says.

There's a pause between us and the questioning feeling from my memories returns. I'm hoping she'll go on to talk about the Clothing. Tell me why she chose that course. But I can't come straight at her or she'll spook. So here we are, locked in a staring contest, blue to blue, waiting to see who blinks first.

Both of us do when the abbey bell rings. It's time for prayer and she must lead the sisters in Lauds and Prime. She rubs the twinge in her knee as she stands.

"Well, I'll leave you to it."

She goes without looking back and shuts the door behind her.

Alone, I take in the collection. It's overwhelming, and it isn't even mine. Or so I think . . .

A flamboyant drawing brings a jolt of nostalgia: the smell of clay crayons, the taste of Nilla wafers, the feel of waxy colors tickling my fingers. It's a picture I made for Aunt Lori in kindergarten. Our teacher had instructed us to place our hands on the craft paper and make an outline. Each finger was colored as a feather. Our thumbs were dotted with black eyes and a yellow beak. A holiday turkey, a rainbow bird. Pride swells in my chest. At five years old, I was sure it was the most beautiful thing I had ever created, and I had sent it to her.

Happy Thanksgiving, Aunt Lori! I love you so troo.

The teacher had written the first sentence on the chalkboard, instructing us to fill in the name of the recipient between the comma and the exclamation point. I'd added the second sentence in the wonky letters of a child wanting to make her feelings known.

Now I place my hand over the drawing, eclipsing the turkey. I'd grown up on the outside, but so much within is the same.

Alongside that drawing are others in markers, colored pencils, and paints; then there are the homemade cards, letters, and notes folded in secret origami shapes; also, class photographs with my height and age penciled on the back by my mom. This is Aunt Lori's life library, but it's also mine.

I fan the items out around me, a color wheel of artifacts. She kept everything I ever sent her just as I kept everything she sent me. My eyes well. It's an extraordinary thing to discover your love is requited. Sure, in storybooks it happens all the time, but rarely in real life. Humans simply aren't hardwired to love unconditionally. Our DNA is conditional.

The singing of the sisters echoes to the closing chant, and I haven't looked beyond the surface yet. I'm as bad as Narcissus.

I put the childhood mementos back in the trunk and dig deeper, opening a journal. The top line reads *Dear Heavenly Father* . . . While these would certainly bear interesting revelations, reading someone's correspondences with God is a line I won't cross. I close it and push on. Newspaper clippings from the *Romeo & Juliet, The Musical* tour. Plane tickets to Rome, Berlin, New York City, L.A. Postcards from Ginny. An out-of-date passport, a driver's license, a restaurant card for a place called Wisteria . . . This is primary-source gold.

Maid Marian pounces into the trunk with claws outstretched. I jump back. They don't call them church mice for nothing. But he has a different prey. He tooths the end of a black satin ribbon and drags it from its nest where it'd been tied around a manila envelope. The clasp, long since broken, allows the envelope to split down the center with the cat's snag. A flood of letters release.

I pick up the closest one. No return address. I'm not sure if Aunt Lori wants me to read these. *Better to ask for forgiveness than permission.* Who said that—was it one of the disciples? I can't recall.

I collect the letters and fight with Maid Marian for the ribbon. He hisses in annoyance but lets me win. I use it to tie the split envelope together.

The quiet clicks of the sisters' feet echo through the abbey. They've finished singing. Quickly, I rearrange the trunk's contents to hide the hole, close the lid, and take the envelope with me back to the Women's Guest House.

Aunt Lori has administrative duties followed by Mass. I promised to meet her in her office after that. I use this time to read the letters, starting at the earliest date. They're all from the same person. A bitter ex-lover, it seems. Some of his letters are zealous in their worship of her, while others are so cold and demanding, they read as if written by a debt collector. All are signed with the single initial T.

This has to be part of why Aunt Lori joined the convent. She was running away from a spurned lover to whom she owed money! But the last letters were in 1967. Over twenty years ago. Why stay if it was just that?

The clock ticks the second hour and moves recklessly toward the next. I rush to put away the letters and tuck the envelope under my mattress, willing myself not to confess to Aunt Lori everything I know. It's not as easy as it sounds. My head pounds with secrets and theories. I want to ask who this man is but I can't. I have to coax her gently into telling me.

I stop and look at my reflection in the wall mirror. A familiar stranger.

"Lucille-Marie," I say hard. "Don't screw it up."

I get my tape recorder and notebook and hurry out.

Part 5

Lori

In the Night

17

Los Angeles
1967

L.A.'s premiere day started with a sizzle: the sound of Nico in the kitchen, which was once again filled with friends. Most of whom I knew from the film. The HMU and wardrobe folks, Pip, a couple of business partners I'd seen floating on set. The afternoon event was the way to go! Hollywood had that figured out. No waiting anxiously for the minutes to slowly crawl toward the bewitching hour when makeup and hairbrushes came to life. Everyone was bubbling with energy and ready from the start. Even Lucas seemed reanimated after a good night's rest.

"Morning, Lovely." He raised his coffee cup to me. "Nico's making breakfast. It's *delizioso*."

"Aww, *cara mia*," welcomed Nico. "How do you feel about lemon ricotta ravioli?"

"I've never had ravioli for breakfast."

He smiled impishly and hummed a little song while tossing handfuls of pasta pillows into the fry pan.

I'd never seen Nico in the villa's kitchen. He was always up at dawn running production. But here, he was quite at home with a chef apron tied around his waist and a hand towel over his shoulder. Directing a dish came as naturally as directing a scene.

His two producer partners, James and Jordan, sat at the breakfast table discussing St. Francis of Assisi.

"I never knew an Italian started the Franciscans. I thought it was a Frenchman," said James.

"Script says that Saint Francis was the first person to receive the stigmata," replied Jordan.

"Is that the blood in the palms thing?"

"Feet too, I believe."

"Interesting. Might we tie a spectral element to the biopic—religious horror or mystery thriller? Those genres are hot right now."

They forked their raviolis in agreement and swallowed with hardly a chew.

"Lorietta, *mangia*!" Nico handed me a plate. "Yesterday's old is today's new with a few *ornamentos*."

He sprinkled cinnamon and powdered sugar over the hot pasta with a zhuzh of lemon juice. To this day, it remains one of the most delicious bites I have ever eaten. I have to think Nico was the secret ingredient.

Three hours later, we were dressed to the nines, standing on the red carpet of Grauman's Chinese Theatre, waving at fans and zealous media the same way we had in New York, Berlin, Moscow, and Rome. The film projected well, just as it had in every other theater. The audience laughed and cried, gasped, and murmured with self-conscious glee at the nude scenes just as every other audience before them had. I knew the reviews would range from genuine praise to sarcastic criticism. Many would comment on the premiere dress I wore but didn't pick out; the hairstyle that I didn't do; the way Lucas gazed lovingly at me, which was how he looked at everyone; how we held hands like besotted lovers—when really it was so we weren't separated in the crowd. Last but not least, that Nico Cellini had put on camera the most perfect Romeo and Juliet of the times, which was the only statement that was even close to the truth.

After the show, limousines whisked us away to the Topanga. If someone had told me that the vineyard was a portal to Italy, I would have believed it. From the herbaceous smell of the night vines to the dome of twinkling constellations above, Nico had once again surpassed my wildest expectations.

The white linen skirts of the banquet tables were held down against the breeze by an army of gleaming candelabras brandishing tapered candles, burning and dripping light at once. Apples, oranges, pears, and pomegranates on grape leaves festooned the tabletops with the artful sheen of produce to be devoured by our eyes not our mouths. A bandstand and dance floor were constructed in front of the cliff drop-off, creating a barricade for tipsy guests and a backdrop for the star surprise. Nico's friend, famed opera singer Luciano Pavarotti, was in attendance with his wife, Adua Veroni, and he'd agreed to sing for our supper.

Nico welcomed his guests with a royal proclamation. One of the wind quintet members stood, switched out his French horn for a herald trumpet, and blew it in royal court fashion.

"*Buonasera!*" said Nico. "I am pleased to see so many of my American friends here to celebrate the love story of all time and the highest global box office sales on record!"

Cheers. Silver spoons pinged against wineglasses. Money had a resounding ring.

"Now, I want you to meet my Juliet. The biggest star in the world. This is her first role. Can you imagine what she will do next? You want to know her—and love her as I do. Lori Lovely!" He extended his arm to me at the foot of the stage.

While I knew his words were genuine, they flashed an anxious sweat across my body. Every eye was on me. I smiled. I nodded. I waited for Nico to please take back the spotlight, for which I was grateful when he did.

"And now, our Romeo, Lucas Wesley! The Sing King of America! He leaves tomorrow morning to finish his new album, on which"—he smiled broadly"""Lovely You' from our film will be the lead-off track!"

More cheers, more silver-spooned wineglasses, more money. The investors in the crowd particularly loved it.

"In the spirit of musical camaraderie—and to save Lucas's voice for the studio—my good friend Luciano will begin our evening with a song from my favorite opera, *La bohème*."

Pavarotti took the stage and the two men kissed in greeting.

"I am no Lucas Wesley." Pavarotti cast a seductive gaze toward the audience. "But I hope you enjoy nonetheless."

Lucas bowed reverentially.

Pavarotti took the mic, and the vineyard was spellbound under the echo of his voice. It was one of those impromptu moments during which you don't realize the extraordinariness until it's over and you feel foolish for not having paid closer attention. At the time, I was distracted by the feeling of someone hovering over my shoulder.

"He sings like an angel." The accent was not quite American, not quite British. Coolly eloquent and old-world. "Wesley might be the Sing King, but Pavarotti is the High C King. There's no one on earth who can do what he does."

I turned to face the man. He was no more than thirty with sandy-colored hair and tanned cheeks, neatly dressed in a slim-cut suit with a thin black tie, and doused in cologne that smelled of sophisticated musk. He was every nameless neighbor in every film, seemingly familiar and yet disconcertingly unknown.

"Hello," he said so close that his breath blew a strand of my hair across my cheek.

"Hello."

"I'm Tony, nice to meet you."

He shook my hand, never breaking his open gaze.

Quickly, he went on to speak with great regard for the artists in attendance, pointing out each in the room. He was a guy who seemed to know everybody, even if he didn't personally know everybody. I assumed, like the rest of us, he was connected to Nico.

When the waiter serpentined through the crowd with a tray of champagne, Tony took two flutes and handed me one without a pause in conversation.

From his jacket pocket he pulled a shiny tin box containing sugar cubes, each with a blue dot. He offered it as casually as a mint.

"For good luck. They say they ward off the devil."

"Sugar cubes?"

He nodded. "These are special. Lucy."

It took me aback. How did he know my name?

"Lucy?" I countered with as much ennui as I could affect.

"LSD," he said.

"What's that?"

"Like five cups of coffee, only stronger. It's the newest perk."

I was completely naïve about the drug, but everybody drank coffee.

He took a cube, dropped it in his glass, and sipped.

Across the room, Lucas raised his glass in my direction with a gaze that asked *Who's the guy?* I liked that he was checking on me. I took a cube, dropped it in my glass, and raised it back with a smile.

"I like perks," I said to Tony before drinking. "What do you do?" I asked, feeling quite sophisticated with the glass in hand.

"I manage talent."

"No kidding! I was just talking to Lucas about that very thing. I need a manager."

"You do? Well, then it's good we met."

I finished my glass of champagne and felt nothing, just the effervescence in my throat.

I was rather proud of myself for being coolheaded. We strolled the vineyard grounds with me pragmatically saying things like "Personally, I prefer the Trebbiano grapes of the Lazio region" and "LBJ is really dropping the ball." When all of a sudden, it was as if the bubbles in my glass had been poured down my back and transformed into a thousand quill feathers tickling, tingling, and growing stronger every second.

Tony smiled knowingly.

Uninhibited, I dove into the cyclone of my own memories. I told him about growing up in North Carolina; about my family coming to the New York party and how terrible I was to them; about the Italia Conti Academy and my best friend, Ginny, who broke her ankle and had to leave, confessing that I didn't want to go back to school now that she was gone. *Why would you need to?* he agreed. The validation was music to my ears.

He told me that he'd lived in Italy and that's how he knew Nico. He'd come to L.A. to make a go of it, fell in love with an actress named Carolyn who subsequently broke his heart. The conversation flowed so easily. It seemed there was nothing we couldn't share, as though we'd known each other for years.

The hallucinatory effects of the LSD were certainly a factor. I distinctly remember looking down at my legs thinking that they had turned into swan's feet. We no longer walked but glided through the rows of vines. The grapes' shiny, ripe faces were near to bursting under the moonlight. And that's when I decided emphatically that I had to kiss Tony. He was confident and worldly, and I thought if I made out with him, I'd prove that I was, too. Maybe I'd even find love and a manager all in one.

"Kiss me," I said.

Without hesitation, he did. But it didn't feel the way it did with Lucas or any of the Pufftown High School boys before him. He was aggressive, nearly violent in his grip. He bit my lips. When I winced, he laughed. I laughed, too, only to mirror his nonplus. He leaned me against the wooden fence of the grape trellis and ran his hand up my skirt. I didn't push him off. My hands had vanished, replaced with swan's wings. He pulled my head back by the hair so that all I could see were the stars pulsating and changing colors like a cosmic pinwheel. I could barely breathe from the alchemy of sensations. I thought I might pass out. It was all happening so fast.

A clear thought: *this is the moment.* I was sure I was going to finally, at long last, be free of my maidenhood.

A shout. "Get off her!"

The familiar voice became a rushing wind, and I was a bird plunging headlong into it. Tony released me, and I landed with a thud. When I found my breath again, my legs and hands returned, too.

Lucas held Tony in a choke hold.

"Stop!" I yelled. "Lucas, what are you doing?"

"Getting this bastard off you!"

"Why?"

"What do you mean, 'why'?" He panted, struggling to keep Tony under his restraint.

I stood on newfound legs and jerked Lucas's arm to release him.

Tony sprang from the grasp sputtering and quickly moved to the other side of the trellis, out of Lucas's reach.

"You're humiliating me." I seethed.

His muscles flexed tight and smooth beneath my grip. I could feel his heart beating fast. Mine was, too.

"Humiliating? I'm saving you from this old creep."

"He's not a creep. And he's not that old."

Lucas scoffed. "He was taking advantage of you."

"No, he wasn't. I wasn't born yesterday."

I knelt beside him so we were face-to-face and our voices were buffered by the fruited vines.

"I know you care about me but . . . nobody's a virgin forever. Not Juliet. Not even the Virgin Mary."

"It doesn't have anything to do with that."

"Doesn't it, though?" I sighed and leaned into his shoulder. "In 1967, a woman gets to decide when and who she sleeps with." I took his hand in mine with a squeeze.

"I just want to make sure it's right for you—if it isn't me, of course." An attempt to hide sincerity with humor.

I wish it was you, I thought, but what I said was "You've read one too many publicity headlines, Romeo."

"Greatest Lover of All Time, I believe is the most recent."

I elbowed him gently.

A cough made us turn. I'd completely forgotten Tony. Lucas stood and helped me up.

"Man, I'm sorry," said Lucas. "I didn't realize . . ."

Tony shook the dust off his jacket.

"He thought you were . . ."

While the initial trip of the stimulant seemed to have passed, my mind and my tongue had the prickling likeness of a cut electrical wire. Thoughts and words were not wholly connected.

"It's cool," said Tony. "I get it. I read the tabloids. You two have a thing going."

"No, we don't," I said.

"We *did.*" Lucas raised his eyebrows at me. "But now we don't."

"I just came out of a bad breakup myself," said Tony. "Can make a guy do crazy things."

"I hope I didn't hurt you," said Lucas.

"I'm fine."

Neither man extended a hand to the other. The disdain between them was palpable.

"Well, we'd better get back up to the party. I think they're serving dinner," said Lucas.

"Tell them we'll be there in a minute." I made eyes at him. I didn't need him chaperoning.

He pushed the curls off his forehead. "Great." Slowly, he started that way.

I waited until he was a good ten paces away before turning to Tony.

"I'm so sorry about that."

He shrugged. "He's a loose cannon. Most actors his age are."

"I hope you won't hold it against me."

I liked Tony, at the beginning. It felt good to have a grown-up, successful man take an interest in me. It told the world that I was a grown-up, successful woman. It told Lucas that, too. He had other women and I would have other men—or, at least, the illusion of other men.

"I only hold grudges against people who earn them." Tony gave a half-hearted smirk. "You didn't do anything."

Then he put his arm on my shoulder, and I was glad for the weight of it. I thought it meant he was taking me under his wing.

❀❀❀

A week later, Tony and I sat together at the Snug Harbor diner counter on Wilshire Boulevard. I'd called the office number he gave me at Nico's party and asked if we could start fresh. It had been a crazy night, I told him, and I was embarrassed that we'd had such an unorthodox meeting. To put it delicately. I didn't want that to stand between us professionally or personally. So I came to the lunch eager to prove that I was a serious actress ready for a serious career handler. Not that I needed to—he'd already typed up a contract.

In retrospect, I should've seen the red flags. But I was young and wrapped up in my own self-consciousness. I figured I'd better sign with him before he realized that I got lucky auditioning for Nico, and I didn't really have a lick of talent. That's what I told myself, anyhow. I was perpetually terrified that people would see past the veil of celebrity and be disappointed with what they found.

Inked on the page, the contract read "Lori Lovely, actress, singer, dancer, and celebrity."

I could hold those words in my hand. They legitimized me and made *me* real.

I signed with a flourish: ***Lori Lovely***

Then he signed: ***Tony Rischio***

The deal was done without my consulting anyone. I thought my family and friends would be impressed that I'd made this wise business decision autonomously. If it made Lucas a little jealous, too, so be it.

We ordered drinks to celebrate. A vanilla malt for me, a Bloody Mary for him. We clinked glasses to our union. It was official, like all the sealed deals in the movies.

"To business," he said. "Do you have any next projects on the burner?"

I didn't.

"Don't worry. That's my job now. I talked to this casting agent yesterday. They're having a hard time finding a lead actress who can carry a studio picture. I think you'd be perfect. It's a comedy."

I'd have said yes to anything in that hour. I felt invincible.

"Sure! What's it about?"

"It's about a married, family man who has an affair with a teenage girl."

I didn't see what was so funny about that. "You said it's a comedy?"

He nodded. "Dark humor. Think Stanley Kubrick meets Mel Brooks. A total stitch."

Kubrick's *Dr. Strangelove* had been nominated for four Academy Awards, but won none. Brooks' *The Producers* had just released and audiences were going gaga for it. Nico had mentioned that he wasn't a fan of these kinds of satires. More than anyone, however, I figured that he'd want me to explore challenging roles.

"It's being done here in Los Angeles," Tony continued. "You'd have to stay for the audition and, if you got it, the shoot. It'd mean skipping the last couple stops on the *Romeo & Juliet* press tour . . ."

My stomach pitted. I couldn't ask to stay in Nico's Malibu home at the expense of his publicity tour. But I didn't want to miss this opportunity. I couldn't be Juliet forever. I couldn't be his Lorietta, either.

"I'll need help finding a place to live."

"A rental. No problem." Tony chomped his celery stirrer. "I know just the place."

I thought I'd won the lottery. Tony seemed too good to be true.

18

Tony helped me move into a converted pool house on the backside of an empty mansion with a panoramic view down Benedict Canyon Drive. It was close to the studios and had been on the market for a year. Tony knew the real estate agent, who offered to lease the place fully furnished until they found a buyer.

"We can work out the payments later," he explained. "Let's get you moved in and working first."

I'd be lying if I said I didn't get a rush out of the forward propulsion of it all. I was too naïve to understand that getting in a cannon and lighting the fuse without knowing your aim is not the way to victory.

I got the part in the dark comedy *Noises in the Night*. It wasn't a hard sell. The director was a writer who sometimes directed. The film he'd made before *Noises* had done modestly well, so they'd given him a bigger budget. Being billed as "up-and-coming" was gold. To studio heads, that meant that the performers (writers, actors, directors, whomever) have the appeal to cash in with audiences but not the precedent contracts of seasoned artists. Basically, they could pay us less and make more. Especially if that up-and-coming director got a high-dollar star in one or more of the lead roles. At that moment in Hollywood, I was the high-dollar star.

Everyone promised me that it would be a low-key shoot. I had a modern wardrobe with modern dialogue in a modern story. I got lines like "You think I'm a bit of a raver, don't you?" After all the vocal coaching to live up to Shakespeare's iambic pentameter, that felt like freedom.

When the deal was announced, I called Nico.

"I'm the lead," I said.

"I heard," he replied. "*Brava*, Lori."

I didn't want to be Nico's *Lorietta* forever, but I also didn't want to lose him as a friend and mentor.

"What do you think?" I ventured.

"I think . . ." He paused. "It is your life, darling. I'll always be your biggest fan whatever you decide to do."

The words comforted while the tone whispered regret. I interpreted it as fatherly disapproval and reminded him that I could not stay eighteen forever. It wasn't humanly possible.

Paramount quietly canceled the last two *Romeo & Juliet* promotional events so I could start filming in L.A. It'd been a year since the musical released, but theaters were still selling out across the globe. People queued up for hours in ticket lines. The film broke all the box office numbers. The capital gains didn't peak release week, they climbed higher than anyone predicted. Which made the fact that I was struggling to pay rent ironic. Where was all the money going if not to me, a star of the film?

Tony explained that the contract I signed with Paramount provided a flat residual compensation according to the SAG union pay scale. The contract did not include royalties on any associated *Romeo & Juliet, The Musical* materials, including movie tickets. So, what I had been paid on completing the acting work was all I was due to receive. I hadn't known to ask about residuals, royalties, or bonuses, and might not have gotten the role if I had. I was simply thrilled to be plucked out of student obscurity at Italia Conti Academy.

"Baby, I could've gotten you so much more. They ripped you off big-time."

The way Tony said it made me ashamed.

"I'm an idiot."

"I won't let it happen again."

He'd ordered takeout after helping me move boxes on my first night at the pool house.

"That's so kind, but I'm not really hungry."

I planned to take a hot bath, wash my hair, read a book, and breathe without a single set of eyes watching me. After the night we met, we'd kept things strictly professional. Still, I felt like the scales could tip at any moment. It put me on edge. It was easy to imagine saying no to a stranger, but what did you do with a person you couldn't afford to lose?

The Styrofoam containers squeaked against each other. He flipped open a clamshell top revealing noodles in shiny garlic sauce.

"The table reading for *Noises in the Night* is in two days. Are you ready?"

"I will be."

"Need help rehearsing?" He took up a slinky forkful.

I shook my head, faked a yawn. "Exhaustion is really my only obstacle. I need rest."

"Beauty sleep is key. We don't want you turning beasty."

Voices trailed outside.

"Go ahead, have a look around, I'll wait for you in the driveway," I heard the real estate agent say.

Prospective buyers for the mansion came and went. Tonight, it was a couple who'd made their way down to the pool to talk.

"I just can't stop thinking about it," said the woman.

"It happened over a year ago. They totally gutted it. Look around. The renovation is gorgeous! And the price is a steal," said the man.

"What about under the floorboards? The newspapers said it was like a swimming pool in the living room—so much blood."

"Sensationalized journalism to sell papers."

"Don't give me that. Four people had their throats cut in the house. Two more in the pool house. Six victims. It's got bad vibes. Look at my arms, the hairs are standing on end."

The man laughed, but it was edged with worry. "Do you hear yourself? You sound like a nutcase."

"I can't do it. The whole place gives me the willies."

"What are we, kindergartners? The willies? Babe, come on."

"There are things of a spiritual nature." She lowered her voice. "Just because we can't explain them doesn't make them any less real. Mark my words, there's something in this place. Something I don't want anything to do with."

The man sighed. "Fine. Let's just say it's too much square footage for two people."

"Yes, and I don't want to live with ghosts."

"We won't mention that part."

They marched back up the patio to where the real estate agent waited.

"What was that about?" I asked Tony.

"You heard about the Newton Temple murders?"

I hadn't.

"It happened while you were filming with Cellini." He took a napkin and wiped the sauce from his lips. "A handful of doped-up cult kids. They broke in during a dinner party, killed the guests, and brought the owners down here." He looked at the floor a beat. "Ran off down Benedict Canyon afterward. Naked. Covered in blood. Yelling out Newton Temple prophesies. A neighbor called the cops. One got hit by an oncoming car. The other two jumped the cliffside."

The room shifted. A clammy draft carried the tang of garlic mixed with Tony's musk cologne. The light changed to a chiaroscuro: broad, contrasting strokes of too bright and too dark. Shadow floaters appeared at the perimeter of my vision. I rubbed them away.

"People died here?"

Tony nodded. "When you think about it, there isn't anywhere that someone hasn't died. It's an old world."

"People were *murdered* here. There's a big difference."

"Want me to hire an exorcist?" He smirked.

It made me feel silly. The offer, the smirk. He'd already done so much to find me somewhere to live. A luxurious pool house on the grounds of a mansion. I was side by side with L.A.'s elite. Who was I to complain?

I dropped the subject. Instead, I thanked Tony for helping me find a place to live, for being my manager, for shepherding me into Hollywood. I pretended not to be afraid. I smiled. I ate the takeout.

In the days to come, the couple's conversation lingered. *There's something in this place. Something I don't want anything to do with.* I didn't want to believe it was true, but suddenly I noticed the doors creaking open and shut. There were footsteps on the floorboards late at night. Once, I left a dirty plate in the sink and returned to find it washed and in the draining rack. I told myself that my imagination was manifesting these things. Why would ghosts do my dirty dishes? I probably rinsed it without thinking. I stopped sleeping, afraid to close my eyes.

At the table reading for *Noises in the Night*, I mentioned that I couldn't sleep to Tony.

"Nerves about the film. Completely normal," he assured me.

He gave me sleeping pills.

"Every actor takes them."

"Yes, I know," I said, staring at the bottle in my hand.

He didn't ask me *how* I knew. I kept that to myself. They helped me sleep, but unlike the pills Lucas shared, these induced a kind of hypnotic delirium. I had recurring dreams. The first was the feeling of someone breathing on top of me. I'd awake smelling burnt hair. The second was that I was dragged to the ceiling and dropped. Falling in terror until the moment my eyes opened.

I told Tony the pills were too strong.

"Only children have bad dreams," he said. "If you want, I can come by at night to check on you—make sure the place is locked up."

That was the last thing I wanted. I shook my head. "It's okay. You're right. They aren't real."

"No trouble. I have the spare key."

I hadn't known about the spare key or how to respond. I was ashamed to have told him about the nightmares and ashamed to say I didn't want him to check on me. The look on his face implied that I ought to be grateful, but my gut told me to be wary. Was the feeling real or a carryover from bad dreams? I had begun to question my own consciousness.

The mania continued in the daylight hours. Things went missing: a pair of shoes, a pajama shirt, my hairbrush, a shower cap; little things that weren't worth mentioning, but still . . . Where had they gone?

I needed more sleep, Tony told me, I told myself. I took more pills.

I was a zombie by the time we started principal photography. I needed to learn my lines, clear my head, be a professional. Nico and the world were watching what I did next. So, I closed myself off from everything and everyone. I spent hours working through scenes in the pool house.

It was a dark film. I played Sal, a teenage actress who has an affair with a much older married stagehand. I found the character more woefully tragic than Juliet. She haunted me as much as the cult's murdered victims. I cried a lot during that film, even though crying was not in the script.

Tony became my single source of contact with the outside world. He offered to send word to my family and explain to friends that I was holed up working. He promised to take care of everything so I could focus.

I thought that would help alleviate my anxiety, but the nightmares persisted. I thrashed in bed, put pillows over my ears, cursed the unseen. *Shut up, shut up, shut up!* I cried into the blackness. Because either I was losing my mind, or I believed in poltergeists. Neither brought me solace.

Lu

Experience

The Abbey, Connecticut
October 1990

"So let me get this all straight. Tony was your manager? And you lived in the house where the Newton Temple murders happened?"

"Only for a brief period when I first went to L.A.," Aunt Lori clarifies. "And it was the pool house, not the mansion."

From high school history class to church Sunday school, a whole generation of us had been warned about the dangers of falling into a religious cult by retellings of the Newton Temple murders.

"So, Tony knew—" I begin but Aunt Lori interrupts me.

"Hand me a Q-tip, Lu."

We're in the barn where the Christmas crèche is kept. The sisters are sweeping and dusting in anticipation of the first Advent Sunday. Foot traffic increases then from a dozen a month to a dozen a week. It's one of the county's most popular attractions. The model figurines are roughly sixteen inches tall, the size of dolls. The holy family, angels, gift bearers, merchants, the three kings, princesses, peasants, farm animals, and even pet dogs and cats are invited to Jesus's birthday party. Not one spec of the original artwork, crafted of wood and terra cotta, has been altered. A gift to a Sardinian king passed down through the ages and bestowed to the sisters as caretakers. So the story goes. A historic artifact. A holy relic.

Aunt Lori feather dusts the miniatures, occasionally using a Q-tip when a spider's web clings religiously. Like the one stuck to Saint Joseph's nose now. I always wondered whatever happened to the guy. He takes the word of his pregnant fiancée that an angel appeared to her one night and *boom*—she's pregnant! He welcomes the baby, not his own but God's, and then isn't even an extra in the rest of the Gospel story. That's a tough role to play.

Aunt Lori gets the cobweb off. Your average housewife might consider dusting a mundane chore, but Aunt Lori insists it's one of the most enjoyable prayer meditations of the year. I'm all for meditation, but my recorder is running. Silence is costing me. Cassette tapes aren't cheap.

"My memory of that time is murky," says Aunt Lori after an extended pause. "Have you ever had an experience that you can say was entirely spiritual?"

The question catches me off guard. She likes to do that. I turn off the tape.

"Come on, Aunt Lori, you know I grew up Southern Baptist."

Spiritual experiences abounded. First, there were baptisms to confirm our spiritual seats in the heavenly theater. Then there were the annual tent revivals of worship singing from dawn to dusk. And of course, the weekly laying of hands, speaking in tongues, fasting, prayer, partaking of Holy Communion, and other supernatural gesticulations.

Aunt Lori looks up from the crèche for the first time and meets my eyes. "That's not what I asked. I asked if you have ever had a spiritual experience."

I hear what she's saying. A fish can live its whole life in a pond and not feel wet.

I think a beat. "It sounds stupid," I begin, "but it was when our first dog, Biscuit, died."

I've never shared this with a soul. It feels too strange, too raw, too real, and far too cherished to have someone flinch with disbelief that I had a paranormal experience with an animal. A *dog.* I mean, if otherworldly realms exist, you'd think they'd make themselves known by some more august representative than a golden retriever. If I hadn't lived it, I wouldn't believe. And if I heard someone tell my same story, I don't think I could restrain a smirk.

Aunt Lori puts down her duster and turns to me with knit fingers. She's listening.

"I looked into Biscuit's eyes and there was this . . . I don't know, light. But it was more than that. Like a rainbow you see through a window. It's not there. Suddenly, it is. And then it's gone. I wasn't sure it happened, but I remember seeing something . . . *feeling* something warm and wonderful like I've never felt before. It made me want to fall into that *whatever*-ness. And that scared me so bad, I started to cry. When the light went away, Biscuit was dead."

I have to give Aunt Lori more credit. Telling is harder than I thought. Tears sting. For Biscuit and for myself—because I wish to God I could feel that light again. I want to know if it was real.

"It sounds dumb, right? Kid's stuff."

Aunt Lori puts her hand gently on mine. "No. It sounds like you saw *through.* There's so much more than this." She taps the crèche figurine on the head. "Temporary relics. You got a glimpse of eternity. That's the most significant spiritual experience a living being can have."

"It's the only time I've seen death close up. Grandpa and Grandma Tibbott were gone by the time I came. Grandpa Hickey died before I can remember. And Grandma Hickey is still kicking it in her eighties. At least the women in our family have good genes, right?"

"Everything's got the same gene when it comes to death," she says softly. "It's Mother Nature's DNA and our Holy Father's promise. Eventually, we'll all have peace from this restless world."

It should make me uncomfortable, all this talk of death. Instead, I feel validated that what I feared was a false memory was no trick of the eye.

I inhale to say more. But then press my tongue to the roof of my mouth and gulp down the words I wish I had the courage to say.

"What is it, Lu?" Aunt Lori asks.

"Nothing." I shake my head. "It's just scary to think the world might not be what you think it is—that there's something bigger. It makes you question yourself."

"Asking questions is the only way to the truth. Isn't that what you're doing here?"

"I'm not here for ideologies. I'm here for historical facts."

"Do you believe that love is a fact?" she asks.

Yes, but I can't say that. She's baiting me. My face must give away my confliction because she continues.

"If you do, then that's all you need to know God and history."

"I guess I don't trust that love won't let me down."

"*Hmm*," she says. "You've nailed the crux of humanity. We struggle to trust because our human examples are notoriously untrustworthy."

She picks up the Joseph figurine. "There's much to the story that we don't know and never will. That's faith. Love takes a whole lot of it."

Sister Candace and another novitiate enter giggling over something.

Seeing Aunt Lori, they reverently bow.

"Good afternoon, Mother Lori," says Sister Candace.

Aunt Lori stands and stretches her back, pushing her chest forward and arching her spine like the ex-dancer she is. She turns her head right and left, shakes out her shoulders. A practice of habit.

"Shift change," she announces.

The novitiates have brought brooms and mops to clean every corner. The barn was a gift from a theologian in Connecticut. His name was Joseph, too. They have his bronze dedication plaque on the wall and scrub it to a shine, taking care of the barn with as much gusto as the Sardinian king's crèche.

Aunt Lori nods for me to follow her outside.

The grass is cool and dewy against my ankles. The light fades early this time of year in the north. I forget how different a day feels up here. By four o'clock, the sky yawns amber into purple, stars wink sleepily through the haze of clouds. The harvest moon appears as a half-eaten boiled egg, making me hungry despite dinner being hours away. The field crickets have already begun their symphony. The Dutch dairy cows softly call to each other in *moos* while grazing on the meadowlands.

Aunt Lori links her arm through mine as we walk the dirt pathway. A pheasant takes flight from a nearby brush, squawking and flapping. I jump back but she holds me steady. We watch the bird rise to flight.

"That didn't scare you?" I ask.

My heart beats as fast as the pheasant's wings.

"No," she says. "We weren't in danger. There's a vibration then. The laity call it divine intuition. You've got a good antenna, Lu. Learn to use it."

"An antenna? I don't remember that in the Bible."

"The Gospels call it the Holy Spirit, I believe. Semantics."

I laugh.

She winks and then picks up the broken heads of asters from the pheasant's flight.

"Poor bird was more scared of us than we of him. And for better reasons."

She collects the purple blooms in the front of her scapular.

"These are great in salads. Makes a good tea for nervous stomachs, too."

We move on toward the abbey with only the sound of our steps crunching on the forest pines. It feels plush, the velvet of quiet company. We go the back way, through the garden gate. A brown bunny disappointedly scurries from the empty vegetable boxes. Someone has already lit a lamp in the kitchen. Its pink glow extends out the open door. Reaching the threshold, Aunt Lori turns to me and kisses my cheek.

"I'm glad you're here," she says.

"Me too."

She drops her apron of asters onto the kitchen table but doesn't set herself to any task. Instead, she pulls up a wooden stool and pats the one beside her.

"Let's talk."

It has a come-to-Jesus feeling, but I don't want another homily. There are more important things to sort out. Quickly, I pull out my tape recorder, place it between us like an amulet, and press record.

"Yes. Let's."

LU:

Date: October 10, 1990. Location, the Abbey in Connecticut. Mother Lori in the kitchen.

(Clears throat.)

Can we talk about your second film, Aunt Lori? I'm sure audiences across the globe were excited to see you cast in another leading role. And no doubt you had unlimited choices. Why *Noises in the Night*? I mean, it's so different—not just from Shakespeare but from you, as a person. If I may speak candidly.

LORI:

Please do. What's the point of being here if not to speak candidly?

LU:

Right. So, *Noises in the Night* is a dark comedy. Your typical kitchen-sink drama directed by—remind me his name.

LORI:

Thomas Gerry.

LU:

Like Tom and Jerry?

LORI:

No, it's spelled differently. And nobody called him Tom. He was always Thomas.

LU:

Okay, Thomas Gerry directed this sordid domestic musical about a bored husband and father who has an affair with a teenager to spice up his life. You played that nymphette teen. Do I have that right?

LORI:

That's putting it in a nutshell.

LU:

(Laughs.)

You can imagine my surprise that you did this film. I mean, it's so alternative to everything you believe in, but maybe you believed in different things then. Care to talk about that?

LORI:

I don't care to, actually.

LU:

Oh... *hmm*... okay, why not?

LORI:

For all of the reasons you just said. It was a dark, sordid, and ultimately forgettable film during a dark, sordid, ultimately forgettable period of my life. I was on that shoot less than a month. One mistake does not define you.

LU:

Do you consider *Noises in the Night* a mistake?

LORI:

If you're asking if I regret doing the film, my answer is no. I am who I am today because of it. All things work together for the good of those who love God and are called according to His purpose. I'm paraphrasing, but that's scripture.

LU:

"All things." That's a bit too all-encompassing for my taste. What about rape, murder, torture, mass genocide, hate? I don't see how those can work for any good.

LORI:

Those are blatantly evil and serve as examples that we can't change what's been done. What we can do is take back our present power and use the experiences for a higher good. The *summum bonum*, to quote Cicero.

LU:

Who defines the higher good?

LORI:

Ah, that's the rub. People love definitions. Rules and regulations to use in the stoning. We see it all the time here. People come under all kinds of pretenses when really, they feel broken—by their own action or what someone has done to them. The shame of that ugly thing makes them believe they aren't worthy of a higher good. We show them that's not true. Grace is love without definition.

LU:

(Audible sigh.)

We've wandered down the sermonizing rabbit hole again. I mean, I hear you, and I appreciate everything you're saying, Aunt Lori. You're a nun. I get it. You think about this stuff every minute. But I'm writing my thesis on your Hollywood career, not the ethics behind it.

LORI:

Aren't they one and the same?

LU:

Okeeee... so then, what does all that have to do with a drama about a pervy husband who seduces a teenager?

LORI:

Well, according to the film script, she seduces him.

LU:

Of course she does! Virgins and vixens. Sheesh, women. For the record, this film sounds really creepy.

LORI:

To this day, I've never seen it. Only a handful of dailies. It was 1967. Counterculture was cool. Despite everyone congratulating each other on the sardonic humor in that movie, I didn't get the comedy. I thought I was losing my mind. I had panic attacks. I wasn't sleeping, as I said...

Part 6

Lori

Archangels

19

Los Angeles to Rome
1967

She's a train wreck," said the grip.

I'd stepped outside to get fresh air before we shot the next scene. A handful of cameramen were on a cigarette break behind the faux boxwoods.

"I have no idea how she pulled off Juliet."

"Cellini is a master, that's how."

"Maybe it wasn't her—maybe it was a stunt double. Like with the singing. I mean, don't get me wrong, her face and body are sexy as hell. I'd screw that in a heartbeat. But we're all screwed if she doesn't get it together."

"Too late. This picture is bad. Have you seen the dailies?"

They all moaned, sucked their cigarettes, blew gray over the hedge.

"Maybe they'll scrap her and recast. More bankable hours for us."

The men chuckled in agreement.

My knees locked. Otherwise, I'd have run. But where? Not back on set. I didn't want to go home to my rental, either.

The pool house had become my private purgatory. Like being trapped inside an hourglass slowly buried by the sands of each second, the dread of accumulating minutes, the anxiety of knowing that darkness was coming to swallow me. No matter how much I told myself that the feeling of being tormented by an unseen *could not be*, I felt the realness in the pit of my stomach. Someone was there. As certain as my own breath moving in and out. Each day when the shadows slanted toward dusk, my terror would rise. I took double the sleeping pills, caught in an endless loop. Hell isn't only for the dead.

Hearing the crew's criticism lit a match of panic. I had to get away from it all.

I went to my dressing room, locked the door, and called Tony's office. His line rang through without answer.

"Miss Lovely?" The production assistant knocked on the door. "They want you on set."

I ignored him.

"Miss Lovely? Please open the door."

I rifled through every bag, binder, and coat pocket in my dressing room until I found an old pizza carry-out receipt with a different number for Tony—his home, I presumed. From the beginning of our relationship, we had crossed lines. Calling his private number seemed a small one in comparison. It was an emergency! So, with fingers trembling, I dialed.

"Hello?" A woman answered to my surprise.

"Oh, hi, is this—is this Tony Rischio's?"

The line dropped.

Maybe I'd dialed wrong. I carefully pressed each digit again.

It rang shrill over and over before the same voice returned.

"Yes?"

"Hi, I'm sorry, I just called—we were disconnected. I'm trying to reach Tony Rischio."

"Tony?" A sob erupted from the other side, and then the moan of the dial tone.

Heat rose to my cheeks. Tony was all I had in L.A. If something happened to him, I needed to know. I redialed. This time, a man answered.

"Whoever this is—*stop* calling! Tony is a goddamn psychopath!" In the background the woman cried on. "Carolyn, I'll take care of this."

"Carolyn?" I whispered.

Tony had mentioned her on our first meeting, the bad-breakup actress.

"Who is this?" the man asked.

"I'm—I'm an actress, too." I didn't want to give my name. "Tony is my manager."

"I bet he is. Just like Carolyn. If you're mixed up with that guy, you're in a world of trouble."

"Please, I need to find him. Is he okay?"

"I hope he's rotting in hell. *Stop calling.* My sister can't take it. She's been through enough."

I wanted to ask what he meant, but before I could, the door handle to my dressing room shook violently.

"Lori! Open this door!" director Thomas Gerry yelled from the other side. "The crew is being paid by the hour!"

The call dropped. The dial tone went on so long that it finally transferred to the switchboard.

"Can I help you?" asked the operator.

"I need . . ." I put my hand over my eyes. I needed to think straight, to figure this out, to make sense of things. "I need help."

"Are you in danger, miss? Should I call the police?"

Fists banged. The yelling became indecipherable.

"No, I don't need the police," I said to the operator. "Thank you."

I hung up. I could've called Marie in New York. I could've called my parents in Pufftown. But there was nothing any of them could do from such a distance. Calling would've made matters worse. After jilting my family at the New York City premiere, leaving my friends at ICA, abandoning Ginny when she'd done so much for me, this was karmic retribution. I had gotten myself into a mess of my own making.

So, I dialed the only other number I knew by heart: Nico's villa in Italy.

"Ciao?"

"Thank God. *Ciao*, it's Lori—Lori Lovely." My voice warbled.

It was noon in L.A. Nine hours ahead in Italy. I imagined the soft plum of evening filtering moonlight through the curtains; the scent of wisteria promising peace and rest. Tears sprang at the memory.

"Is Nico there? I need to talk to him, *per favore.*"

"Nico non c'è. Vengo solo a spazzare la casa. È in Marocco per un film."

"I don't speak Italian. English?"

"*No Nico,*" the man enunciated slowly. "*È in Mar-o-cco.*"

My jaw tightened. I could barely breathe. "Morocco?"

"Si, si."

"Do you know when he'll return?"

"Ritorno? No lo so."

Then came an ear-piercing sound like a thousand bees set to sting. The metal door handle fell to the floor with a thud. The door swung open. The entire production crew peered through in silent consternation. A tech held a drill. Thomas's neck and face were mottled red with rage.

"I'm sorry," I whispered and looked away shamefully. "I'm not well."

They called the doctor. The same one who came for every cough, bone break, finger cut, and neurosis on set. His entire practice consisted of concierge consults for Paramount. I don't recall his name. *The doc is here* was all they told me. He gave me a sedative shot and arranged for a car to take me home. I slept fifteen blissful, dreamless hours and woke to ringing in my head and in real life. I hoped it was Tony and everything from the day before was merely another nightmare.

"Tony?" I answered.

"It's Linda, Mr. Gerry's personal assistant. I'm calling to make sure you are up."

It was before dawn by the light and the sound of the birds. Juliet's words came to mind: *It is the lark that sings so out of tune, straining harsh discords and unpleasing sharps.*

"Lark? What lark?" parroted Linda.

I hadn't realized I'd said the lines aloud, and suddenly I missed Lucas so much it made my chest ache.

"Never mind."

She cleared her throat of irritation. "Mr. Gerry hopes you're feeling better. He told everyone that you were dehydrated, fatigued, and just needed a day's rest. He can't cancel another day of shooting though. I have a car arriving in twenty minutes. Dawn is here."

I wanted the doctor to give me another shot. Put me back to sleep. Being awake was exhausting. I fumbled on my bedside table to find my watch, but it'd gone missing, too. Then the words rejiggered: not *dawn* of the day but *Dawn* of the hair and makeup team.

"Miss Lovely, everyone is waiting."

The sharp edge to Linda's voice reminded me that if I didn't show up, there would be repercussions. It was a known fact that our studio had one of the highest financial penalties in the business for actors, directors, and production staff who didn't complete their projects. I needed the paycheck. My only choice was to walk myself out to the curb and get in the car, which I did in a haze.

No one spoke a word when I arrived. The awkward pretense of turning a blind eye clamored louder than if they had simply said what they were thinking: *Lori Lovely has cracked up. Lori Lovely isn't a real actress. Lori Lovely is a failure.*

I heard their whispers. I headed to my dressing room.

Inside, Dawn sat flipping through Vogue magazine. She was a decade older than me, a painter who came from Georgia to join the West Coast Jesus hippies and eded up doing hair and makeup on film sets. God works in mysterious ways was one of her signature aphorisms.

Seeing me, she stood and threw the magazine on the love seat. "Hey-ya. I heard about yesterday." She closed the dressing room door and gently ushered me into the makeup chair, both hands on my shoulders.

"What's going on with you, Lovely?"

There's an unparalleled intimacy between a person and their stylist. An odd thing to admit, but it doesn't make it less true. I'd argue that a stylist can be as significant as a parent, physician, or priest. This person welcomes your natural state of unkemptness with the promise to help you look and feel your best. You give them permission to touch you. It's why a gentle hand on the face feels so primally loving—and a slap, so destructive.

It's a noble calling, and I can honestly say that every time I've sat in a hair and makeup chair, I was my most vulnerable self.

That's probably why I unburdened myself talking to Dawn that day.

"The house I'm living in is cursed. I think I am, too. And my manager . . ." Saying the awfulness aloud made my whole body quake. "I've never felt so scared and lonely."

Dawn wrapped her arms around me and leaned her head against mine. Her dark hair draped like a comforting curtain. Under her shield, I let the tears fall. She rocked me wordlessly until I was done sobbing.

Then she dabbed my cheeks with cotton tissues, washed away the salt with a wet cloth, and rolled cool jade stones under my eyes. I pressed into the tenderness of her hands.

"Lovely, I see no curse on you," she said. "Being alone is one thing. Being lonely is a whole other. Loneliness can feel like a curse."

She combed my hair away from my face with a soft-bristled brush that made a hushing sound with each sweep.

"Do you have people in town? I mean real people, not show people—trusted friends, a distant cousin or something?"

I shook my head. "I called everyone I know yesterday." My voice choked on the memory. The desperation was still raw.

Dawn put down the brush and turned the chair so we were face-to-face. "It's not much, but I have a couch. We can come to work and go home together. It'll be like a slumber party."

I knew I ought to reply *Thank you for the gracious offer, but I couldn't impose.* I heard the socially polite response in my mind, but I needed someone to hand me a miracle. In that moment, Dawn was as good as an archangel. It's no hyperbole to say, that act of kindness saved me.

I never went back to the pool house on Benedict Canyon Drive. I heard it was eventually demolished. Every splinter gone. For some things, that's the only way forward.

All my belongings fit in three boxes, which Dawn picked up for me and brought to her one-bedroom apartment in Glendale. The setup was similar to Marie's, but instead of skyscrapers outside the fire escape, there were palm trees. The first few days, Dawn apologized for the dishes in the sink, the lumpy couch, her tabby cat named Delilah who left hair on everything. I didn't mind any of it. I was sleeping again. Deep, full, glorious nights without drugs. I'd wake to the smell of Dawn making Bisquick pancakes and Delilah rubbing my bare feet with her cheek.

"She's putting her pheromones on your skin to claim you as part of her clowder," Dawn explained. "You're family now."

I liked the feel of it. I needed to be loved. I was alive and exposed, but healing. Our trinity: Dawn, Delilah, and me.

Noises in the Night wrapped quickly. To my relief, they opted for a body double on all the sex scenes. Thomas Gerry didn't want to risk me having another meltdown. Also, I heard later that they wanted someone bustier. I didn't call Tony again. Part of me was glad that he hadn't answered his office phone. What Carolyn's brother told me made me question everything about Tony.

Dawn said I could stay with her while I looked for a new place. The rental market was brutal. I offered to pay for my keep. She refused.

"I own the place! You can buy groceries. We need more butter and Bisquick mix."

I loved those days of butter and Bisquick. One night, the three of us sat in a mess of patchwork quilts and floppy pillows with a bucket of popcorn. *I Dream of Jeannie* was on TV. Barbara Eden had us laughing so hard, we scared Delilah under the covers.

"I hate that I love this show," admitted Dawn. "A scantily clad woman in a bottle granting wishes to a man. I mean, it's ridiculous. Still . . ." She crunched a handful of popcorn. "There's something to a woman with power, and Barbara is a comedic wizard."

I saw it from a professional standpoint. There was so little on television or in film with female characters as the headliners. It seemed a triumph of the times to have *I Dream of Jeannie* be the title marquee and not, say, *Captain Tony's Genie*. Barbara's slapstick was genius. I wish I had an ounce of it.

"There are worse places to live than a magic bottle," I said. "Imagine the silk tapestries, satin pajamas, puffy pillows . . . A private sanctuary with everything at your blink and call. Sounds rather nice."

"Except for someone to share it with," said Dawn. "People are communal creatures. We need each other."

Commercial break: a wedding scene with a young bride floating to sensual music and the tagline *As the day lingers on, a Dial shower has staying power.*

Dawn cleared her throat. "So, this Tuesday, I'm going out."

"Out? Oh, yes, of course."

She'd given me a refuge when I needed it most, but she had a life! A beautiful, single woman in L.A., no doubt she was popular on the dating scene. I was ashamed for having impinged on her.

"Please don't think you have to babysit me." I put on my perkiest smile. "I'll be totally fine while you're on a date."

She laughed. "It isn't a date. I'm volunteering at the St. Joseph's soup kitchen. A group of French nuns run it. Tuesday nights are cassoulet. It's free dinner for the volunteers. I was hoping you might want to come along."

I was familiar with soup kitchens. My mom and the church ladies served holiday meals. Turkey and biscuits at Thanksgiving. Roast beef and sweet potatoes at Christmas. Ham and macaroni at Easter. These were the staples. I had never had cassoulet in any kitchen.

The only people who served in our Southern Baptist church kitchen were full-fledged Southern Baptist church members. There were membership classes you had to take that included a volunteer training program.

Not just anybody could walk in off the street and give a handout. It simply wasn't done. At least not where I came from.

"But I'm not a member of their church."

"Sweetheart, do I look like a Catholic?" Dawn pointed at her face, brightly shaded with blue eyeshadow and magenta lipstick.

I wasn't sure what a Catholic should look like, so I refrained from answering.

"Hungry bellies don't discriminate," she continued. "And neither do the sisters. They can use all the help they can get. Plus, the food is good eating. Come, it'll be fun."

I wasn't keen on it. I'd developed social anxiety when it came to public gatherings. Being in a kitchen full of strangers was the opposite of fun. I would've much preferred to stay on the couch with Delilah. But it was Dawn's home, and I appreciated her kindness. So if she wanted me to go with her to help French nuns dish out cassoulet, then that's what I'd do. She was the only friend I had in Los Angeles, and truth be told, I was curious.

20

The only indication that the building was not abandoned was a wooden sign hung over the door reading *John 17:21*. A name. A set of numbers. A cryptic message to most, including myself. No one would ever suspect the feast within.

We were greeted first by the aromatic smell of rich spices, stewed meats, and fresh-cut vegetables. Three pots the size of wizards' cauldrons bubbled merrily on an industrial range. My stomach cartwheeled. It'd been so long since I'd had anything besides pancakes, popcorn, and potted meats. Dawn's fry pan was a thing of wonder, but I hadn't realized until that moment how much more I craved.

"*Bonjour*, sisters," said Dawn.

Bonneted and aproned, the room of nuns turned in joyous unison.

"*Bonjour,* Dawn! The Lord be with you," they called out from their stations.

A handful welcomed her with an embrace.

"This is Lori." Dawn introduced me. "Lori, this is Sister Mary Janet, Sister Anthony, and Sister Tabitha."

I was surprised by how young they were. Dawn's age, if not a little younger. I'd always thought of nuns as wizened ancients. But these three were not at all.

"We were so excited when Dawn said she was bringing an extra set of hands," said Sister Mary Janet.

"Did you also bring the"—Sister Anthony eyed the nuns behind her—"goods?"

"I'd never forget those!" Dawn opened her purse and pulled out a tube of the lightest shade of pink lipstick. "Bonne Bell's Ski Pink."

Sister Anthony gave what could only be described as a squeal and effusively thanked Dawn before slipping it into her tunic pocket.

"Don't let Sister Michael see or you'll have her tsking all night," warned Sister Tabitha.

"It's medicated," defended Sister Anthony. "You know how dry my lips get. This is the only product that keeps them from cracking."

"That color will complement your complexion, too," Dawn added.

Sister Anthony's eyes twinkled impishly.

"I have another sample at home. Honey Bun. It's got golden undertones. I think that would look beautiful on you, Sister Tabitha."

Sister Tabitha gave a cautious grin. "This California weather is soooo dry. I thank you for providing us relief."

"Sisters!" called an older nun from the stove. "The cassoulet won't make itself! We've got hungry people waiting!"

"Coming, Sister Michael." Sister Tabitha winked at us before turning with an innocent hum.

Sister Anthony joined her on cue. The sound harmonized, and soon it seemed the whole kitchen was infused with the wordless melody. The recognizable tune brought a knot to my throat.

"How great thou art, how great thou art," Sister Mary Janet sang quietly beside me.

Time seemed to turn inside out like a sock, and I was suddenly back at the Troubadour hearing Lucas sing. My bones vibrated like the tines of a tuning fork. Did I unconsciously know that night how much of my future he would become? How could I? And yet, like with so many things we can't explain in life, I knew without knowing.

Sister Mary Janet stitched her arm to mine and led me to a wooden prep table.

"I have to tell you what a joy it is to have you here. A little group of us went to see *Romeo & Juliet, The Musical* and absolutely loved it."

It shocked me. Nuns in the theater watching me and Lucas play lovers. But I supposed holy vows didn't stop a person from feeling.

"I'm honored," I said.

"And we're honored to have you serving supper."

"What should I do?" I asked.

She pointed to a giant slab of butter and a tray of baguettes cut into diamond slices. "The bread needs buttering if you would."

I took my position slathering slices with fresh butter. Dawn was right, the simple act of working with my hands and serving others gave me a peace I hadn't felt in months.

When the sisters opened the doors for the dinner crowd, the makeshift cafeteria filled with men, women, children, elderly couples, and teens too young to be on their own.

Over the dinner service, I learned that the nuns belonged to the Sisters of St. Joseph of Carondelet, a monastic congregation that began in seventeenth-century France. A group came to the United States two centuries later and established Los Angeles as the providential headquarters in 1903. The women were from everywhere—France to Hawaii, Japan to Idaho. Some had master's degrees in science and the arts, and others, like me, had barely finished high school. None of their differences mattered. They came together as one sisterhood to serve the community and each other. The Bible verse over the building's doorway was, in fact, their sacred motto: *May all be one.* A dedication to unconditional equality. I never imagined people lived like that outside of ancient texts. But these were modern women doing modern things. There were bottles of wine being poured into the stewpot and tubes of lipstick being traded.

On the serving line, Sister Mary Janet struck up a conversation with a young man who'd lost his arm in Vietnam. She had a brother there. Sister Tabitha, too. They asked the young man for suggestions of things to send to their brothers in the field. "Socks, shampoo, and chewing gum are gold," he told them. On the spot, they decided to put together packages of these items for their brothers' regiments along with cookies, hard candies, and sunscreen. It was inspiring to be part of their activism.

"Thank you for inviting me," I said to Dawn on the drive home.

"Tuesday cassoulet always hits the spot. You can come with me again if you want."

"I think I will."

But the next week, Dawn got a job on a sci-fi film. The actors' hair and makeup were extensive, as were the hours. So I took the bus and went by myself, honored when the sisters turned to me with a collective *Bonjour, Lori*! I didn't need to be shown what to do. I put on my apron and got to work. After that, it wasn't just Tuesdays. I came as often as possible. The kitchen was open daily. People needed fuel for their bodies and their spirits. Hope was as much an ingredient as the trinity of celery, onion, and peppers. And it wasn't just for the diners. Chopping mise en place became my own therapy. My anxiety dissipated into tiny dices of green, white, and red, and I often found myself dreaming of days in Italy with Lucas. I'd look down and see an Italian flag in the rows of vegetables, a mirepoix miracle.

The tabloids said Lucas was in Hawaii filming a musical. There were photos of him romping through the sand with a flock of bikini-clad girls. Staged production stills, but that didn't stop the twinge in my chest. I wished I could talk to him but knew it'd be impossible to reach him on set. After the awkward parting at Nico's party, I wasn't sure he wanted to hear from me, either. So, I sent a postcard to his Memphis address. The recording studio was his anchor. He'd go back at some point.

Lucas, lovely you, I'm still in L.A. I think you were right about Tony. Not a good fit. Staying with a friend currently but looking for a new place. Promise to send address as soon as I have one. Miss you.

Love, LL

21

Noises in the Night tanked at the box office. No one was surprised. The studio flung it out like a fast-food hamburger. It was a distasteful, overcooked film. I knew I was terrible even before the critics lambasted me in their reviews. I wanted to forget about it and move on. The sisters were there to help me do just that.

"Are you still looking for a place to rent?" Sister Mary Janet asked one day when I was in the kitchen chopping fennel.

I'd mentioned my need to Sister Tabitha in passing.

"Yes. Dawn's been incredibly kind to let me room with her, but I can't stay forever."

Sister Mary Janet nodded. "There's a couple in our parish, the Raymonds. They own a home in Westwood with a garden cottage. The previous renter was a poet, but she took a job teaching in Florida. I thought of you. If you like, I can put you in touch with Tina and Joel."

I was grateful, but also apprehensive.

"I had a bad experience with a pool house," I explained to Tina when we spoke on the phone.

"Oh, there's no pool. Unless you count the frog pond. Why don't you come over for supper and get a sense?"

That following Sunday, while Dawn was on an actual date, I taxied over to the Westwood address, shocked when the driver pulled up outside the gate of a restored Georgian. The plush garden acted as a privacy screen around the grounds, with the cottage's shingled roof just visible past the desert willows and gum trees.

What everyone had failed to mention, and I soon discovered, was that Tina was an heir to the Beringer wine fortune. She had married her college sweetheart, Joel, a mixed-media artist from Monterey. Tina and Joel graciously donated barrels of sacramental wine to the local Catholic churches and affiliates. The wine that the sisters of St. Joseph used in the kitchen was from their vineyard, which happened to be the same vineyard of Nico's party.

Some people believe in happenstance, not fate. I beg to differ. The interconnected elements of my ending up in Tina and Joel's home could only have been the hand of God.

It was a nice day, as were most days in L.A., so we ate Sunday supper on the veranda overlooking the backyard garden.

"Your home is beautiful," I said. "Your vineyard, too."

"You've been?" asked Tina, who fed their dog, Corky, scraps of leftover egg from the Cobb salads.

"Yes, Nico Cellini had a party there."

"Pavarotti sang, didn't he?" asked Joel.

I nodded.

"What I wouldn't pay to hear him and Lucas Wesley do a duet," said Tina.

"I imagine Pavarotti's opera and Lucas Wesley's rock and roll might not be a good mesh."

"We've seen stranger pairings that ended up well. Look at us!" quipped Tina.

"Touché, my dear, touché." He kissed her cheek and clinked his wineglass to hers.

They had an ease about them. A comfortable kind of intimacy that made those around them feel comfortable, too. I liked them immediately.

"Why don't you ramble down to the cottage while we clear the dishes," suggested Tina. "I keep forgetting that you aren't just our dinner company. You're here to do reconnaissance!"

Joel took up our plates and clicked his tongue for Corky to follow. "I've got a big piece of bacon fat with your name on it."

Corky wagged her tail merrily at the promise.

Tina pointed to the pebbled path. "Just keep going until you come to the front door. You can't miss it." Then she patted my hand like a kindly aunt and sent me on my way.

It was one of those early summer evenings when the temperature is bathwater right and every step feels like floating. Be it in California, Italy, or North Carolina, golden afternoons hold no geographic distinctions. The stones gave a satisfying crunch underfoot. Bordering lavender, phlox, coneflowers, and primroses scented each step with green sweetness. The air was alive with the buzz of bees and ladybugs, their wings aerating honey nectar. Every breath tasted of dessert. When the cottage bloomed from the thicket of butterfly bushes, I gasped at the purple wisteria growing around the arched doorway.

I was half expecting a symphony of flowers, dancing woodland creatures, and merry dwarves to swoop in. Disneyland was only thirty miles away. However, the interior was far from cartoonish. Decorated in a chic Grecian mode of periwinkle and white. The double-hung windows had been left open. The tapestries billowed like sails. If I hadn't had a favorite color before then, I did after. Blue violet still evokes the warmth of summer, sanctuary, and the everyday saints who led me there.

I ambled around dreaming of where I'd put a bed, a three-legged table, a cozy chair for reading, a bench to stack books. I didn't own any of those items, but somehow I knew I would. The cottage made me believe that anything was possible. So when a dove landed on the window ledge and cooed, I wouldn't dismiss the signs any longer.

I had a small amount saved from *Romeo & Juliet, The Musical* and had finally been paid for *Noises in the Night*. I collected the check in person and took it directly from the studio offices to the bank district for depositing. I didn't trust Tony as the middleman anymore.

I needed a fresh start. Tina and Joel's cottage felt exactly that. We agreed on the rental fees. It was important to me that I pay my own way. But on move-in day, Tina threw me a curveball.

"We want someone we trust on our property. So if you give us two hundred dollars for the first month's rent, we'll hold that as a security deposit against any shenanigans." She winked. "We won't worry too much about monthly fees. Take good care of the place, pay when you can, and it's yours for as long as you wish."

Her graciousness was impossible to decline.

Dawn was sad to see me go.

"Delilah and I will miss you, but we'll always have these . . ."

She gave me a box of Bisquick and a twelve-inch fry pan as a housewarming gift. She had been a steadfast ship between two harbors. Only a selfish friend would've overstayed the welcome.

Quickly, I made the cottage my home. The first meal I cooked myself was pancakes for dinner. I ate them with blackberries picked off a garden bush. The purple juice stained my fingers and lips. It was exhilarating—being alone to do as I pleased.

Those were days of simple pleasures. I cooked and decorated. I worked at the soup kitchen and went to Sunday suppers with Tina and Joel, who turned out to be wonderful landlords. Tina frequently dropped off baskets of herbs, vases of flowers, jars of honey, and books she thought I'd enjoy. Little things that made me feel less like a tenant and more like a friend.

When a skunk having a midnight feast on the almond tree outside my open window decided to crawl into my bedroom, I called the main house in a panic. Joel came right down with a flashlight.

"Their eyes are light sensitive so this should scare it off." He shone the light so that the skunk skittered out the way it'd come.

"What if it returns?" I asked.

The night terrors of the pool house remained fresh in my mind, but I couldn't explain that to Joel. Didn't need to. He saw my hands trembling and heard the fear in my voice. So, despite the late hour, he walked me around the garden swaying the flashlight back and forth, while giving me the horticultural history of skunks on vineyards.

"They keep the mice, raccoons, and other vermin away. They don't bother with the vines. The grapes make them sick."

"What about their spray?"

"Skunks are gentle as kittens unless they feel endangered. People aren't much different. Now, how about you get some sleep?" He put the flashlight in my hand. "Keep this. I know the way home."

I watched his figure meander through the darkness until he reached the lit patio where Tina greeted him with a kiss that parted with laughter seen even from a distance. It made me sigh and think, *That's love.*

For a full month, I didn't worry about work. I didn't read the reviews of *Noises in the Night* or watch the celebrity variety shows. I let Hollywood be Hollywood and me be me. It was what I needed at the time—to embrace the routine of stillness. To cease striving. Sometimes retreating isn't hiding, it's healing. When it's safe and you're ready, the universe gives you the green light.

Mine came on an August afternoon when the ocean air made its way up the hills and laced everything with the salt of the sea. The phone rang.

"Hello?" I answered.

"*Ciao*, darling, it's Nico."

"Nico!"

When I moved into the cottage, Dawn suggested I open a box at the post office for correspondences. It was cheap and allowed me to keep my residence a secret. I only sent my new address and phone number to a handful of people: my parents, Marie and Bill, Lucas, and Nico. After the hysterical phone call I'd made to Nico's house sitter, I felt I owed them both a *scusi* with an explanation: *I wasn't well, but now I am! I have a new home in L.A. Here's my address and phone number*.

I didn't expect to hear from Nico. I'd let him down or, at the very least, disappointed him. *Noises in the Night* was a massive flop and as career damaging as he foresaw. But the moment I heard his voice, I knew all was forgiven.

"I've just returned from Morocco. Fabulous place, have you been?"

"Never."

"I must take you. It's all hanging lanterns and spice souks, tagine feasts, mint tea, cats, and gold everywhere! Absolutely splendid."

My pulse raced at the confidence of his invitation.

"We're in postproduction. Tedious business." He sighed, a thousand soft scratches across the miles. "To avoid the uninspiring stuff, I jumped from the frying pan into the fire. My next film is shooting here, thank God. So much easier. You know how I love having everyone at the villa. Unfortunately, I am fortune's fool—to borrow from Romeo. That's why I'm calling. Are you free?"

He said it as if he were just down the road in Santa Monica and not halfway across the globe.

"You see," he went on at my pause, "we're a week from principal photography and one of my lead actresses just broke her arm in a waterskiing accident. I can do a lot of tricks with a camera, but I can't disguise a casted arm! Waiting for her to heal is not an option. We can't hold up production because she decided to have a misguided swim the week before. *Faccia tosta!*"

It was one of the few times I ever heard Nico frustrated. His voice took on a frenetic pitch that intensified his accent.

"Will you . . ."

"You're breaking up, Nico." I had a hard time hearing him. "What did you say?"

"The film, darling! It's called *Roman Ragazzi.* It's about four college girls on spring break in Rome. Ivonne Thibodeaux, Francis O'Connelly, and Pauline Tiss are the other three. Luana Patterson was the fourth but now she's up to her elbow in plaster of Paris!" He huffed into the phone. "Will you come and save me from this debacle? *Per favore, mio Lorietta?*"

I didn't wait a beat.

"Of course, *sì*, anything for you!"

"Aww, *bene, bene*! I'll have your room ready. It will be like old times. Don't worry about anything. My assistant will coordinate. We'll get you a plane ticket and the script. You must be in Rome by Friday."

That was in four days. I could hardly believe the speed of it all. Like a shooting star, like movie magic, like Nico! I couldn't resist the compulsive power. And just like that, I was back.

22

September in the Lazio region was a cascade of blue-skied mornings visited by the occasional rain cloud that left wet kisses atop the needled cypress trees. Then the sun would make its triumphant return, crowning everything in bright heat until dusk's breeze brought the cool reminder of the Mediterranean just out of sight. A season of self-contradiction, the weather couldn't decide if it wanted to be hot or cold. It was easy for us to pretend it was autumn's converse, spring.

I loved being back at Nico's villa. Back in his good graces, as well. To my delight, a familiar face had joined the coterie.

"Flynn Winston!"

"'Ello, Lovely!" He pulled off his large sunglasses and greeted me with a peck on each cheek. He'd been there long enough to bake himself bronze.

"Dashing as always. What are you doing here?"

"I'm a spring-breaker." He winked.

"I bet you are. In the film or in real life?"

He shrugged. "Does it matter? I'm Method acting."

I laughed.

"I've moved up in the world," said Flynn. "Nico invited me to stay at the villa this go."

He took the crook of my arm, and we walked the sandstone gravel leading to the villa's double-door entrance where Nico stood waving arms in welcoming salute.

"Can you keep a secret?" Flynn whispered. "It seems I've found favor with the king."

It didn't surprise me. Flynn was insatiably charming beneath his cynical quips.

"Good on you," I whispered back.

"*Lorietta!*" Nico called. "Darling, you are a vision! We've been waiting for you. Come and meet your co-stars."

Evie, Frannie, Pollie, and I hit it off immediately.

"*Mio Quartett-ies*," he called us.

"Another nickname?"

"I always want my actors to feel . . ." He searched the sky for the word and, having found it, turned back to me. "*Intimo. Sì?*"

Intimate. Yes.

"Everybody wishes for endearment," he continued. "Even if they don't think they do."

I'd never thought of it that way. He was right. The nickname made us feel like we belonged together.

We were the *Quartetties*, a quartet of performers, a foursome of women living in the world of *Roman Ragazzi.* Despite being in their late twenties, the girls treated me as an equal. I confessed to them that I'd never gone on spring break. I did less than a year at Italia Conti Academy. Oh—and I totally bombed at comedy in *Noises in the Night*! No doubt, a true veteran actress would've used more self-discretion. But I so earnestly wanted them to like me. I was starved for female friendship. My time on that film was full of truth, laughter, and rapport in the way only experience has in bringing people together. I would always call them friends, though our paths never crossed again.

All of the lead and supporting actors as well as a majority of the male dancers were staying at Nico's.

"What would spring break be without boys?" Nico said with a wink.

As with *Romeo & Juliet, The Musical*, he transformed his estate into the film's setting. In this case, a Roman holiday. The barn that once held Juliet's boudoir and the scene of my unofficial defloration was now the college girls' hotel room decked out with twin beds and palm frond–printed decor. No need to build make-believe backdrops. The alleyways and hidden backstreets near the Spanish Steps, Castel Sant'Angelo, and Trevi Fountain were used in the hours when foot traffic was low. Ensemble scenes started in the evening and went to dawn. *Student holiday hours*, we joked.

On our off days at the villa, Nico threw elaborate parties. He loved a theme: flower fairies, spaghetti western, Mad Hatter tea, card games, gelato social, pajama bingo . . . He enthusiastically evoked the zeitgeist of the film while keeping his cast from roving the town.

Sadly, Frannie and Pollie had to leave immediately after their scenes were shot. Both were trained singers and augmented their films with music gigs. Frannie was particularly popular and slated to sing on a Macy's Thanksgiving Day Parade float in New York City. Nico graciously offered that anyone not committed to other engagements was welcome to remain for the Feast Day of the Immaculate Conception.

"No better way to kick off the holidays than with an Italian feast!" he said and then picked up a *grissini* and conducted the table in a round of "Buon Natale."

He wanted the company as much as the company wanted him.

"Oh, please stay, Lori," begged Flynn. "It'll be tremendous fun!"

My parents had already decided that they were giving themselves the Christmas gift of a two-week cruise. They'd never traveled out of the country and Mexico was as far as they were willing to venture. Marie and Bill never left the photography shop during the holidays, their busiest season. Tina and Joel would look after my belongings at the cottage. So really, there was nothing waiting for me on the other side of the ocean and nothing holding me back from staying.

"Sure," I told Flynn. "Why not?"

❃ ❃ ❃

There's a reason that actual spring breaks last one week. It allows young people to give in to hedonism with the security of its promised end. No one can live perpetually on spring break. It isn't humanly possible. Without boundaries, what's to stop us from exhausting ourselves? I learned that on the *Roman Ragazzi* shoot.

Fresh out of party themes, Nico made the grand announcement one night: "We're having Lori's half-birthday bash!"

I daggered my eyes at Flynn. He was the only one who knew my birth date, and he was weeks off.

"It's not—" I began, but Nico waved a hand as to imply that the factual didn't matter. We were commemorating the spirit of my half birthday.

"Growing old is notoriously difficult no matter what age you are," he continued. "So we must celebrate! I've arranged everything." Nico waved a hand like a magician. "The chef is working on an American Lane Cake, which I've been told is as lovely as our Lori!"

I softened with the memory of my mom aproned in the Canary House kitchen whipping butter, sugar, and flour to ribbons. The scent of the vanilla milk soak and bourbon frosting would permeate every nook and corner. Lane Cake was her signature. Even the church ladies couldn't resist. Many a Bible study went giggly over empty plates. On my last call home, Mom had just finished making one for the annual Pufftown Library Cake Raffle, and I'd rhapsodized its unrivaled delights to Nico. It touched me that he'd taken note.

Two days later, HMU came to my room with orders to style me. My long hair was teased and twisted into a beehive befitting Marie Antoinette. My cheeks, eyes, and lips were painted lavishly. Nico sent over three Mary Quant minidresses. I chose the shamrock green with the racer stripe around the waist. White go-go boots and a corresponding emerald hairpin finished the style.

Outside, rainbowed streamers hung from the pergola. Tufts of silk flowers filled the vases. Elaborate cream laces stretched out over the wooden tables. Candles twinkling everywhere, not merely on the cake, which wasn't the traditional layer cake but a five-tiered tower. Though it was innocently covered in white coconut, anyone passing could smell the whiskey. There must've been a hundred guests, but I only recognized a handful. Nico called them all to his attention.

"Who said we can't have dessert first!"

Flynn ceremoniously handed me the blade used in Juliet's death scene. I raised the knife with dramatic flair and cut the closest tier.

"To our Lori Lovely, may she age to perfection!" Nico took up the slice and ate it out of his hand.

I followed his lead, licking the bourbon buttercream off my fingers. The oaky sweetness made my vision feather.

The band played a catchy jazz beat that brought partygoers to the dance floor. Nico wouldn't serve dinner until everyone had danced enough to sit without fidgeting. He, most especially, grew fidgety at the table. But I needed more than a handful of canapés and a fistful of frosting to hold me steady. I waded through the crowd of small-talkers, thanking them for their good wishes, on my way to the kitchen.

With each step came a mounting déjà vu. I'd walked this exact path with Lucas. An aching fondness washed over me. I missed him. Someone who saw me, the real me. At that moment, I wanted nothing more than to scrape off the makeup, pull down my hair, and eat scrambled eggs out of a skillet. But it was more than Lucas. I also missed suppers with Tina and Joel, Dawn and Delilah, dancing with Ginny, Marie and Bill, my parents' voices whispering good morning and good night. I wondered where they were and wished I could have them by my side.

Footsteps and the familiar sharpness of a man's cologne made me turn.

"*Ciao*, Lori."

"Tony! What are you doing here?"

"I came back to Rome." He shrugged offhandedly, but his eyes held a fierce intensity.

"I didn't hear from you for months! I moved out of that awful pool house and finished that awful film. You disappeared!"

He shook his head. "No, no. *You* disappeared. I get you a job with an up-and-coming director and then I find out that my actress nearly ruins the whole production with diva antics."

"Excuse me?"

"They had to saw off your door lock, Lori."

"I tried to call you!" I started to defend myself and then stopped. It was a futile endeavor to argue. Nothing he told me about himself was true. "You're not my manager anymore."

"You're overreacting," he scoffed and pulled me into his embrace, clammy with perspiration.

"Don't touch me!"

He didn't release me. Instead, he gripped me tighter. "We signed a contract. I represent your interests and this decision is not being made with a clear mind."

His pupils were wide and dark. He was on something.

"You're high," I said and tried to pull out of his grip.

"You know what happens to liars." He put a finger to the tip of my nose. "Their noses grow too big for their faces."

Every touch was a trigger. I hated that I'd let him get so close, physically and professionally. I hated that I'd pushed others aside on his behalf. I hated that he'd made me distrustful of my own intuition. Mostly, I hated that he stood here now acting as if he had any right to show up like this, to treat me like this, to touch me like this.

"I mean it. You don't work for me. We're done." I forcefully pushed his hands off.

He gave a disturbing grin, and I realized he liked it. The fight. It turned him on. Carolyn and her brother had been right. In a flash of awareness, I knew it was him in the pool house. He'd been the one taking my things; the one breathing over me at night; the one drugging me with his pills. I wasn't crazy and I wasn't being haunted. I was being stalked.

Everything inside me wanted to run, but I knew a chase would not end well.

"It's not that simple," he continued. "You owe me the percentage on the film I booked you and months of pool house rental fees. I have the paperwork with your signature. Who do you think paid that every month?"

That damned house. I had signed the lease, but I would've ended it properly if I'd been able to reach him. As for the managerial fees, I was guilty. I didn't know what to say except . . .

"I'll find a way to pay you back. When I'm home in L.A. I can't do anything right now. So I think it's best if we walk away from each other."

I started back to the party as calmly as I could when suddenly, he grabbed me by the elbow with such force it tore the sleeve of my dress. Months of pent-up fear erupted. I torqued and flailed as if I were fighting off the nightmares again. He put a hand over my mouth to shush me, and I reared my head back. Momentarily stunned, he let go and brought his hand to his cheek.

My emerald hairpin had gouged his face. The blood seeped through his fingers. I thought of the mansion on Benedict Canyon Drive. Before a drop hit the floor, I ran as fast as I could.

Finding Nico in the crowd, I threw myself into his arms. He touched the rip in my sleeve and smoothed the mess of my hair.

"What's happened?"

"He's crazy . . ." I said, trying to catch my breath.

"Let's get you inside." He waved for his assistant. "Get security but keep it quiet. We don't want to incite hysteria."

Nico ushered me into the villa and up to his bedroom. There, he set me down on his dressing chair.

"You need water."

The water ran in the bathroom sink. A cup was placed on the vanity beside me. The cool night air settled onto my exposed shoulder where the dress had split. I shivered and Nico draped a shawl over me. Someone banged on the bedroom door. I startled and knocked the cup over.

"I'm sorry."

"It's only water." He opened the door to Flynn.

"What's happened? You both left?" asked Flynn.

"Someone's hurt her," said Nico.

Flynn's eyes widened in alarm.

"I'm okay," I assured them.

A flood of questions: "What? When? Where?"

I didn't have answers, except to "Who?"

"Tony Rischio."

Nico's face was blank.

"The talent manager I met at your party in L.A."

Dark anxiety crawled over my shoulders. I pulled the shawl tighter around me.

"I told him I don't want to work together anymore, and then he grabbed me."

Nico paused, and I filled in the hesitation with self-doubt. Hosts know their guests. Reputation meant so much in the industry. I could see the tabloids: *Juliet actress loses her mind and disfigures manager. Beware of the mad ingénue!*

Imagination can be the harshest hangman.

"Tony Rischio?" Nico turned to Flynn. "Get my assistant. I want every production member's name. Lori, darling, what else do you know about this man?"

I told Nico how I met Tony at the vineyard party and about the phone call with Carolyn to the moment I left him bleeding by the kitchen door. He listened with growing concern.

The *polizia* were called. The assistant brought the production payroll list. They meticulously went over every name, but there was no Tony Rischio. The officers had better luck with the phone book. They were able to locate an Anthony J. Rischio and an Anthony Z. Rischio. At the station, they could pull the corresponding addresses and make visits for questioning. However, they warned us that an arrest was unlikely given that it was my word against his.

With the *polizia* scavenging the grounds, an eerie disquiet seeped through the partygoers. Whispers replaced cheers. By the time the patrol cars departed, the villa was silent. If that had been the end of it, perhaps we could've looked back on that night as an *un*happy half birthday. But it was only the beginning.

Two days later, an envelope was slipped under the front door of Nico's villa on formal stationery: a typed letter of intent to sue from Tony. Nico called his lawyer, and we gathered in his study around the phone.

"You owe him money?"

"I do." I explained the situation.

"I can lend you the amount," Nico offered. "Pay this guy and be done."

"But how does she pay someone who slides a threatening letter under the door?" asked Flynn.

"What's the address on the letter?" asked the lawyer. "We could have a court-appointed courier deliver the cash."

"There's no address," I said.

The lawyer balked. "It isn't legitimate then. He's just trying to scare you."

"So what do we do to make him go away?" I asked.

The men quieted. No one had an answer.

"I think this is about more than money," said Nico. "I know his type. *Un molestatore.*"

Nico amped up security. I was assigned a bodyguard named Arturo, who looked every bit his name. Still, I couldn't shake my perpetual anxiety.

The *polizia* reported back that they'd gone to both Rischio residences. Anthony J. Rischio was a sixty-year-old shoemaker whose hands were so arthritic from his vocation that he could barely open the door. He had no facial wounds and no children or namesakes to his knowledge. At the address of Anthony Z. Rischio, they found the Mancinis, a couple with a young child who said that they bought the place two years prior from Tony Rischio, who'd moved to America. He'd left no forwarding address. For all intents and purposes, he was a free-floating phantom. All we could do was wait until he made himself known again.

Flynn took me shopping to try to take my mind off things. I had a panic attack in the middle of the *mercato* when I saw a passerby who looked like Tony. Flynn and Arturo had to practically carry me home.

"I'm sorry," I told them. "I really thought . . . I don't know what."

I couldn't truthfully say what was real. It was like at the pool house. I was trapped within walls I could touch and ones I could not. It was a great relief when we officially wrapped and I could avoid all public settings. For two weeks, I stayed inside Nico's villa, playing bocce ball with Flynn and Nico, reading books, and swimming. I gave myself permission to feel safe.

Then one morning, we awoke to another note under the door. This one was handwritten.

We need to talk. You owe me.-T

"Darling, there's not much more we can do here," said Nico. "Is there someplace else you can go?"

I called Marie.

"Come," she said.

I was on a flight the next day.

Lu

Women's Retreat

The Abbey, Connecticut
October 1990

The abbey is hosting its annual Women's Retreat. In decades past, it lasted weeks. Now it's only Thursday through Sunday. Guests could petition for an extension if they wished, but a long weekend was the most time that contemporary women had to spare.

Truthfully, if I had known it was happening during my visit, I would've planned a trip to New York City as an excuse to be absent.

"'Silent meditation, fasting, nature walks, mineral baths, farm work, chants, prayer . . .'" I read the agenda aloud. "This is supposed to be fun?"

My cynicism is not lost on my aunt.

"It's supposed to be what it is—a *kenosis*," Aunt Lori replies. "Have you ever experienced one?"

"I've never even heard the word."

We're in the abbey's laundry room, steamy from the electric irons. They're pressing blue denims fashioned after the local farmhands' apparel. I can't say they're stylish, but I suppose they're more modern than tunics and scapulars. Each attendee receives one along with muslin bedding, a schedule of the daily prayer hours, and a group activity itinerary neatly nestled in a welcome basket like Moses in the woven reeds. The sisters do a nice job gussying up the presentation; otherwise, they'd look like the parcels prisoners receive upon incarceration.

"A kenosis," Aunt Lori explains, "is an emptying of the Self so as to receive the Divine Calling."

She folds a denim button-down shirt, then tucks dried lavender into the collar.

"How do you know which is which?" I ask.

"It's hard to decipher when the world is clattering on. Particularly for women. Our voices have been subjugated for centuries."

"Doesn't the church subjugate as much—hush and obey God the *Father*?" I dare.

"God has no gender. You know that, right? We assign gender because our human language has limited pronouns," she continues. "But He/She is equal parts. Humankind has placed people in hierarchies, and, unfortunately, women are still second fiddle. So, we provide space for them to shut out discriminating factors and unrealistic expectations. A place to commune with the Divine without barriers."

"A cloister is barricaded by definition. Seems self-contradictory."

She laughs. "It isn't Plato, Lu. It's Wellness 101. Clear the mind and body so the heart can lead the way."

I shrug. "If I wanted to clear my mind and body, I'd go to a tropical beach and have a fruity cocktail. I wouldn't sign up to do chores, pray, and keno-whatever—and I wouldn't pay for it."

"They don't pay," Aunt Lori corrects. "They give an offering."

"Tomato, tomahto."

She darts her eyes but doesn't argue.

We fold the rest of the garments in silence while in my mind I hear Ella Fitzgerald and Louis Armstrong singing "Let's Call the Whole Thing Off."

When we finish the laundry, I pull out my tape recorder. We've fallen into a routine. I give her what she wants: abbey chores. She gives me what I want: her story.

"Back to where we left off?"

The night before, I'd been the one to cut the interview short. I saw how it wore her down—retelling was reliving the trauma. At one point, her fists closed tight defensively. It's hard to be dispassionate when we have such a close relationship. I feel every heartbeat of her distress—then and now. I'd turned off the tape and said I was tired. She'd exhaled in relief and agreed.

But there's no going around it. This is a pivotal part of her past.

"So . . . Tony. Did he turn out to be a stalker, part of a cult, or a psycho creep at the very least?"

No one could blame her for defending herself. I'd have done worse if a guy showed up out of nowhere, threatening and grabbing me. I'd have gouged his . . .

"Blessed bells!" Aunt Lori jerks her finger to her mouth.

A rough piece of the handwoven basket stuck her. She pulls it back, pinches to inspect.

"A splinter."

I wince on reflex. "That stings."

"It's not so painful. The splinter'll make its way out. But if it bleeds, it'll ruin the clean laundry."

She stands and waves for me to follow.

"Sister Mary Clare, would you be so kind as to finish the welcoming baskets?"

"My pleasure!" says Sister Mary Clare with such cheer that I think she might sincerely believe it to be a *pleasure*.

Aunt Lori goes to the closet where the First Aid kit is kept. A cotton swab with hydrogen peroxide, a Band-Aid, and she's set. Maid Marian is concerned. He *meows* around her ankles and looks accusatorially at me.

"I didn't do it," I tell him.

On our way to Aunt Lori's office, a hubbub echoes from the public entry. Guests have begun to arrive.

There's a kind of rolling admission. The retreat officially begins tonight with the welcoming Compline and chants before bed. Up until now, I've had to sit alone during the Divine Office hours. An iron grille separates the holy of holies from . . . well, me. I don't attend the other liturgical gatherings, but Compline appeals to me like a bedtime fairy tale.

Each night the sisters pray aloud in unison: *May your holy angels dwell herein, may they watch over us in peace, and may your blessing be always upon us.*

Candles are lit. Hymns are sung under a stained-glass window of a fiery red Madonna with flaming doves. The Crux Sacra is recited: *May the holy cross be my light; may no dragon be my guide. Get back, Satan!*

It's supposed to drive out demonic forces leaching onto a person so that they can sleep peacefully. I can't say for certain if the incantations work, but I've slept like a baby since I came. So I'm all for it.

I linger in the hall to see the early birds. It's not even noon Sext. Compline is hours away.

Sister Evangelista welcomes three middle-aged women with possible family ties. They share a similar smile and tone of voice, but that's just as easily regional as it is biological. Dressed in matching cardigans and belted khakis, one carries a Longaberger basket with a lid as a purse.

My mom attended Longaberger parties in our Pufftown neighborhood and even hosted a saleswoman once. Neighbors came to see and order the newest maple wood weaves and pottery wonders from the catalog. The saleswoman insisted that a perfectly woven basket suggested a perfectly woven household. We had the entire line of dishes in the cornflower-blue pattern. Matching dinnerware and expensive baskets were the benchmarks of suburban success.

The baskets at the abbey have wonky edges and splinters. The pottery is beautiful, but an occasional fingerprint is left behind. They hand-make everything, which means no two are alike. Somehow, that makes each item feel more costly.

"Welcome!" bellows Sister Evangelista. "You'll be staying at the Women's Guest House. Here are your room assignments."

She hands them their welcome baskets. The woman with the Longaberger now juggles two and looks like an extra from *Little House on the Prairie.* They each thank Sister Evangelista and titter nervously. First-timers, they're in for a ride.

Sister Candace escorts them to the Women's Guest House on the opposite side of the pine copse. The house is visible from the main monastery, but you can't get there directly. The leafless bottom branches of the evergreens have formed an impenetrable wicket gate of Mother Nature's making. Guests must walk the giant U-shape path to get from one to the other. And trust me, it is no short trip.

Sister Evangelista waves to me. "Are ya ready for the retreat?"

I smile and put my hands in prayer pose. "It's a writing retreat for me." God knows, I need to keep every word I have, not empty them out.

The sisters' routine of song, prayer, and silent meditation provides many hours to explore the abbey's ample, albeit cluttered, library. They'd lined a concrete storage room with hand-hewn shelves, giving the space a mountain-cabin vibe and the old-woods scent that comes with it. A knotty oak table with knobby legs is pushed against one wall with two mismatched cushioned chairs, castoffs from the communal sitting room. Their cushions droop in the center, and it looks as if a cat used the back of one as a scratching pole. Yet somehow the room retains a hospitable aura, a silent beckoning of whispered pages and shared secrets. It's the only place in the abbey that's nearly soundproof from the church bells and Gregorian chants.

The nuns have a wealth of information on the church's development, the saints of yore, Bibles of every translation, and, to my surprise, an eclectic range of fiction from Jane Austen to Danielle Steele. One tiered shelf contains the diaries of sisters gone to Glory or back to the secular life, as well as the administrative inner workings of the abbey. The names of the novitiates in residence and details of their Clothing ceremonies are itemized alongside how many chickens are in the coop and favored bread and stew recipes. The diaries also recount their private prayers, praises, and petitions. It's strange that such intimate correspondences with the

Almighty are saved. Reason has it that an omniscient God would have no need for such historical records. The decade of 1965 to 1975 contained the most. It was then that the Second Vatican rulings were put into practice. Many sisters left the monastic life feeling demoted and unwilling to embrace the new order of flexible freedoms.

Aunt Lori entered during the exact period when most were exiting. A curious incongruity. Religious sisterhood was certainly not a popular vocation at the time. Though, it was difficult for me to imagine when it was. I took as many books as I could carry back to the Women's Guest House so I could study after silent hours. The night before, I'd stayed up past midnight attempting to align Aunt Lori's story with the primary documents. All in vain, because the giant niggling question remains: *Why did she join the order when she did?*

Now, Sister Evangelista turns as a black limousine pulls up slowly, inch by stretched inch. I find myself inching closer, too. It stops and the driver comes around to open the door.

A strikingly tall woman steps out with a bouffant of curly, bottle-platinum hair and a slash of red lipstick. She's wearing acid-washed jeans, canvas sneakers, and a men's tuxedo jacket cuffed to display a cascade of glittering bangles on each forearm. Under a brimmed hat and oversized sunglasses, it's clear she's trying to conceal her identity. But anyone who's turned on a television or walked by the magazine rack would recognize her. She looks exactly like she does on film, exactly like Aunt Lori described.

It's Ginny Wilde.

My stomach drops to my knees and bounces back up to my throat. She's breathtaking in every way we wish celebrities to be. Despite being double my age, she carries herself in a manner that makes me want to be her best friend—to lie in bed beside her like Aunt Lori and look up at the ceiling of stars, laughing and dreaming together. The magnetism is undeniable.

She pulls down her sunglasses a beat. Her eyes are red, raw, and rubbed makeup-less.

I should look away, give her privacy, let her be. But I can't. It's Ginny Wilde. GW. Goddess Wilde. Lady Wilde. The Holy G.

I step closer. I'm gawking. I know it. My heart thumps madly, and I can't get the monkey grin off my face.

Sister Evangelista feels my approach and gives a warning glare. Then her eyes move past me. "Mother Lori," she says.

I turn to Aunt Lori, then back to Ginny, then back to Aunt Lori. "It's GW," I whisper.

"No," she says.

"It is! It's Ginny Wilde!" I repeat.

"It's not." Aunt Lori puts a hand on my arm. "That woman is Jennifer Cockburn. We know her well."

We lock gazes. I understand.

"Everyone needs a place where they can be as God made them."

Sister Evangelista goes out to greet her while the driver unloads the luggage.

"So, you're saying I should *not* call her Goddess or Lady or the Holy G?"

"Those titles don't mean anything," she says. "She's a woman looking for refuge."

"Refuge from what? She's got the world on a string!"

I stop, suddenly remembering one of the radio disc jockeys talking about her while I was driving up from North Carolina. It'd gone in one ear and out the other. A romantic scandal of some sort. Ginny had been married and divorced a handful of times and was rumored to have been with men and women from New York to New Zealand. I wasn't sure if any of that was true or merely told to sell a boatload of movie tickets. The primary sources were conflicting. History was slippery. I should know. I was getting my degree in it and having a hard time pinning it down with my own family. My notebook was a jumble of unanswered questions and secret speculations.

Aunt Lori takes me by the hand. "Let me introduce you."

Before we reach her, Ginny sees us and spreads her arms wide like a great egret.

"Lovely!"

She embraces Aunt Lori with me caught awkwardly between. Their voices chime like birdsong.

"You look tired," Aunt Lori whispers.

"I took a red-eye from L.A." Ginny lets out a long sigh that seems to settle her body even closer to Aunt Lori's. "I'm here and that's all that matters."

They pull back, smile at each other, and then Ginny turns to me.

"This must be your Lu." With a manicured finger, she pushes my bang behind my ear. "I'd recognize those blue eyes anywhere."

I am speechless.

Part 7

Lori

Callings

23

New York to Connecticut
1967

When I arrived in New York, Marie didn't mince words.

"You look like the living dead," she said as a hello.

"Looks do not deceive," I replied.

"What's going on?"

I'd been up for nearly forty-eight hours, wired on caffeine and the fear that Tony, or some specter of him, would appear the moment I closed my eyes.

I dug my nails into my palm and rubbed my forehead with my fist. A simple question that would take too much to answer.

The seconds of my hesitation ticked on. Wordlessly, Marie pulled me into her shoulder, and I let my head rest.

"Stress isn't good for the body. My doctor says it can be as crippling as any other disease."

I craned my neck up to her face. "Are you sick, Marie?"

"No, not in the typical way." She patted my hand in reassurance. "Bill and I still aren't able to conceive."

It wasn't something that our family talked about directly. Children, yes: *God's little blessings*. However, the science of creating children was left to the imagination. When I was very young, I'd gleaned what I could from the backyard bunnies. As a teenager, I obsessed over Marie's *How to Have a Love Affair* book. As an adult, I'd turned to films, my portrayal of

Juliet included. But for the most part, it was the blind leading the blind. Yet even I knew you couldn't make a baby out of fantasy. There was biology involved. If that failed . . .

"I can't sustain a pregnancy past the first term," explained Marie. "Stress, the doctor says, is passed down through the maternal side. I have had nine miscarriages since we got married."

I leaned in closer. "Oh, Marie, nine? I didn't know . . ."

"It's not really something one goes on and on about. You sort of hope the next time will stick and you won't need to think about what came before"—her voice caught—"because it will have been worth it." She cleared her throat firmly. "I wouldn't even be telling you if you hadn't come now. I'm leaving tomorrow, driving up to an abbey in Connecticut. Once a year, the nuns host a Women's Retreat for guests to take in the mountain air, herbal remedies, healthy foods, prayer, rest . . . a kind of cleansing. It's open to anyone. You don't have to be Catholic. A client of ours did it last year and got pregnant as soon as she got back. We took her baby's first photo."

"Do you think it'll work?"

"I've tried everything else," she said. "Why don't you come with me?"

"To an abbey?"

"Yes."

There really was no safer place than a convent. No one on earth would think to look for me there. I could rest—really rest! And I'd be with Marie. It seemed a blaze on a trail just when I was looking for a path.

"Okay." I shook my head with disbelief. "Okay," I repeated to make myself believe.

❀❀❀

We took the bus from Manhattan to Waterbury and then a taxicab from the station to the abbey. I slept most of the way in the throes of jet lag. When we arrived, the Portress checked us in. There was no official cost for the retreat. They operated on the order of *first donate, first served.* So, despite being unexpected, my attendance was well received.

An elderly woman named Sister Uma saw to adding a cot in Marie's room. A nun nearer to my age, Sister Evangelista, gave us each a change of clothing and bedding.

"You can wear these or your own clothes. Whatever you like, but knees and shoulders gotta be covered. The Second Vatican Council might've loosened things up, but modesty is still the cardinal rule," she explained. "Not that anybody would wear a polka-dot bikini in late November—to a nunnery! But ya never know. Fashion is notorious for bucking common sense." She stretched her arms, so the fabric of her tunic billowed like sails. "I'm sticking with the monochromatic mod. Never goes outta style."

She made me laugh, and I knew we'd be fast friends. Sister Evangelista escorted us to the room that Marie and I would share at the Women's Guest House, a white clapboard with an apple tree out front laden with bright green fruit. It was clean and neat and made the world feel similar. I kicked off my shoes and made up my cot.

"Remember that summer camp we used to go to as kids?"

"Camp MacMerri," said Marie. "In the Blue Ridge."

I hadn't thought of it in years. It was an all-girls camp. Two weeks each summer, Marie and I would pack our duffel bags and join girls of similar ages in cabin tribes. We'd ride horses, learn to whittle, hike, play bingo, and sing "Kumbaya" around the campfire at night. The abbey had a similar vibe and there's powerful comfort in familiarity.

So, I slid my suitcase under my bed like I used to do, washed my face, braided my hair back, and changed into the cotton denims.

"I never knew nuns wore blue jeans."

"If Grace Kelly can pull it off, I guess they can, too," said Marie.

She pointed out the window to a shepherdess in blues guiding a handful of sheep across the meadow. The sunlight fell just so through the surrounding forest trees, lacing them with a halo of gold.

I threaded my fingers through hers and we stood, silently awed, as each woolly head bent and lifted, bent and lifted in lullaby cadence. I couldn't remember the last time I'd felt so unburdened. Maybe this was all that was needed. Time away to reset. If I disappeared from the world for a bit, maybe all my troubles would, too. We could all move on.

"I hope this works." Marie sighed.

"Me too." I squeezed her arm.

Wishful thinking, hopes, prayers—call it what you will. We had faith.

I learned quickly that the Queen of Praise Benedictine Abbey was lauded as an enclave of vestal artists. Music, theater, painting, sculpture, farming, gardening, cooking, herbalism, and most important, the art of quiet meditation. Guests were encouraged to rotate through each of these disciplines while also participating in the communal gathering of chants, chores, and meals.

There was a rhythm to the hour by hour that appealed to me. I hadn't expected to attune to it as quickly or enjoy it as much. After years of feeling like a kite without a string, I finally had a pull of direction. I grew stronger, and closer to Marie. Closer to the unknown, too.

One day, I was weeding the garden when something drew me out past the stone fence into the fields. A white cat, I thought, but its ears were too round. A silver rabbit? But it didn't hop. It sauntered, looking back over its shoulder at me as if to lead the way. I followed, curious.

Alone in the pasture, tufts of dandelion seeds caught in the breeze and flew like musical notes. The bell of the abbey rang for the next incantation, and at a distance the sisters' voices echoed. The birds and breeze and dandelion seeds seemed to take the cue and harmonized. A single billowing cloud stretched a hand across the sun. The light canted directly on my face, and I felt the queerest sensation. I'd describe it as a rising or a bubbling up from a well I hadn't realized was within. I knew with all certainty—and no proof—that it was God.

Not the God who caused folks to shake and faint at tent revivals. Or the God whose black leather Bible thumped like a smack. Not even the God my mom and the church ladies wore their finest Easter hats to celebrate.

I'd never felt that God. I'd nodded my head to keep people from thinking badly of me, or worse, trying to convert my heart to their will. I'd never been convinced it was real, and I wasn't convinced that those who said they believed were either.

But in the symphony of that meadow, I had what I can only describe as an *experience*. It dawned on me that humanity had it upside down. We zealously climb to peaks of success thinking it will give us happiness, and that's where we're most endangered. I knew that place. So close to the stars, if I reached up I'd burn my fingers on them. But one loss of balance, one mislaid step, and the fall was catastrophic.

I thought about Tina and Joel, Ginny, Lucas, my parents, and about Marie, wanting a baby so badly that she'd offer any oblation to get one. And me, here on a whim because of her, battling my own fears in an altogether different way.

I sat in that patch of wild clover for hours, talking to God, asking questions, feeling the close tremor of the bees passing and the rustle of woodland creatures in the thicket. When the sun set, a chill descended so I made my way back to the abbey's hearth. I'd been gone all day, but none of the sisters asked why or where. Instead, they welcomed me to the supper table with gracious smiles as if privy to the secret I carried. Sister Uma ladled out hot fish stew capped with a mountain of cheese. It salted our spirits and filled our stomachs so fully that by the time I lay down in my cot, I could barely keep my eyes open to answer Marie.

"Where were you all day?"

"In the field."

"By yourself?"

"Yes . . . no." I yawned. "I don't know."

Then the rising came again. Only this time, it was the weight of an extra blanket being pulled from my toes to my shoulders. The gentle warmth of my sister's kiss on my forehead, and I slept.

❀ ❀ ❀

In a flash, the two weeks were over. Marie was on pins and needles to get back to Bill, hopeful that the tinctures, exercise, and holy hands had opened her womb to a miracle. I did not share her enthusiasm to return to the world at large. The thought filled me with dread and brought with it old devils.

I walked the garden pathways for hours the days before our farewell, mulling inwardly. The abbey had been the sanctuary I needed, but I never could've imagined how badly I'd want to stay. I had responsibilities in Los Angeles. Tina and Joel were expecting me—and not just them. Nico wanted to see me taken care of in the wake of everything, so he recommended me to his friend John Guglielmo, who was directing a loose musical adaptation of an Agatha Christie novel. Nico had staked his reputation on me, and John had agreed without asking for an audition.

Besides all of that, it was coming on Christmas. The sisters couldn't have guests lingering during the busy Advent season. All rational thought said I needed to shove off, but I couldn't shake the deep-seated feeling that I was meant to be here. I wanted the chants, the chores, the topsoil beneath my fingernails, meditation walks, and silent prayers. I wanted to follow the sheep shepherded by the light. Did that make me crazy?

Mother Abbess saw me marching figure eights the night before our departure.

"May I join you?" she asked.

While the retreat guests communed with the sisters, we rarely saw Mother Abbess outside of liturgical activities. I heard she was a great reader and spent hours engaged in that. So it took me by surprise that she sought my company.

"Of course, yes, please," I stuttered.

She picked up where I had paused my pacing so that I had to skip a little to catch up.

"I get the impression you are troubled, my child. Care to share?"

Straight to the heart.

"I—well, yes."

I was troubled, but I wasn't sure I cared to share.

The sound of our feet on the gravel came into one. She waited for me to speak.

"Being here has been life-changing," I said. "I don't want to go back to the way things used to be."

"Who says you have to? That's the goal of kenosis. To change forever."

Hope fluttered in my throat.

"That's just it . . ." I gulped. "I want to stay. With you and the sisters."

"Oh." Mother Abbess slowed her pace. "I see."

"I don't know what that means, but this place feels right."

She nodded slowly.

"You feel God's Calling here. Is that what I'm hearing?"

I nodded. "Yes."

"All of us do." She smiled. "But each of us has her own unique gift—a strength that is meant to be used for the will of God. You, Lori, are a celebrated and talented actress. You have the world's eye on you. Think of all the good that empowers you to do."

Even the kindest rejection stings. I dropped my chin to my chest.

"You were created and chosen for such a time as this. That's Esther 4:14." She lifted my face with a gentle touch so that our eyes met. "You are a child of God. Don't ever doubt how significant you are in the universe. Consider that."

We stood there under the crescent moon. I wish I could say that her words brought divine illumination, but in the moment, all I heard was that she didn't want me. The demons of my own making told me that she must see the awfulness in me—the things I had done and the things I had yet to do.

Suddenly, the white creature crouched by the garden gate.

I gasped. "What is it?" I'd thought it a figment of my imagination.

"That's Pearl." Mother Abbess clucked her tongue and Pearl raised her nose in hello. "An albino skunk. The sisters found her. Lost, abandoned, or simply looking for a new home, we'll never know. But we fed her and she stayed. She thinks this is her private Eden."

"A skunk?" I shook my head. "They seem to be following me coast to coast."

She looked at me curiously, but before I could explain, Pearl scaled the garden rock wall, blending in so seamlessly that she looked like a slow-moving stone. The only tell was the flick of her tail in stealthy pursuit.

"I'm told they keep other predators away," I said.

"They do, indeed," said Mother Abbess. "We all have a job. God will never ask us to remit the purpose for which we were created. A fruit tree must bear fruit. A skunk must protect its garden. You must go back to Hollywood to finish what you started. Drifting in a sea of what-ifs is a fate far worse than death. Never let fear be the reason for anything. We act despite the fear. Promise me?"

I sighed. "Yes."

She put an assuring arm around my waist.

"Our doors will always be open. But God isn't in one place. God is in people. In you, Lori."

So, I packed my bags and got on the bus with Marie the next day. With each turn of the wheels farther from the abbey, I couldn't help but feel my spirit falling . . . falling . . . falling.

24

Marie and Bill graciously invited me to stay for Christmas, but they needed privacy. The apartment was small, and I knew Marie was eagerly counting the Advent days for her own miraculous conception. New York wasn't where I was meant to be. Before flying to the West Coast, I visited Ginny's old landlords, Mr. and Mrs. Finkelstein. On the phone, Fern had said that Ginny left them as her forwarding address, so I hoped they might be able to tell me where she was.

"She went to Paris," said Mr. Finkelstein.

"No, she went to London," Mrs. Finkelstein corrected.

"Yes, I was in London with Ginny, but do you know where she is now?"

"She went to Paris!" Mr. Finkelstein insisted.

"He's practically deaf," said Mrs. Finkelstein.

"And you're blind as an old bat!" he returned.

Mrs. Finkelstein ignored him and continued. "Ginny's going to be a famous actress. She's on tour now. Chicago, maybe? Hollywood? Toronto? I'm not sure. She sends us postcards." She rose and rifled through a captain's desk stuffed with papers. "I think the last one was from . . . *hmm* . . ."

"Paris!" yelled Mr. Finkelstein.

And what do you know, when Mrs. Finkelstein turned over the card, it was a picture of the Eiffel Tower.

"So maybe it was Paris." Mrs. Finkelstein passed me the card.

My fingertips tingled at the sight of Ginny's handwriting:

Dearest Finkelsteins—I'm in Paris! Dancing and singing mostly but I just got a part in the new Shirley MacLaine film shooting here. I'm pinching myself! Avec beaucoup d'amour, G

No address. The timestamp was blurred beyond legibility. A Shirley MacLaine film was a big break.

"If you see her again, please tell her that Lori came," I said. "Here's my Los Angeles number and post address."

I wrote it all down.

"Los Angeles?" She handed it to Mr. Finkelstein, who was still gloating over being right about Paris. "I think I recognize you. Are you an actress, too?"

"I'm an old friend of Ginny's."

"Give her the postcard," Mr. Finkelstein told his wife.

"I couldn't," I argued, but they insisted.

I took the postcard as a sign. I would find a way to see her again. It was in my coat pocket when I landed at LAX.

To welcome me, Tina and Joel decorated the cottage with evergreen garlands, red holly berries, and tinsel draped over everything. It looked pretty as a Bing Crosby film scene. Tina baked snickerdoodles and left them under cling wrap on a plate. Condensation beaded from the cookies' warm middles while the scent of cinnamon sweetened the room.

"We're so glad you're back!" said Tina.

"It's been a whirlwind. Thank you for all of this." I pointed to the garlands, the cookies, my freshly made bed, and the potted Christmas cactus on the table that hadn't been there before.

They'd really gone out of their way to make the place feel like home. So why didn't it? I sat on the couch in a kind of shell-shocked exhaustion. I was back, but so much had happened that I hadn't the energy to explain to them.

I rubbed my head. "I'm sorry. It was a long flight. I'm out of sorts."

"Of course you are!" said Tina. She patted my hand. "You'll have the holidays to rest."

"When do you start shooting *Murder on the Nile*?" asked Joel. "I've always loved Agatha Christie."

I'd mentioned it to them after giving Guglielmo's assistant the cottage's phone number with instructions to let the line ring until someone picked up. Which the assistant had done and Joel had run down from the main house to answer after a couple dozen jingles.

"We begin filming in January."

"Wow, 1968." He whistled. "The years fly by faster and faster. I remember when summer felt like an eternity."

Living in L.A., it practically was.

"I put your phone messages with your mail," said Joel, pointing to a paper bag of envelopes. "Mostly Christmas cards and fan letters."

I'd left my PO box key with them, and they'd kindly collected everything.

"It's late," said Tina. "Take a hot bath and get in pajamas. There's a casserole in the oven and you've already spied dessert." She winked.

I sighed. "That sounds divine."

"It really is." She chuckled. "Chicken Divine!" She took Joel gently by the arm. "Come on, let's give Lori her space."

They bid me goodnight and strolled up the footpath to the main house. The Santa Ana winds blew gusts of warmth despite the twinkling Christmas lights strung to mimic icicles. I stood in the doorway breathing in the scent of desert and ocean, two natural rivals that met in perfect symmetry here. This magic land of make-believe come true. This California.

I thought of what Mother Abbess had said before I left. I knew she was right. I had a job to do. I slipped my hand into my pocket and found the soft edges of Ginny's postcard. Thinking of her in Paris made me smile. She was using her gifts for a purpose. It was time I got back to doing the same.

I closed the door and did as Tina suggested. I took a long, hot bath. Afterward, I hadn't the appetite for casserole, so I took the cookies to the couch. Leaving a trail of cinnamon-sugar crumbs, I casually sorted through the correspondences.

Joel was correct, it was mostly fan mail with some familiars. Marie had already sent a Christmas greeting. On the back flap she'd written *Missing you!* I fished out Mom and Dad's postcard: *Feliz Navidad para Tulum!* These epistles put me in the merry spirit. But then, the slanted script on an envelope caught my eye. It had no return address. I dragged my fingernail under the flap and opened it. It was from Tony.

The brown bag had more. Letter after letter. Dozens of them in his handwriting. The tears mounted, but I stifled them. Instead, I collected the letters and took them out to the brick firepit, where Joel had neatly stacked a pyramid of pine logs. I threw in a log and then four more. My day job might've been glamorous, but I aced Camp Bonfire 101. I tucked dried underbrush, twigs, and leaves in the crevices, struck a match, and blew it forward until the wood crackled and spit to embers. Then I took a seat in one of the Adirondack chairs. I wasn't going to run and hide anymore. I promised Mother Abbess I would act despite my fear. So I lifted the first sealed letter to the light and ripped the envelope open.

Tony repeatedly referred to my outstanding financial responsibilities and the contract we signed. He stamped out demands: *tell me where you are*; *you owe me*; *I must see you*. Most disturbing were Tony's declarations of love, which he claimed to have since our romantic encounter in Topanga. He wrote that we had a long-standing love affair. He was obviously delusional, but if taken as fact, these letters rewrote the reality of our history. All of the letters were signed with the initial T.

I thought about calling the police, but what would I tell them? There was nothing incriminating. No threats of bodily injury. No blackmail. Not a single expletive. The language was controlled, even reasonable. I did owe him money for neglecting my lease. I did sign a contract for him to manage my business deals. Nothing in the letters positively identified him, either. In singularity, a reader might overlook the cumulative madness. I worried the police would take Tony's side, and I hadn't the financial assets to pay my debt. The money from my two films had barely been enough to cover the checks I wrote.

I blamed myself for being imprudent. Some might argue that I'd led him on, left him with my financial obligations, and assaulted him when he came to see me at Nico's villa. Only I knew the truth. I never consented to any part of his abuse.

So I didn't call the police. I put all the letters in a manila folder and stowed them away. I took a sleeping pill. Old habits die hard. Everything in moderation, I told myself. Out of sight, out of mind. All the adages, all the reasons, all were partly true.

❁❁❁

We filmed *Murder on the Nile* in ten weeks. Italian American director John Guglielmo had the artistic drive of an Italian painter and the efficiency of an American banker. The production was by the book, efficient as a well-oiled clock. I presumed that kind of precision would be stifling but found myself thriving in the order. When shooting hours began, the actors and crew clocked in. When they ended, we clocked out. As simple as that. The set was secure. Everyone was professional from good morning to good night. I didn't have to worry about Tony showing up unexpectedly or the grips discussing me on a cigarette break. There wasn't a spare minute. John expected me on my cue with no excuses, which made me on my cue with no excuses. I was a better actor for it. More confident, too.

After principal photography wrapped, I came in once for postproduction, but the film needed little polishing. It was Agatha Christie's masterpiece with a few ditties and do-si-dos thrown in. The studio planned to release it in the UK sometime the following year and in the US after that, but no promotional tour was scheduled.

So, I was in a predestined lull when I got the call from Jordan, the producer I had met at Nico's Santa Monica house. He asked if I'd be interested in auditioning for the biography film *St. Francis's Fire.* Work was always welcome, especially when it came from a trusted source. I hadn't anything else lined up, and I hadn't found a new agent.

"I'd love to!" I said. "Should I read up on Saint Frances' writings?"

"I suppose you could, but you don't really fit the part of Saint Francis."

My heart sank. Why didn't I fit? Too Juliet demur? Too *Noises in the Night* risqué? This or that, and never enough.

"Brad Faulkner is already signed on," he explained. "This is Saint Fran-C-I-S of Assisi, not Saint Fran-C-E-S of Rome."

My face went hot. I hadn't known there were two saints, Francis and Frances. Who could've, if they'd never seen the names written out? The only distinguishing factor was a vowel. Same name, same God, same flesh and blood christened to sainthood through toil. But one was a man, and one was a woman.

"You'll audition for the role of Clare, a young aristocrat. She was so enamored with the mystic Saint Francis that she became a nun instead of marrying a count. The film chronicles the lifelong battle for her affection between the two men."

I understood Clare's yearning to be close to something otherworldly. That love transcended every other, but at what cost? While I didn't have two men fighting for my affections, I empathized with how awful it felt to disappoint people you loved. I used that feeling to propel me through the audition.

Before I left the room, they told me I got the part.

"I had a good feeling about you in this role," said Jordan. "Clare of Assisi is the *séducteur* and the Madonna."

There it was. The paradoxical female archetypes. Part compliment, part insult couched in a smile. I templed my palms and bowed like the woman I was to portray. That act of gratitude felt truer than words. I wanted to be Clare, and through her I was determined to disavow the stereotype of us both.

"We're shooting in Italy," he continued. "It's a tight turnaround, but we want to make use of the summer weather. The sets are almost finished being built. You're familiar with the Cinecittà Studios."

"Rome?"

It was a double-edged sword. When once it had been my place of refuge, now thoughts of Tony made me clench my fists. In a panic, I considered refusing for personal reasons, thereby declining the role. But Tony's letters were postmarked from the year before, and I hadn't received any since returning to L.A. *What if he finds me*? I thought. *What if he comes after me again?* Then I remembered what Mother Abbess had said about drifting in a sea of what-ifs. She was right, it was worse than death. I promised I wouldn't let fear keep me from acting, and I would make good on my word to her.

"I assure you, security is top priority," Jordan continued at my hesitation. "Nico shared a little about what you've been through . . . I want to put your mind at ease."

"Thank you," I said, more confident knowing I didn't have to hide.

Secrets have a way of shackling while truth gives strength to do the bold thing, the hard thing, the scary thing. That's the thing with lasting impact. It's stepping into your sovereign power. That's how I felt about Clare of Assisi.

"So, what do you think?"

"There's no part I feel more right for."

Lu

Media

The Abbey, Connecticut
October 1990

While I'm told that everyone is familiar with Jennifer Cockburn (aka Ginny Wilde), her attendance at this year's Women's Retreat is unexpected. The press had photographs of her fourth husband canoodling with a Las Vegas showgirl. The damning evidence of his two-timing was confirmed in a TV interview with the showgirl, who was now pregnant with his child. Within twelve hours of Ginny's arrival, the tabloids have every detail of the affair in print. Even Sally Jessy Raphael is saying, "Oh my God, can you believe Gin and Ren?" to her live studio audience.

Sister Evangelista has an old five-inch portable TV that gets five channels. *One for every inch,* she jokes. She insists it's for national emergencies and to watch the Pope when he makes appearances. That said, she and Sister Mary Clare are notably absent every day during the hour of *Guiding Light*. No judgment from me. We've all got secrets. It's only when those come to light that you ever understand . . . anything, really.

So, when Ginny and Aunt Lori say they're going on an evening stroll to see the newly constructed theater that Ginny helped fund, I join them. As if I would miss a minute . . .

"A Vegas showgirl—such a cliché!" Ginny exasperates. "Ren couldn't even have an original affair."

Ren is short for Henry Beatty, one of Hollywood's hottest up-and-coming actors and sixteen years younger than his celebrity wife, aka GW.

"It's like I'm in a scuzzy B movie!"

Ginny dramatically paces the amphitheater stage while we sit in two folding chairs, her captive audience. Aunt Lori says this is part of her kenosis and neither one of us is to interrupt.

"She's emptying her frustrations," Aunt Lori tells me under her breath.

Ginny sounds like a scorned woman in the rightful throes of scorning. I can barely blink. She's glorious, even in rage. I want to rage with her and all I know of Ren Beatty is that he plays a Don Juan bellhop on the TV show *Bed and Breakfast.* Art imitating life?

"The worst part is that I can't breathe a word of this to anyone," Ginny goes on. "Nobody told me there's a non-disclosure in our prenup! My own lawyer is in the old boys' club and agreed to it—pack of rats, all of them!" She kicks a fallen poplar leaf off the stage. "I know what the press will say. What happens in Vegas really does stay in Vegas. The irony isn't lost on me."

Ren and Ginny got married less than a year ago in a walk-in chapel on the Las Vegas strip.

"I guess, I hoped"—she pauses, turns her cheek away—"that we'd be different."

The stifled sob in her voice is so perfectly pitched, so poignantly delivered, so masterfully enunciated, that I feel myself choke up, too. I want to jump onto the stage to hold her. I want to battle Ren to the death. I want to do whatever it takes to make Ginny smile again. But before anyone can, she turns and stands to the fullness of her height, eyes blazing.

"The selfish prick!" She pulls a pack of cigarettes out of her denim pocket. Gently lifts one to her lips and fires the end with a lighter. She is amazingly talented.

"He never stops to think how his actions reflect on others," she continues, using the cigarette as a kind of enunciating pointer. "He's my *fourth* husband! People automatically assume it's my fault—I'm the spoiled fruit—even if all the facts say otherwise. It's men-rule-the-world bullshit."

At the expletive, Aunt Lori inhales long through her nose. The sound of it seems to resonate out the open theater into the woods beyond.

Ginny puts her palms up, cigarette dangling between her index and middle fingers. "Sorry, sorry."

Aunt Lori exhales with a sympathetic nod. "If Ren wants a divorce, give it to him."

I balk momentarily. Technically, Catholics don't believe in divorce. I guess it depends on the circumstance, the people, the interpretation, et cetera. Like so much else.

"Life is short," Aunt Lori continues. "Nobody remembers the details in the end. Just thank the Lord it didn't go on longer."

I can't tell if she means the affair, the marriage, or both.

Ginny takes a deep breath. She steps off the stage, still smoking her cigarette, and sits next to Aunt Lori. They lean into each other like one of those heart necklaces partitioned in two.

"Did you really think he was forever?" Aunt Lori asks.

"No." Ginny sighs. "But the story you tell yourself feels good."

Aunt Lori nods.

I do, too. This is real life. The off-the-record stuff isn't the public's business.

That's how most of Ginny's weekend visit goes. I leave my tape recorder in my room. No need to substantiate her realness. The truth is here. I'm living it.

The women laugh and reminisce, spend hours in the garden, and sing songs on evening walks. The guests and sisters rotate meal preparation. Cooking is considered a culinary art. I help Aunt Lori and Ginny make roasted chicken and vegetables, cacio e pepe pasta, and tiramisu for dessert. We eat family style.

When I visited with my parents, I never saw this lighthearted side of the sisters. I assumed that the solemnity I witnessed during Mass or the holy days was the everyday of their existence. I was wrong. Yes, there were hours of silent meditation, weeping, and tearing down. But there were just as many hours of music, laughter, and building up—the latter often being overlooked. History is written with a bloody knife, not a flower stem. It's the way of the world.

How Aunt Lori and Ginny found each other after years of estrangement is a prime example. There was no epic saga of reunion. Nothing that would even make a good teatime story. When it was officially announced that Aunt Lori had joined the monastic life, the media had a field day. The news spread from Los Angeles to New York and across the pond to France, where Ginny had just wrapped her breakout film with Shirley MacLaine. She'd immediately sent a letter to Aunt Lori at the abbey, and the rest, as they say, is history. The two reconnected and stayed connected.

"Past was past. We're so lucky to have found each other again. Simple as that. Ockham's razor," Aunt Lori says. "William of Ockham was a Franciscan friar and theologian, you know."

I didn't, and I yawn as I shake my head. It's now Monday, and we're up early to say goodbye to Ginny.

"I got to skedaddle before the media crew shows up. Flying monkeys will be unleashed if they see me." Ginny pulls me in for a hug, and my pulse gallops at the smell of her floral shampoo. "Your aunt has been telling me about you for years and you're just as she said. Perfect."

I am far from it but love that she thinks so.

She hugs Aunt Lori, and the women exchange kisses.

"Peace be with you," says Aunt Lori.

Ginny smiles. "Peace is in short supply where I'm headed."

"There is a time for peace and a time for war." Aunt Lori winks. "Ecclesiastes 3:8."

The two embrace one last time before Ginny gets into her car. She rolls down the window and waves. "Good luck with the interview today!"

Aunt Lori waves back. "Send me a postcard from San Francisco. I think this could be your best role yet!"

Ginny is shooting a film about a group of singing nuns. Whoopi Goldberg is a co-star.

Meantime, an NBC crew will be at the abbey any minute. They're running a Lucas Wesley movie marathon in honor of his birthday, November 8. The programming will culminate with a Prime-Time News Hour featuring close friends and fellow co-stars. Aunt Lori is the headliner interviewee.

Permissions were granted for one reporter and one videographer. News anchor Sadie Joric and her cameraman were dispatched. Media is not allowed to reveal the convent's sanctum spaces. Those are abbey rules and the sisters keep to them. So the outdoor amphitheater was suggested.

A nod to Aunt Lori's past, a peek into her present. The network ate it up.

"It's a beautiful spot," Aunt Lori told the production assistant on the phone, but I know it's more than that.

The theater gives her a buffer from the well-meaning ears of the sisters. Whenever Lucas Wesley comes up, his ghost enters the room. Her eyes dim. Is it sorrow? Regret? Longing? I can't say for certain, but I hope to suss it out before long.

Time's ticking. I've been here two weeks. My December deadline is approaching, and I still have to transcribe the tape recordings and notes into a coherent thesis. Even if Professor Proctor is willing to give me a pass on the occasional typo, Dr. Gibbons is out for blood. He expects every *i* dotted and *t* crossed. I may not give a flip about the academic system, but I want this to be my best effort for Aunt Lori and for everyone who played a role in her story.

Anchor Sadie Joric and her cameraman, Grady, set up exactly where Aunt Lori, Ginny, and I sat a couple of days prior.

"Can I mic you up?" Grady cautiously asks Aunt Lori.

"Feel free," she says. She lifts the collar of her wimple so he can clip on the microphone.

Aunt Lori sits across from Sadie, who is more dazzling in person than she appears on TV. She is a few years older than me, her cheeks smooth as a freckled egg. With a high forehead and perky lips, she could've been Aunt Lori's co-star in another decade. The best friend role: she gave off that spunky sidekick vibe.

"Are you comfortable? Do you need water before we start?" she asks.

"I should be asking you," Aunt Lori replies. "You're the guest."

"I've got to be honest with you. I'm a huge fan. I could barely sleep last night knowing I'd meet you today."

Aunt Lori grins kindly. "Underneath the habit, I'm just a person. And like you, thinking about this interview kept me up late, too."

She hadn't mentioned that. I take a step closer and see the lilac shadows under her eyes. My movement catches her attention. She beckons with a hand.

"Have you met my niece, Lu?" she asks Sadie. "She's here writing her History thesis for college."

Sadie turns, smiles electric-white teeth, and shakes my hand. "You're writing about the abbey?"

"About Mother Lori," I reply.

Sadie tilts her head with interest. "I always felt that history and journalism were rather synonymous. What do you think?"

Asking for my opinion: she's good at her job.

"Since both history and journalism have foundations in the study of primary sources, I suppose they could be interpreted as one and the same."

Sadie gives an impressed nod. "I'll have to keep my eye out for your work. Do you have a job lined up?"

I hadn't thought past getting my degree. "I'm not sure what my plan is after graduation."

"Well, when you figure it out, give me a call. I know some people."

Sadie hands me a business card from her pocket. It has the NBC rainbow peacock at the top. It doesn't bend easily. There's weight to the stock. It feels powerful.

Aunt Lori clears her throat. "Shall we?"

I step out of the camera frame. Grady gives a countdown with his fingers, then points to the red recording button. I push the same on my tape recorder. Hey, why not? Two birds with one stone.

SADIE:
What was it like working with Lucas Wesley?

LORI:
Pure joy. Lucas was the most genuine, kindhearted person. A true gentleman. My career wouldn't have taken the trajectory it did without him. My life, either.

SADIE:
Can you tell us about your favorite memory with Lucas?

LORI:
I couldn't pick one. There are too many. Every minute together filming in Italy. Every laugh we shared. Every kiss. Every everything. I look back in awe and gratitude that we had him in the world. Even for as short a time as we did.

SADIE:
So very short. Lucas was only twenty-five when he died. The circumstances of his accident continue to haunt fans across the globe.
(Silence.)
I'm sure his death is still very painful for you, being so close with him.

LORI:
(Nods.)

Only I can tell that her eyes have taken on the color of deep ocean water. The flesh around them has gone seashell pink.

SADIE:
(Clears throat and faces the camera for a tight shot.)
Lucas Wesley died in a car accident on Highway 1, near Castellammare, California, on Friday, September 13th, 1968, fueling rumors that the curve of the road there is cursed. Sources confirmed that Lucas had dinner at

> Wisteria Ristorante with friends, including you, Mother Lori. Forensics indicated that his AMC Marlin was speeding at the time that it careened off the road and hit a tree. Lucas was thrown from the car. There was speculation as to drug and alcohol use; however, the autopsy report found no evidence of drugs and only a small amount of alcohol in his system. Authorities all agreed that Lucas Wesley died of his injuries. Do I have that correct?

Sadie's doing her job: giving the audience the key points they need to understand the context of Aunt Lori's story. I get it. But in the moment, it feels like ripping open an old wound and watching it bleed. I want to turn off Sadie's tape. Turn off mine, too. The grief is too tangible.

Aunt Lori lifts a hand to wipe the corner of her eye. There's a tremor in it. Sadie sees it, too. She gestures to Grady.

"Let's pause a moment. I have a tickle in my throat. That water might be a good idea now."

She's lying, and I love her for it.

"I'll get it!"

There's a pitcher and paper cups set aside by Sister Candace. I pour two and return to find Aunt Lori storytelling off the record.

"We put a pony onstage for *Oklahoma!* but it started eating the waves-of-grain scenery. So Sister Evangelista gave it a heap of chamomile. Next thing we knew, it was snoring in the middle of the grand finale! A show-stopper. Literally."

It's a relief to hear Aunt Lori chuckling over kinder memories. I give them the water. Aunt Lori sips. Sadie gulps.

"Thanks, I was parched," she says.

Then, right as rain, they continue the interview with questions mindfully chosen to celebrate Lucas's life, work, and close ties with Aunt Lori.

An hour before Vespers, the NBC crew drives away and Aunt Lori suggests we take the long pathway back to the abbey instead of cutting through the meadow. It's one of my favorite views, especially at dusk. There's an ethereal haze over the wintering fields: the flutter of lady beetles, grasshoppers, boxelder bugs, and bees collecting food as fast as their wings can carry. The brittle chill in the shadows foretells the first frost on the way.

Aunt Lori takes my arm to steady her cloaked walk, and I'm grateful for the warmth of her. We don't speak for a little while, just amble and listen to the whirl of nature changing seasons. I'm working up the courage to ask the question Sadie could not.

"Were you in love with Lucas Wesley?"

She smiles, but it's a fragile thing. "The whole world was in love with him."

Part 8

Lori

Fortune's Fools

25

Rome to Los Angeles
1968

That summer was supposed to be rainier than usual, or so we were told by the old Italian farmers who sat outside their village homes watching the sky's steady spin.

Each night before I went to bed, I'd look out and remember the childhood rhyme: *Ring around the moon means rain soon.* Folks who grew up on North Carolina's farmlands understood that seeing the moon's halo meant we'd best pull in the dried tobacco or lose it to weather. Without fail and thousands of miles away, the proverb rang true. The rains came in bursts, waves, and then mists that crawled up from the ground and made everything sticky.

Despite the gloomy conditions, I felt better than I had in months, baptized by the water and revitalized by the work. We shot the *St. Francis's Fire* indoor scenes at Cinecittà Studios and the outdoor scenes in a village to the south of Assisi.

While the farmers were keen on predicting the weather for the season, the farmers' wives had their own brand of clairvoyance with a tighter forecast window: clotheslines. When wash hung out, the weather would be dry. That day, clothes across the village were put to lines before dawn, so director Mike Curtis had everyone up on a similar timetable to make good while the skies were fair. The sunshine hadn't lasted long. By afternoon, the winds had picked up, the dried laundry fluttered like parade flags as their owners pulled them in window after window. No sooner had their shutters clapped shut than we felt the first drops.

"Everyone, get inside!" Mike called. "It's about to come down!"

The camera people scrambled to protect their equipment. The extras took sanctuary within the parish church. The costume designer opened a large umbrella and led me to my trailer parked on the perimeter of the set. By the time we reached it, the downpour had turned the paths to mud. The hem of my costume was sopping.

He shook his head in despair. "Please, I take."

I stripped off the nun's habit and handed it over piece by piece. He inspected his workmanship for stains, pulled stitches and loose threads. I felt awful for not avoiding the puddles better.

"I clean for tomorrow," he said and left.

The rain cascaded over the tin trailer in a thousand thrumming fingers. There was little to do inside. I spent a lot of time alone on the *St. Francis's Fire* set, which I didn't mind so much. It allowed me to concentrate on becoming Clare of Assisi. The only book readily available in English was a prop Bible. So I casually thumbed through the stories I'd learned as a child. Along the way, I stumbled into ones that were *not* played out in Vacation Bible School puppetry. Like the heroine Jael, who put a tent stake through a sleeping general's head. And Deborah, a prophet judge who made her courtroom beneath a date tree. So much I hadn't known.

I tried talking about the religious context of our characters with Brad Faulkner under the assumption that portraying Saint Francis would evoke similar introspective questions. But he said he knew as much about the Bible as a Bible salesman—the paper, ink, price, and production. Interpretation was left to the user. He read it like he would any other self-help tome. I got the impression that I perplexed him. None of the philosophical layering was of concern to Brad. He was a dedicated character actor. He could morph into whatever form was necessary to play the part without it affecting his real person.

"The Method is all well and good for those who want to *be* the character," he told me just before he was to shoot the scene where Saint Francis receives the stigmata. "My aim is far less righteous. I act for the moviegoer who bought a ticket and expects a couple hours of entertainment."

When Mike said *Action!* Brad raised his corn syrup–bloody hands to the sky, glycerin tears streaming, and called on God to anoint him with the power to change the world for the greater Kingdom of Heaven.

It was magnificent.

When Mike called *Cut!*, Brad stood, wiped his face, and asked the cameraman if he knew the score of the Yankees game.

I never learned the art of turning on and off the emotional pipeline between myself and the characters I embodied. They were all one wellspring. While I was acting Clare, I had also become her in ways. Prior to visiting the abbey with Marie, visiting a church had felt like a virtuous deed one did, a kind of spiritual hygiene that showed you as a person of good standing in society. I go to church: I'm a good person. That was the prevailing sentiment where I grew up. But the older I got, the more I wanted to understand the underlying beliefs and relational qualities that made religion so alluring.

That day the storm muddied my habit, I'd just filmed the scene where Clare defied her parents' wishes that she marry a count and cut her hair off as a declaration that she would not be ruled by any man. She'd have only one lover, and his touch would be of the spirit, not of the flesh. The scene was interrupted by the rains.

So I sat alone in my trailer, emotionally suspended. The wheels of my mind churned on Clare's pronouncement. My pulse quickened at her impulsivity and wild longing for an alternative life. Freedom or ruination? It was a toss-up. And all for what? It had to be more than an infatuation with Francis of Assisi or Jesus of Nazareth. More than a prop Bible, too. I smoothed my hand over the leather cover. The book was meant to be a record. Evidence of God. Simple, complicated, and real as gravity. Clare of Assisi believed it and took radical action.

Belief is not all pixie dust, rainbows, and bursting into song. With it comes a strange sort of heaviness. The *what now* of the revelation. Real life out of frame. That's where I was in that hour. Out of frame in my own *what now* of the soul, when there came a knock on my trailer door.

My heart pounded. I was always afraid it would be Tony. But I'd been working in Italy for weeks without any incidents, and I wasn't about to let paranoia get a foothold. I figured that Mike had arranged for cars to drive us back to our *pensiones* in Terni. He wouldn't risk filming in these conditions. Someone could slip and get hurt. Replacing an actor was a director's worst nightmare, and the liability insurance was a producer's hell.

I cracked open the door against the pelting rain. Outside, a figure dressed in black made me inhale sharply. He lifted his hooded head with a smile.

"Lucas!" I launched myself into his wet arms. "What on earth!"

"Hello, Lovely," he said and half carried me back inside the trailer, closing the submarine-style door tightly and shaking off water like a happy puppy.

"Thank God for whoever invented the leather jacket." He laughed and took off his coat. "This thing saved my skin. I rode all the way from Rome on a Vespa. The skies were clear there."

I was ecstatic. Lucas was here!

"You must be soaked to the bone." I grabbed a towel from the trailer's bathroom and handed it to him.

"I could say I am, but I'd be lying. I only hit the end of the storm. It's headed the other way. Dry as a cracker until about five minutes ago." He ran the towel over his head. His dark hair sprang free and flopped casually over his forehead.

"Sit, sit, I'll make us something to drink. Is tea okay?"

"Whatever you got so long as it's hot."

I put on the electric kettle. The trailer was no more than four feet wide, so even with my back to him we were practically on top of each other.

"What are you doing in Italy?"

"I'm filming the musical *Casanova* in Rome."

He slid onto the pop-out dining bench and slung one arm around the back. I forgot how beautiful he was. His eyes were like blue skies. His smile, like sunshine. His voice, like the lark. How I'd missed my Romeo. Nostalgia is a powerful force. Suddenly, we were back at the beginning with no emotional baggage, fame, or failure. All my fears and *what-ifs* burned away in his presence. The effortlessness of *us* was intoxicating. I was unprepared for the swell of emotions, the love I felt.

"I got here yesterday," he went on. "I'm off my rocker with jet lag. It's my first time back in Europe since *Romeo & Juliet.* We don't start shooting *Casanova* until Friday."

"How did you know where to find me?"

"I called the number you sent me, and your landlady—Tina?—told me you were in Rome filming with Mike Curtis. Sweet lady, she didn't believe who I was at first. Wouldn't tell me a thing until I sang her a song. Afterward, all she kept saying was *Joel, it's Lucas Wesley! Lucas Wesley!*"

"They're such good people. You'd really like them."

"I already do. Tina made me promise to come for Sunday supper the next time I'm in L.A."

"Sounds about right."

"From there it was relatively easy to find you. I just had to bribe a few crew members, steal a Vespa, sneak off the set, and battle a rainstorm. All worth it."

"Good Lord! You practically sold your soul to the devil," I teased.

"And I would've, had he offered to spare me the rainstorm."

"I wouldn't have let you do that. Here." I handed him a cup. "It's aster tea. The sisters showed me how to make it."

"*Sisters*? I thought you only had one."

"Not Marie. The sisters at the abbey in Connecticut."

His eyes went wide.

I waved my hand. "It's a long story."

"The Method, I got you." He grinned. "I may not be a graduate of the Actors Studio, but I know thespian-y things."

He patted the bench beside him for me to sit. Our knees knocked, as familiar as ever. The last time we'd seen each other was at the vineyard in Topanga, and we'd parted on strained terms. He'd been right in his intuitions about Tony, but that didn't make following my own wrong. Life is about choices. Right or wrong, the point is who you become in light of the choices you make.

Lucas gave me the highlight reel of his last year. There were moments when he paused mid-thought, and I knew there was more to the story. He was editing and rearranging, adding details for flourish and subtracting ones too dull, or too painful, to recount. He was telling the past the way he wanted it remembered. I did the same, omitting Tony.

It wasn't that we were hiding anything. Hiding is a form of entrapment, while selective sharing is liberating. Some might argue they are two sides of the same coin. But here's how I saw it: I could not control any of the terrible events that had transpired, but I would not let them define me. Tony would not be the star of my highlight reel.

After we'd drunk our tea and laughed our bellies to sloshing, we noticed that the rain had quieted.

"What do you say?" asked Lucas. "Wanna hop on the Vespa and go for a ride? I can take you back to your hotel while the weather holds off."

I pulled on my jacket before he'd finished his sentence. "Only if we can grab something to eat on the way."

"Deal."

I waved to the assistant director across the lot. "I'm going back to Terni—I got a ride!" I pointed to Lucas as the AD's mouth dropped open.

Before the rest of the cast and crew had a chance to circle, we jumped onto the Vespa. Lucas revved the engine. I wrapped my arms around his waist. The leather of his jacket was slick and cool against my cheek. Off we went! The vibration and speed of our twosome made us feel invincible.

We picked up salty prosciutto, pecorino cheese, jarred mushrooms, and a bottle of Frascati wine at a *pizzicheria* shop. A quarter of a mile from my hotel, the sky cracked open again. We were drenched and tipsy on lost inhibition by the time he parked the Vespa. Instead of rushing out of the storm, I took his hand and chasséd into a turn. My feet slipped on the cobblestones. He pulled me close to keep me from falling and attempted to sing the opening lyrics of "Lovely You."

"I would kill and die . . ." He choked on the rainwater. "I just might! Gene Kelly made this look easy."

"*Singin' in the Rain* was filmed with a sprinkler system. Totally fake!" I reminded him.

We threw back our heads, faces to the cloudburst, daring the heavens to drown us. Good Italian food, however, could not perish as such.

"The prosciutto is getting wet!"

"Save the prosciutto!"

The grocer's paper bag had turned to mush. We salvaged the goods and sprinted for the hotel.

With hearts racing and water squishing inside our shoes, we giggled our way through the lobby. The husband-and-wife owners side-eyed each other.

Inside my room, the dampness quickly settled under my skin. Waves of shivers made my teeth chatter. I changed into a robe.

"You can't stay like that. You'll get sick," I told Lucas. "Put your wet things on the radiator to dry."

I didn't have a second robe to offer so I handed him a blanket. Even after being romantically involved both on- and off-screen, Lucas had a shy side that not many people knew. He went into the en suite to change and returned wrapped like a cannoli. We nestled together on the room's settee. A glass of wine helped the heat return to my cheeks, but the edges of Lucas's lips remained violet. I couldn't look away from them or him.

"I was always cold on set," I said. "Remember how thin those modesty coverings were?"

"Yeah. They weren't much. I worried we might accidentally slip into, y'know, doing it."

"Sometimes I imagined we were." My tongue was a loose pinwheel, thoughts unbridled. "That was the closest I'd ever come."

A bolt of memory: his body on mine, the white fabric draped about, the Italian breeze sweeping through the room with the scent of wisteria. So soft, so sweet. Full of unmet desire. We were Romeo and Juliet. Just like the film. Only we weren't. We were Lucas and Lori.

This was our chance to reclaim a moment.

Lucas leaned forward or I leaned forward, I can't remember. We kissed, but it wasn't like our prior kisses. It was messy and wild and long of countless seconds. My wet hair splayed across our faces. His lips pulled mine to aching. He laughed and kissed my nose.

"Lori," he whispered with a musical lilt.

A request, a question, a calling.

I answered by undoing my robe and then his blanket. This time, I pulled him directly to me, skin to skin. The softness I remembered. The boldness I forgot.

"Make love to me," I whispered.

And when he did, I felt the sting of tears. Pain ebbed slowly, turning inward on itself like a rolling wave, and resurfacing as pleasure. Chills rose up under my fingertips. I clasped him tighter. I wanted my fever to make him warm. I wanted us to be borne away to that place that knows no bounds. Love without fear or judgment or ownership. Two people. Simple. Complicated. Holy unto itself.

❁❁❁

We made love three times but even then, Lucas was restless. He hadn't expected to stay the night so he hadn't brought his sleeping pills and I had none to offer. I'd been off them since visiting the abbey.

So he tucked the sheet over my shoulder in the dark. "I'll be back."

I awoke hours later to the scent of bread and his return.

"G'morning, Lovely! The rain stopped." He pushed aside the drapes and opened the balcony door to a swath of buttered light.

"Where'd you go?" I yawned.

"If you can believe, I ran into a shepherd."

"A shepherd?"

"He was the only one awake, too. He told me to go to the Rovina La Roccaccia, the ancient ruins. It was like a fairy tale! Are there fairies in Italy? You've got to check it out."

He was whirling with energy. I dared not ask the source. Instead, I pointed to the bag he carried. "Was the shepherd also a baker?"

He pulled out two cornetti, set them on the balcony table, and licked the flakes from his fingers. "I got these on the way back. First ones out of the oven. Had to wait for the *panetteria* to open."

My belly grumbled. We'd eaten the prosciutto and cheese at midnight, but it hadn't sated my hunger. My head throbbed slightly from the wine. My lips were swollen, my body tender. The sensations prickled with all the best of life. I stretched my toes toward Lucas, bare feet outside the sheet.

"I asked the landlady where I might pick up coffees," he went on. "She offered to bring cappuccinos to the room. I thanked her, but then wasn't sure if you were comfortable . . ." He looked away bashfully and scratched the back of his neck.

Chivalrous to a fault. What he was really asking was *Are you okay?*

I rose, letting the morning light bathe me before pulling on my robe.

"I couldn't wish for anything more. Cappuccinos, pastries, and you."

I wrapped my arms around his waist, and I tilted my face up so our gazes met.

"Thank you."

He smiled in understanding.

The intimacy we'd share was ours to define. There was freeness in that kind of love. No shame. No burden to make ourselves what we weren't. No compulsion to explain our actions to the world. We were best friends. We were lovers. We were something I'd never known in life and never would again.

The landlady knocked. "*Buongiorno, caffè* drinking?"

I let her in, and she set the cappuccinos on the table, and then paused with bated breath. We did the same. I should've asked if overnight guests were permitted. I didn't want to disrespect.

Instead of admonishment, she exclaimed, "*Amo Romeo e Giulietta!*"

She clutched her chest. "*Molto bello! Ho pianto tanto.*" She hummed the film's theme song and danced her hands in the air like a conductor.

On her cue, Lucas sang the chorus of "Lovely You." She gave a mouse shriek. Tears sprang to her eyes. He kissed her cheek after the final lyric. I thought the poor woman might faint on the spot.

"*Bellissimo, grazie, benedizioni.*" Beautiful, thank you, bless you.

She excused herself still clutching her heart.

I learned in that moment that people will surprise you with kindness, if you let them.

Lucas and I sat on the balcony dipping our pastries into milky cappuccinos, filling up on each other's company. We knew it couldn't last.

A dove perched nearby, aroused by the smell of our simple feast. The storm clouds of yesterday were nowhere to be seen. The sky was as blue as the ocean turned upside down. The daylight grew bolder. The village below awakened. A man pushing a wheelbarrow of melons clattered down the lane. Two children in uniforms skipped into the schoolhouse holding hands. A young woman on a bike called *Buongiorno, Gianni!* to a young man in the *mercato* who waved back with a tomato in his hand. *Buongiorno, Sofia!*

I could live a hundred years and never know a morning so perfect. Even in the moment, hearing the dove coo, I longed to relive the moment. Because I knew it was impossible to hold on to. With each breath, time turned on the axis. Like sea surf and rainbows and first love, the most precious prizes of human existence are ephemeral, then gone forever.

Terni's Church of St. Francis chimed the new hour. Lucas swept the last crumbs of our croissants over the balcony. The dove gave chase. Its moment had come.

"I better get back before folks get crazy. The director's probably called the *carabinieri*. He's a real nervous Nellie."

"I can't blame him. You're America's biggest star . . . jet-lagged . . . in a country where you don't speak the language . . . on a stolen Vespa!"

"Borrowed. I'm bringing it back."

I sighed. "I'm due on set in an hour, too."

We had to finish the scene interrupted by yesterday's rain.

Lucas slung his leather jacket over his shoulder with one hand and then pulled my chin gently to him with the other. "No regrets?"

"No regrets."

He kissed me long in goodbye, tasting of sweet milk and coffee.

"I'll see you soon. I'm headed to L.A. after we finish filming. House-hunting!"

"You're moving to L.A.?"

My heart practically leaped out of my chest.

"Uncle Tim thinks it'd be smart to have my own place so I don't have to stay at the hotel. The paps know every Peeping Tom–hole at the Miramar Hotel. Truthfully, I've never been crazy about the town, but if *you're* there . . ." He winked. "I'll call you as soon as I'm back."

"You might beat me. With all these weather delays, this film is taking twice as long to shoot. You know how it is—a game of hurry up and wait. Some days you're the tortoise and other days, the hare."

"I guess we're old hands now. Let's try not to let it ruin us, eh?" He gave that rakish grin I first saw in the ICA audition room. "Be safe, Lovely you."

"Same, lovely you."

Shorthand for what we felt but weren't brave enough to say: *I love you.*

26

We wrapped principal photography when the sparrows began to hop like popcorn across the freshly threshed wheat fields. A telltale sign of winter's approach. They saw from afar what we could not from the still-warm Lazio valley.

I flew back to Los Angeles. En route, I became violently ill and blamed the salmon served over Indiana. I wobbled off the plane and vomited in the closest trash can. The taxi driver who drove me home skittishly eyed me through the rearview mirror. I imagined I looked as putrid as I felt. I went straight to bed. A week later, I was still there.

Every time I got up, the room spun. The only thing that helped was to lie very still with a cold cloth over my eyes. Any pronounced sensation was accosting: the pungency of garden sage, the brightness of car headlights, the roughness of my hair against the back of my neck, the sound of Corky barking at a squirrel. My stomach would turn and my head with it, and back to the bowl I'd dive.

"Is it the flu? I always catch a bug when I travel," said Tina.

She and Joel came down with an aluminum-foiled lasagna. The gamy smell of the meat put me over the edge. Tina held my hair back while I dry-heaved.

"Food poisoning wouldn't last this long." She laid the back of her hand to my cheek. "No fever. Are you in pain, dear?"

I sat up, wiped my mouth, and shook my head. "Just queasy."

"Maybe it's a migraine," said Joel. "That's how mine go."

Tina furrowed her brow. "Or a bacterial infection."

Joel nodded. "Should we take her to the emergency room?"

"Noooo," I said.

The last thing I needed was the paparazzi splashing my green face across the headlines with exaggerated theories as to the state of my health. For actresses, rumors of being anything less than bright-eyed and bushy-tailed could shut doors forever.

Tina rubbed my back. "If you're not feeling better soon, we'll call our primary care guy. You might need antibiotics."

"Okay," I promised.

The next morning, Dawn brought me scones from the Sisters of St. Joseph. I told her to thank them for me, but the swaying didn't abate. Maybe Tina was right and this was something more serious. A migraine, an infection, parasites, cancer . . . The list of ways a body could go wonky was endless.

So that Monday, I went to the Westwood walk-in clinic. Tina and Joel were off to Santa Clarita to meet a wine merchant. I didn't want to make a fuss out of it like I knew they would. So I called Dawn. She picked me up within the hour and sat in the waiting room crocheting yarn loops.

The doctor was an older gentleman with softly wrinkled hands. Quirky in an endearing way, he wore penny loafers with actual pennies in them. He listened to my heart, checked my blood pressure, shone a light into my eyes and ears and down my throat. Then he asked me to pee in a cup and give it to the nurse. He'd be back in a moment with his diagnosis.

The wait felt interminable. The overhead fluorescent lights were stingingly bright and there was a pungent fruity smell trapped in the room with me. Hand soap or something spoiling in the trash. Every minute I counted my breaths and prayed for him to return before my nausea did.

When the door handle finally turned, I exhaled. "Thank God."

"I'm sorry for the delay," he apologized. "People don't like to spend their weekends at the doctor's—no matter how sick they are. Mondays are chaotic." He cleared his throat and flipped the page on my chart. "Good news. Everything looks normal. You don't need antibiotics. Just a good multivitamin."

"Oh?" As easy as that?

He scribbled on his Rx pad. "Yes, a prenatal."

The room did a cartwheel, and I vomited on his shiny pennies.

❃❃❃

As children, girls are encouraged to play make-believe house. The practice is deemed infantile in pubescence, even sinful if we engage a male playmate, but then firmly demanded in adulthood. A frustrating seesaw I never got on.

I was not one of those girls who dreamed of being a mother. I never wanted Marie's hand-me-down baby dolls. Never portrayed a mother in a film, either. And despite all the erotic scenes I *had* portrayed, the biological repercussions remained firmly off camera. Rarely was a pregnant woman part of the narrative. In effect, pregnancy was practically nonexistent in film.

In real life, sex was similarly taboo. One of Marie's schoolmates got a copy of *How to Have a Love Affair*: *A Guide to Sex for the Girl Who Says "Yes!"* and passed it around their friend circle. Each girl underlined and wrote comments in the margins. Marie kept the book under her mattress, and when she was out one afternoon I fished it from its hiding place. The author gave advice such as not to shower at a lover's apartment unless one was ready to be "seduced" and to let him handle taxi drivers and waiters. When it came to birth control, the calendar method was recommended. Procuring other forms of contraception might harm an unmarried woman's reputation. She was not to mention them to her lover, however, as it was a sure-fire way to kill the mood. Marie's friends had underlined these rules. With Lucas, it had flickered through my mind, but the math of ovulation was hard to do in the heat of the moment.

"I'm knocked up," I told Dawn in the car.

The strain of vomiting made my eyes bloodshot and burn. My clammy hands clutched the doctor's prescription.

Dawn silently stared at the brake lights of the car in front of us. The traffic across Wilshire Boulevard was at a standstill.

"I worried that might be it," she said. "I saw the signs."

"This shouldn't be happening. I keep a calendar or . . . I did."

I tried to count back the weeks since my last cycle, but between travel, time zone changes, sleep deprivation, days on set, days in bed . . . What month was it now?

Dawn pushed her hair back so that it feathered with the tracks of her fingers. "Promise not to think badly of me?"

Think badly of her? *I* was the one in trouble.

"Before I met you on *Noises in the Night*, I was in a similar situation." A quiver in her lip. She bit it back. "I was with this actor." She blew her bangs and rolled her eyes. "He broke up with me and went back to Idaho to marry his high school sweetheart."

"You never mentioned him."

"It had all just happened when we met. I was your hair and makeup stylist. I had a job to do, and I wanted to keep doing it."

It was hard to remember when we first met. The present us eclipsed the past. She hadn't appeared pregnant on set but, to borrow from Aesop, *Appearances are often deceiving.*

"What happened?"

"A baby out of wedlock would've been a nuclear bomb to my family, my career, my church . . ." She gripped the steering wheel tighter. "I went to Tijuana. There's a surgeon who has a clinic. He's discreet and very kind. He helps a lot of the girls around here."

The song ended and the radio crackled with the disc jockey's next play. The traffic crawled forward.

"To be clear, we're talking about an abortion." I didn't want code language.

She turned to me, long enough to meet my stare. "We are."

There were so many things and people to consider. So many future ramifications. The choice I made would be the past I looked back on. I needed to think.

"God." I exhaled aloud. "What am I going to do?"

"How far along did the doctor say you are?"

"He didn't."

"We can do the math. It's basic biology. Do you know when you might've conceived?"

I nodded. "In Italy."

"Good on you, an Italian *amore*." Dawn cracked a smile, attempting to lighten the mood. "So, you're still in the first trimester—that's the cutoff."

"Okay," I said.

"Whatever you decide. I'm here." She squeezed my hand reassuringly and didn't ask about the father. I was grateful.

I didn't regret being with Lucas. I loved him. What we did was the definition of making love, and the sisters had shown me that God is love. So it couldn't be wrong. That was the only truth I knew for certain.

27

Hey, Lovely you," Lucas said a few days later. The echo of the phone amplified his silvery tenor.

Dawn had gone to the grocery store to buy me ginger ale, crackers, tinned Vienna sausages, and prenatal multivitamins. She picked up a copy of the daily tabloid when she saw Lucas on the cover with the actress Skylar Wood, his co-star in *Casanova*. Lucas had been photographed with dozens of speculated love interests, including me. It was good press to promote films. Audiences wanted to believe that the chemistry they saw on-screen was happening off-screen as well. They wanted the magic to be real. So, while the headline read "Is Skylar Wood Lucas's New Love?," I knew enough not to believe a word except for the fact that he was in Los Angeles. I was anticipating his call.

"Hey, lovely you," I answered.

"I'm in L.A."

"I saw. The paparazzi have a flip-book of your every move."

"Don't I know it. I can't scratch my keister without a camera up it."

I laughed, and it jostled the quiet thing growing inside me. Before I knew it was there, all I had felt was indigestion. After, I couldn't stop envisioning tiny feet and hands. Impossible, it was too early. According to the fetal fruit chart in the doctor's office, it was barely the size of a strawberry. Yet here I was, talking to its biological father and feeling tiny *thumps* like bubbles rising. Was I imagining it? Was it real? Only God knew.

"So how about I pick you up and we grab dinner?" Lucas asked.

"Fried chicken?"

Our first meal together at his flat in London.

"I was hoping to up the ante this time. Something . . . romantic."

It warmed me. Despite all the acclaim, coronation as Sing King and Romeo to the world, Lucas retained his polite, country boy manners. Even with me.

"Are you asking me on a date, Lucas Wesley?"

He hemmed and hawed, and then confidently said, "Yeah. You're a good girl so I want to treat you good."

It undid me. Was I . . . a good girl? I was secretly carrying his child. I had to tell him, but I didn't want to tell him. It would change everything. It would change us. He'd ask me to marry him. That was what nice Southern boys like him were raised to do. I would decline. I couldn't take marriage vows just to be a good girl. But I couldn't enter motherhood for that reason, either. Love is a choice. But how can love be love when all choices lead to heartbreak?

"Tomorrow night, I'll pick you up?" he went on.

"Okay," I said.

"G'night, g'night, parting is such sweet sorrow."

A lump in my throat kept me from speaking. I looked down at my belly. I could pretend for now, but our course was as inevitable as Romeo and Juliet's. I swallowed hard.

"I'll say goodnight till it be morrow."

❁❁❁

It was a balmy September Friday. The Santa Anas blew helter-skelter, so I wore a fuchsia A-line dress that stayed put against the winds and gave my midsection room to breathe. Kitten heels on my feet and my hair in a French twist. I wanted to feel pretty. Not for a camera, a director, or even Lucas, but for me. A kind of ritualistic preparation that helped set my resolve. I hadn't made up my mind if I wanted to keep the baby or not, but I would tell Lucas.

Just as the first glimmers of twilight pinked the sky, he pulled up in a polished blue AMC Marlin with the windows rolled down.

"Hello, Lovely," he greeted.

After parking the car, he came round with a nervous energy that could've just as well been my own.

"New car?"

"You like?" He grinned and took my hand, gently weaving his fingers through mine. "I missed you. Did you miss me?"

"You know I did."

He pulled me tenderly to him in a kiss. My chest tightened with the breathless force of his lips on mine. I put my hands on his chest, and he wrapped his arms around me. Time elongated and retracted, like a moonbeam. God, I loved him. If only we could be suspended as we were, frozen in time.

He pulled back reluctantly and eyed his watch. "We're going to be late. I made reservations at Wisteria Ristorante."

"Wisteria?"

It was one of the most-celebrated restaurants in Malibu. I had never been, but I'd seen it featured in enough magazines to feel like I had. The Who's Who of L.A. were photographed dining al fresco against the scenic coastline. It looked like something out of a movie. It looked like Italy.

On the drive there, Lucas's new song, "Heartbreak Rock," came on, and he thrummed the blue steering wheel. "What do you think?"

"Another hit." Truthfully, I was too preoccupied with my own roving thoughts to listen. The chorus lyrics were stabbing: *There's only one to whom I'll be true. But you'll break my heart, baby, you'll break my heart soooo how can I . . .*

"Uncle Tim is putting together a big show for the new record. Planning to do a holiday tour in November. Always a good sales bump for albums."

November. I'd be in my second trimester by then. I doubted that was the kind of bump he'd welcome in the middle of a big tour.

"Have you ever been to Las Vegas?" Lucas continued.

"No."

"You'll love it." He winked. "Always more fun to have your girlfriend on the tour bus."

My earlobes went hot. "Is that what I am—your girlfriend?"

"Naw, you're more than that."

A car came around Highway 1's curve too fast and Lucas swerved. The motion caused my stomach to drop. Nausea set in. The sight of the serpentine road brought a sour taste up the back of my throat.

"You okay, Lovely? Looking green around the gills."

"It's just . . ." I closed my eyes and inhaled. *One-Mississippi, two-Mississippi, three-Mississippi*. Exhale. "My stomach."

"I got Dramamine if you want. It helps me stay calm. Works for motion sickness, too."

I was willing to take anything to keep from vomiting in his new car.

"Okay," I said.

He popped open the glove compartment. Inside was a pharmacy of prescription pills. I rooted through it, reading the labels until I came to the Dramamine. I swallowed it back without water and prayed for it to go to work quickly.

By the time we parked in Wisteria's back lot, my prayers were answered. The nausea had abated. A strange placidity swept me along and made telling Lucas feel less like scaling a castle wall. A very good thing given the onslaught of sharp-shooting cameras that met us on the sidewalk.

Lucas took my hand. "I've got you."

Through the haze of camera flashes, I saw the subject of their frenzied attention: Lucas's co-star, Skylar Wood, and her boyfriend Paolo Mazzola, an Italian football player, posed at the restaurant's entrance.

Seeing our approach, the paparazzi turned.

"Look, Lucas and Lori!" said one.

"Are the world's greatest lovers back together?" asked another.

"Kiss! Come on, kiss!"

Instead of giving them their shot as we had during publicity junkets, Lucas put a hand up to block the lenses.

"Come on, we're here to meet friends for dinner. Can't a guy have a normal date night?"

"So, you *are* dating again!" The crowd buzzed. "Lori and Lucas reunited!"

But all I heard was *We're here to meet friends.*

"I thought it'd be just the two of us," I whispered.

"Figured it was a good way to put rumors to bed. Skylar's a great girl but . . . there's only one Lovely for me. You don't mind, do you?"

I couldn't fault him. His intentions were honorable. But I had other plans for tonight. What I had to tell him couldn't wait.

"I'd hoped for some alone time is all."

"Oh, we will—after." He nestled his lips into the side of my neck. Goose bumps spilled down my back.

The cameras swung: *flash-flash, flash-flash.* The flares burned my eyes. I shielded myself under Luca's arm, constricting tighter and tighter until I imagined myself as small as the knot in my belly.

The doorman did his best to usher us inside unscathed, but he was no match for the encroaching paparazzi. Lucas flagged down the maître d', who came to our aid.

"*Scuse, scuse,*" he said, knocking cameras to the floor.

Finally inside, he shook his head and apologetically took my hand. "*Mi scusi, bella.* We call them the *pazzo-gazzi*—crazy boys." He grimaced. "Please, come with me. It's safe now."

He led us through the packed restaurant. On the way, introductions were made.

"Hi, I'm Skylar, and this is Paolo."

"Nice to meet you both, I'm Lori."

Skylar giggled. "You don't need to tell me who you are. I know! *Romeo & Juliet, The Musical* is my favorite film ever! I'm a huge fan. I was so excited to meet you tonight, Paolo had to give me a roadie just to calm down." She held up a little tin flask.

Four years younger than me, she was part of the next wave of fresh eighteen-year-olds Ginny had spoken of at my first audition. She was young and impressionable, and I knew exactly how that felt. I liked her for being transparent, and I also felt protective. So I took her by the arm like a big sister.

"*Shh*, put that in your purse or you'll have the paps reporting that you're a wild child of ill repute."

"Ill repute," she giggled. "That's so Juliet!"

The maître d' led us to a private table on the terrace, strung with overhead fairy lights under a pergola of grapevines.

Waiters came directly with cocktails.

"A welcoming drink. Negronis on the house. My apologies for that crazy bunch at the door," said the maître d'.

He didn't ask for anyone's ID, simply placed the drinks in the center of the table and left. I winced when Skylar took a glass but wasn't about to chastise her. I had my own sins. We raised our cups to friends and lovers and Italy that brought us all together.

Dinner was served family style off big platters: Caesar salad, angel hair pasta in tomato sauce, veal scaloppine studded with bright lemons, plus another round of complimentary drinks. I passed on the second Negroni. The first had been intensified by the Dramamine. The worries at the forefront of my mind slipped to the back and nearly vanished by the time the cannoli were served. It felt good to forget the secret growing inside me, if only for a few hours.

We stayed at the table telling stories of Italian escapades until we were the only people left in Wisteria. A little after midnight, my yawns chased me down. I could barely keep my eyes open.

"I'll call a cab," offered the maître d'.

So as not to overstay our welcome, we waited outside while the tired kitchen staff did a last sweep of the restaurant and went home. The sidewalk was empty. The only flashes came from the constellations above reminding me that the earth was a giant marble rolling through the universe. One Negroni had made me languid and philosophical.

Two, and a flask of whatever she'd come carrying, had been too much for Skylar. She leaned into Paolo's embrace with eyes half-hooded. He was no better, and I suspected they'd shared potions.

The taxi pulled up.

Skylar and Paolo twined each other like overcooked noodles. We helped them into the cab, but when I slid in beside them, Lucas gave me a funny look.

"I can't leave my new car here," he said. "It isn't safe."

It was true. Car theft in Los Angeles was as common as sunburns.

I got out of the cab.

"Coming or going?" asked the cabbie. It was late and he had little patience for passengers dithering away the minutes.

"Going," Skylar mumbled from her slump. "Surfrider Hotel."

I shut the door and the taxi took off down the road.

In the silence, I turned to Lucas. "So, what do you want to do?"

"I can drive us."

I gave him a dubious look. He'd had two Negronis and shared a bottle of wine with Paolo. Lucas could hold his own, but I wasn't keen on him behind the wheel. I'd only had the one and that'd been at the beginning of our meal hours before.

"How about I drive?"

He smirked. "I think this is your way of testing out my new car."

No, it was my way of getting his undivided attention.

The last time I'd driven was the summer I left North Carolina. I'd never had the time to get an official license, but I'd been driving my dad's flatbed truck since I was fifteen. The Marlin was a sporty baby blue with matching plush interior. A definite upgrade. We got in and the car purred new and jumpy as a kitten.

"This is nice," I said.

"Have it!" he said.

"I like your car, but I can buy my own."

"I know you can, but what's mine is yours."

I laughed. "See now, this is why I'm driving. Me thinkest thou has had one too many-eth, Romeo."

He pulled me close and kissed me. My heart raced. My hand went to his chest, drawn to the skin-to-skin memory of his heart beating in time.

"Your place?" he whispered.

It was on my mind, too. We wanted to be together—to make love the way we had the first time, the last time we'd seen each other. But how could we with this secret between us? It felt like a betrayal. If I pushed him away without explanation, he would think I cared less for him. The only solution was to tell him about the baby, and I had the twenty-minute drive home to do it.

I took a deep breath and we started south on Highway 1. While I drove, Lucas hummed to a slow ballad on the radio. He rolled down his window to let in the ocean breeze. The beach was empty, and the clear night gave a magical view of the sea rippling out to places unseen.

"Lucas . . ." I cleared my throat and knuckled the steering wheel. "I need to talk to you about something."

"*Mm-hmm?*"

He leaned his head slightly out the window so that the wind ruffled his curly brown hair. His sleepy blue eyes shimmered like a waning moon. He never looked more beautiful. It was impossible to love someone more than I did in that moment. And suddenly, I thought, *Why not?* Why not make a go of being a family? A child was a better reason than many. Far better than a reckless union by a friar with a plan. People longed for children. Look at Marie and Bill. They'd been trying to conceive for years. So maybe I was meant to come back to work and love Lucas and create this new, amazing thing together. Maybe this was God's plan as Mother Abbess had divined. A marriage and child would mean sacrifice, but didn't all great things come by suffering?

At my pause, Lucas smiled, took my right hand off the steering wheel, and kissed it.

"What is it, Lovely?"

I didn't know how best to say it. I caught a glimpse of myself in the rearview mirror. My face was ashen and my pupils dilated too large. I looked like a deer in headlights. I felt similarly.

So, I closed my eyes, only for a moment, to collect courage.

"I'm pregnant. With your baby."

Then I turned to him and saw the shock-turned-joy spread like blue starlight across his face.

What neither of us saw was the husk of a fallen palm frond caught on the wind. It thwacked the windshield suddenly, and I jerked the steering wheel. The car torqued. I slammed on the brakes, sending us into a tailspin. My body was thrown against the steering wheel, which anchored me to the car and saved my life. We weren't wearing seat belts. On impact, there was a sharp squeal of metal followed by a burst of silver sand that filled my throat and burned my vision. Everything came to a stop. My ears rang pitchy. Smoke crawled in ghoulish shades of violet. Gasoline and engine oil. The car had wrapped around a sycamore tree with the back wheels precariously teetering over the ravine.

"We've got to get out," I croaked. My throat was sandpaper raw.

I turned to Lucas, but all that remained was the crumpled metal frame of the rolled-down window. I climbed over the seat covered in silver soot, filaments from the interior pulled apart on impact.

Outside, the winds brought the sobering salt of the ocean. That's when I saw him, body twisted unnaturally with arms and legs outstretched like a star.

"Lucas!"

I crawled to his side. His breath was labored but his eyes met mine.

I took his hand. "I'm here . . ."

"We're having a baby," he whispered.

I nodded and started to cry.

"Lovely." He smiled briefly before choking for air.

I feared moving him would cause more injury and pain. So I lay by his side, my eyes inches from his, my body close enough for warmth.

"Someone will come. Any minute," I assured him. "We'll get you to a hospital and they'll take care of you."

But a minute passed and then another. The night seemed darker than ever. I saw no more stars. The expansive nothingness was above, the hard dirt below, and we two trapped between.

I checked his breath, held his hand, and willed my pulse to be his.

"Sing to me?" he asked after a time.

Music was his balm.

"*I would . . .*" My voice gave out. So I spoke the words as best I could. "Just to hold you by my side, let the sun and moon collide, all for my lovely . . ."

I stopped to bite back the sob. Words fail in times like that. He knew the ones on my heart.

"I love you," he whispered.

"I love you." I kissed him.

Then he closed his eyes and was gone.

Lu

Forbidden Fruit

The Abbey, Connecticut
October 1990

"Oh my God." It slips out without my meaning to.

I turn off the tape recorder.

Aunt Lori was driving the car in the accident that killed Lucas. Not to mention that she was pregnant! Or had been. Those were the facts. But I'd never read either of those in the accident reports. The tabloids would've had a field day! I have so many questions—off the record.

Before we can continue, the telephone in Aunt Lori's office rings. I startle and drop my pen. I'm on edge, protective of Aunt Lori and her secrets.

She leans down to retrieve the pen and hands it back to me. For once, I can't read her expression, and I hate the veil between us.

The metal phone clatters on its base. She pauses a beat before answering, "Hello." She looks to me, then covers the mouthpiece. "Let's take a break."

I nod like Aunt Lori's parrot. Clarence perches atop the bookcase, gawking down with those big bird eyes. We're locked in a game of stare.

Aunt Lori moves her hand from the phone to mine and squeezes. A gracious way of telling me to go. I blink away first. Clarence gives a tweet of victory.

Clergy-penitent privilege, like attorney-client privilege, is legally binding and a sacred vow of secret keeping. I get it. She can't talk to the caller with me there.

I rise in a kind of fugue state and take my things with me.

"*Hm*, yes, I think that wise," I hear her say as she closes the door behind me.

On my way around the U-shaped gravel path separating the monastic residence from the Women's Guest House, I bump into Sister Mary Clare carrying a basket of spotted apples, green, pink, and red.

"Applesauce for dessert tonight. These are the last of the pickings."

She has no idea that I've just taken a bite of forbidden fruit, and the knowledge is lodged in my throat.

I stare at the apples without responding.

"Are you all right, Lu?" Her voice is a hundred miles away.

"*Uh-huh*," I mumble and hurry on to my room.

Only behind the locked door do I realize I'm clutching the tape recorder like a grenade. I push eject and pop the cassette tape into my palm. Such a small thing with so much potential to blow up everything. It would be easy to rewind and record over the confession—her driving the car that night, telling Lucas about the baby, negligence being the cause of the accident . . . *Negligence.* I wince. While a judge and jury might be understanding of inattentiveness, they would never pardon a lack of a driver's license, no seat belt, driving while under the influence of Dramamine and alcohol. All while pregnant! It was vehicular manslaughter, third-degree murder. A jail sentence, at the very least. There was no way the law or popular opinion would offer her clemency or forgiveness. But the church—the church would! That had to have been why she came here.

In my thesis, I could simply state the accident's date and time, inferring that it was a painful and private memory. It wouldn't be a lie so much as a filtering of the truth.

Who would question it? Except me.

When do I make something known and when is it best forgotten? In my single-minded pursuit to sleuth out the details of Aunt Lori's past, I hadn't expected to be derailed by a moral dilemma. Knowledge is power. If those with it selectively edit, future generations get a watered-down version of someone else's truth. Rendering all of history bogus.

How the hell am I supposed to write a History dissertation withholding what I know? But then, why did I assume that anybody ever got it right?

The unofficial oath of the historian is to tell the objective truth; to research, interpret, and share the past by studying primary sources. Aunt Lori is my primary source. My head throbs with frustration.

Where do I go from here? I put the tape on the table and walk as far away as possible, which is only to the opposite side of the room. I need space to think. This evidence impacts so much more than whether I graduate. It incriminates Aunt Lori.

No matter the discrepancy of facts, one night should not damn an entire life. The car crash *was* an accident. So that's what I'm going to write in my thesis. Lucas's death is penalty enough. Their tragic love story doesn't need to be dragged out for public scrutiny again. But the pregnancy. That's the revelation that interests me most.

What happened after the crash? How did she go from being a pregnant starlet with her unborn child's celebrity father lying on the side of a dark California highway to being clothed in holy vestment as Mother Abbess in a Connecticut monastery? There's a wide divide between.

These are my *who*, *what*, *when*, *where*, and *how* without even broaching the iceberg tip of *why*. I don't write these in my notebook. I don't need to. I have enough theories about Aunt Lori. I've been stewing on them my whole life! They're the real reason I'm here. I've reconciled with the fact that I may never get the whole truth, but I need answers to my questions. No more pussyfooting around.

I march back to her office. She's off the phone, but the door is still closed. I collect my breath before knocking. My heart pounds in my ears.

"Aunt Lori?"

"Come in."

I raise my empty palms. "Off the record. I need you to tell me."

She looks at me a long beat. Blue eyes like steel. I meet them. She sees my unwavering intent and doesn't argue.

"Sit down, honey. It's time you know the rest . . ."

Part 9

Lori

Testimonial

28

Los Angeles
1968

I sat in that rubble beside Lucas and willed my spirit to follow him into the darkness. But every time I closed my eyes, I saw his smile and eyes, alive inside me. I heard his voice in the wind whistling through the sycamore leaves overhead. *Livvve, Lovely, livvve.*

"I can't leave you," I cried to the cold.

Livvve, Lovely, livvve the wind sang.

So, I forced myself to rise. Shaking and nearly blind, I climbed down to the beach to wash the soot from my face. So thick the seawater turned it to paste. I walked into the ocean. The calming sway of the currents did not pull me deep but rather, made me buoyant. When I came up for air, I could see again. The stars. The moon. The darkness was not infinite but laced with silver threads. A living spindle turning in one direction—forward.

The waves propelled me to shore where I sat in the sand dunes, webbed in kelp and clammy with night. The spraying surf scoured my arms and legs. I needed to get somewhere safe. Down the beach, I could just make out the pink and green of Nico's house shimmering in moonlight. He wasn't in town, but I knew the secret way.

I walked the shoreline, step by step, each a heavy sink against the tide. At the rock garden gate, I entered the code: 1-1-1-1. The number of the angels. The key was exactly where I remembered, under the fake prickly pear. I let myself in, showered, and took care to wash the sand down the drain, not wishing to be both uninvited *and* untidy. I put the remnants of my dress, smelling of electric fire and ocean, in the outdoor trash bin and borrowed a T-shirt and shorts from his dresser.

I was sure that Nico would've welcomed me if he had been there. Did that make my actions permissible? I'm still not sure.

In the moment, I felt flayed open. It hurt to breathe, to blink, to think. My body was a vacuum of pain. The quickening in my womb had gone still. Exhaustion held me in a state of cycling hysteria.

In Nico's medicine cabinet was a bottle of prescription codeine. I tapped out two and took them with a swallow of water. Like being inside a theater, the lights dimmed. *Thy drugs are quick.* Lucas appeared in my mind, a projection larger than life. Vivid and beautiful, he finished the line: *Thus with a kiss I die.*

29

I woke up in the late afternoon on Nico's sofa. This nightmare couldn't be real, I told myself. It mustn't. How could I live if it were? I was in shock. I know now. But at the time, it was as if I were on a film set watching the crew and actors run scenes. All the action was happening around me while I was off camera.

I locked the door, put the key back under the prickly pear, and walked to Santa Monica Boulevard where the cabs circled for tourists. I caught one to Westwood. The driver was an older man who said he'd been to New York once and loved the pizza. I didn't realize until later that the T-shirt I'd pulled from Nico's dresser was emblazoned with *New York City*.

At home, I didn't turn on the television or the radio. I didn't speak. I couldn't sleep. I took looping walks around the garden. It wasn't big, but one could circle endlessly. A meditation labyrinth of my own creation. Over and over, I replayed the night. What if I'd not taken the nausea medication? What if I'd not drunk the drink? What if I'd not offered to drive? What if I'd not closed my eyes? What if I'd not told Lucas about the baby? So many singular choices that could've made the whole difference. I blamed myself.

I was expecting retribution when there was a knock on the cottage door on Sunday. But it wasn't the smiting hand of God or the Los Angeles Police Department. It was Tina, just come from Mass.

"Lori, dear, have you heard the news?" She took my hand. "Lucas Wesley is dead."

It's one thing to know a silent truth. It takes on a different form when spoken aloud. The words punched like an iron fist. I stopped breathing. The heat rushed to my head. The room tunneled. I doubled over into her.

"I'm so sorry." She rocked me.

I didn't pull away. I needed to be held.

"Apparently, he was in a car accident," she continued. "Some detectives are up at the house with Joel. They spoke to a number of people already. I'm sure they'll explain. We told them we saw you in the garden walking early this morning, so I didn't think you knew yet. I thought it best if I broke the news first."

I readied myself for punishment. Tina led me up the path. I had a dazed moment of vertigo. The earth was moving while I stood still. Tina held me steady.

On the veranda, the detectives sighed heavily and shifted their weight from heel to heel.

"Our condolences, Miss Lovely," said the taller one. "We hate having to question you now. But we've got to get the record straight, you understand."

I nodded.

Joel came from the kitchen carrying a glass of something. "Let's sit her down."

"Of course, of course." The officers shuffled over to the patio table.

"Take a drink," said Tina.

I drank, tasting nothing.

The soft-spoken detective with sad eyes sat across from me. His mouth moved, but all I heard was a stream of monotone. I took another sip. It was sour and sweet. Lemonade.

"You were with Lucas Wesley at Wisteria Ristorante meeting Skylar Wood and Paolo Mazzola on Friday night. Is that correct?"

His voice was suddenly clear as a bell.

I nodded.

"Was Mr. Wesley drinking?"

"We all were." It came out as a croak.

He scribbled on his notepad.

"Thank you. The maître d' corroborates that multiple rounds of alcohol were served to your table. That you were the last patrons at the restaurant. And that he called a cab to ensure you left safely. We've spoken to Miss Wood and Mr. Mazzola. Unfortunately, their recollections are vague and somewhat contradictory due to"—he cleared his throat—"inebriation. However, the Surfrider Hotel verifies that the cab dropped off Miss Wood and Mr. Mazzola. Miss Wood remembers you in the cab with them, but not Mr. Wesley. Mr. Mazzola said he refused to leave his car . . ." He flipped a page back on the notepad. "The AMC Marlin at the scene of the crash."

I saw the car again, the metal twisted around the tree. Lucas twisted on the side of the road. I opened my mouth to say *I did it, it was me,* but the detective continued quickly.

"We needed to confirm that the cab brought you home safely. Would've been here sooner, but it took some digging to find your physical address. All we had on file was the PO box. Luckily, Tina and Joel were able to help us out."

"I called the station when we heard the news," Joel explained. "You know how rumors are in this town. We didn't want to give you misinformation."

I clenched my fists. Purple crescents studded my palms.

Tina took my hand and rubbed her thumb along the creases. "We're here for you, Lori." She turned to the detective. "How much more do you need?"

The detective tapped his notepad.

"One last question, and I only ask because we need it on file." He cleared his throat modestly. "What exactly was your relationship with Mr. Wesley?"

"I . . . he was . . ." I crossed my arms over myself. How could I begin to answer. Tears came instead of words.

"They were clearly in a relationship!" Tina interjected with tears budded at the sight of mine.

The detective scribbled and then clicked his pen away. "Yes, again, I'm sorry to have to do this now. You know the media, they'll make up stories if we don't give them facts." He stood apologetically. "If we need anything else for the investigation, we'll be in touch."

And then they were gone, and Tina and Joel were on either side of me, walking me back to the cottage, helping me into bed, insisting that I rest, promising to bring dinner, pulling the curtains closed . . .

"Thank God she wasn't in that car." Tina sniffled to Joel before the click of the door shut.

Thank God? How could I? No one had lied, but there was a false belief. The truth would come to light, I told myself. It always does. I leaned into the darkness and cried until my body seemed wrung of life. That's when I felt it. A strange flutter just below my navel. I put a hand to the spot, the lightest tremble through my skin, like butterfly wings.

Lucas was still in the world.

❋❋❋

The police instructed me to stay as inconspicuous as possible until they finished their investigation. Lucas's death had sparked a media frenzy from Los Angeles to New York. Dawn called. Marie and my parents, too. Tina and Joel brought over tin-foiled dishes and wine. I thanked them but didn't touch any of it. Joel picked up my mail at the post office. Fans around the world wrote their condolences. I didn't open them.

In the public's mind, I would always be Juliet, and Lucas was Romeo. We were lovers with a tragic ending on-screen and off. The totality of the world's grief was a wave growing in strength each day, my guilt along with it. Together, they threatened to swallow me up.

I waited for the phone to ring and the authorities to say, "*Ah-ha*, gotcha—you killed him!" I had nightmares of the crash. In them, our car didn't stop. There was no sycamore tree. We fell over the edge together. I'd wake in sweat-soaked pajamas and then cry that it hadn't been true.

I stopped walking in the garden. I stayed in bed all hours. Two weeks passed like that. Finally, it was Tina who pulled me out of the pit.

"Come with us to Mass," she said. "Church is for the brokenhearted. 'No more death or mourning or crying or pain.' That's Revelation."

I went because I wanted those words to be true. I wanted revelation.

My skirt was tight. I wore a cardigan to hide the undone buttons. It was the first time I'd been out in public since the accident. The sanctuary was filled bent knee to bent knee and thick with the haze of incense. When the priest asked everyone to turn to the book of Luke, I knew I'd made a mistake. What was I doing there? I wasn't even Catholic. I had to get out. I needed air, space, solitude . . . I tried to step over the kneeling parishioners, but my skirt wouldn't allow the bend. Instead, I fell forward onto a praying congregant. The seam of my skirt split.

It caused exactly what I wanted to avoid: a scene. People gasped. Women gestured with their chins. Men shook their heads in alarm. The priest paused in his proceedings.

I pulled my knees to my chest, trying to hide the bulge, while gazing up at the stained-glass saints whose eyes fixed sympathetically on me.

"'Saints do not move, though grant for prayers' sake.'"

"What did she say?" a man in the pew behind me asked.

"That's Shakespeare," said his wife.

No, I thought, *that's Lucas.*

Tina and Joel took me home without mentioning any of it. I was grateful, but pretending that it hadn't happened deepened the sting. I saw the look on their faces. Their confidence in my soundness was faltering. Mine was, too.

So when Dawn phoned, I did all in my power to keep it together. Not an easy task when the first thing out of her mouth was "Did someone from the LAPD contact you?"

I had to take a seat on the kitchen stool before answering. "No, not since they came over."

"I'm sure they've got their hands full. They just finished the press conference. That's why I called. The investigation is closed. They ruled the crash an accident with Lucas at fault. They found prescription drugs in his car. Lots of them."

"No, he didn't . . . " I began, and then realized that I didn't know if he'd taken any that night but I certainly knew he did use them, and I'd seen the bottles in his glove compartment. My stomach knotted, and I put a hand to the kink and rubbed until it relented.

"Of course, they kept it all hush-hush," Dawn continued. "The coroner said he died of his injuries from the car crash. Lucas's manager spoke in support of the police force and advocating for driver safety. I think they're trying to calm the public and avoid all the drugs and alcohol stuff. They don't want to tarnish his memory. Fans are pretty distraught. They're holding vigils from coast to coast. So many people have gone to the crash site that it nearly shut down Highway 1! You need to get out of L.A. Can you go home for a bit?"

Home was not an option. I couldn't face my family like this. Where could I go in my condition?

The memory of a meadow, dandelion seeds blowing like sacred wishes, the rising toll of the abbey bell, light falling on my face . . . It was my only hope. I hung up and slept for the first full night in weeks.

❁ ❁ ❁

Early the next morning, I telephoned the abbey. The Portress put Mother Abbess on.

"Lori," Mother Abbess welcomed. "I've prayed for you every hour since the news broke. How are you, my child?"

I didn't beat around the bush. There was no time, and I didn't see the point.

"I'm pregnant," I told her.

She paused, absorbing the shock. She expected me to say something about the accident and Lucas, but not this. I readied myself for a word of admonishment—disappointment, at the very least. She surprised me.

"Tell me how I can help."

At her kindness, I cracked open, like a clam taking in water.

"I considered an abortion," I confessed. "But then, the accident changed everything. I have to have it, but I can't have it. The father"—*Lucas*, I kept his name to myself—"isn't here anymore. I don't know what to do."

There was the tap of something in the background: a pen on paper, a finger on a desk, a moth against a light bulb.

"You'd be surprised how many women come to us in similar circumstances," she replied. "Sister Evangelista was a social worker at the New York Foundling Hospital before taking her vows. Our relationship with them is strong and continues to this day. Everything is kept confidential. If that's an option you'd consider, you could stay here at the abbey until the baby arrives. The hospital would then place the child with adoptive parents or a family of your choosing."

The abbey. I pressed my ear to the phone, willing the sound of bells and meadow wind to flow through and fill me.

I inhaled. "Yes," I exhaled.

The strength came suddenly, and with it an epiphany. My sister remained childless. Maybe this was a way. Unconventional and unexpected, but unlike all the other *un*'s, this one was unique. And *unique* was the stuff of blessings.

"I need to make a call," I told Mother Abbess.

"I need to do the same," she echoed. "Send word when you are to arrive, and we'll be waiting."

I got off and dialed Marie before I lost my nerve. I used the same strategy. No small talk, straight to it.

She gasped into the phone. "Pregnant? I am, too! Only nine weeks. But still. I haven't told anyone because of, well, how it's turned out in the past. But we hope each time . . ."

The catch in her voice mirrored the catch in mine.

"Oh, Marie, that's so wonderful."

"If they're girls, they'll be like sisters. Like us."

"That's *my* hope." And then I poured out my plan and my heart.

She listened without asking who or how, what or why. Her only response was "Yes."

One word had the power to transform everything.

We hung up, and I booked a flight to New York City. I was down to a single skirt and a pair of trousers. The rest of my clothes didn't fit, not even with the buttons undone. I couldn't wait any longer.

Dawn drove me to the airport the next day.

"You're doing the right thing," she said at the terminal drop-off.

"I wish it felt better."

"We act regardless of our fear. That's what makes it right."

She said she'd try to write. I said I'd do the same. We both knew if we didn't, our bond would remain. That kind of love gives wing.

30

New York to Connecticut
1968

Marie and Bill met me at JFK International Airport.

"Hi, hey." I stuttered on what to say, suddenly worried that they'd changed their minds about me and the baby.

But then, Marie put her hand on my belly, and I put my hand on hers. We leaned into each other so our foreheads touched. Our breaths aligned. Such a small margin between us, and yet its significance was immense. We were between the past and the future. Fully present. So maybe I wasn't lost after all. Just between two miracles.

We took the train up to the abbey, where Mother Abbess and the sisters had prepared a room, a hot bath, a change of clothes, and herbal salves. The ease with which they received me made it clear that they'd done this before, many times. Just as she did at the Women's Retreat, Sister Evangelista delivered a welcoming basket: a jar of pickled radishes, unleavened crackers, and honeycomb to sweeten cups of raspberry leaf tea. An itinerary was left on my bed inviting me to the Divine Office sung throughout the day. I was settling back into rhythm: Mass, Sext, Nones, Vespers, Compline; eat, sleep, wake, and repeat. Like being rocked by a deeper power, it gave my life order; and with order came peace.

Marie returned the following weekend, but it was hard for her and Bill to leave the shop. I appreciated the sacrifices they made for me. It meant even more that they never saw them as such. Soon enough, however, her doctor put her on bedrest. We made regular phone calls in lieu of visits.

"Tell me about the woods and the meadow and the sisters," Marie would ask. "There's nothing but gray outside my window."

In her own way, she was more confined than I was at the abbey. I told her about my long walks in the autumn woods. The kitten I found stealing scraps from the compost bucket. I named her Robin of the Hood. About the Shakespearean scenes that the sisters read aloud after dinner. Quite cheeky—and good fun! And the barn I thought would make an excellent stage. Maybe we'd even put on a little play.

When the snows came, the sisters decorated the Women's Guest House with pine branches from the forest and kept a hot kettle on the stove for tea. Sweet buns with apple butter were baked each morning and the hearth burned bright with yule logs all day. It was like being tucked inside an ecclesiastically flavored Louisa May Alcott novel. She liked the sound of that.

We talked of the quickenings we felt, the food cravings, leaky bladders, and swollen feet, too.

"I can't wait to meet them. I can't wait for them to meet each other," said Marie.

I couldn't speak of Lucas. Even the thought of his death sent me spiraling into darkness. During which I wouldn't leave my bed for days. The sisters faithfully coaxed me back to the light with gentle song, warm soups, and the silent promise that I would never have to explain myself. Grace in practice. It strengthened me in ways that surpassed the physical.

We had just welcomed the new year when Sister Mary Clare woke me one afternoon. I'd fallen asleep by the fire reading *Little Women*.

"Lori, you have a call. It's your brother-in-law, Bill."

I wasn't expecting him and nearly toppled over attempting to stand. My belly was cumbersome by that point. Sister Mary Clare helped me to the Portress Office.

"Hello, Bill?"

"The baby's gone," he murmured with the voice of a man long past tears. "They can't find a heartbeat. It was a girl."

There was no comfort to give. Marie had miscarried again. I shared her heartbreak and mourned their loss as my own. I wanted to put my hands on her empty and hers on my full like we had before. So that she would know . . . we would not let sorrow be our history or our future.

There is a space between what happens in life and our response. In that expanse is the power to choose who we will become. I knew then with all certainty that this was my calling.

"How can I help?" I asked Bill.

"You already are helping," he said.

On April 7, 1969, I gave birth to a baby girl. I saw Lucas in the curl of her hair, the dimple of her chin. How I missed him. I saw pieces of myself, as well. Her tiny toes and fingers were mine; her bright eyes and unconventional spirit, too. I loved her more than I ever could've imagined. As firmly as I understood that immense love, I understood that Marie was her mom and Bill was her dad.

The sisters called them when my water broke, and they immediately trained up. Marie was the first to hold the child while the sisters christened her. I didn't have one moment when I doubted my decision, nor do I feel any regret. What some may call a mistake was repurposed into a miracle.

Marie and Bill took their daughter back to New York, while I requested to stay at the abbey and perform the Rite of Christian Initiation, officially converting to Catholicism. Mother Abbess was welcoming. The goal, after all, is to convert skeptics to the Gospel. But from the beginning, she knew my ulterior motives. I wore the denims of the sisters and worked by their sides in the fields, kitchen, and barns. I took my meals with them and joined them in prayer practices as much as allowed.

Marie and Bill invited me down to the city to visit and see how the baby had grown, but I didn't want to be caught by a reporter's lens, nor did I wish to bring an unwanted public spotlight. They were supportive of my conversion. They'd witnessed my journey. But my parents knew only their daughter Lucille who wanted to be the actress Lori Lovely. This new incarnation was a stranger.

"It seems so out of the blue," Mom said over the phone.

"A Catholic?" Dad was on the second line. "Are you sure about this?"

"I am."

"A Catholic," Dad repeated, stymied. "Does that mean your mom has to take the ham hock out of the beans now?"

"That's Judaism, Bert," Mom corrected.

"And Islam," I said. "We only do meatless Fridays."

"I thought it was Meatless Tuesday."

"And Wheatless Wednesdays."

"I've never heard of either of those."

"It was for the war effort," Dad explained. "FDR. Anyhow—that's neither here nor there."

"It's your life, Lucille," Mom said. "We lived ours. Now you live yours."

It was the final blessing I needed.

As soon as I finished my Rites, I petitioned again for Mother Abbess to allow me to become a sister. This time, she didn't send me away. Instead, she invited me into the office and shut the door.

"You must understand, the religious institute forbids a person from joining the monastic community if the individual has a spouse, children, or debts. Although we are an institution of tradition, we must be open to expanding our constructs for new generations." Mother Abbess cleared her throat. "I see you as part of that new generation. While many of our good sisters have chosen to depart since the reforms of the Second Vatican, you are choosing to arrive. God is making a way where there was no way. Isaiah 43:19. You have no husband. Your child has been adopted. So, if you promise to pay off your debts as you know them, I will write to the Archdiocese with my endorsement for you to begin your novitiate."

I threw myself into her embrace.

Those were the terms we agreed to. I entered my postulancy. I don't think my family or anyone else believed I would see it through. They assumed it was a phase, an emotional response to the trauma of Lucas's death and having lived extravagantly as a young actress. The presumption was that I was doing self-imposed penance. The tabloids plastered my Juliet photographs on their covers for sales. *Get Thee to The Nunnery: Is Lovely's Next Role in* Hamlet? When I didn't respond, they lost interest.

Old friends reached out through more private means, letters and phone calls to Marie, who played gatekeeper: Nico and Flynn, Fern and Kitty, Mrs. Crawford and troubadours from ICA, Dawn, even Ginny hunted me down. They all believed that I'd return—if not to film, then at least to the world at large. Only the sisters knew the totality of my intent. I don't think *I* was even fully aware. I was more afraid that someone would stop me.

With each obstacle, I fought harder. From the Archdiocese's hesitant approval of an actress joining the order to the physical examination, wherein I was convinced that the doctor would take one glance and know I was not a chaste woman. Thankfully, he was a general practitioner with a shy nature. He didn't venture farther than the stethoscope's reach. My bloodwork came back clean, and he deemed me healthy.

It was announced that my Clothing ceremony would be in June of the following year. Only then did the outside world take my next role seriously.

I borrowed Marie's white wedding dress and short lace veil for the ceremony and picked a handful of lavender from the abbey garden on my way into the sanctuary. I was shocked to see my niece in a matching smocked frock. She looked like a living blossom in the front row, swinging her legs and leaning into Marie's side. It was a sign. I was on my destined path. Down the aisle, I confidently took my vows and received my consecration as Sister Jude, although I would choose to be called Sister Lori. I turned to my family, who weren't sure if they ought to stand or kneel, clap or pray. So I came to them with open arms.

Marie, Bill, and my niece met me with cheer. Mom put on a brave face. "You look as beautiful as any bride." Dad, however, was notably shaken. He'd imagined giving his girls in holy unions, but never this kind.

He held me a long minute. His breath came in painful spurts, and his bones seemed to stick through his skin. Cancer, but we didn't know it yet.

"It's not too late to jump on the train," he whispered in my ear. "First class all the way down to North Carolina."

I held him closer, held the memory of him. "Life's a one-way ticket, Dad."

"That is true."

When we pulled back, the tears in his eyes were undisguised. The tears in mine were, too.

Connecticut in June is hot, sticky, and still. There was no air-conditioning at the abbey then. It relied on an old, wooden exhaust fan that clicked round and round with little payoff. Everything dripped with humid uncertainty. Thankfully, the sisters had prepared for that and set a picnic table of refreshments in the garden.

"There's iced tea and beignets," I told my family.

My niece looked to her mother curiously.

"Beignets are special nun buns." Marie winked.

"Nu-bu," my niece repeated.

"Yes," I said. "Some are heaped with powdered sugar and others are filled with the most delicious hazelnut chocolate."

Her eyes sparkled wide. I ran my hand over her crown of curls. Soft as new petals.

"Shall we try them together?"

She nodded and shyly slipped her hand into mine.

Marie met my eye with a look only a sister could give, and the three of us made our way out to the garden, blooming every good thing.

❁❁❁

THE LOS ANGELES ENQUIRER

JUNE 29, 1970

NEWS FLASH

STAR DRIVEN INTO NUNNERY BY HER LOVE FOR LUCAS WESLEY.
SOURCES CONFIRM THAT LORI LOVELY IS OFFICIALLY SISTER LORI!
SHE HAS TAKEN THE VOWS OF POVERTY, CHASTITY, AND OBEDIENCE,
SHORN HER HAIR, GIVEN UP HER WORLDLY GOODS, AND WALKED
THE AISLE AS A BRIDE OF THE CHURCH—AT 24 YEARS OLD! THE
ANNOUNCEMENT HAS SET HOLLYWOOD ABUZZ. FAITHFUL FANS
AROUND THE GLOBE WILL BE ASKING FOR YEARS TO COME, WHATEVER
HAPPENED TO LORI LOVELY?

Lu

Truth

The Abbey, Connecticut
November 1990

I turn off the tape recorder. My heart beats wildly.

"So, you joined the convent because . . . you had a child out of wedlock."

Aunt Lori doesn't reply. She stares at me with watery eyes, making their blue even more ethereal.

"You didn't say your daughter's name," I press.

Enough of the cat-and-mouse game. My hands are shaking. I ball them into fists. I need to hear her say it.

"Lucille-Marie."

On the surface, the naming seemed a benevolent act of sisterly devotion. My mom named her only child after her sister, Aunt Lori, being a nun who didn't have children. She was my godmother, a living fairy tale. But it was a half-truth, and deep down I knew it. That's the real reason I came to the abbey. My whole life, I felt like a boat lost in the darkness and she was the beacon in the distance, the candle in the lighthouse. Finally, I'd reached the shore.

Lori Lovely is my mother. Lucas Wesley is my father.

I'm shocked and not. I'm validated and not. I'm elated and not. I'm angry and not. My emotions are a strobe light, blinking hard and fast in the moment.

"I thought so," I say, "but I had doubts. I needed to hear it from you."

"Yes," she says. "I had my doubts, too. I needed to make sure you were ready."

"You knew I came for more than my thesis?"

She smiles tenderly. "Of course. I saw it in your eyes the minute you arrived."

"What about my mom—your sister?" I ask.

She looks to the phone briefly. "She's the one who encouraged me to tell you now. We've been waiting for this day. We always knew it would come."

I thought I was in control. Lu the historian rooting out Aunt Lori's story. But the tables have turned. It isn't about Aunt Lori anymore. It's about me. It's about us.

I stand, unsure of where I'm going, but I can't sit here anymore. I'm the one under the magnifying glass, and it's uncomfortable.

"I need a minute." I leave before she has a chance to respond.

Outside, the wind hints of burning pine. The last remaining orange and red foliage clings weakly to the tree tips. The clouds lumber across the sky, blocking the sun and glimmering of unborn snow. The garden is empty now, minus a little house sparrow that cocks its head side to side, trying to figure me out. I'm doing the same.

It's an unsettling thing to have your narrative of reality challenged. We want to believe that we are the author of our own stories, if nothing else.

As a little girl, I'd sometimes do this thing where I'd stare into my mom's vanity mirror and think, *What if you aren't really here? What if you aren't you?* I'd say it over and over in my mind until the belief became palpable. The terror would mount, but I wouldn't relent: *You aren't here! You aren't you!*

I'd mentally provoke myself to sobs and only then would I close my eyes against the reflection. I had no logical reason for engaging in this behavior except that it made the hours after more vibrant than the ones before. *I am here! I am me!* I would think during dinner or while getting ready for bed, and a swell of giddiness would wash over me. A kind of confident relief that the world was as it should be. That *I* was as I should be.

I breathe in, tasting copper. The air burns my throat and prickles icy inside my chest. Suddenly, Aunt Lori is at my side, placing a thick coat over my shoulders. The weight of it and the promise of warmth bring instant comfort.

"What's going through your mind?" she asks.

I pause to consider. Anger that this knowledge was kept from me. Remorse that I never knew my biological father. Righteous validation, perhaps? *My suspicions were correct!* One of these or all of these, you would think. But I only feel that wash of relief. Because I wouldn't change my past. Not even how I came to this moment. So what's going through my mind is . . .

"I am here. I am me."

She takes my hand in hers, just as she's done all my life. But for the first time, I see. They're identical.

One of the last leaves on the wild apple tree catches wind. It flitters up and then down, landing so softly that the sparrow doesn't blink.

"For God's eye is on the sparrow, and I know He watches me," says Aunt Lori.

I believe there is something watching us. I feel that truth. Is God real? I imagine the answer in mirrored response: *I am* . . .

❀❀❀

"Lucille-Marie Tibbott." Professor Proctor announces my name.

I stand and walk across the graduation stage to his outstretched hand. We shake, and he gives me my rolled diploma and bound thesis.

"Well done," he says. "I knew you had it in you."

I turn to the crowd.

Mom and Dad stand to their feet cheering. "Lu! Lu!"

The audience applauds. Cameras flash. I am my mothers' daughter.

"Your thesis was fascinating," Professor Proctor says after the ceremony. "A tragic love story inside a tragic love story. It's worthy of the Bard. Art reflecting life. Life reflecting art. As I say to my students, we couldn't make this stuff up if we tried!"

Oh, but we do. History is the way we tell it, and I told it the best I could. Was it fact or fiction? Both and neither.

One thing I know for sure, humankind loves to be right in its assumptions. We live like we're reading a novel, trying to guess where the clues are leading and how it will turn out. We come up with theories and imaginings that satisfy. We want to be clever. We want to raise our hand to the questions and have the teacher say, "You are correct!" When we aren't, we're disappointed. When we are . . . we're disappointed. Because while we want to be right, we also want to be surprised.

I put my rolled diploma between the pages of my bound thesis. The cover presses it into a misshapen roll. It's an imitation anyhow. The real one gets mailed later.

Life isn't about trophies or benchmarks. It's not about the mistakes or obstacles, either. It's about the course that leads to them and more importantly, what you do after. That's the calling, and I guess you can say, I found mine.

AUTHOR'S LETTER TO THE READER

Dear Reader,

This book is a work of fiction and wholly my invention. As with most of my historical novels, it's loosely inspired by real life. Specifically, three actresses. Feel free to speculate on which those might be. Each found worldwide stardom at the tender age when childhood turns to womanhood. They were everything we wanted and everything we wanted to be. I found it curious that, according to public statements, all three asked themselves a similar question at the height of their celebrity: "What now?"

By society's definition, they had achieved the pinnacle of success, global admiration, and dream manifestation. They had *Made It.* But *Made It* is a fragile peak. One wrong step and the fall is irreversible, and it's often memorialized by the public more than the summit, proving old Jimmy Durante wasn't lying when he sang that fame comes and goes in a minute.

This is what hooked my imagination. So I cast my line into history's fathoms, reeled it in, and let it out again. I became a "fisher of stories," a term bestowed on me by one of Lori Lovely's living inspirations. A woman who was once a Hollywood starlet, and then a Sister, and now a Mother.

In July of 2023, I ventured to the Benedictine Abbey of Regina Laudis where Mother Dolores Hart lives and practices her religious calling. After seven years of corresponding through letters, it was our first face-to-face meeting. I am not Catholic. So I must stop and thank Mother Abbess and the sisters for permitting my visit and welcoming me with grace and love. From hello, my Mother of inspiration and I felt as if we'd been holding each other's hands all our lives. We spoke uncensored for hours. She is an octogenarian. I worried I would tire her, but her energy only increased the longer we were together. Finally, I dared to bring up the book you hold.

"I'm writing a novel," I told her. "It's absolutely not the facts of your life but it is the essence of you in part. I want to honor your choices as a woman and a seeker."

She turned a twinkling eye to me and replied, "Write what you want. I've lived my life. Now go write your book."

It dawned on me suddenly and with her blessing: Yes, this is my story, my journey, my calling. This is my way of inhabiting the people, places, and reality so that I might connect the facts to the feelings. For me, it's the only way to know history's truth. All errors of fact in this book, intentional or not, are my own.

I tell you this so that my honest aim in writing *Whatever Happened to Lori Lovely?* will be remembered in the end.

With love,

Sarah McCoy

Sarah McCoy

ACKNOWLEDGMENTS

The idea for this book came to me while watching a classic film literary adaptation. The movie left me with an unrelenting desire to know more about its starring actress. In my search for her, I discovered other young actresses lionized by audiences who similarly seemed to dazzle and then . . . *poof*! Gone, but not.

Whatever happened to them? I asked myself.

Lori Lovely answered the question.

I greatly admire the writer Nora Ephron for her mastery of illuminating the heart of her characters in just about every story format. She said, "The crucial questions any storyteller must answer: Where does it begin? Where does the beginning start to end and the middle begin? Where does the middle start to end and the end begin?"

I think of that quote often. Because everything truly is the beginning of something else. There are no endings. Even now, you are reading this at *The End*, but it's just the beginning of how Lori Lovely's story will impact your own world, as I hope it will. A miraculous circle. Books to stage to films and back again. The art of inventing, reinventing, and releasing these mythical medleys of true life, hoped life, and pure imagination are gifts from God. So I must start there and thank the higher power of love that fills my inner dimensions with inspiration and provides all of the subsequent guides and kindred spirits to help me on my outer journey.

Thank you, dear reader, for being one of those friends. You continue to shepherd me through the years, to share my stories with your family members, reading buddies, neighbors, and strangers alike. Your support of me is an answer to my prayers. Each of you is a blessing. I wish I could be in all places at once to hug you. I hope you feel my warmth in the form of this book.

I'm equally grateful to the legions of incredible librarians, schoolteachers, and booksellers who are the true guardians of the never-ending story kingdom. Thank you for giving us a lifetime of beginnings with every book you place in each reader's hand. I can't wait to connect with all your reading communities again through this novel.

Dearest book bloggers, podcasters, influencers, readers, and reviewers, you are the beating heart of our literary nation. Thank you for waving around my books on social media, hosting book clubs, and sending private messages of love. I'll never be able to express how very much you mean to me: Robin Kall Homonoff and Emily Homonoff; Carol, Tom, and Greg Fitzgerald; Anne Bogel; Pamela Klinger-Horn; Jennifer Tropea O'Regan; Andrea Peskind Katz; Zibby Owens; Susan Weinstein Leopold; Jamie Martin; Susan McBeth; Carol Schmiedecke; Ron Block; Dallas Strawn; Laura Beth Vietor, Annissa Joy Armstrong, and Beyond the Pages Book Club; all the online book club leaders who've welcomed me to their chat rooms; the book festival organizers who've invited me to their cities; and so many more! If I've forgotten to mention anyone, I promise to thank you face-to-face the next time we are together.

Thank you to my family circle (of blood and of heart) who've seen me scribbling away since I could first hold a pencil: my parents, Curtis and Eleane McCoy; my brothers, Jason and Andrew; sisters-in-law, Khristina and Bianca; delicious new nephew, Luca Christian McCoy, the apple of his titi Sarah's eye; grandparents Wilfredo and Maria Norat; my beloved aunts, Titi Gloria and Titi Ivonne; Stacy Rich, Eric, and sweet nephews Louis and Charlie Schatten; Christy, JC, and darling nieces Kelsey Grace and Lainey Faith Fore. I love you all.

Heaps of gratitude to my beta readers and dear friends Mary Laura Philpott and Beth Seufer Buss, who braved the unfiltered jungles of my imagination to help me wrangle the cheetahs and wild turtles on the page. The next round of vegan Diet Cokes are on me.

Thanks to my local bookseller tribe in Winston-Salem: at Bookmarks, Jamie Southern, Beth Seufer Buss, Kate Storhoff, Caleb Masters, Lisa Yee Swope, Morgan Wehrkamp, Lera Shawver, Teresa Dampier, Cat VanOrder, Becca Naylor, Sarah Blackwell, Juliana Reyes, and the rest of the amazing team; at The Bookhouse, owners, sisters, and frontline saleswomen Tara Cool and Meghan Brown. Hurray, bookstores!

There are fellow authors in this business who become your spirit sisters and brothers. They walk the path with you word by word, sentence by sentence, page by page. They call you when you need to talk about the work. They call you when you need to talk about everything *but* the work. They check in by email, texts, and private messages to remind you to wash your hair, go for a walk, take a deep breath, laugh. This is vital for an author when she's so far down the writing rabbit hole that she doesn't feel human anymore. If it weren't for them, I might write, but the fullness of this life would lack its sparkle. So I thank the following for bringing light to my shadows: Paula McLain, Jenna Blum, Jane Green, Mary Laura Philpott, Christina Baker Kline, Allison Pataki, Patti Callahan Henry, Therese Anne Fowler, Lisa Wingate, Pam Jenoff, Chris Bohjalian, Jamie Ford, Charmaine Wilkerson, Kristin Harmel, and Adriana Trigiani.

A special shout-out to Martha Hall Kelly, who welcomed me up to Litchfield County the summer I visited the Abbey of Regina Laudis. You are divine and I adore you. Thank you for the relic postcards of Regina Laudis. They stayed on my desk for the last two years of finishing this book.

Thank you to my literary spouse and one of the strongest hearts on Earth, my agent, Mollie Glick. Across the seas, through the valleys, and up the mountains, we journey together. You, Gabe, and Griffin are chosen family. Thanks also to my wonderful CAA team: Via Romano, Kate Childs-Jones, Ali Ehrlich, Jamie Stockton, Michelle Weiner, Berni Vann; Nicki Kennedy, Katherine West, Alice Natali, and everyone at International Literary Agency for sharing my work abroad.

This book would be nowhere near as lovely without my editor, Rachel Kahan. Thank you for believing in the greatness of this story and for being its champion in the world. Thank you for doing the same for me. It's a godsend to have a creative partner who shares your vision, big dreams, and high aims. Immense gratitude to my publishing team at William Morrow: Alexandra Bassette, editorial assistant extraordinaire; John Simko, copyeditor; Michelle Meredith, production editor; Lainey Mays and Virginia Stanley at Library Love Fest; Kim Racon at Harper Academic; Corey Beatty at HarperCollins Canada; and all the Morrow book cheerleaders in marketing and publicity who are shouting *Lori Lovely!* from the mountaintops.

As ever, I'm grateful to my husband, Brian Waterman (aka Doc B), who didn't bat an eyelash when I told him I was writing about a young Hollywood star who joins a cloistered abbey, and I needed to follow her trail from L.A. to Rome to a Connecticut nunnery. He merely raised a puckish eyebrow and smiled. Game on. Brian, thank you for rolling suitcases through city streets and sitting outside convent doors for hours while I took notes, did interviews, and let my imagination absorb all the details that manifested this book. This life . . . this incredible life we have together has taken us further than we ever could've imagined. I wouldn't change a thing. I love you beyond all words, which is *a lot*.

Lastly, I must thank the Abbey of Regina Laudis for allowing me entry into its sacred circle: Mother David, Mother Lucia, Mother Lioba, and all the sisters who welcomed me with warmth and sincere affection. While I'm not Catholic, you embraced me as one of your own, demonstrating through action that God has no denomination distinctions. The heart is all that matters.

My eternal homage to Mother Dolores Hart. Thank you for faithfully writing me since 2016. I was overjoyed to tears when you answered my first letter. I've kept every correspondence since. They are treasures chock-full of wisdom, divine insight, and supernatural confirmation. I'm continually amazed at how our words seeded and grew into a deeply loving friendship. I count you as one of God's greatest gifts to me.

So now I pen back what you wrote to me when I visited in July 2023:

How beautiful you are. I think I have known you for a long time, but what a gift God gives us to be in one's presence! Bless you and all your work—your life—your marriage. You are of God. With love . . . a beginning.

A beautiful ending. A beautiful beginning. May this be the blessing over this book and each person who reads it.

FURTHER READING AND ENTERTAINMENT

NONFICTION

Cannon, Doris Rollins. *Grabtown Girl: Ava Gardner's North Carolina Childhood and Her Enduring Ties to Home.* Down Home Press. 2001.

Hart, Dolores, and Richard DeNeut. *The Ear of the Heart: An Actress' Journey from Hollywood to Holy Vows.* Ignatius Press. 2013.

Hussey, Olivia, with Alexander Martin. *The Girl on the Balcony: Olivia Hussey Finds Life After* Romeo & Juliet. Kensington. 2018.

Longworth, Karina. *Seduction: Sex, Lies, and Stardom in Howard Hughes's Hollywood.* Mariner Books. 2018.

MUSIC

Presley, Elvis. *The 50 Greatest Hits.* 2000.

The Choir of Benedictine Nuns at the Abbey of Regina Laudis. *Women in Chant: Gregorian Chants for the Festal Celebrations of Virgin Martyrs and Our Lady of Sorrows.* 1997.

Roto, Nino. *Romeo & Juliet.* Original Motion Picture Soundtrack. Film by Franco Zeffirelli. 1968.

Various artists. *William Shakespeare's Romeo + Juliet: Music from the Motion Picture.* 1996.